HOWE·LIBRARY

HANOVER
NEW HAMPSHIRE

## ALSO BY BUDD SCHULBERG

### FICTION

*What Makes Sammy Run?*
*The Harder They Fall*
*The Disenchanted*
*Waterfront*
*Some Faces in the Crowd*
*Sanctuary V*
*Everything That Moves*
*Love, Action, Laughter and Other Sad Tales*

### NONFICTION

*Loser and Still Champion: Muhammad Ali*
*The Four Seasons of Success*
*Swan Watch* (with Geraldine Brooks)
*Moving Pictures: Memories of a Hollywood Prince*
*Writers in America*
*(Four Seasons,* revised and updated)

### PUBLISHED PLAYS AND SCREENPLAYS

*A Face in the Crowd*
(screenplay, with an introduction by Elia Kazan)
*Across the Everglades*
(screenplay, with an introduction)
*The Disenchanted*
(play, with Harvey Breit)
*What Makes Sammy Run?*
(musical libretto, with Stuart Schulberg)
*On the Waterfront*
(with an afterword)

### ANTHOLOGY

*From the Ashes—Voices of Watts*
(edited, with an introduction)

■

# LOVE,
# ACTION,
# LAUGHTER
*and other sad tales*

# LOVE, ACTION, LAUGHTER

*and other sad tales*

■     ■     ■

## BUDD SCHULBERG

RANDOM HOUSE
NEW YORK

■

Copyright © 1989 by Budd Schulberg

All rights reserved under International and Pan-American
Copyright Conventions. Published in the United States by
Random House, Inc., New York, and simultaneously in
Canada by Random House of Canada Limited, Toronto.

Some stories in this work
originally appeared in the following publications:
*Collier's, The Dartmouth, Ellery Queen Mystery Magazine,
Esquire, Liberty, Playboy, Redbook,* and *Story.*

Library of Congress Cataloging-in-Publication Data

Schulberg, Budd. Love, Action, Laughter and Other Sad Tales
p. cm.
ISBN 0-394-57619-5
I. Title.
PS3537.C7114S4        1990
813'.52—dc20         89-42780

Book design by Debbie Glasserman

Manufactured in the United States of America
24689753
First Edition

105250

C✓

FOR STAN SILVERMAN

who, as editor of the *Dartmouth Jack-o'Lantern,* gave me early encouragement laced with tough but constructive criticism and who, half a century later, is still with me and at me

# PREFACE

## BY KURT VONNEGUT

The enthusiasm for stories told with nothing but words on paper was so intense in the United States during the first half of this century that a beginning writer used to look on someone who had published a marvelous tale as a literary ancestor, even though the age difference between the tyro and the master might be minuscule. Thus did it come to pass that I, born in 1922, thought of Budd Schulberg, born in 1914, as a member of another generation at the end of World War II, although he was actually one year younger than my brother Bernard. He had by then published the small, hard-edged, one-hundred-percent-American masterpiece *What Makes Sammy Run?*

Amazingly, he is now my friend, and in all respects, like my brother, a clear-headed and healthy contemporary. But I will never stop thinking of him as a member of another generation to which my own owes a lot. Mine is Norman Mailer and William Styron and Richard Yates and James Jones and Vance

∎

Bourjaily and Gore Vidal and so on. His is William Saroyan and Nelson Algren and Irwin Shaw and John O'Hara and John Cheever and so on most gloriously. I do not know if Schulberg in turn looks on me as my brother always will, as a little kid. I doubt it, since I myself, when thinking of writers old enough to be my own kid brothers and sisters, perceive no clear break between them and me, although they surely do. This is self-protection. I do not want to be an elder, a graybeard, a dean.

Schulberg himself, of course, has written brilliantly in the persona of a kid about "ancestors" of his own whom he came to know just as I have come to know him—most notably F. Scott Fitzgerald and Sinclair Lewis. Granted: They were more senior to him than he is to me.

Let us grant, too, that the popularity of stories told with nothing but words, no matter what age the author, is in sickeningly steep decline. New technologies now send beloved actors and convincing illusions of love and hate and weather and catastrophes and so on, underscored with appropriate music and other sound effects, to every corner of the planet where there is disciplined electricity. So that even the forty million United States citizens who are said to be able to read very little, if at all, still have stories coming out of their kazoos, so to speak.

What is being missed by those who cannot read or will not read? Nothing less than the most profound and influential form of meditation yet stumbled upon by humankind. The invention of the printing press was as cold-bloodedly technical in its intentions as TV and computers and xerography and fax, and who can say what's coming next? But a person getting information from a book, purely by accident, simply because a book requires this, achieves isolation and a body state recommended by Oriental holy persons as ideal for meditation. I ask that reading a book not only be recognized as a form of meditation, and treasured as such, but that those who do it celebrate it as being superior to the Oriental varieties, which I have likened elsewhere to scuba diving in lukewarm bouillon. Not much happens when a person meditates in the Oriental style, and I have done it, and I still do it from time to time. I think better of life after I have done it. Life is sweeter and I am sweeter, but not much else has changed.

But I say to the literate person who holds this book of fine stories by Budd Schulberg: Be aware that you are about to engage in Western-style meditation, which is not only refreshing but instructive, since it allows you into the brain of a highly intelligent and gifted person who has seen things you may have seen, but in a very different light, and seen things you will never see, and had thoughts you yourself would never have shared if you had not engaged in Western-style meditation.

# CONTENTS

▪

# INTRODUCTION

I'm not the best short-story writer in the world. But I can tell you what I am. I'm a short-story reader. It's one of my favorite forms. Some say it's essentially an American form, like our musicals. *Oklahoma! Guys and Dolls.* But of course there's de Maupassant and Chekhov, and Dostoyevsky, Tolstoy, Isaak Babel, where do we stop, the Irish storytellers, O'Faoláin, O'Connor, O'God, those Irish know how to tell 'em! And how about our *Latino* friends, Carlos Fuentes, Borges, García Márquez . . . ? An endless list of wonders. Short stories are great for good-night reading, and on planes and trains—easier to read a short story than a novel in a subway. I don't only mean that a short story is short—a twenty-, thirty-minute read. A short story is also something you can reexperience, relive, reflect on—whatever you want to do with it—while waiting for your plane to be called, or letting your watch warn you that your ferry from Orient Point is approaching New London. That would distract you from thinking about a novel, say *1984*

■

or *The Old Gringo*. But it gives you just enough time to ask yourself, Why did I like that story? Why did it hold me? What does it make me think about? Good stories are to enjoy. *Tell me a story, Daddy. Well, once upon a time . . .* Fun. But very good stories do more. First they entertain you, then they add to knowledge you already think you knew. They stretch you. Aesthetic aerobics.

Any collection of short stories or tales is a kind of map, with lines indicating where the traveler has journeyed, and this group of tales is no exception. There are Hollywood stories, not because "Hollywood" lends any special glamour to this assemblage—quite the contrary—but because Hollywood happens to be this writer's hometown, where he was raised, where he ran a mediocre half-mile for L. A. High, put out a daily newspaper there and learned to meet deadlines, and where he first began writing the poetry that soon convinced him he should try his hand at prose.

The Hollywood tales in this book are not particularly happy ones because no one is happy in Hollywood unless he or she is very successful, and no one in Hollywood can stay very successful. As this is written, I can think of at least three of Hollywood's most brilliant directors, Elia Kazan, Billy Wilder, and Robert Wise—with all their Oscars and all their marbles—who can't get a job. Apparently it's okay to run a country at seventy-five or over, but direct a movie? The kids in short pants running the studios will tell you, "Forget it!"

There are a number of Mexican stories, because I have not only kept an apartment in Mexico since 1960 but left a part of my heart there indefinitely. Sentimental? Damn right. One day in the plaza of an old village I saw a scribe at a typewriter that looked like a relic of the 1910 revolution quietly typing a letter being dictated to him by an illiterate *borracho* whose complexion suggested the chemistry of red peppers, *tequila* and uncontrollable temper. As I watched them, "Señor Discretion" began to write itself into this book. A minor archaeological rip-off in Taxco, followed by chance associations with some serious pre-Columbian digs, provided still another little Mexican play on moralities. And the counterintelligence story, as extreme as it may read, actually came to me through a glass of Dos Equis in a pungent Mexican *cantina,* extravagantly named the Transatlantico, where a Mexican cop in the grip of *tequila añejo* was closing in on a pair of unsuspecting peasants from the mountains. So, picaresque these Mexican tales may be, but I had to hold back several more to try to keep this book in balance. The trouble with Mexico is you trip over the picaresque. Even their philosophers, like Octavio Paz, have to dig deep into their seriousness so as not to become *pícaros.*

Some of these tales spring from hobbies, like deep-sea fishing and boxing, and some from lifelong obligations, like having to keep up with the waterfront. And a few are country stories, like "Say Good Night to Owl," because my novels have always been the city novels of a country boy. Los Angeles was country when I was growing up amid palm trees, fig and pepper trees, and the blossoms of grapefruit and oranges. I have lived on farms in Bucks County and beaches on the west coast of Florida and now on eastern Long Island.

A great blue heron just flew by my window. Where was it going, in the dead of winter? The germ of a story, or a tale. That's how they begin. Of course a large bird flying by your window is simply a fact. An odd or interesting fact. A paragraph for *Audubon* magazine. What would make it a story? Well, if this large pale-blue bird is an anthropomorphic creature, he could be a symbol of a lost soul in a changing world. Why hasn't he gone south to the warmer climes self-respecting blue herons expect and deserve? Is he a symbol of the greenhouse effect: He thinks or senses that our winters are getting warmer? Is he a metaphor for climatic aberration leading to social alienation? Or could this be the story of a bird whose mate has been killed by man or some other marauder? Many birds, from racing pigeons to swans, mate for life. Will this one continue to search for his lost mate until he freezes or starves to death? Or will a human sympathizer get involved? Will he or she try to get to the bottom of this mystery of the great blue heron who chose to stay, or simply was left behind? How does the human character we've brought into the story cope with this problem? Do the intervention and the coping change it from a fleeting event to a story? The possibilities, we begin to see, are limitless. A story is not an event, but a series of related events, one drawing on the previous one, and building to a climax. It doesn't have to be a big payoff climax like a smoochy clinch or a screeching car-chase at the end of a movie. It can be quiet and almost deceptively uneventful. Chekhov comes to mind as the master of such an ending, and so does Hemingway, whose novels may date a little but whose short stories are still wonderful on rereading. Any student of the short story would do well to study their endings.

Short stories have played an important part in my life. My childhood in Hollywood was enriched by my father's enjoyment in reading to us (his children) from the classics on Sunday mornings. Very un-Hollywood, you might think, for Father ran a big movie studio when I was in grammar and high school. But short-story writing, oddly enough, had helped us get to Hollywood: B.P. (all big producers used initials in those days) had won a New York City high-school short-story contest. It helped him get a job as a copyboy with Franklin Pierce Adams, F.P.A. (forgotten now, famous columnist then), on the old, still-lamented New York *World.* One day my sister Sonya (a gifted but underpublished short-story writer) found a copy of Father's prizewinning story in the attic of our house in Hollywood. It was called "The Man from the North" and it was terrible, worse than Jack London when he was bad. But at least it was a story, with a beginning, middle and end, and it drew a picture, it set a mood and it had a theme, even if rather a simplistic one.

"The Man from the North" did two good things: It established Father as a professional who became one of the movies' first "photoplay" writers, and it encouraged his own appreciation of short stories, an interest that he (and our mother, a would-be librarian) passed on to us through reading aloud and urging us to read everything from O. Henry and Stephen Crane to Tolstoy and Thomas Mann.

In my early teens, I was in thrall to the Russians and my first short story, "Ugly," was written under their influence—about an outcast in Eastern Europe, so disfigured that he only ventured to appear in public at carnival time, when he could wear a mask and disport in disguise. I was also in thrall, you might say, to my father's writers. When sound and the need for dialogue turned Hollywood upside down, B.P. threw a net around as many eastern writers—novelists, playwrights, even poets—as he could pull in. Out came Herman Mankiewicz, who had collaborated with George S. Kaufman and was later to write *Citizen Kane,* Ben Hecht, John V. A. Weaver and Edwin Justus Mayer, who had written two Broadway plays— *The Firebrand* and *Children of Darkness*—that were surprisingly successful considering their wit and poetry. And B.P.'s favorite, Vincent Lawrence, another Broadway playwright, earning twenty-five hundred dollars a week in Hollywood, cynical but conscientious about the movie work he had contracted to do, and at the same time devoted to the art of the printed word. When Vinnie got drunk, he would lapse into near-total recall of *The Great Gatsby,* and it was eerie to hear him recite the precise opening, or the haunting coda.

In my late teens I showed a story called "Busman's Holiday" to my father, a fairly tough critic, who thought it good enough to try on Vinnie Lawrence. A tall, gaunt, driven Scotsman who still kept reaching for creative perfection, for what he called "that blue sky-rack," Vinnie was down at his writing shack, in Topanga Canyon, built out on stilts over the ocean.

"V-V-Vinnie," I stammered, "I just finished a story and D-D-Dad thought I—I—"

"OK, laddie, don't tell me about it. Lemme read it for myself."

Vinnie, my hero, took my story, retreated to the bedroom and shut the door. I stepped out onto a long, narrow balcony above the white water of the waves crashing against the rocks. I watched the aquatic commotion below, paced the precarious balcony and, every few minutes, glanced at my watch. Ten minutes, fifteen, twenty . . . When half an hour had passed, I began to worry. The story was a mere seventeen pages. Vinnie was a fast reader. What if something terrible had happened to him? He was high-strung, worked hard on top of drinking hard, and was under all sorts of pressure. Jesus, maybe he was dead!

I went to the bedroom door and knocked. Gently at first. "Vinnie . . . Vinnie . . ." Then harder and harder: "Vinnie! *Vinnie!*" After a long pause, he opened the door. He looked terrible. Blotchy white. Holding his throat. Then he grabbed me in that fierce way I was used to. "Laddie," he burst out, "you know what you did to me, laddie?" Without waiting for an answer, he gave it to me: "That story is so lousy it made me throw up." That's what had taken so long. Not the reading, the retching.

Now *that,* my friends, is criticism. I still don't think "Busman's Holiday" was that bad. I'd find things to praise in it if I were teaching a creative-writing class again. But I have passed on this Vinnie Lawrencism to my students as an example of what writers should be ready for when they remove their clothes in public—which, as every writer knows, is not unrelated to the telling of tales in and out of school.

Despite Vinnie Lawrence, or maybe thanks to his help, I learned from those youthful experiences that I enjoyed telling stories, stories that fired my imagination, and that I had an urge to tell my friends, or readers. As for style, I discovered I was something of a chameleon. Not that I copied anybody or wrote to please anybody. But my style was decided by my subject matter. If *What Makes Sammy Run?* was a tough story, it demanded a tough style. A more contemplative subject, like *The Disenchanted,* would obviously demand a "softer," more subjective style.

This book of tales is written in what may seem quite different voices: tough, whimsical, realistic, quixotic. My way of writing is to choose a subject that appeals to me and then reach for the voice (in my repertoire) that serves it best. A shoemaker doesn't always make the same kind of shoe. There are plain, snub-toed shoes for hard walking, and fancy-toed, shiny shoes for dancing.

Readers of these tales, and an earlier collection, *Some Faces in the Crowd,* will either enjoy or accept the fact that I favor what may be called today the old-fashioned story; in other words, like my father's "The Man from the North," they tend to have a beginning, a middle and an end. Camp-fire stories, I call them. Maybe they go all the way back to the caves. Or forward to Chaucer, and then fast-forward to Mary McCarthy, Cheever and Updike. I love McCarthy's "The Man in the Brooks Brothers Suit," just as I do "The Bear" and "In the Penal Colony." And somewhere you have to find a place for Welty and Katherine Anne Porter, for the uncanny ear of John O'Hara, for a solid, reliable teller of tales-with-a-purpose like Irwin Shaw, and for the magic of Salinger, who has made himself—but fortunately not his stories—disappear.

This haphazard roll of short-story writers is called not only to suggest their originality but their craftsmanship. The live stuff of creation balanced in the hands of people who know how to use the tools of their craft. F. Scott Fitzgerald had that, and Dorothy Parker and Pietro di Donato, briefly, as in his short story "Christ in Concrete."

Someone who didn't have it as a rule, but only accidentally, or subconsciously, was William Saroyan. I will never forget first reading him in *Story* magazine. Ah, *Story*! For twenty-five dollars, if you wrote a story those connoisseurs Whit Burnett and Martha Foley accepted, you broke into *Story.* We all read *Story.* Established and newly discovered short-story writers every month! Not just one or two as in *Harper's* or *The New Yorker* or *Esquire.* An entire magazine devoted exclusively to the short story.

It was the dream of every aspiring writer to make the cover of *Story* (where the contents were boldly listed). Its Intercollegiate Short Story Contest gave me my chance. One of the winners was "Passport to Nowhere," now included here. Since it fell into a fancy category *Story* liked to call "novellas," it earned the mighty sum of fifty dollars. That I had to wait eleven months for my check in no way dimmed my exultation. Acceptance by *Story* was the *Good Housekeeping* seal of approval for neophyte writers. Thanks to a combination of nepotism and early promise, while still in college I had a job lined up as a reader and junior writer with David O. Selznick, the ebullient producer of *Gone With the Wind,* who had been my old man's assistant at Paramount, and for whom I had done a little film-writing the summer before I left for Dartmouth. That I could report to D.O.S. as a published short-story writer (in a few other "little" magazines besides the *Story* breakthrough) helped check my sensitivity to the nepotism issue, for I had been openly critical of the family favoritism practiced at Universal, MGM and other major studios.

But back to Saroyan in *Story:* The first time I read his "Seventy Thousand Assyrians" and "Aspirin Is a Member of the NRA," I knew I had discovered a new voice. I don't mean I had discovered him for the world, I mean for myself. Yes, there were beginnings, middles and ends, but they were beautifully hidden in a style all his own. Since my father was a movie producer as well as someone with a taste for good prose, I showed him Saroyan's stories. He urged me to find him and offer him a job as a dialogue writer. I tracked Bill down in San Francisco and offered him B.P.'s two hundred fifty a week. *Story* wasn't even covering Bill's two-dollar racetrack bets, so he grabbed the job. Soon he was writing movie scenes by day and his own stuff by night.

In Hollywood, Stanley Rose, who owned our favorite bookstore, had a small printing press, and he and I got the idea (well before Random House brought out *The Daring Young Man on the Flying Trapeze*) of publishing a collection, the first, of Bill's short stories. (Bill wrote at least three pieces a day. I call them "pieces" advisedly because some were stories, some little sketches, some of them merely creative doodling.) I thought I had separated wheat from chaff, worked up a table of contents, and Stanley and I were ready to go—when Bill dumped at least two dozen more pieces on us. I went through them, selected and discarded, drew up a revised table of contents, and—you guessed it. It kept happening, more and more from Bill Saroyan: now and then a little gem of a story or a poignant tale, but mixed in with his very own, original style of rambling. The master storyteller could also be a master rambler and the trouble was, he never knew the difference.

Bottom line: Our book, which would have been the first Saroyan, never got to press. A lot of what I took out, Bill later poured into *Inhale and Exhale,* a short-story volume that our long-suffering Random House editor, Saxe Commins, tried in vain to pare in half.

For Bill Saroyan, an *enfant terrible* writer all his life, even in half-defeated, half-defiant old age, inhaling and exhaling was all the stimulus he needed to start writing whatever popped into his fanciful head. This writer was always slower and needed more, first the faces, then what Fitzgerald wisely equated with plot: characters in action; finally that good old beginning, middle and end. And beyond the structure that holds it all together, there should be something more, the reason you're telling this tale. If characters-in-action equals plot, then plot-to-a-purpose equals theme. Take the theme away and we're just out there juggling for the hell of it.

Meanwhile, end of the overture, up with the curtain, on

with the juggling—only in this case, instead of barbells or bottles, we're using people we know, in places we've been.

Or, as the late and too-soon-forgotten "Wild Bill" Saroyan would put it, "Love, here is my hat."

Budd Schulberg
Brookside
Quiogue, Long Island
N.Y.
May 16, 1989

# LOVE,
# ACTION,
# LAUGHTER
*and other sad tales*

■

# SAY
# GOOD NIGHT
# TO OWL

■      ■      ■

"Read me Owl," the little boy said.

"Benjy, I just finished reading you Owl," his father tried to reason with him.

Benjy was four, and not easy to convince. He began pressing his lips together, threatening to cry. It was a bit of emotional blackmail he had learned how to perform before he was two. In the past year he had developed the Benjy Pout, as Carl called it, into a fine art. Carl could never bear to see his little boy curl his lip that way. He hated to see him cry.

Carl's own father had been very firm with him and had smacked him if he didn't hop into bed on time; his father had even smacked him for forgetting to say his prayers. Carl had grown up not particularly liking his father and not at all convinced that a strong arm directed against one's small, trembling backside builds character. He worked all day in an advertising office, where he made a great deal of money but did not like the people he worked with or the work he had to

■

do. He had signed up with Belgore, Bristow and Ryan right out of college because he had thought the copywriting position would give him enough money to write his novel. The novel had been rejected by thirteen publishers, and Carl had accepted this as a sign pointing to his resignation from novel-writing.

Meanwhile Mr. Ryan, the only partner still active, had called him into the big office for a drink, the crowning B.B.&R. accolade, and told him he had "the making of one helluva copywriter." That was fifteen years ago, and now Carl was only a year or so away from tacking his last name to the end of the formidable chain.

To be honest with himself, Carl hated Belgore, Bristow and Ryan, individually and collectively. He hated his suburban house—a disturbingly expensive split-level—even with its full acre of gardens and lawns. It was almost an estate. It was almost in the country. That's what he used to tell his clients when they asked where he lived—way out, beyond Scarsdale, almost in the country.

"Read me Owl, Da-da," his son was saying, blinking his eyes as if to cry.

Of the many books Benjy had, Owl was his favorite. His mother wanted him to be a reader. Already she had dreams of his becoming the writer Carl had wanted to be. She bought him a new picture book almost every day. Benjy would like the one about taffy clouds one week and about the peppermint tiger another week, but all summer long, to their amazement—yes, and pride—he had been faithful to Owl. It was about a baby owl, round as a dumpling, not at all a solemn owl but one with a big, happy, infectious smile on its face. Peg liked to dabble in children's books. She drew quite well, and often thought she could make a better book than the one she was buying. But she had to admit that Owl was a stroke of child-book genius. "He's so completely *owl;* everything about him is *owl,*" she would say to Carl.

The surprising thing was that Benjy agreed. He became owl-minded and finally was owl-obsessed. His mother bought him rubber owls and pictures of owls and plates and glasses with an owl motif. The first sounds Benjy made every morning were *"Hoo-hoo-hoo . . ."* With variations he could keep this up contentedly until his parents awakened. And at night he would *hoo-hoo-hoo* himself to sleep. Carl and Peg would tiptoe up to his bedroom and look at each other with soft smiles as this slumber music died away. It had become an evening ritual.

So now when Benjy begged once again to hear the Owl book that already had been read to him three times that evening, Carl said, "Benjy, wait till you see the great big surprise Mommy and Daddy have for you. We're going to leave this house and move out to a better house, a real *farmhouse.* We're going to have pigs and chickens and there's a great big old barn. And, Benjy, the main reason I'm buying the place is— guess who lives in the barn."

"Owl?" Benjy said.

"Owl," Carl said. "Not just a little book owl, but an honest-to-goodness friendly barn owl for you to talk to. You can say, 'Good night, Owl,' and he'll answer back, *'Hoo-hoo,* Benjy, *hoo-hoo-hoo'*—which is friendly owl talk for 'Nighty-night, see you in the morning.' So off to sleep you go now. . . ." Carl tucked the little boy in and kissed him on the forehead.

"Maybe sometime the friendly owl can come in my bed and sleep with me," Benjy said.

"Maybe, if you're very nice and gentle with him," his father said.

"I'll make a nice nest for him in my pillow," Benjy said, and he began to *hoo-hoo-hoo* himself to sleep.

The idea of moving from the lower Westchester suburbs to the remote wilds of upper Westchester had come to Carl quite suddenly one Sunday afternoon when he and Peg were visiting a college friend, a playwright who lived beyond Katonah.

"George is so mad about his new tractor I'm afraid he's going to give up his typewriter," the playwright's wife had said, to make easy visiting conversation.

George had tapped tobacco into his pipe and looked thoughtful. "Well, not *quite.* But, Carl, they may laugh at us intellectual country boys, but when I've plowed a ten-acre field and I look back at that lovely turned-over earth, fresh and waiting for the seed, I feel I've *done* something—not just written another scene those bloody actors will probably louse up a few months from now, but done something with my own hands."

The wives had tried to turn off the rather solemn pronouncement with politely mocking repartee, but Carl had become just as serious. "I know exactly what George means. Look at *my* life. Everything so clean, so antiseptic. Everything is done for me—aluminum foil and garbage disposals . . ."

"Oh, we have aluminum foil and a garbage disposal," said the playwright's wife. "I mean, we didn't exactly come out here in a covered wagon."

"Yes, I see the station wagon—it's a beauty," Carl said. "But I also see the tractor and the Jeep. If you were snowbound, you could live from your own corn and tomatoes, your own eggs every morning. I think that's what living was meant to be. I don't mean full time—I'm not a romantic."

"Oh, but you are, hopelessly—always have been," Peg said.

"Well, I mean . . . not losing our ties with our old roots . . . our hold, I mean—" George had been using a heavy hand on the sour-mash bourbon and Carl was feeling not exactly drunk but a little loose, a little wild, a little angry at—what? What does a successful advertising executive happy with his second wife and crazy about his four-year-old kid (his first son; the girls were with their mother) have to be angry at?

"Carl, I'll get you a windbreaker and we'll go for a walk," George suggested.

■

Conspiratorially they stopped for another shot of the sour mash in George's rustic bar off the big Early American living room. "I know what you're trying to say," George assured his long-time but not really close friend. "Modern life is a crock. You do great at it and what have you got? We've lost something. Even if we never find it, at least the searching is a positive act of faith. Out here in the real country you feel as if your soul has room to search and *stretch.*"

Benjy ran toward them, twitchy with excitement. "Da-da, look, look!" He opened his hand, moist with discovery. Nesting there was a small, uneven egg.

"That's an egg from a young hen," George explained. "That's the way they lay them at first—small and uneven."

"You see, even a chicken has to learn to make eggs." Carl took delight in instructing his four-year-old. Suddenly a warm, undersized, uneven egg was a symbol of escape from their overcivilized world.

"Can I save it, Da-da? Can I?"

"If you put a pin in it and suck out the inside," George answered for Carl. "Take it into the kitchen. Mrs. Enright will show you."

Benjy hurried off, with the egg held out importantly in front of him. "Careful you don't drop it," his father called after him.

The kitchen door swung shut behind Benjy. A moment later they heard piercing howls of anguish. The men found Benjy disconsolate in the pantry, the crushed egg leaking through his fingers.

"That's all right—there are lots more," George consoled him. "You see, Benjy, eggs from these new little hens still have very soft shells."

"There are so many things to learn on a farm, aren't there, Benjy?" Carl kept at his educational approach, kissing his son's damp cheek.

"Read me Owl," Benjy said.

"Uncle George and I are going for a walk. Maybe Mommy will read you Owl."

The two men followed a winding dirt road that led through a pasture where sleek, well-fed Holsteins were grazing. The sun was low, but would linger for another half hour. The breeze was soft and the air was a sweet mixture of clover and cow dung and fresh-cut hay.

"Mmmm, the air smells like—perfume," Carl said.

George smiled. "You advertising fellers," he chided him. "Got to improve on everything. To me the air smells like good country air."

"Wish I could bottle it and take it back to the office," Carl said, breathing in and out with exaggerated heartiness.

"You might have a new product there," George said. "Fresh air in the new container with the easy-open, snap-off top."

They were approaching the sprawling ruin of a barn that long ago had been painted red. Now it was faded to weathered rust. The big door was off its hinges, the windows were broken and the barnyard was fenced in by an eccentric collection of bedsprings, ramshackle boards, gnarled barbed wire—whatever the owner could patch together. In the barn doorway appeared a tall, unshaven, unkempt figure that impressed Carl as an apparition haunting the place from some previous century. It was difficult to describe just what the man was wearing as a shirt—"tatters" would probably say it best—strips of limp gray cloth that hung down like worn skins. His shapeless pants were tucked into torn high rubber boots. Under the wild beard and the grime Carl could detect a long-boned, noble head and dark, intelligent, angry eyes.

"That's Mr. Bassey," George told him, and called out as a greeting, "Bassey?"

The big countryman gave a grunt of recognition, an animal throating that sounded like "Hmmmmmp."

"Friendly cuss," Carl said.

George nodded proudly. "A real character. I'm seriously thinking of doing a play about him." Then in his special gruff, country voice he called, "How you doing, Bassey?"

"Can't complain," Bassey barked at them. From a large, dirty pail he tossed the slops to his pigs.

"Bassey, this is an old friend of mine, Mr. Aarons," George said.

"Hmmmmmpf," Bassey said, taking a stick to swing out the very last of the slops to the pigs. "What line of work *you* in?"

"I'm in advertising," Carl said.

The hulking countryman shrugged and his lips parted in a kind of malevolent grin. Then he said, "Craaw," or something that sounded like a crow's mirthful but humorless laugh. "Reason I ask, I write up a colyum for the weekly paper, the Hoopville *Sentinel.* Thought maybe I'd put you in it. Don't have too much to write about out here."

Carl and his playwright friend walked on. George was smoking his pipe and swinging his walking stick with what seemed to Carl ostentatious contentment. They were approaching a once beautiful but now dilapidated story-and-a-half stone house.

"Seventeen forty-seven," Carl said in awe as he read the chimney date stone.

"That's when the original Bassey built the place," George said. "Captain Bassey. This character's great-great-great-grandfather. They called him Captain Bassey because he organized a local militia in the Rebellion—that's what this Bassey still calls the Revolutionary War. In the country's first depression, 1786—I get my local American history straight from Bassey—when veterans like Captain Bassey were desperate for paper money to save their farms, he raised a little army of destitute farmers and tried to overthrow the governor. Sort of a local Shays' Rebellion. In fact, Captain Bassey and Daniel Shays were friends. I've actually seen the letters. Bassey's got some stuff in that cluttered farmhouse of his that belongs in a museum. A fascinating character, Bassey. Looking at him, would you ever believe that he's a college man? He knows Latin and Greek, and that funny column of his sounds right out of a Jeffersonian Republican paper. Bassey knows more about Jefferson than What's-his-name at Princeton. And with it all, I don't think he ever takes his clothes off or takes a bath—"

George stopped. Bassey was right behind them. Somehow, high boots and all, he had crept up within hearing distance.

"You want to buy the Bassey house?"

Carl stared at the man. "What makes you think so?"

"I was watchin' how you looked at the sign."

Carl tried to fit a word to the look in Bassey's eyes. Craven? Mendacious? Country-shrewd? In the unkempt yard in front of the house was a faded "For Sale" sign.

"Are you moving away?" Carl asked.

"Craaw," came the harsh laughter. "Us Basseys got our own cemetery up there on the hill. Cheapest funeral I could possibly get, so I'm aimin' to use it. Not right away, though."

Carl wondered if he ever could get to like Bassey.

"Bassey sleeps in the old carriage house," George said. "There are four separate houses here at Basseydale, as the old estate used to be called. But this is the earliest one."

"Oldest house in the county," Bassey said. "I've got the original deed."

From the dark silhouette of the barn behind the house, in the dying light of sunset's final minutes, came a hoarse *hoo-wah,* like a snoring man choking out a cry in a troubled dream. *Hoo-wah, hoo-wah . . .*

"What on earth is that?" Carl asked.

"Barn owls," Bassey said. "Got a whole family of 'em in the barn."

"Are they friendly?" Carl asked.

Bassey looked at him. "Well, sure, I guess you could call 'em that. As friendly as any of us."

"I've never seen an owl," Carl said.

"Well, they go with the place," Bassey said. "No extra charge."

Carl would never admit it, not even to his wife Peg, but it was the owls that persuaded him to buy the place. That's why, when Benjy had asked him to read Owl once again, Carl put him off by letting him in on the surprise—a farmhouse of their own with their very own Owl.

They moved in before the remodeling was finished. They were having the house repointed to restore the original stone facing, and they were taking old pine planks from the barn to panel a study for Carl. Dormer windows were inserted in the slanting walls of the attic, and Peg had begun to transform it into a wonderland nursery for Benjy, painting a prettified barnyard fresco dominated by a charming owl that smiled down on Benjy protectively.

Near Benjy's window was an old maple tree, and it was there that Benjy decided his real Owl was to sleep. Carl had taken him into the barn and told him to look up and see if he could find any owls. He thought he could see them way, way up at the top.

"See their little white faces?" Carl asked.

"I want Owl to sleep in the tree by my window," Benjy said.

"All right, I'll tell him," Carl answered. "If you're a good boy and go to bed without complaining every night, Owl will watch over you in the big tree by your window."

It was an ideal arrangement. Just about the time Benjy started fretting that he didn't want to go to bed, Carl would say, "It's time to say good night to Owl." It was magic. Nothing in any of their child-psychology books worked so swiftly and satisfyingly as Owl. Benjy would begin his delaying action in prayer: "God bless Mommy and Da-da and Grandpa and Grandma and Mr. Milkman and Mr. Postman . . . and Mr. Moon ["Now you're getting silly," Carl or Peg would reprimand him] and Owl." Then when the jig was up, Benjy would go to the window and peer out. "Good night, Owl," he would say into the dark.

Outside, the night was full of country sounds, the *oohs* and *moos* of barn life busily settling down for the night, which might easily have been mistaken for Owl's end of the good-night ritual. Satisfied, Benjy would climb into bed and fall asleep. At breakfast, before Carl caught the commuter train to the city, Benjy often described his Owl dreams. He would be locked up in a cave by a Bad Giant, and Owl would fly in when the ogre went out to catch other little boys. In Owl's mouth was a doughnut so Benjy wouldn't be hungry. Because Owl could see in the dark he was able to show Benjy a secret passageway in the back of the cave. By the time the Bad Giant returned, Benjy was already back safe and cozy in his bed.

"There's nothing like the country for a little boy," Carl boasted to the head of one of the big companies for whom he was laying out a new advertising program. They were lunching in the Oak Room of the Plaza, and subconsciously Carl was using his new country experiences to charm his client. "I mean, in the suburbs all my son could do was read about wildlife. Out at the farm he can actually live with it. You begin to get a feeling of what Thoreau was talking about . . ." The charm-of-the-country talk was not only a pleasing respite for the client, but it made Carl feel there was some sense to this Madison Avenue martini race.

During his first days in the country Carl was so green that he had just left the garbage cans out by the kitchen door and expected them to disappear as magically as they had in Scarsdale. But when he got home for dinner Peg described how George and his wife had laughed at their city ways when they stopped by that afternoon. "Out here we have to handle it ourselves," George had explained. "We throw the slop to our pigs and bury the trash in a trench at the far end of the corn-field."

The idea of buying young pigs to fatten with table scraps was a novelty that Carl found himself enjoying. But the disposal trench turned out to be more than he bargained for. The ground was much harder than he had expected it to be, and after hacking at it for half an hour he managed only a shallow wedge barely two feet deep. There, rather proud of this pioneering effort, he deposited the trash. It looked quite neat when covered over with loose earth and then tamped down with the new boots he had brought home the day before from Abercrombie & Fitch. But that evening Peg reported that Bounder, their German shepherd, had dragged discarded chicken bones back to the kitchen door and had scattered shreds of brown paper. Carl went out with a flashlight and studied the mess strewn along the edge of the woods. He had been late getting home because the client had turned down the whole new ad campaign and there had been a long crisis conference in his office. The last thing in the world he needed was to be digging a garbage trench at night. In fact, his associates in the office would never believe it if he told them how he was spending his evenings in the country.

"Craaw . . . need any help?"

Carl was so concentrated on his labors that he had not heard Bassey coming up behind him. Carl had placed his flashlight on the ground at the edge of his crude ditch, and Bassey, in his baggy clothes, big floppy hat, and hip boots rolled to the knee, looked like a magnified long black shadow.

"Good evening, Mr. Bassey," Carl said, trying to put that certain country heartiness into it.

Bassey just stood at the edge of Carl's shallow trench. "Ain't much of a hole, is she? Guess you city fellers could use a lesson in old-fashion' diggin'." With a brusque gesture Bassey took the shovel from Carl's hand and stepped down into the hole. "Dig a hole around you—it's a lot easier on your back."

Carl felt the blisters that were beginning to rise on his palms. "Thanks, Mr. Bassey. This is very kind of you."

"Craaw." Bassey dug in silence for a few minutes with

awesome efficiency. Then he paused with his heavy foot poised on the spar of the shovel. "Tom Jefferson," he barked.

"Pardon?" Carl said.

"Yessiree. He's been to this farm. Come t' see Cap'n Bassey when he was runnin' for president. Tom helped get him his pardon after the Rebellion. Even loaned him a little money. After a spell Bassey got back on his feet and even got himself elected to Congress. Guess you remember that Tom only beat out Aaron Burr by one vote. So you could reckon it was Cap'n Bassey put him in the White House. Over in the historical museum you c'n see the letter Tom sent my kin. One of the first letters written by the President from his new capital in Washington."

Carl liked American history, but never before had he felt it wrapped intimately around him like this. The way Bassey talked, it was no longer mere history, but something altogether personal that had just happened to him. He was beginning to appreciate Bassey. Here was your true early American in the flesh, Carl thought, almost a lost type—actually a throwback to the days when a man could be a thinker, a scholar, a writer and at the same time live by his own muscle, sweat and skill of hand.

It had been cold, and now a wind was building up. An enormous, shapeless cloud was blacking out the moon. "You better get back to your house," Bassey said. "The weatherman is fixin' to spit."

"That's awfully kind of you," Carl said again.

Bassey hunched his big shoulders. "Well, we're neighbors, ain't we? If we don't scratch each other's backs, it's a pretty sad day."

Pleased with Bassey's quaint phrases and neighborly service, Carl bent into the wind and walked back to his house through the gaunt November field. As he passed his huge, empty barn he heard the *hoo-wah hoo-wah* of the barn owls. Upstairs he found Benjy already in bed but, as usual, resisting sleep.

"I want to say good night to Owl," the child begged.

"Now, Benjy, dear, you said good night to Owl ten minutes ago," Peg said impatiently.

"But I want to say good night to Owl with Da-da," Benjy insisted.

"Well, all right, but after that no nonsense," Carl said, giving in as always. The boy was irresistible in his flannel bunny pajamas. Carl carried him to the window, and Benjy looked out as if he could really see his nocturnal friend. "Good night, Owl," he said, and then he added something new: "I love you, Owl."

Carl felt his eyes going wet. It had been such a perfect country evening. First Bassey's gesture of warm, neighborly spirit, and now the simple love of a child for his wildlife friend. "It restores my faith," Carl said to Peg in bed that night. "After a day with those elegant cutthroats who've got the ethics of sewer rats, little things like this restore your faith."

Carl was late getting back to the country next evening. B.B.&R. had lost a big account, some eight million dollars' worth, and Carl had worked very late. Peg met him at the door, nervous and upset.

"Oh, Carl, I'm glad you're here. That terrible man has been waiting for you in the den."

"Oh?" Carl's mind was still on his bleak afternoon with the dissatisfied client. "What terrible man?"

"He came in through the kitchen and tracked mud all the way through the house. You can follow his tracks. He's such an *animal*. It's like having one of his filthy pigs in the house."

"Oh, so that's it—Bassey's here. Now, Peg, it isn't anything to cry about."

"I can't help it. That man makes me terribly upset."

"Now, darling, don't get yourself into a mood. Bassey is a character, but he certainly isn't dangerous. I'm sorry about the mud he tracks in, but the way he lives American history is—"

"You know what they say about him around here? That he's

crazy. That insanity runs in his family. His mother used to keep a loaded shotgun handy because she was afraid the British were coming to burn her house down."

Carl smiled. "Well, you never can tell. They did set fire to the White House not so long ago—1814, to be exact."

"I don't think it's a bit funny. Did you ever notice his eyes? He gets an awfully peculiar look. From now on I want you to keep your quaint Mr. Bassey out of our house and back in the pigpen where he belongs."

Carl never liked Peg when she got this way. She had a childish way of heaping personal blame on him when she was upset with things that neither of them could help.

"Benjy all right?"

"He tried to wait up for you but he finally fell asleep. He was simply darling with Owl tonight. He said his usual good night, and then he went back to the window and said, 'Don't forget now, if you get lonely out there, you can come in and sleep with me.' Everytime I get to thinking that living in the country is more trouble than it's worth, I think of Benjy and Owl and I begin to feel better about everything."

"Mmmm-hmmmm," Carl agreed. "Every kid needs something like that, an old spaniel to boss or an imaginary owl to talk to."

"Imaginary? Benjy makes Owl so real I find myself talking to him too!"

As if in agreement there came the haunting, familiar call from the barn.

"I love that sound," Peg said. "It makes Benjy feel Owl is really talking to him. I'm sure he'll remember it all his life."

"Bassey says barn owls are better than cats for keeping rats away."

"Wouldn't it be fun if we could tame one and keep it in the house, like a parrot?"

Carl smiled again. "Maybe. Meanwhile, let's see if we can tame Mr. Bassey." He kissed his wife on the cheek as a sign of truce and went on into the study he had paneled in golden pine lovingly removed from the barn. This time Peg had not been exaggerating. You could follow Bassey's mud tracks, all right. The man did have a maddening contempt for civilized living. He was a fascinating old character—Carl could see him in one of George's future plays—if only someone could house-break him.

In the study Bassey was sitting in Carl's favorite red leather reading chair, his large, unkempt, bearded head bent toward a book in his lap.

"Got some good books here," Bassey said. It sounded as if he were barking angrily at Carl.

Carl noticed that Bassey had selected Beard's *The Economic Origins of Jeffersonian Democracy*

"This fella Beard knows his Jefferson," Bassey said approvingly. "Mind if I borra this book?"

It was a rare book, long out of print, and Carl had a thing about lending books. "Well, I never like to . . ."

"Neighbors is neighbors, ain't they?"

"You came to see me about something?"

"That's right. My money."

"Your money?"

"For the slop trench I dug for you. Ten dollars."

"Ten dollars! I thought you were doing it out of the goodness—as a neighbor."

"Craaw. We've got to watch you city fellers. You'll skin us every time."

"Just how do you figure ten dollars?"

"I put in three and a half hours last night. The rate's two dollars an hour, after dark. If I was in a union, I'd be getting overtime."

"Now, Mr. Bassey—"

"Then I come back this afternoon and hauled away today's garbage and dug—"

"Did Mrs. Aarons ask you to?"

"She saw me doin' it and she sure didn't stop me."

Carl felt that captains of industry were easier to deal with.

"Now if you'll give me my money, I'll be getting home to supper."

Carl swallowed hard and handed him a ten-dollar bill.

"You've got a fine ditch there," Bassey barked as he shambled through the living room to the kitchen. "Four foot deep and ten foot long. You don't have to worry. From now on I'll look after your garbage."

"At those prices we could put in an automatic disposal system," Carl said. But Bassey didn't seem to hear him. He just kept on tracking mud through the kitchen to the back door. It was only when Carl stood looking after him that he realized Bassey had taken the Jefferson book with him.

At the end of the first week Carl had paid Bassey twenty-seven dollars for a few hours of hauling and digging. Carl was sure he was exaggerating about the hours he was putting in. But it was too much for Carl to take care of and still make his morning train.

"It's getting ridiculous," he said to Peg at dinner on Monday of the second week. "In Scarsdale we paid the garbage collector ten dollars a month. Talk about city slickers—he's the country slicker taking us big-city hicks!"

"And in Scarsdale the garbage collector didn't track mud through the living room," Peg said.

"And he didn't borrow my books." Carl said.

"Well, you were the one who said he was so fascinating," Peg reminded him.

"I hate him," Carl said.

*"Carl."* Peg had a finicky theory that hate created bile in the stomach and led to ulcers. This was all wrong, Carl thought. If it was ulcers he was in for, he was supposed to get them from those madmen on Madison Avenue. The country stood for Thoreau and peace and inner growth, a sense of being in

harmony with the elements. That's what he liked to tell associates at the office. But Bassey was the black bootprint of mud across the harmonious carpet. If only Bassey would change his clothes! If only Bassey would work for an equitable minimum wage like an accommodating suburban hired hand! Damn Bassey. Bassey was beginning to take up too much of his conscious time. Carl had come into possession of Bassey's house; but Bassey—unless Carl could find some way of fighting back—was beginning to possess the possessor.

These troubled thoughts were interrupted by the cries of *hoo-wah hoo-wah* they had grown accustomed to hearing from the barn. Only this time the sound seemed louder, closer, as if one of the barn owls were actually perched in the two hundred-year-old maple tree that spread toward the house. When Carl went up to say good night to Benjy the little boy was excited by the closeness of the owl sound. "Owl wants to come in," Benjy said. "I think maybe he's getting cold outside."

"Owl has nice warm feathers," Carl said. "Owl is fine. He's been sleeping in the barn all day and now he's getting up to have his breakfast."

"Owl has his breakfast when it gets dark and I have my breakfast when it gets light," Benjy said.

"Right," Carl said. "Now say good night and hop into bed."

"Good night, Owl," Benjy said, his face serious. And then, with his nose against the glass for a hoped-for last glimpse of his friend, he said, "I love you, Owl. Forever and ever."

Carl picked the boy up and hugged him hard, carried him to his bed and lovingly tucked him in. "Now get under the covers, like a good little owl."

"Owl doesn't have covers; he has feathers," Benjy corrected him. "Nice soft warm feathers. I want Owl to come in the house so I can pet him on his nice soft feathers."

"All right. Someday you can do that. Off to dreamland, now."

"I love him," Benjy said.

Carl kissed the little boy on his warm, sweet-smelling forehead. "And he loves you. Now close your eyes. Owl says, 'Sweet dreams, Benjy-boy.' "

On his way down the stairs Carl could hear Benjy contentedly *hoo-hoo-hoo*ing himself to sleep.

When Carl came home from the office next evening, the big country kitchen looked warm and inviting. A fire was blazing in the corner fireplace, and Peg was busy at the old-fashioned eight-burner stove she had carted home triumphantly after overbidding at a back-road auction. She was making her own cranberry sauce for the turkey George had given them from his flock down the hill. Benjy was playing on the floor with one of the empty glass jars Peg had sterilized for the cranberries. He had discovered that when he put his mouth to the open neck of the jar and blew, he could make a deep, echoing sound like a real owl. *"Hoooooo, hooooo,"* he kept repeating.

Carl made himself a highball. It had been another jagged day at the office.

"All right, Benjy, dear, that's enough Owl for one night," Peg pleaded as she poured the steaming cranberry juice.

"Benjy, *please,* give Owl a rest," Carl seconded.

Stubbornly concentrating on his discovery, Benjy was just putting his mouth to the lip of the jar again when Bassey burst in. Peg glared at his filthy boots. The smell of him seemed too strong to be human. His small, shiny eyes in his heavy, bristled face made him look like a giant boar reared up on its hind legs. He wasn't as erect as usual. He was weaving slightly, and Carl was sure he had been swigging homemade applejack.

"Mr. Bassey," Peg said boldly, "we're trying to keep this kitchen clean for the holidays."

"Craaw," Bassey said. "Got something for the boy."

Carl looked at him, from his muddy boots to his unwashed, unshaven face, and wondered what he was up to.

"Y'know how he's always talkin' about owls. Well, I went 'n' fetched him one."

In an unexpected, cat-quick movement he shut the kitchen door behind him and was gone. But in an instant he was back, carrying a cage. In it was a wild, clawing something that made a hideous, hoarse, rasping sound. A rapacious hooked beak was slashing at the bars of the cage, which was being shaken violently by powerful talons. The face was a spectra white Halloween mask come savagely to life. The eyes were large and black and full of fury.

It all happened so quickly that it seemed a jumble of discontinuity, but Bassey extended the cage toward Benjy as if to present to him the captured barn owl, and in surprise, or to ward off an enemy, the boy moved his hand toward the cage. The angry bird lurched forward and—whether with his talons or his beak, Carl wasn't sure—ripped the flesh from the tips of Benjy's fingers. Benjy's scream was shriller than the owl's. Blood was spurting along his fingers. He was screaming hysterically when Peg grabbed him up and ran out of the room with him.

"See how deep it is—maybe we should call a doctor," Carl called after them. Then he turned on Bassey. "You son of a—"

"He ain't hurt. Just a little scratch on his finger."

The owl was screeching and flailing to fight free of its cage.

"Take that damn thing out of here!"

"I thought he'd like to see what a real owl looks like."

"Bassey, that was a mean, despicable thing to do. I never want you to set foot on this place again."

"All right by me. Just pay me the twelve dollars you owe me and we'll be even."

"Twelve dollars! I don't owe you a nickel."

"Two hours a day for the last three days. Don't worry—I keep track."

"You can sue me for it, damn it."

"I'll get the constable on you, that's what I'll do. City people comin' in here, hoggin' everything . . ."

"Damn it, Bassey, what you did to that boy . . . Now get out of here."

The barn owl was still flapping, hissing, struggling to get out of its cage.

"And take that goddamn owl with you!"

Bassey hulked out of the door with his ferocious prisoner gnashing at its bars. Through the small square window in the kitchen door Carl watched his atavistic neighbor trudge across the lawn into the field that separated this house from the squalid carriage house. Carl bolted the kitchen door and went up to the nursery. Benjy was still whimpering and staring moodily at his bandaged hand.

"That wasn't the good owl that lives in your tree," Carl said. "That was the bad owl who lives in the barn."

Benjy didn't say anything. Carl offered to piggyback him around the room, but Benjy didn't want to. He sat on his bed, staring at his fingers.

Carl tried again. "Don't you want to say good night to Owl—the good owl?"

The little boy was silent.

"The *good* owl is waiting for you to say good night to him," Peg said weakly.

Benjy's silence made them want to keep talking, but they couldn't fool Benjy any more. There weren't any friendly owls. Owls had feet to grab and claw you with, and hard, angry mouths to tear at your flesh and eat you up. Real owls had mean, fighting eyes and all they wanted to do was hurt you and kill you.

The next day Benjy did not mention Owl. He had cut him out of his vocabulary as one painfully omits the mention of an old friend who has betrayed him. Sometimes he would just sit at the window and stare out for ten or fifteen minutes at a time, something he had never done in his going-on-five-year-old life. Carl would have been relieved if he had said, "I hate that old owl," but he never did. Owl was a closed chapter in a life that Carl darkly imagined as an accordionlike unfolding of disenchantments.

With Bassey gone, Carl went back to burying the garbage in inadequate holes he never had the time or the patience to dig. To add to his country woes, he was no longer on speaking terms with his neighbor George. George had taken Bassey's side of the argument over the twelve dollars, and Carl accused George of becoming a professional country snob. George went back to his luxurious farmhouse in angry silence.

Sometimes Benjy would wake up crying at the sound of the barn owls, and Peg complained that their constant hooting was disturbing her sleep too. To top it off, the R. of B.B.&R.—Mr. Ryan—had retired, and Carl found himself saddled with major responsibilities for replacing lost accounts, which required after-dinner meetings in town two or three times a week. Before the end of winter he and Peg began searching through the Sunday *Times* real-estate section. Carl could hear Bassey saying, "Craaw!" and George muttering something over his pipe about summer soldiers. Well, to hell with them. At least if he and Peg moved closer in, there would be no physical threat from those hideous barn owls to give Benjy nightmares and jangle their peace of mind. But as he checked off, with a nagging sense of surrender, half a dozen promising locations in Scarsdale, Larchmont, Mamaroneck, picturing quiet tree-lined streets far from mud, garbage ditches and Basseys, a sound even more threatening than the scream of the owls grew louder and louder in his head: "Craaw! Craaw *craaw* CRAAW!"

# THE REAL VIENNESE SCHMALTZ

Harold Edson Brown's indignation could be heard throughout the entire studio. The only thing that was louder than his voice was the sports coat on which a couple of gag men had once played a game of checkers.

It was an outrage. Here he was, Harold Edson Brown, the highest-paid writer on the lot, the only Pulitzer Prize winner on contract (though that winning play had been written twenty years ago with an enthusiasm and intensity which had sickened and died before he ever reached Hollywood), the man who had juggled such themes as mother love, camaraderie and sex for over ten years without ever dropping a script, being denied the fattest assignment of the year.

"What d'ya mean I can't write it?" Brown demanded in that golden voice that had gilded some of the most wilted Hollywood lilies of the past decade. "I didn't do so bad with *Mardi Gras. At the Pole* ain't exactly a stinker either. I got range."

(Actually Harold Edson Brown was one of the town's bet-

ter-educated writers. Bad grammar was an affectation he enjoyed because he knew everybody else knew he knew better.)

"But you don't know Vienna," the producer repeated. "I'm
going to throw millions into *The Blue Danube.* I've got to have
the real Vienna—the old Viennese schmaltz."

"The real Vienna—that's right down my alley. Don't you
think I've ever been to Vienna?"

"Sure. For two days. The only time you left your hotel room
was when you chased that dame into the lobby. I happen to
know. I was with you."

"But I'm an expert on Vienna. I didn't spend seventeen
months on *The First Waltz* for nothing."

"I should say not! Not at two grand a week. But *The Blue
Danube* has to make *First Waltz* look like a quickie! I want the
whole picture to sway like a beautiful waltz from start to finish.
It's got to be absolutely lousy with the real Viennese
schmaltz."

"And just who is going to supply this R.V.S.?" Brown asked
irritably.

The producer spoke the name with the proper air of mystery. "Hannes Dreher."

"Hannes Dreher! Never even heard of him. What are his
credits?"

"Myron Selznick sold him to me. He's come straight from
Europe. He's written Vienna's favorite operettas for years.
This picture has got to be authentic. So it's going to be written
by a one hundred percent genuine Viennese."

Harold Edson Brown sat at the head of the writers' table in
the commissary dishing out the latest inside dope like the
man-about-studio he was, when a funny little stranger edged
himself into the room.

"Who's that penguin with a hat on?" asked a gag man.

Harold Edson Brown prided himself on being a one-man
studio bulletin. He always knew who had just been hired and

who was about to be fired. He was supposed to have an *in* with
the producers. "That must be Hannes Dreher," he announced. "He's the Austrian genius they imported for *The
Blue Danube*. I'll get him over."

The lunch hour was at its height and the commissary vibrated with rapid talk punctuated by the grating clatter of
many plates. Hannes Dreher was still standing close to the
door, like a bewildered child arriving at boarding school for
the first time. His coat looked as if it had started out to be a
cutaway and changed its mind, and beneath it he wore the
old-fashioned white vest which gave him the penguin look.
His heavy gray fedora was balanced on his head like a book.
The eyes were a gentle, light watery blue, and the only
weapon he had developed throughout his half-century on this
earth was the vagueness which drew a screen of gauze between
him and the brashness of life.

As Harold Edson Brown strode toward him with his two-
thousand-dollar-a-week smile and his hand outstretched in the
manner that had earned him the nickname Ward Boss of Writers' Row, Dreher shied like a horse that had been whipped.

"You must be Hannes Dreher. Glad to meetcha, boy. I'm
Harold Edson Brown."

Dreher smiled at him gratefully, bringing his heels together
so gently that they produced no *click*. Because he always tried
to be kind, he did his best to act as if he had heard Brown's
name before.

"The same gang put on the feed bag here together every
day. Make yourself at home."

Dreher bowed timidly. "*Dankeschön,* Herr Brown, you are
very nice."

As Dreher ate, Brown nudged him familiarly. "Well, kid,
you're running into plenty of luck. Just between you and me
and Louella O. Parsons, the boss is throwing Jeanette Mac-
Donald and Nelson Eddy into *The Blue Danube*. Which means
you grab yourself an A credit right off the bat."

*"The Blue Danube,"* Dreher reflected. *"Die schöne, blaue Donau."* He looked out, through the window, and Brown's eyes followed, but there was nothing out there to see.

"You're in a great spot, baby," Brown continued. "We've had plenty of these Viennese horse-operas but they've always been strictly phonies. The boss tells me you're going to give it the real Viennese schmaltz."

"The real Viennese schmaltz," Dreher repeated with a slow smile his eyes did not reflect. *"Ach,* that is very hard to give, *ja?"*

"You sure you wouldn't kid me, Mr. Strauss?" Brown laughed. "I'll bet you do your typing in three-quarter time."

Brown looked in on Dreher on his way to lunch next day. "Well, how's the beautiful blue Danube?" he asked. "Rolling along?"

Dreher looked up from his desk wearily. He hadn't written a line all morning and there were tight lines of worry around his eyes. *"Nein, nein,* she moves very slow," he answered.

"Oh, you'll hit it," Brown said. "How about ducking out for a little lunchee?" As the self-appointed good-will ambassador of the writers, he had to make the screwy little foreigner feel at home. And of course it wouldn't do him any harm to be chummy with Dreher, just in case he got a sole credit on *Danube* and became a big shot.

*"Dankeschön,* Herr Brown," Dreher said. "But when I write I am never hungry. See, I have brought a sandwich with me."

From that moment on Brown had Dreher pegged as an all-day sucker. He couldn't figure him at all. In his ten years in the business he had seen hundreds of writers come and go, but he had never seen one take a job so hard. Believe you me, he would tell his pals, the little Austrian sausage is doing it the hard way, strictly from torture.

Brown himself was the town's champion horizontal writer. He was one of the last holdouts against the Screen Writers

Guild because he didn't believe a writer should have ethics. He had a well-developed memory and a great gift for other writers' phrases. All he ever did was stretch out on a divan between the hours of ten and five and dictate last year's story with a new twisteroo. So you could have knocked him over with a paper clip when he found out that Dreher was checking in at eight-thirty every morning and pounding away until seven or eight at night. And he was even more flabbergasted when he got news straight from Leah of the stenographic department that Dreher hadn't turned in a single page. Since the new efficiency move was a minimum of five pages a day, this sounded like professional hara-kiri.

Next time Brown saw the producer he couldn't resist giving Dreher a stab in the back, just a little one for luck.

"What's Dreher been doing?—Dozing on the banks of the Danube?"

But the producer only nodded like Solomon. "Give him time. A man who loves Vienna like him! For the real Viennese schmaltz—I'm willing to wait."

When Brown had to stop back at his office late one night to pick up a script, he was amazed to find Dreher still plugging away, his office full of smoke, an atmosphere of desperation, his hand pushing and pulling a cigarette into his mouth in a series of twitching gestures. The floor around his typewriter was cluttered with pages he had rolled up into nervous little balls and thrown away.

"How's she coming, pal?" Brown asked.

Dreher put out the cigarette he had just lit and tried to smile the way he had heard you should in a studio. "This is the . . . how you say . . . toughest . . . story I ever wrote," he said.

"I don't get it," Brown said. "A real Viennese like you. It oughta be a cakewalk. Old Vienna in the springtime! Waltzing in the streets! Love on the banks of the Danube! You oughta be able to write it with your eyes closed!"

Dreher closed his eyes slowly. *"Ja,* the blue Danube," he sighed. "The lovely streets of Vienna—and the waltzes." He stopped short; his fingers stiffened. After too long he said, *"Ach,* no, it is no . . . cakewalk."

Brown perched on the edge of his desk and waved his cigar around. "How's this for an angle? I'm just thinking out loud, see, but suppose we've got a charming young Viennese student. Nelson Eddy. You know, like the *Student Prince?* Well, Nelson's in love with the barmaid, Jeanette MacDonald, only he can't marry her because he's engaged to some princess he's never seen. But Jeannette's really the princess who ran away from the castle to find *life,* only she don't want to tell Nelson because she wants to be sure he loves her—for herself, see?

"So . . . well anyway, you can pick it up from there—and how do you like this for the topper at the finish?—Nelson and Jeanette doing a duet alone in a little sailboat floating down the blue Danube, and suddenly their song is echoed by thousands of voices, and you're into a terrific number with all the lords and ladies paired off in little boats singing "The Blue Danube" like it's never been sung before?"

Brown built his climax at the top of his voice, emphasizing its power by thumping Dreher's chest. Dreher had tried to listen attentively. Even though he recognized Brown's angle all too well. He looked from Brown's confident face to the labored, tediously crossed-out manuscript beside his typewriter. It was bad enough for Brown to appropriate a famous old plot. But when a man begins to plagiarize his own work! For Dreher couldn't fool himself any longer. Brown's enthusiasm-coated clichés had jolted him into realizing that the story he was working on was nothing more than a feeble carbon copy of his first operetta.

*"Dankeschön,"* he said miserably. "You are very . . . helpful."

"Aw, don't mention it, Hans. Just let the plot take care of

itself." And from the door: "Just give it that real Viennese schmaltz."

Dreher stared after him for a moment, absently shredding the cigarette he was about to light. Then he was grabbing everything he had written these last two weeks, viciously tearing it in two, flinging it into the wastebasket, and crazily twirling another blank sheet into his typewriter.

He began again, slowly, tentatively, as if every word were being wrung from it—peck, peck-peck, pause, peck-peck. The typing faltered and stopped. As he pressed his small fists against his forehead, he could still hear Brown walking down the hall whistling "The Blue Danube." Then his keys beat another slow-motion staccato, until finally page after page was being torn from the roller and thrown among the heap that lay crushed on the floor.

Harold Edson Brown stopped looking in on Dreher after that, because he had seen the handwriting on the producer's desk. The finger was on Hannes Dreher.

"One month and I haven't seen a page," the producer grumbled to Brown. "I think he's a fake. For my money he's never even seen Vienna."

Impulsively the producer got Dreher on the phone. "I don't want any more stalling, Dreher. If you got something I can read, get it up here. If you haven't, get out. I'll give you twenty-four hours."

Next morning Dreher knocked shyly on the door and presented the producer with a manuscript the size of a telephone book. His hand trembled with strain and fatigue as he laid it on the desk. For the last twenty-four hours he hadn't even left his office. He had written faster and faster, pounding feverishly into his typewriter the words that came rushing, the most furious labor of his career, attacking his story the way Van Gogh slashed color at his canvases.

The producer fingered through Dreher's script dubiously, and only said, "I'll call you back in an hour."

An hour later when the producer told his secretary to call Mr. Dreher down again, Dreher was still sitting anxiously in his reception room.

The producer had impressed him with his club-room informality at their first meeting. Now he was barely polite, and his voice sounded crisp and anxious to get it over. "Dreher, I only had to read the first fifty pages to know it was all wrong. It's not what I wanted at all. It's got no life, no charm, it reads like a horror story. It doesn't sound as if you've ever been to Vienna. I'm afraid we'll have to close you out as of today."

By the time they were shaking hands, the producer was already getting Brown on the phone.

At the threshold Dreher's only response was to smile with amusement but no joy, and to bring his heels together in a weary *click,* as he said good-bye.

On his way out of the studio, Dreher had to pass the projection room, where they were testing sound tracks of Jeanette MacDonald singing "The Blue Danube." The lilting rhythm almost seemed to make his head sway, but the movement was mostly in his mind.

That lovely spring afternoon in Vienna. He had just finished his new play and was celebrating with friends at a sidewalk café. Over the radio had come the strains of "The Blue Danube," and just as it seemed as if the entire place was beginning to sway, the waltz was harshly cut off. Suddenly, in a nightmare, they were listening to the trembling voice of Chancellor Schussnigg. *This day has placed us in a tragic and decisive situation . . . the German Government . . . ultimatum . . . we have yielded to force . . . God protect Austria!*

That had been the signal for the explosion . . . *the thunder of Nazi threats and Nazi boots along the cobblestones . . . the last night . . . full of hoarse screams futile cries the death-rattle of old Vienna . . . and there was Lothar, Lothar my only son just turned twenty-one a scholarship student at the university still wearing the red-and-white ribbon of the Republic . . . my Lothar tying some clothes and books into a hasty bundle whispering: They are hunting every leader of our Fatherland Front . . . I must get out.* Remembering. *The mad rush to the station . . . the fear-crazed crowd fighting for places on the train . . . and the new conquerors of Vienna dragging them off . . . Then the last hope of freedom, the steamer anchored in the Danube ready to sail for Prague . . .* Remembering: *the small boat the muffled oars the friendly Danube the beautiful blue Danube where Lothar learned to swim . . . then the angry putt-putt-putt-putt of the motorboat full of the cruel young faces of Lothar's classmates and Lothar slipping over into the dark water diving down to leave behind the ghastly path of their searchlight . . . and the beam always flashing across the darkness to pick him out again . . . the sound of steel winging along the surface like ducks . . . the grotesque pizzicato of the bullets plunk-plunk-plunking into the river . . .*

Harold Edson Brown was reading Dreher's script. "You don't have to read it," the producer had told him. "Unless you want an idea of what I don't want." Brown had looked at the title, *Last Waltz in Vienna,* and had only meant to skim through the first couple of pages, but here he was on one hundred and two, feeling every second of Dreher's last night in Vienna. For a moment the power of Dreher's script drove so deep it reached the evaporating pool of integrity buried within him. He still knew real writing when he saw it. He was going to rush up to the producer, slam this script on his desk and shout the truth. "The climax where the old musician is playing a Strauss waltz in a Viennese beer garden as the tramp of Nazi troops and the sound of their drums begin to drown him out—the old Viennese playing louder and louder as if trying to make the voice of old Vienna heard above the tumult—until finally nothing but brown shirts and the roar of their feet, voices and martial music fills the screen and sound track—that will be one of the most terrific moments in the history of pictures!"

But when Brown finished reading he shoved the manuscript under a bunch of loose papers in his bottom drawer, violently pushing it out of his mind. He wondered if he was going to let it lie buried there forever. One of these days (maybe), when he couldn't look his fat check in the face any more, he was going to pull it out and fight for it and watch it blast his piddling little comedies off the screen.

He tilted his chair back, sprawled his feet across the desk and pulled out a bottle of whiskey. *What's the matter with me today? I'm getting soft, I'm sitting around mooning like a goddamn sophomore,* he lashed himself as he washed ideas out of his head with a healthy slug.

At the same moment Hannes Dreher was slowly climbing off a bus in Hollywood, wondering how to tell his family that the money they were waiting for to buy their way out of Vienna might not be coming for a long, long time.

Harold Edson Brown took his customary place at the writers' table. He was completely recovered. He wore a smile the way a winning racehorse wears a wreath.

"What's the big grin for?" the gag man asked him. "You look like the cat who just swallowed a producer."

"Better than that," Brown laughed. "Just got a new assignment. And I'm tickled to death. *The Blue Danube.*"

"Don't forget to change the names of the characters from *First Waltz,*" the gagman said, "so the audience won't know it's a rehash."

"Rehash hell!" Brown said. "Wait'll you hear the new angle I got on it—a twist on the *Student Prince.* I'm going to give it that real Viennese schmaltz!"

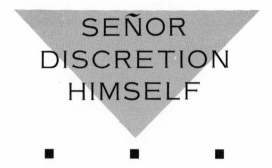

# SEÑOR DISCRETION HIMSELF

For as many years as the townspeople of Tepalcingo could remember, Alfonso (Pancito) Perez had been the proprietor of one of the smallest, poorest and most bedraggled bakeries. The Panadería Perez was a shabby little square in the wall of one-story faded-pastel storefronts that ran along a side street leading from the plaza. The back half of the bakery, thinly partitioned, was a hot, cluttered kitchen where the *bolillos, pan blanco* and *panes dulces* were made fresh every morning. Pancito always dominated the baking, barking out instructions as if his daughters had never learned how to prepare the dough and form it into the familiar shapes that decorated the fly-specked shelves until the end of the day.

In the morning a few old customers would make their purchases while the bread was still warm and fresh. In the evening the crumpled poor, barely a notch below Pancito on the local totem, would creep into the dark little shop just before closing time and buy the cold, stiffening unsold bread for half its original price, only a few centavos more than it had cost Pancito to produce it. The only way Pancito stayed in business at all, and maintained his thirty-five-pesos- or three-dollar-a-day profit, was because the genetic fates had been kind to him. If he had been a farmer he would have needed sons, but in the little bakery daughters served him very well, and here he enjoyed his only inheritance—María Cristina, age twenty-one, Rosita, nineteen, Esperanza, seventeen, and Guadalupe, the youngest, the one they called Lupita, a precocious fifteen.

María Cristina, Rosita and Esperanza were not exactly ugly. They were more what people, out of charity, like to call "plain." All three resembled their dead mother, thin and dry and dutiful. They were good girls. They did as they were told. They worked hard and went to mass on Sunday; and although they were still very young, they seemed already to be in training to become very old. María Cristina was rather advanced in years for a maiden in Tepalcingo. She was the homeliest of the four and the most strongly possessed by sense of duty. She had mothered the others, was a veteran at the job before she was twelve, had cooked for all of them and mended the clothes and prepared the home remedies when they were sick. She was a deeply religious girl and had wanted to become a nun, but Pancito had not been able to spare her. The family would have fallen apart.

Pancito, which can be literally translated as "Little Bread," was a good father, within his limitations. But his limitations were considerable. After his wife, Beneficencia, had died— suddenly, it seemed to him, though neighbors could see she had been slowly wasting away—Pancito had felt extremely sorry for himself and had gone from the Panadería Perez to his favorite *cantina*, The Bass Drum of God, where he would drink *mescal* beyond his capacity and describe Beneficencia in terms far more glowing than ever he had granted her during her brief tour of duty on earth. "But thank God," he would say to Celestino the bartender, the only one who would listen,

"He has seen fit to bless me with hardworking daughters who respect their father and who do not throw their dresses over their heads for the first little hoodlum who comes along. *Rebeldes sin causa,* that is what they are," he would shout over his shoulder at the domino players who were always in the same booth minding their rattly business across from the bar. *"Rebeldes sin causa."*

Pancito had heard that phrase read to him by his youngest daughter, Lupita, from the local newspaper in connection with an assault of *hampones* on the Panadería Cortez, the proud establishment of Hilario Cortez, who had a bakery three times as large as Pancito's. To the unrelenting envy of Pancito, the Panadería Cortez had just installed overhead neon lights. The *hampones,* or young hoodlums, had managed to break into the modernized bakery of Hilario Cortez and had thrown empty beer bottles at the new-style neon tubing, but had disdained stealing any of the bread. Not even a single *pan dulce.* They had smashed Hilario Cortez's pride-and-joy neon lights merely for the sake of smashing, a strange, nihilistic disease that seemed to be spreading south from the monster *gringo* republic beyond the Rio Grande.

*"Rebeldes sin causa,* rebels without cause, just like in the movies," Lupita had said.

"A decent young girl of fifteen should not have any knowledge of such degrading movies," Pancito had scolded. "How many times must I tell you—you are forbidden to see the *gringo* movies."

"Papa, where could I get the *pesetas* to see the movie?"

"Then what has made you such an expert on this shameless *pelicula?"*

"My teacher spoke about it in school. Maestro Martínez."

"Martínez! He is an atheist! He taught school two years in California. He is a *pocho.* I have a good mind to go to that school and hit him such a crack with my cane on his know-it-all skull that—" Pancito was fond of launching grandiose threats of violence that he had difficulty in rounding out rhetorically. He was short, barely five and a half feet high, and it was his potbelly as much as his profession that had given him his nickname. He also had a slight limp from a touch of rickets in his childhood, but this did not discourage him from threatening bodily harm to people half his age and twice his size. Although his cane was a crutch, it could quickly become his lance. Undersized, put upon, easily triggered to anger, Pancito Perez saw himself as a mailed champion of his own right to be alive, to have a place in this world, be it ever so humble, as long as it was not without dignity. Since Pancito could not read, he had only a hearsay acquaintance with Don Quixote, and so was not truly aware of how closely he reflected Cervantes's true knight. But Don Pancito was ever ready to raise his cane and charge into battle against the human windmills arrayed against him.

"Papa," Lupita reminded him, "only last week you were praising Maestro Martínez and telling me how much I could learn from him if only I would study harder."

"Don't contradict your father," Pancito shouted, outraged at his daughter's logic. "Can't a man praise someone for his intelligence and knowledge of books and at the same time damn him for his atheism and his worldliness? Now get on with your studies. I must get back to the bakery before those lazy sisters of yours destroy what little is left of my business."

"Very well, Father," Lupita said, and opened her mathematics book that had to do with mysterious letters as well as numbers and made Pancito feel both proud and inferior in the presence of her unexpected scholarship. That and her inexplicable beauty gave Pancito twinges of anxiety. Lupita was a strange fruit on the tree of Perez. She was full-bosomed and ripe rather than plump, like a mango ready for plucking when the skin has turned from green to yellow gold and its firmness gives satisfying form to the softening yellow fruit that waits within. Often when he looked at her, Pancito wondered if she could be truly his. It did not seem possible that his shy, hard-working, life-drained Beneficencia could have put horns on him. Even if she had had the inclination, when could she have found the time, and what *cabrón* would have taken the trouble? Yet, when Pancito looked into the voluptuous, high-cheek-boned face of his youngest daughter, he recognized not a single feature of his own, and certainly none of Beneficencia's. Guadalupe, his rapidly maturing Lupita, was a lush mango hanging from a dried-up pepper tree. All of the beauty of the family Perez had funneled into her, and all of the brains. Neither Pancito nor his wife nor the three older sisters had been able to read and write, and so Pancito had decided that Lupita would be the first member of the family to break the literacy barrier.

When she read the local newspaper aloud to him, Pancito's feelings ran against each other like the opposing currents of a riptide. He felt a puffer's pride in her unique achievement and at the same time a resentment that this near-child fifteen-year-old already knew so much more than her father. It made her sassy and difficult to manage. Just the same, the virtues of higher education outweighed the personal disadvantages to Pancito, and he had begun to hope she could finish the *secundaria* and even move on to become a teacher. Since Pancito was resigned to the hard fact that he would never be more than fifty pesos ahead of himself, that he would never have a bakery even half the size of the grand Panadería Cortez, status meant everything to him. To have a daughter who could rise above menial labor, who could be elevated into the professional class as a *maestra,* this was the star to which Pancito might hitch his wobbly little wagon.

"Well, no rest for the weary," Pancito said as he drained the glass of dark beer with which he always washed down the meager midafternoon *comida.* "I'm off to catch another eagle." On every silver peso was engraved the Mexican *águila,* and Pancito was fond of describing his financial pressure as "too

many mouths and not enough eagles." Like many men who
cannot read or write, Pancito was inclined to outbursts of
eloquence. In his youth he had been a partisan of the Obregón
revolution, and two of his favorite postures were politically
oratorical and verbally combative. When he was addressing an
audience of three or four half-listeners in The Bass Drum of
God, or when he was tongue-lashing some absent enemy (and
the farther away the target the more ferocious his attack),
Pancito was able to put out of mind his petty-bourgeois poverty and the insufficiencies of his figure and his position. Self-
propelled by his own anger or rhetoric, the roly-poly baker in
his tight, threadbare double-breasted suit (a one-hundred-peso
secondhand acquisition necessary as a symbol of shopkeeper
status) was no longer earth-bound or bakery-bound or bound
to the faded walls of the sour-smelling Bass Drum of God.

Pancito was cooped up in his cell-like *panadería* with his
solemn-faced daughters a minimum of ten hours a day. He
unlocked his shop every morning at five A.M. (including Sundays) to start the baking with the heavy but shapeless resentment of a man serving a life sentence for a crime he not only
did not commit but cannot even identify. Yet he felt strangely
guilty, guilty for having been born, guilty for having been a
spindly and undernourished child, guilty for having grown up
short and pudgy and slightly lame, guilty for having lost his
wife to the graveyard before the four girls were fully reared,
guilty for having what was generally acknowledged as the
sorriest bakery in Tepalcingo, guilty, inexplicably and inexora-
bly guilty of being Pancito Perez. Pancito Perez the Failure.
Waking up in the dark to face the same day he had endured
the day before, he could almost hear that defeatist phrase
forming in his mind. Only quick gulps of *mescal* and the release
of shouted anger had the power to change Pancito Perez the
Failure into Pancito Perez the Man.

When summer came, waves of heat from the oven rolled out
to embrace the heat waves from the sun-fried cobblestones of

the narrow street; by noonday Pancito felt like one of his steaming loaves ready to burst its crust. The three daughters worked quietly, stoically, managing to triumph over perspiration, perhaps because there was not enough juice in them to pour out in protest against their fate. But Pancito made up for them. He groaned, he cursed, he pitied himself, he called on the Holy Virgin to take a little belated interest in the Panadería Perez. He kept up such a commotion that finally María Cristina said, "Papa, instead of suffering here with your *dolor de cabeza,* your sorrow of the head, why don't you go home and put a cool towel on your face and try to calm yourself. There will be very little to do here until the sun is low."

Ordinarily, Pancito would have argued that his presence was essential, that María Cristina could not count well enough to make proper change, that she was not an aggressive enough salesman in urging a customer to buy an extra *pan dulce,* that she was not strong enough to ward off the blandishments of Faustino, the unshaven policeman who never paid for his purchases and who came around behind the counter and peacocked in his unpressed, dirty brown uniform. If given enough time, Pancito could think of a hundred reasons for not entrusting the Panadería Perez to his three well-meaning but ineffectual daughters. But this time his head was pounding with the heat and with such a sense of failure that he hardly cared whether María Cristina sold an extra *pan dulce* or not, or whether Patrolman Faustino raped the daughters one by one or all together. This was a monumental headache, a milestone of a headache, and his unexpected decision to give in to it and quit the shop early put certain forces into motion that were to change the entire chemistry of his life.

The phenomenon began when Pancito, holding his small, fat hands to his temples, pushed open the door of his house with his foot and saw something that made him forget his headache like *that.* There at the table where Pancito always sat down to his private *comida* was Hilario Cortez, whose prosperity he had always resented but whom he now hated with righteous passion for daring to violate his precious virgin Lupita. To be factual, Hilario Cortez was only sitting at the same table with Lupita and feeling his way very carefully, as befitted a man about town. But Pancito knew that a forty-year-old man does not come to discuss the agrarian problem or civic betterment with a ripe and uninitiated fifteen-year-old *guapa.*

"Get out! Get out!" Pancito screamed, waving his cane in the air like a righteous flag. "Out, you lecher, you rapist, you pervert, you despoiler of children!" Hilario Cortez managed to duck the wild swings of the cane as he ran out of the house, with Pancito shouting after him, "Help! Police! Rape! Rape!" Hilario Cortez turned the corner on the run while Pancito loudly expressed to the entire street his moral objections to this unnatural assignation between the depraved Señor Cortez and his innocent Lupita. As soon as he stepped back into the house, however, his attitude toward his precious darling shot into reverse. "Lupita, you little tramp, for *this* I struggle and sacrifice and get up in the middle of the night to get a head start on the eagles so that you can go to school—for *this,* so you can whore around with an old man who has enough years to be your grandfather!"

Lupita was trying to explain that Señor Cortez was a fine-looking gentleman who had not yet laid a hand on her. But it was difficult to talk back when Pancito was slapping her across the face, pushing her and cuffing her and shouting the most vile insults he could think of, until finally Lupita sank to her knees, her face reddened from blows and shameful language.

"Please, Papa, if you will only listen a moment! I will tell you everything that happened. I was turning the corner from the school to our street with my arms full of books when hurrying the other way was Señor Cortez and, *zas,* we bump into each other like two taxicabs and my books go flying into the street and—"

"The scoundrel," Pancito shouted. "Seducer. I know that little game."

"Papa! Señor Cortez was very polite. Very *suave*. He apologized and picked up all my books and dusted me off—"

"Patted your little behind, isn't that closer to the truth?" Pancito shouted, and raised his cane to strike out sin.

"Papa—don't hit me—all he did was walk me home. Then he asked if he could sit down a moment, out of the sun, and then you walked in—"

"And not a moment too soon!" Pancito shouted. "Everybody knows Hilario Cortez is the cleverest seducer and virgin-grabber in our entire *municipio*. If I ever catch him here again I'll—Oh, I mean it. I'll . . ."

To admit the truth, Pancito Perez wasn't quite sure what he would do to Hilario Cortez. After the spontaneous combustion of his first face-to-face confrontation with this rival baker, Pancito began to consider the reality of this physical complication: Hilario was as tall, lean and broad-chested as Pancito was short and potbellied. A few inches less and Pancito would have been a dwarf; a few inches more and Hilario would be a giant. He was almost six feet tall and known for the feats of strength he liked to demonstrate at fiestas. He could ride a horse like Zapata and, in fact, he somewhat resembled the legendary hero of Morelos, even to the ferocious black bristle of a mustache around his upper lip. Obviously, Pancito could not beat his rival in a contest of physical prowess. He would have to play the fox to the lion. He would have to outwit his enemy Hilario Cortez.

He went to The Bass Drum of God to think it over, and staggering home from the *cantina* he was still pondering it when he happened to pass the small, immaculate house of Maestro Martínez, the schoolteacher of Lupita. Under his name was a sign that read: LECCIONES PRIVADAS, private lessons, and beneath that. PUBLIC STENOGRAPHER—LETTERS WRITTEN IN YOUR OWN WORDS. The pay for a public schoolteacher was not enough to marry on or raise a family, and many teachers had to use their outside hours to keep a few *águilas* in their trousers.

The moment Pancito saw that sign he knew what he should do. He would send Hilario Cortez such a threatening letter that the big, self-important Don Juan of a baker would never dare to come near Pancito's prize little guava again. In the plaza there were always a few *evangelistas*—the common nickname for the public letter-writers who dozed all day by their ancient typewriters waiting for an *analfebeto,* as illiterates were called, to dictate letters of the heart or urgent requests for money. Often when sitting on one of the park benches watching an *evangelista* at work, Pancito had thought of sending someone a letter. But the plaza was the favorite haunt of the *sabelotodos,* the know-it-alls who would enjoy seeing Pancito exposed before the town as a self-confessed illiterate. This was particularly embarrassing for Pancito, as he never would admit that he was an *analfabeto.* Sometimes, when a piece of printed matter was shoved in front of his face at the *panadería,* he would pretend that he had left his reading glasses at home. Sometimes, having absorbed Lupita's digest of the local paper for him, he would pick up the sheet, scan it thoughtfully and announce. "Well, I see the *municipio* is going to fill the potholes on Hidalgo Street. It's about time . . ."

So it was a welcome sight to see the public-stenographer sign on Maestro Martínez's gate. Pancito could turn in here without anyone knowing his secret. To acquaintances who might see him enter he could swear he had an appointment to discuss the schoolwork of his daughter Lupita.

Maestro Martínez was still in his twenties, with a slight, wiry build, stooped beyond his years, with rimless eyeglasses that lent a fussy, male old-maid look to a face that otherwise would have seemed attractively vigorous and lean. The house was small but exceptionally clean, the tile floor immaculate—none of the clutter of Mexican lower-class life. With Maestro Mar-

tínez, cleanliness and order were signs of modernity and progress. They spoke for a man who scoffed at the miracle of the
Virgin of Guadalupe, whose goals were pure reason and science, a world swept clean of superstition and blind emotion.
A product of the state university, he was the sort of Mexican
progressive who advocates such iconoclastic ideas as honest
elections and planned parenthood. One whole wall of the
front room was lined with books: neighbors gossiped that
Maestro Martínez sat up reading books until three or four in
the morning. Only on the national holidays, Independence
Day, Cinco de Mayo, the Anniversary of the Revolution of
1910, would Maestro Martínez be seen in the *cantina,* and
then he would drink a few beers and explain to willing listen-
ers the historical background of the days they were celebrating
in a state of profound inebriation. A thoughtful fellow was
Maestro Martínez, with passionate convictions held in dispas-
sionate check. For the *maestro's* strongest conviction was in
pacific solution to man's problems. "Man is the most violent
of all the animals," he liked to lecture his classes. "Faced with
a problem, man's first instinct is to attack it violently. A man
strikes out by instinct. He must be taught to negotiate. He will
never be thoroughly civilized until he learns to operate in the
light of reason rather than from the dark caves of emotion
where he still lives."

Maestro Martínez was buttressing this favorite theory with
some pertinent reading from Auguste Comte when Pancito
burst in on him. "Good evening, Señor Perez, won't you sit
down?" the young teacher said pleasantly as he rose and
bowed. "Here is Maestro Martínez at your service."

"I am too goddamn mad to sit down," Pancito shouted,
brandishing his cane and almost losing his balance. "I want to
send a letter that will tell a rotten skunk why he should crawl
into his hole and die like a dog in the final stages of rabies."

"Please. Señor Perez, you are mixing your metaphors, you
must compose yourself," Maestro Martínez said quietly.

"The devil with my—whatever you call them," Pancito shouted. "When the honor of my daughter is at stake, I must use words that will chop the snake down like a machete, not tickle him like a feather."

"At your service." Maestro Martínez shrugged as he sat down to his fifty-year-old *máquina de escribir* that should have been in a typewriter museum.

"To Señor Hilario Cortez—" Pancito shouted as if he were face to face with the nemesis of Lupita, in fact even a little more aggressively, because he would have been slightly intimidated by the overpowering physical presence of Hilario Cortez.

"To *el estimado* Señor," Maestro Martínez corrected gently, adding the conventional courtesy.

"To hell with that *estimado,*" Pancito shouted. "That I should be courteous to the thief of the one jewel in my humble crown? I did not come here to argue with you about courtesy. I came to tell you a letter that will shoot into his heart like a poisoned arrow."

"OK—no *estimado*—proceed," said the *maestro,* who was rather proud of his *gringo* slang. "Shoot."

Pancito cleared his throat and launched his dictation: "Listen to me, you mangy son of a homeless bitch, this is Pancito Perez talking—no, change that 'Pancito' to 'Don Alfonso'—If you do not stay away from my Lupita I will shoot you in a place where you will have no further interest in molesting innocent children. This is no idle threat. Poke your lecherous head in my house once more and I will chop it off with my machete and stick it on the gatepost outside my house so all the people in Tepalcingo can see what happens to whoremongering old bats who suck the lifeblood from innocent little girls like my angelic Lupita. You filthy rapist, beware!"

Pancito was so carried away that he seemed on the point of attacking Maestro Martínez with his cane. "Type my name at the bottom, 'An outraged father bent on vengeance, Don

Alfonso Perez,' and then I will sign it," he instructed. He had learned to sign his name with a flourish that made forming individual letters unnecessary.

The fingers of Maestro Martínez worked rapidly to keep pace with Pancito's rage. His efficient, objective manner gave no hint of his personal reaction to the content of Pancito's message. When he finished, he read it back to Pancito in a dry, academic tone that lent a curious malice to Pancito's honest outpouring of parental wrath. Satisfied that he had said what he had come to say, Pancito affixed his furious signature. "Now I will type a clean copy double-spaced," Maestro Martínez said. "Then you can sign the official one and drop it in the mailbox on your way home. I hope it will bring you the results you desire."

Pancito was on his way back to the bakery after lunch next afternoon when he happened to see Hilario Cortez coming toward him. The rival baker looked particularly big that afternoon and Pancito found himself nervously slowing his steps. But Hilario surprised him by calling out, "Good afternoon, my friend, how very nice to see you today," and passing by with a cordial smile. Pancito resumed his normal pace with growing confidence. Hah, isn't that typical of bullies, he nodded to himself. You stand up to them and threaten to put them in their place and the wolves turn into frightened sheep.

But on his way home for lunch the following day, he was quite sure he saw Hilario hurriedly leaving and rushing down the street in the opposite direction. Again he cursed and cuffed Lupita and stormed off to The Bass Drum of God to fuel rather than drown his anger. Then he went again to Maestro Martínez. This time he put it even stronger. He called on the foulest language he could remember. Maestro Martínez abandoned his professional objectivity long enough to question whether such obscenities should be allowed to go through the mail.

"Put it down, Maestro, word for word. I know what I am

doing," Pancito insisted. "There is only one way to deal with monsters."

Maestro Martínez sighed, eloquently, and typed away. Pancito studied the finished product carefully, as if he could read every word of it, and signed it with a furious flourish, the tail of the final "o" on Alfonso surging across the page like the savage thrust of an avenging sword.

The next time Hilario Cortez spied Pancito, he not only waved to him but made a point of crossing the street to intercept him. Still apprehensive, Pancito took a tighter grip on his cane, but Hilario could not have been friendlier. "I just received your second letter," he began, "and I want to tell you how much I appreciate it. I must confess that I have had an almost uncontrollable desire to possess Lupita. But your letters have moved me to reconsider. You are clearly a man of the most unusual intelligence and tact."

Pancito simply did not know what to say. He stared at Hilario in stunned amazement. Finally he summoned up all the dignity he could find for the occasion, muttered a "Thank you, sir, and good afternoon," and walked on. He walked straight to The Bass Drum of God to celebrate his victory. On his third *mescal* he began to feel he had not gone far enough. Obviously, he had his old enemy on the run. But Hilario Cortez was a shrewd one. He was *muy listo.* Now he was trying to get around Pancito with flattery and honeyed words. But Pancito Perez would show him who was boss. He had a fourth *mescal* and was ready to face the formidable typewriter of Maestro Martínez.

"Rapist Hilario, you depraved son of a rutting she-goat," he began his mescalated dictation.

"Señor Perez, are you sure you are in a condition to write another letter tonight?"

"Stop interrupting how my mind is thinking," shouted the inspired Pancito. "Put it down. Every word. Just as I say it—You don't fool me with your lying mouth, you whoring son of a two-peso *puta*—"

"Señor Perez!"

"Every word," Pancito shouted, waving his cane like General Santa Anna leading his troops on the Alamo.

Maestro Martínez gave another philosophical shrug and went on typing. When it was ready, Pancito looked it over with exhausted satisfaction and signed it with another angry scrawl. "That will keep the depraved beast from turning this whole town into a red-light district," Pancito said, handing Maestro Martínez a soiled, hard-earned ten-peso bill.

"Thank you, Don Pancito. I hope my poor efforts to reflect your true feelings will bring the moral solution you desire," said the schoolteacher with the Oriental humbleness that is also in the Mexican.

Results were soon in coming, and they could not have surprised Pancito more if the Virgin of Guadalupe had swooped down and personally invited him to dance a *paso doble.*

Two days later Pancito was just locking up his shop when he saw Hilario coming toward him. Pancito's first impulse was to duck back into his shop, lock the door and sneak out the back way. For in the sober headache of morning, Pancito knew that even for him he had gone a little too far. Such words as he had spewed in rage and frustration and anti-Goliathism invited the challenge of violence, of pistol fire and the metallic clashing of machetes. But it was too late for Pancito to escape. The long, well-shaped legs of Hilario quickened their pace and the rival was upon him.

"Pancito—wait—I must speak to you."

In fear Pancito waited. Hilario came to him with a great smile of affection such as Pancito had never seen before. "Pancito, my dear fellow, I must speak to you. Your last letter convinces me beyond any doubt. You are surely the wisest man in Tepalcingo. Won't you join me for a *copita* at The Three Kings?"

Pancito hesitated, but the seeming sincerity of Hilario's invitation was beguiling. A little wary, Pancito accompanied the towering Hilario to the most respectable sidewalk café on the plaza. There Hilario ordered not *tequila* or *mescal* but whiskey *escocés,* to express the solemnity and high quality of the occasion.

"To our friendship, begun in strife, may it mature and ripen into prosperous brotherhood." Hilario toasted.

Pancito merely touched glasses with a half-swallowed *"Salud."* He was confused to the point of stupidity. What was Hilario's game? Was he simply fattening Pancito up for the kill? One night he had seen this happen in The Bass Drum of God. The editor of the local paper was invited to sit down and have a drink with a local politico who thought the journalist had insulted him in print. They had three ostensibly friendly drinks together when suddenly the politico went berserk, grabbed the journalist with a terrible oath and started pounding his head against the wall with one hand while he slapped him viciously with the other until blood began to spurt from his victim's face. It had been an ugly and frightening spectacle, at the same time *muy mexicano,* and Pancito feared that any moment he might suffer the same shift in emotional weather.

But if Hilario felt any resentment at Pancito's latest effort at literary violence, he concealed it convincingly. In fact, he startled the anxious Pancito by saying, "Don Alfonso, I am a man who likes to come right to the point. I must confess I am charmed by your letters. They are little masterpieces."

"I—try to write as I talk—say what I think," Pancito muttered.

"Then let me say I like the way you think. You are obviously much more a man of the world than, no offense intended, you would seem to be at first appearance. Your letters have convinced me that you are Señor Discretion Himself."

"A thousand thank-yous," Pancito said, taking heart and signaling to the waiter for another round. "Now it is my turn to buy you a drink. You see, I had thought you might be offended—"

"Offended! My good fellow, my good friend, I should call

you. I was flattered. I'm not sure I didn't go back for a final
visit with Lupita just so I could receive another of your extraor-
dinary letters. Look"—Hilario patted the inside pocket of his
jacket—"I keep them right here. Once in a while I take them
out and reread them, as I would a poem by Octavio Paz."

Pancito paid for the new round of whiskies *escocés,* a new
alcoholic experience which he found not at all to his taste,
thought of all the insulting names with which he had assaulted
Hilario and wondered if his "new friend" had gone mad.
Well, maybe the man thrived on insults. Pancito had heard
about those types—were they not called *masoquistas?*

"But now to the point, as two practical men of commerce."
Hilario snapped Pancito back to attention. "I have a business
proposition to make to you."

Pancito sipped his Scotch with a clumsy effort of poise to
cover his confusion.

"You have a small bakery, I have a somewhat larger one,
and they are on the same street, only a block and a half apart,"
Hilario Cortez began. "So every day I take a good deal of
business away from you, but you also take a little business away
from me. I am a baker and you are a baker, but frankly, I am
a man of ambition, a little too restless, a little too modern to
spend all my life peering into an oven or measuring out *panes
dulces* for pimply adolescents. In other words, I do not have the
temperament to spend the next twenty-five years—or fifty, if
I live as long as my father—in a hot kitchen or behind a
counter."

Hilario raised his glass and touched it to Pancito's with an
appreciative smile. "Health—and money, lots of money, to
the two of us."

"To the two of us," Pancito mumbled, a little high on the
foreign whisky and the heady talk.

"So I began to speculate," Hilario went on. "The more I
thought about your letters, the more strongly I asked myself,
perhaps the man who is the soul of discretion, of understand-

ing, and with such intellectual control of his capacities, and at
the same time an excellent baker with a lifetime of experience,
who knows how to make a *pan dulce* that melts in the mouth
and to write a letter as sweet to the mind, is he not the perfect
partner I have been looking for?"

Pancito wanted to sip his Scotch like the man of the world
Hilario was determined to think him, but he gulped and a few
drops of the unfamiliar liquid went down his windpipe, caus-
ing him to choke and cough in a most undignified way. Hilario
pounded him on the back attentively. Pancito muttered some
spastic apology, but if the pudgy little baker was, in the eyes
of Hilario, the soul of discretion, the younger, more prosperous baker was the soul of solicitude.

"There, there, drink a little water. I realize you are a sober,
conscientious man not used to so much alcoholic refreshment
in the middle of the day. But as I was saying, if we were to
merge our bakeries, Panaderías Cortez *y* Perez, you could
manage the big shop, keep an eye on your daughters in your
old one, and leave me free to wander around and search for
new locations. You see, I am looking to the future. I am
thinking big, I see a chain of *panaderías,* not just here in our
little city, but Cuernavaca, Chilpancingo . . ." Hilario's expan-
sive wave of the hand seemed to take in the entire map of
Mexico.

"Don Hilario, you are indeed a man of great vision," Pancito managed to say.

"Cortez *y* Perez," Hilario intoned. "No longer little hole-
in-the-wall bakeries, but first-rate, modern establishments. As
a bachelor, I will make the perfect outside man, *advance man*
I believe the smart *gringos* call it. Your oldest daughter is a
solid, responsible girl—teach her to run the little bakery, it will
cater to the poor, no use wasting expensive sweets and egg
twists on the centavo pinchers. But there is a profit in quantity,
we can send down the leftover morning bread to your evening
bargain hunters. First we'll invest our profits in new equip-

ment, new facilities; later we can put our earnings to work for us with ten-percent bonds—someday we might even go into the restaurant business, coffeeshops, like I have seen when I went to visit my great-uncle in Texas—the waitresses will have starched orange dresses—we will add coffeecakes and *hamburguesas . . .*"

In this Scotch haze of optimism the partnership was consummated. Cortez *y* Perez it was, and this was perhaps the only time in the history of *El Bar de los Tres Reyes,* of The Three Kings, when the splendid dreams of a long afternoon's congenial drinking were to be translated into cash-money reality. For the mysterious letters in Hilario's pocket worked their magic like the lamp of Aladdin, and lo, it was even as Hilario Cortez had promised. Pancito seemed to find himself in the larger *panadería.* He supervised the baking rather than doing it all himself and he managed both bakeries with a newly discovered authority, an executive ability he had never been aware of before but that must have been in him all the time. Now he was flowing like an underground stream that Hilario had discovered, tapped and channeled up to the surface. He became very sure of himself, but in a quiet and controlled way. The old rages and outbursts of frustration were left behind him, like the cramped and poverty-drab rooms where he had raised his daughters around the corner from his shabby little bakery. After the first year of his partnership with Hilario Cortez, he was able to purchase a small stucco, modernistic house, two stories, with a small patio and balcony. His partner Hilario still liked to refer to him as Señor Discretion, and the name not only caught on around Pancito, but within Pancito as well. He became each day more what Hilario believed him to be. Customers would say, "It is such a pleasure to deal with Pancito"—although more often now they referred to him as Don Alfonso—"If you wish to feel the bread to make sure it is warm before you buy it he never flies into a tantrum, and you can even return loaves you are not perfectly satisfied with and he will accept them with a smile and let you pick out something fresher in its place, or even hand you back your money. Señor Discretion he certainly is, from the top of his bald head to the very heel of his poor lame foot." Old customers who knew the earlier, irritable, unprepossessing Pancito thought it was a miracle, no less than the healing kiss of the blessed dark Virgin of Guadalupe.

As if to reward Pancito for this growth of character, fortune continued to smile on him—no, not merely smile but laugh, roar with a laughter of largess as Hilario outdid his original promise and there were modernized bakeries and branches and finally, on the main square of Cuernavaca, a spick-and-span chrome-and-plastic C & P Coffee Shop with Hot Doggies and *hamburguesas* "King-Size" and, yes, waitresses with flared-out, starched orange dresses, as splendid as anything you could find in Texas. To celebrate the addition of this restaurant business to their chain of bakeries, Don Hilario and Pancito, excuse us—Don Alfonso—went to Cuernavaca for the grand opening and took a suite together at the plushiest hotel they could find in that *gringo*-plush, Old Spanish-Indian resort. There were elegant individual cottages overlooking a small private lake on which swam in graceful self-assurance redheaded pintail ducks and stately black swans. The two partners were relaxing on the latticed portico of their bungalow suite as the white-jacketed waiter served them their Scotch, which had been for some time Pancito's favorite drink. He often told his employees he could not understand how they could tolerate that vile *mescal,* but of course it was their stomachs, if they wanted to burn out the linings, that was their business.

"Don Alfonso, I have a little memento for you," the graying but still flat-bellied Hilario said to his now portly rather than paunchy partner, tailored clothes making the difference. He reached into his attaché case and produced a silver frame in which a neatly typed letter was carefully preserved under glass. "A small token of my regard for you, dear friend and partner," said Hilario, handing over the original letter he had received from Pancito. Pancito knew instinctively what it was. He squinted at it and said, "Hilario, my *compañero,* my reading glasses are inside in the bathroom—for old times' sake, will you read me the letter?"

Actually, Pancito was curious to hear the magic letter. So much had happened that he remembered only dimly what he had written, or rather dictated to Maestro Martínez.

"It will be an honor to read it," said Hilario, and he began enthusiastically:

" 'My dear, esteemed friend Señor Cortez, it has come to my attention, as a result of your recent visit, that you are an admirer of the charm and beauty of my daughter Guadalupe. I salute you on your evident good taste and also on your gentlemanly conduct during your visit to our humble home. What my daughter may not have told you, out of inevitable regard for a suitor so distinguished and attractive as yourself, is that she is barely fifteen years old. If you were a lesser man I might feel I have to appeal to you personally, but I fully appreciate that in the case of a gentleman so gallant and blessed with the true chivalric spirit as you are so well known in the community to be, I have only to mention the fact of my daughter's tender age and leave it to your profound sense of courtesy, maturity and understanding to guide your kind heart and noble soul in lieu of a widower-father's paternal concern. As gentleman to gentleman, I am, then, ever your humble servant, Alfonso Perez.' "

Hilario Cortez lowered the silver-framed masterpiece with a feeling of tears blinked back behind his eyes. "When I first received this letter, it filled me with the most unbearable guilt," Hilario said. "For I realized it was you, not I, who possessed that 'profound sense of courtesy, maturity and understanding.' After our little 'altercation' at your house the first time you found me there—a self-invited intruder—oh, you were quite right to express yourself that forcibly—imagine what you might have written, the names you might have called me, the rude phrases, the insults . . ."

"Yes, imagine," Pancito agreed. And he was not trying to dissimulate. He was not sure he had said all *that*, not quite; there were, in fact, a few words he did not even understand, but he decided the young, owlish schoolteacher must have put those in to dress the letter up a bit, as a photographer touches up a portrait.

"Those letters, so full of warmth and wisdom, convinced me to stop trying to woo Lupita into bed and to woo her father into business instead," Hilario laughed. "But now, time has moved on. Lupita is no longer only fifteen, but almost twenty, an accomplished young lady, graduate of the high school, able to read and write and be the legal mistress of one of the leaders of the community. In other words, dear friend, I ask no less than the hand of Guadalupe in formal marriage."

"Dear Hilario, I am a man who likes to come straight to the point," said Pancito, borrowing a phrase from his partner, as he frequently did. "In the entire city of Tepalcingo, in fact, in the entire state of Morelos, I cannot think of a husband better suited to the station and happiness of Guadalupe than Don Hilario Cortez. I will break the good news to my obedient daughter the moment I return."

When he arrived home from the C & P Coffee Shop ceremonies in Cuernavaca, Pancito found Lupita combing her hair in her dressing room. She had oil-black hair flowing to her waist and she could sit before her long mirror and comb it sensuously for an hour without becoming the least bit bored. When Pancito told her what he had announced as wonderful news, Lupita threw her hairbrush at him. Since those threadbare years of the little bakery, she had grown into a handsome and stately and self-possessed young lady of whom Pancito was extremely proud, when not wondering whether it was the fault of too much education that had made her so unmanageable.

"If you think I am going to marry that ridiculous old man,

you are even more stupid than I think you are," Lupita screamed, for she had a quick-trigger personality, not unlike her father's in his primitive, prediscretion period.

"Old man, he's a full ten years younger than I am," Pancito argued.

"After one is thirty, it makes no difference," Lupita said.

"But five years ago I had to keep him away from the house. And you were encouraging him, you little hussy."

"Five years ago I was a child, it was flattering," Lupita said. "And when you wrote those stupid letters and he stopped coming, I lost all respect for him. A real man would have found ways to get around you, to make secret rendezvous, to carry me off by force."

"Thank the Virgin he was too much of a gentleman for that," said the frustrated Pancito.

"You can have him. You seem very happy together. I have made my own choice," Lupita said.

"And just who, may I ask, is this fortunate fellow?" asked Pancito with some touch of his prediscretion sarcasm creeping into his voice.

"Maestro Martínez," Lupita said.

"Maestro Martínez, that bent-over little hunchback of a schoolteacher!" Pancito exploded. "He's a pauper! You'll both starve to death! I'll break his eyeglasses! I'll smash his big dictionary over his head. I'll—I'll—have him arrested and packed off to the prison island, I'll—"

Maestro Martínez was standing in the doorway. His hair was slightly streaked with gray and he was a little more bent over from so much study and writing, but otherwise he was the same wiry, intense, birdlike man, surprisingly handsome behind his rimless glasses and his studious expression.

"Señor Perez, I am happy to find you here. I have come to talk to you," Maestro Martínez began.

"*Cabrón!*" Pancito shouted. "You dirty, double-dealing cradle-snatcher, son of a two-peso whore, you—"

At the first oath, Lupita had run from the living room into the kitchen, not merely shocked by her father's obscene language, but so she could eavesdrop unseen behind the kitchen door.

"Well, Señor Discretion, I see that the years have not changed you after all," Maestro Martínez said quietly.

"What do you mean? What are you talking about?" Pancito asked.

"The foul names you call me for daring to admire your daughter are practically the same ones you dictated to me against Hilario Cortez," Maestro Martínez explained.

"Never—I knew I could appeal to my dear friend Hilario as a man of reason and honor," Pancito said. "To the discretion I showed in dealing with that problem I owe my entire success in life."

"I think you mean to the discretion *I* showed in dealing with that problem," Maestro Martínez corrected him, and he drew from his pocket some worn pieces of paper. "Perhaps this will refresh your memory—'Listen to me, you mangy son of a homeless bitch . . . If you do not stay away from my Lupita I will shoot you in a place where you will have no further interest in molesting innocent children . . .'"

Pancito shut his eyes. Were those really his words? Yes, some faint echo from the furious poverty of his past warned him not to protest too strongly against the evidence in the hands of Maestro Martínez.

"This is the actual letter you dictated and had read back to you and signed. You remember you waited half an hour to re-sign the clean copy double-spaced? The second letter was not a duplicate. When I read your outburst, I thought to myself, if Señor Cortez receives this intemperate letter he can turn it over to the police and they will arrest Pancito Perez for threatening to commit assault and battery, even murder. And furthermore, you remember my theory that man is at the crossroads—he can be the most vicious, the most brutal and deadly of all the animals—or he can use his superior intelligence to reason and negotiate and solve his problems in peace. So I rewrote your letter in those terms. You have seen how Señor Cortez responded. It has proved my theory. But I still have your original letters, signed by you to acknowledge that I had put down exactly what you said, insult by insult, obscenity by obscenity, just as you insisted. If you wish, I could send them to Señor Cortez, explaining that the man he valued so highly that he wished to make him a lifelong associate is not really you at all—actually Señor Discretion Himself is me."

Now Pancito bent over his cane, feeling weary and humiliated. Maestro Martínez observed that this made him look more like the earlier Pancito of the shabby, fly-specked Panadería Perez. The Don Alfonso he had become walked erect on his cane, as if the cane were actually a gentleman's accoutrement maneuvered with a sense of grandeur, rather than a crutch to be leaned on in disability.

"Maestro Martínez," Pancito said in a hoarse, defeated whisper, "are you trying to blackmail me?"

The slender, wire-bent *maestro* seemed to smile behind his frown. "Perhaps. Or you might say I am trying to white-mail you. I mean, I am not threatening you with a black lie, but with the pure truth. Lupita and I wish to leave Tepalcingo and go to the capital, to the city of Mexico. We can both attend the national university, where I can work for my master's degree in philosophy and she can complete her college education and become a teacher as you have always hoped she would."

"I thought it was better for her than doing menial labor," Pancito protested. "But it's hardly in a class with becoming the wife of a leading citizen."

This time Maestro Martínez seemed to frown behind his smile. "Ten thousand pesos will see us comfortably through the first year at the university."

"Ten thousand pesos—" Pancito shouted. "Because Hilario Cortez and I own a few bakeries together, you think I am a millionaire?"

Maestro Martínez glanced at the threatening letters he held in his hand. "So far I have only read you the first letter," he said. "The third, as you may remember, was even stronger. 'Rapist Hilario, you depraved son of a rutting she-goat—' "

"Stop—stop!" Pancito shouted. "I no longer know whether I ever used such vile language or not—all I know is, I cannot bear to hear it now. You will have your ten thousand, yes, and Lupita in the bargain. I say good riddance to both of you."

"We will make you very proud of us at the university, Father," Maestro Martínez bowed.

By the time Pancito saw his partner Hilario again, he had somewhat composed himself and was walking a little straighter on his cane. "Hilario, my dear friend, I am covered with apologies. I do not understand what devil possesses the young ladies growing up today. They are unruly and disobedient. It seems to be a curse of this modern age. *Rebeldes sin causa.* Lupita chooses to run off to the university with that little lizard of a schoolteacher, Maestro Martínez. Ay, don't think I couldn't stop them, don't think I couldn't box their heads, get our good friend the chief of police to—"

"I know. I know," Hilario said soothingly. "But you are too civilized, too much the man of peace. If we must use force to gain the things we want, is it not better to do without? You taught me that lesson years ago, Don Alfonso, and I have never forgotten it. That is why I cherished your remarkable letters."

"Please, please, you embarrass me with so much flattery about those old letters," Pancito muttered. "Hilario, perhaps you would do us the honor of coming home for dinner to-night. My daughter Maria Cristina is only a handful of years older than Lupita, she is an excellent manager as you have observed, she cooks like an angel, she plays Chopin on the piano most agreeably and I have a father's intuition that one reason she has never married is that she holds you in such high respect."

"Señor Discretion Himself," Hilario said, in what had now become a ceremonial accolade, and he put his arm around the shoulder of his dearest and most trusted friend, and thus they walked to their favorite street-corner table at the bar of The Three Kings, and in the finest Scotch whiskey available they toasted themselves and all that is reasonable and wise, harmonious and peaceful in the reach of humankind. And a warm glow came over Pancito, excuse us again, Don Alfonso Perez, as he luxuriated in the admiration of his old partner who so loved him for his moderation and humanity that it was no trick at all for Pancito to accept and believe every word of it himself.

# PASSPORT
# TO
# NOWHERE

■          ■          ■

Nathan Solomon loved to paint. He was young, blond and large-muscled; he was a Jew and he wanted to paint Poland. Nathan wanted to paint his Poland vibrant and gay with color, but solemn too, streaked with the solemnity of Jewish beards and Jewish *yarmulkes*. Sad too, blackened with the sadness of broken windows in the synagogue, the long sad lines of old man Gutterman, whose wife was stoned into her grave, guilty of having a son who ran off with the narrow-hipped wife of the village merchant Pokanski. And mad too, the madness of the Jew Garnitsky, who plodded down the street mumbling the psalms into his long white beard. And mean. Mean as the grasping little child hands that pulled that beard with innocent, self-righteous and frenzied anger.

Ten years before, Nathan's pictures might have been brighter. The sadness and the meanness and the madness were growing. Each year the Jews in Minsk seemed to pray more and more and each year they drew further into their historic

■

shells and each year there were more stones, more taunts, more hate. Each year old man Gutterman bent his head lower and the gleam in Garnitsky's eye flashed more wildly and Nathan's pictures grew blacker and blacker, until finally they made Rouault look like Van Gogh, and he would shake his head, and throw his paints away and then begin again.

"Look, Irma, black again. Always I paint my Poland yellow and green, and it comes out looking like something from the coal bin."

And Irma would say, "Leave it black. I like it black, Nathan. It is like a picture of beautiful, healthy Poland, covered with ashes."

"But I want to get through the ashes."

"The ashes are truth."

Once Nathan had painted Irma in yellow and green. She was all lovely yellow and green when he first met her by the fountain several years before. He had set his easel there. He was painting the pigeons that came to drink. As she stood there, her loveliness swept over his canvas like pigeons soaring. He began to paint her among the pigeons. It seemed as if they were all about to take wing. Nathan would not have been surprised if suddenly, when he waved his arms, she led them winging over the roofs into the sky.

"Please, do you mind standing just a moment longer? You see I began to paint you and . . .''

Nathan walked toward her. The pigeons flew away. He didn't notice them. He didn't want to paint this girl any more. He wanted to kiss her. Paint was too cold, too far away. He wanted to find if those small, pink lips were as warm and alive as they looked.

She looked at the picture.

"You're a painter?" she asked teasingly.

"I try to be," Nathan said, a little too seriously.

"But the pigeons have gone."

"They will come back tomorrow. Will you?"

She looked more closely at the canvas.

"You've started well," she said.

Irma kept her appointment with the pigeons next day. And the next. She was like a little motorboat, the way she skirted around this big, slow, friendly artist. She could zigzag in and out through his course and leave a wake that would rock him. She had the glorious knack of loving Nathan in a matter-of-fact, motorboat sort of way. You paint well, you kiss well, you love well. She was the teacher, the best kind, learning with him. She would grade him fairly. And when she praised him, Nathan would paw her and wag his tail like an overjoyed St. Bernard.

Irma still praised him. But now Nathan's canvases were always black, dull and lifeless, and he didn't know why. Only Irma knew why. She knew they were black for Gutterman and Garnitsky, black for the Jews.

"Look, Nathan darling, they will always be black," she would say, "always and always, unless you Jews escape from your bondage again."

Nathan put down his canvas in despair. "Hush, Irma, none of your socialist talk. Only in more trouble that gets us. For you it is safe. No, they will not touch a pretty young girl with a face like a madonna. But for me, a Jew, stones in the face—and finally stones in the heart."

Some nights they would walk down into the fields, lie in the fresh hay, and listen to the river. There were only two moments when Nathan did not feel his Jewishness would choke him to death, when he felt himself a man on this earth, when he could breathe the air without thinking, I am breathing *goyische* air. Those moments were when he was painting, and when he was there in the dark with Irma, the fire of her body crashing over him like tidal waves of heat.

"Now the darkness *is* beautiful, Irmishka. Now it is like the walls of our home, walling out the ugliness."

"Poor Nathan. Always looking for walls. Most Jews look for

walls, either to cry against or to hide behind. But I don't want
you like most Jews, darling.''

"Jews, Jews." Nathan took his hands from her as he always
did when anger rushed to his head. Irma did not have to look
at him to see that face, his large, soft cow-eyes fighting hurt and
tears, his strange, animal mouth trying to be strong.

When he turned to her again he did not talk. He suddenly
plunged his feeling, red mouth to hers. She took him quickly,
joyous in his strength.

Later they hung their feet over the edge of the riverbank.
They felt their bodies free, flowing like this water below them.

"That's how I want you always, strong, unafraid," she said
quietly.

"Marry me, Irma," he answered. "I can paint. You can help.
We will manage. I want you always."

Suddenly Irma felt bent and gray. Wise, and almost conde-
scending. Nathan was a weight tugging at her sleeve. This was
not a world of riverbanks and warm bodies in the hay. This life
was peasants starving, strikes in the city, greedy wars, and
more Jews crucified. Irma listened to the river and recognized
this rhythm.

"Poor Nathan."

"Then you won't?"

"It isn't won't, it's can't."

"You don't love me. You love those masses. It isn't natural.
A young girl like you loving a million people she's never
seen."

"I love you, Nathan. Too much to fool you. Too much to
fool myself."

"But not enough to fight with me."

"Nathan darling, you don't want to fight. You want to
escape. You and I on an island of canvas and color. You want
us to sail off on a private adventure, way, way down into
ourselves, somewhere where there are no Jews, no Jew-haters,
no problems."

"I want us."

"You want us on the moon, Nathan. Up and down this river tonight there are thousands of *us*, little Irmas and their Nathans saying 'We want us, nothing else matters but us.' But something else does matter. Power matters. Power that thrives on hate, power that blackens your canvas, power that we must fight."

"Jews always fight. Nothing is ever right for them. Jews were stoned three thousand years ago. They will be stoned three thousand years from now. Irma, all we have is this minute, today, tomorrow. For God's sake, don't steal this from us."

"I steal nothing from you, Nathan dear. I only show you what you never had."

"I haven't got you?"

"You haven't got life."

"I won't live without you."

"They won't let you live with me."

It was true. Already village tongues were beginning to wag. Nathan could hear them, a tail of buzzing sound behind him, as he walked home with his easel slung over his shoulder. Day after day, the sound increased. Nathan would see the spiteful gentile faces in his dreams, their tongues darting out like snake-fangs. "That Jew ruins one of our Christian girls. That Jew dares. Jew, Jew, Jew."

It made Nathan want to laugh. Nathan Solomon. His father used to say, "You are too easy with people. You will never be a trader."

Nathan Solomon, artist, with a sickness for friendship, who wanted only to paint Poland yellow and green.

It made Nathan shrug his shoulders. "No? What is to do? To fight like Irma? To get killed? Life is short enough. So you go down another street where they won't bother you. Soon they will stop. . . . When they see you want to bother nobody, they will stop soon enough."

The next day Nathan hiked five miles up into the hills to do a landscape. It was summer and the sun was hot. The intense heat ate through his heart and into the canvas. The sun scorched his palette with gold. See, Nathan, the painter thought, life can be golden. Only you must get away from the streets, from the people who spit. Here on the mountain life is always golden. Irma is wrong. Her peasants and Jew-haters are not truth. This is truth, truth to outlive us all, truth to make my canvas light at last.

Then he slung the easel over his shoulder, and went down the mountainside, his mountainside, with joyous unmusical songs in his throat.

The town was strangely quiet, so he walked down the main street. He was a man, this Nathan, he thought, not knowing that those who must think this are slightly less than men. He locked the door of his little room and sat at the window, washing rye bread down with milk.

It is good, this being a Jew, painting good pictures and being a Jew. These *goyim,* they drift through life. Everything comes easy. Yes, for us life is sharpened, Nathan thought, suddenly pleased with himself. When life is hard, the flowers are redder and their fragrance sweeter. So why worry? Why fight like Irma? It was meant to be this way. He held the last gulp of milk in his mouth a moment and let it trickle slowly down his throat in a warm, satisfying stream.

It was growing dark. Nathan gave himself up to the cool evening. The cool evening was fate. He could not fight against the dark. You take it, make the most of it, paint it perhaps, use it. That's the Jew in me. I stand by and look at life. If I look at it well enough I catch it on my canvas.

There was a knock on the door. It was Irma. Irma's face. But Irma's face in a nightmare, eyes like hot rivets, snakes in her hair. The lines in her face were hard and angry. A face free from fear but full of frenzy.

"Nathan, hurry, get your things together."

"Darling, sit down, what is the matter?"

"No time. Pogrom. The Jews in the next village stoned a bully. The crowd is crazy. They're coming this way. Killing every Jew. Nathan, hurry, they'll kill you."

"Irma—for God's sake—where will we go?"

"*You* go, Nathan. I am staying. Hurry, hurry."

Nathan threw his few clothes into a bag, grabbed his thumbed copy of Plato, tied them to his easel. So a pogrom. A pogrom rolls over the land like lava, human eruption of hate. So Irma was right. "You want us on the moon." It was all so foolish. Even at this moment, Nathan could not help thinking it was foolish. Some men want power, money, castles built with bones of fellow men. What do I want?—Irma, a room to paint in, milk and rye bread. I want the cheapest thing in the world, life—and they won't let me have it.

"Hurry, Nathan, hurry."

"Then you won't come with me?"

"No."

"Your people?"

"Yes. Don't you see, Nathan, there is still a chance. Some of these peasants and village workers—they learn their class. They begin to learn these anti-Jewish raids are but the first attack on *them.* There is still time."

"I will stay with you. I will try to fight."

"No. Not you. Without conviction a gun in your hand is like a water pistol. It is too late. You can only watch and paint. Hurry."

Nathan hated her for saying that. Because it was true.

"I will go to my uncle in Warsaw. Will you meet me?"

"Yes, yes."

"When?"

"When I can."

"Good-bye, Irmishka."

"Good-bye, Nathan."

She stood there loving him and despising him. She stood

there so right he wanted to hurl himself at her and beat her with his fists. He ran over and kissed her. She held the back of his head, pressing his mouth against hers. For a moment he forgot the Jews, the pogroms, as their mouths held each other. Then, suddenly, she pushed him away.

"I must go, Nathan. Good luck. Some day you will know I was right."

She ran down the stairs. He could hear her strong little feet taking them three at a time. He tried to say over and over, "This is the last time. That sound on the step is the end of her."

But he could not take it seriously.

So many times, there by the river, Irma had warned him. But their bodies had clung then, and nothing had seemed true except their love. Now she was gone, and it was too casual. She had gone to join her revolutionary peasants as young girls skip off to meet their beaux. It takes only courage to face catastrophes. It takes a genius for living to take them in stride. Irma had that genius. She could risk her life with the same ease and spontaneity that marked her graceful dive into the river in the spring. Nathan loved her for that. That made him laugh too. He loved Irma because she could run off to help the peasants when she should have been with him. Nathan laughed too long. Tears rolled down his cheeks. He was many miles from Minsk, safe and very sad.

But not far enough to be free from the pain of stones flung with the force of prejudice, free from the mad faces, the sadistic havoc of self-righteousness, the broken windows, the broken heads, the broken vows. No distance was great enough. No time. He was held forever to this torture and torment by some umbilical cord. He could never cut it. He could only tug.

When Nathan reached his uncle's room in Warsaw, the old man was praying. It seemed to Nathan that he had never seen Uncle Max when he was not praying. Uncle Max was a tailor, one of Warsaw's million little tailors. The room was cold and disorderly. The tablecloth was spotted with crumbs and stained with red wine. Furniture was sparse. The rug was gone. For in Warsaw it is slow death. Jews come to market to sell each other things they can't buy. There is a strict boycott against the Jews. They live on an island of fear.

Nathan sat down and waited patiently for his uncle to finish his one-sided conversation with Jehovah. When he was finished Max turned toward him wearily. He was a spindly little man, tubercular, with shoulders hunched by half a century of sewing. Nathan felt his uncle's small hand in his. It was soft and wet.

"So, Nathan, my boy, you have come to the big city."

He could not make his voice glad. The room was too small for another. It was hot now, and there was not enough tea. But Max was lonely and his damp white face was splotched with darkness, like the blackness that streaked Nathan's yellows and greens. Slowly the old heat of family affection began to tingle in his old body.

"Nathan, you grow like a weed. Praise God, you are in good health, you are a man now, twenty-two, yes?"

"Twenty-seven, Uncle Max. How is everything, how is your health?"

Max shook his head sadly.

"A fine thing to ask. All day we sew for two zlotys. Thank God it is soon over."

Max took the tea from the stove, and poured it into a glass. Then he poured some into a saucer and sipped it noisily through his skimpy beard.

"So why have you come, Nathan, you have something to sell?"

"I ran from the village. Pogrom."

"Ugh, ugh," Max groaned painfully, raising his shoulders in a gesture of futility. "Don't tell me."

They sat in silence. Don't tell Uncle Max about pogroms. Let him squirm further up into his shell. Let him cry five minutes longer to Jehovah. Let him try to forget the word that splits his simple heart.

They sat in silence. The poverty seemed to gag them both. Everywhere it was the same, sweat all day, pray all night, starve and hide from hooligans screaming "Jew," then die, a good Jewish funeral, everybody sobbing for their own misfortunes.

Uncle Max rocked awhile. Then he put on his little *yarmulke* and threw a shawl around his shoulders.

"Come, it is time to go to *schul.*"

The *schul* was a cellar, one small room, where the poor Jews tried to forget their hunger and the bad air as they made their peace with God. Nathan shuddered to see these old men, their sons, and their pasty-faced grandchildren swaying together and droning in unison their mournful incantations. The air was soggy with sweat and heavy breaths. The faces were pinched, yellow, pockmarked with poverty, yet flooded with faith. Nathan wanted to laugh. He always wanted to laugh at the wrong time. But it seemed so obvious, so horribly obvious that God was not in this place.

Max rushed home after the service. He had to have a pair of pants mended by morning. Nathan walked along slowly through the ghetto. A barefoot beggar boy followed him for a block, burdening him with an involved tale of misfortune. Too timid to order him away, Nathan gave him five kronen to get rid of him.

"And what will you do with it?" he asked, hoping for some spark of warmth ("bread for momma") seeking the human touch.

"Vodka," said the brat and ran away.

As Nathan turned the corner, the wind sprang up. The shrill, rasping tones of a woman's voice came to his ears. A moment later a policeman passed, dragging a smeary-faced woman. Nathan had heard stuck pigs howl like that in the village, when they were dragged along for the blood to spill out.

"Let me go, you fat ape, you stuffed pig—I won't—I won't any more, I promise."

And Nathan had to laugh again.

Here was Warsaw, squirming with lies, every gutter gushing depravity, great swindles, misused power, the filth of corruption. And all the police could do was arrest this woman, this mascara-madonna, willing to sell the only thing she owned.

Nathan spent six days in Warsaw, sleeping on the floor of his uncle's room. Every day Max grunted a heartless good morning, prayed, drank his tea, sewed all day, grunting only, "Ugh, how it goes with us! Better we should all be dead."

Nathan was anxious to hear from Irma, anxious to get away. He felt he was dying, here in the slums of the Jews. He looked into the pale faces of little boys shadowed with TB, smelled the horrible grime of the crowded market place, walked through this prison without bars and felt he would die.

On the sixth day a note came from Minsk. It was signed by one of Irma's comrades.

She had asked for him, at the end, it said.

"Tell him not to wait for me," it said.

"Bad news," nodded Uncle Max complacently, not looking around from his sewing machine. Here in the ghetto Uncle Max had heard bad news for sixty years, and his father before him and his father's father. All news is bad news in Warsaw and also no news is bad news.

Nathan folded the note and slowly put it in his inside pocket.

"Mind if I paint here, Uncle, just today? Then I'll be gone."

Max shrugged his shoulders and went on sewing.

Nu, a painter, a loafer, making pictures when he could be sewing.

Nathan set up his easel in the middle of the room and sketched quickly. It was Irma, Irma on every inch of the canvas, Irma standing with the pigeons, Irma laughing, Irma holding him to her in the dark, Irma talking to the river, Irma

singing, Irma saying, "They won't let you live with me," Irma
fierce, leading the peasants with her hair flying, Irma telling
him to go, Irma on the stairs, Irma in his heart, Irma in the sky.

The picture was all Irma, all the Irmas that make one life,
all the lives that make one Irma. The picture danced with
yellow and green, the colors flirting together, jumping together like kittens. Irma was dead and Nathan was soggy with
sorrow, and the picture was gay, a leaping peasant mazurka.
And Nathan thought this is strange, Irma dead so soon, and
her picture happy and yellow like the one on the mountainside. And Nathan thought, I am a fine lover, nauseous with
grief and painting her joyous as the morning I met her.

And the more Nathan wondered about this, the blacker
grew the picture, like rain clouds sweeping over a perfect sky,
until finally only specks of yellow and green peeked out
through the murky black. And this was true. Nathan knew it
was finally true. Here was the blackness, the fight, the unfamiliar forms of hate, and through the murk shone the bright
moments, moving like colored searchlights in a fog. They
shone through, lighting Nathan's face, then piercing him like
an X ray, exposing the truth that flowed in him, bits of happiness flowing in this black river, salvaged from the wreck of life.
He knew in that moment why men struggle, what light colors
really meant, why Irma had died. It was all so clear at this
moment, why the Jews wander like tumbleweed, how he must
fight, whom he must help. Irma had made it clear.

Nathan shoved the easel away and wiped the sweat from
his neck and forehead. The sewing machine wheezed on
monotonously. He mopped his face again with his handkerchief. Sweat flooded his eyeballs and moved like tiny glaciers
down his nose and across his cheek.

He rose and went out without a word. Uncle Max never
looked up. The sewing machine hummed.

Nathan strolled over to the market. The street was a human
stew, pushcarts, garbage, screeching, haunted faces, selling,

selling. It was all one face, all one smell. The stink of the street and the anxious breath sickened Nathan to the realization that this was modern Jewry, pushed down into this alley, not a unified, fighting force but a giant severed in a million pieces, with each part beating at the other with its bloody stump.

Then someone threw a tomato. It flooded his philosophizing and his unsuspecting head in a mess of ripened pulp. Before he could recover he was surrounded by a ring of white faces, bulging with hunger and hate.

"Nazi, Nazi!" they screamed.

Nathan laughed. This was a new joke. These city Jews had little bodies, swarthy complexions, pale faces. Nathan was tall, tanned and blond. He knew the same suffering: taunted, hunted, hated. He had come to market to be with them, to smile with them, to move with this crowd. Irma had died for this, believing this to be right. He wiped the tomato pulp away with the edge of his sleeve. This is the Jew today. A ripe tomato thrown in a friendly face.

Slowly he walked back to Max's room. Max was still sewing. Nathan looked at his picture. So that was knowing Irma! Look back. How could anyone know Irma? I love one village. She loves the world. I love one human being. She loves a billion. Irma was a shadow. A shadow of the future. A shadow behind a bad portrait. Think back. Did you see Irma? Did you feel her? Did you ever understand?

Save humanity! Two billion people, two billion pulses beating at different rates. Save the Jews! Sixteen million people. Sixteen million different people. Black and blond, rich and poor, atheist and orthodox.

No, Irma had not made it clear after all. Irma had only died. Unity is a mirage. The fight is Don Quixote's. I, Nathan Solomon, must walk alone.

"So you go, Nathan? Home to the village, yes?"

"No, Uncle, thank you. You have been good."

"But where do you go, Nathan?"

"With the tumbleweed, Uncle Max."

The door closed. The rounded shoulders shrugged. The sewing began again.

Nathan sat on the hard board seat of a third-class carriage rolling into Germany. Next to him sat two well-fed American boys who were roughing it. Across the way was a beefy German woman with a sad-eyed little boy whose nose seemed to run a steady stream into his mouth.

When they reached Berlin, Nathan waited in the station for the train to Paris. The station swarmed with brown-shirts, posters and swastikas. It was a bristling, foreign world he was glimpsing, and he felt alternately a giant and a pygmy. He sat down on the bench, drew his head in and waited. There was no curiosity, no struggle. There was only Christ, making his way through a German railway station, the holes in his feet trailing blood.

It was different in Paris.

Nathan drifted to the Latin Quarter. The third day, he was earning his board, sketching in the restaurants. Tourists brought their faces down, and the restaurants filled them and Nathan sketched them, and everybody seemed well satisfied.

Nathan had never met anyone as satisfied as Jacques.

"So we paint, and we eat enough to fight and tomorrow, tomorrow comes the revolution," said Jacques. Jacques was slightly drunk. Jacques was a painter, surrealist, and a revolutionary, Leninist. He could slap you on the back, like Gauguin, he could drink like Gauguin, he could live like Gauguin. He could do everything but paint like Gauguin. After all the customers had left, Nathan and Jacques sat drinking absinthe with the oval-bodied, square-headed little proprietor.

"Meet Nathan—he has escaped a pogrom," Jacques shouted. He was extremely proud of his new friend, seeing in him a political martyr. "In the People's Front," yelled Jacques to an imaginary audience, "nobody crawls. The workingman gets up on his legs and walks. The Jew gets off his belly. In the People's Front we are all brothers."

The little proprietor yawned. Several loitering waiters held up their fists. Nathan and Jacques left the restaurant arm in arm.

Jacques lived in one room above a bakery shop, a one-room suite, Jacques called it.

"Here in the corner is my art gallery, there is my library, over beyond the bookcase is my bedroom, and way across on the other side is the most important room of the whole suite, the meeting room."

And Jacques would laugh so loud Nathan would fear the floor would crack and the bakery downstairs would be added to his friend's imposing list of rooms.

They talked and drank red wine, Nathan all warm with the Jewish excitement of being accepted, Jacques never knowing his surprise, a philosopher, a lover of men. Jacques told him of the revolution, of mobs walking like men, running the Fascists into the trees like monkeys chattering.

Soon Mr. Tandry, the baker, entered and settled his plump little body into the only soft chair.

"Comrade Tandry," said Jacques in a booming voice, "meet Comrade Solomon. Two heroes. Tandry the *petit bourgeois* who will gamble his bakery on the working class. And Solomon, child of the universe, a Christ of the People's Front."

The two men looked at each other embarrassed and pleased. That Jacques, he is a fool, their eyes said; that Jacques, he has a tongue like a flag, but it waves the right color. They smiled, and Nathan was a long way from Warsaw, a long way from rows of pushcarts and lonely Jews.

The door opened again, and a young couple came in. The boy's face was dirty, but there was something about the rakish angle of his hat and the laugh in his eyes that seemed to bring elegance to the room. The girl was exciting. She came in shouting hello, and shook hands all around, a strong grip, a strong grip for a shapely young girl with eyes like black lights.

"Make room for the proletariat," Jacques called. "Maude and Louis, this is Nathan, our new comrade."

Nathan laughed, taking their hands, then he suddenly grew quiet, realizing how long it had been since he had laughed.

"Come, Nathan, we are all friends, why so quiet?" Jacques called, and Nathan started to laugh again, louder and louder, upsetting his wine glass, until finally M. Tandry began clumping him firmly on the back. He coughed then, and washed his cough down with more wine, hiccuping contentedly to himself.

In a few moments three more entered. Nathan found himself looking up into their faces gladly, eager to meet them, new friends, wishing Irma could see him, thinking he would paint this room, with the smoke hanging over it, a fine happy red, and through the red the yellow laughter of Jacques, and the flaming black hair of Maude. Red friendship filtering like smoke through the room.

When a bald, broad-shouldered man with a briefcase entered, even Jacques became quiet. This was Paul, Jacques explained to Nathan, a Communist leader here to tell them of their tasks in the mass meeting tomorrow. Paul smiled at them methodically, took several papers from his briefcase, and explained in a low, patient voice what each one of them must do when they met at the Arc de Triomphe.

"There will be one hundred thousand people marching. The Fascists will try to disrupt, to provoke violence. It is up to the Communists to maintain discipline, to explain to the people that their strength lies in peace, unity."

There was not a sound in the room but the quiet buzz of instructions. Nathan leaned forward, magnetized by Paul's quiet force, his lack of heroics. He leaned forward, feeling himself part of the group, part of one hundred thousand, spellbound, knowing again that Irma *had* made it clear, the part he must play, the price, the goal.

The next day belonged to Nathan. For the first time in his life, he saw men march for life instead of death. Before had been the pogroms and the soldiers. Before, ten men on a street corner meant trouble, rocks through Jewish windows. Safety was in the hills, going your own way, painting your own pictures. Today Nathan did not merely see one hundred thousand Frenchmen, shouting for freedom, cheering a Jew because he was one of them, marching for millions, down from the cross to lead democracy; today he was one hundred thousand, faces smiling, frenzy of friendship, one great heart beating, the People's Front, the People, yes, marching down the Champs Elysées. He found his answer in the quick smiles of strangers, the borrowed cigarette, the ready handshake, the contagious spread of song, the single laughter of many throats.

When it was finally over, the line broke, filtering into the sidewalk cafes. Jacques ordered a cheap white wine, and Nathan gaily poured the cold liquid down his burning throat.

"Well, Nathan, now you are a Frenchman, one of us. Let's drink on that."

Nathan drank, one of us, held the first gulp in his mouth a moment, then let it trickle down. He was clinging to the toast.

Then he sat quietly looking out at the holiday crowd.

"Come, Nathan, you old owl! Have another! What were you thinking?"

"At home if a Jew drank on the street like this, they would say he was a flaunter, a show-off," Nathan said.

"You could never show off drinking the way you do," said Jacques critically. "Nathan, I take back what I said about you being a Frenchman. You still drink like a Pole."

"I can never be a Pole again," said Nathan seriously.

"Today I am a Frenchman. You don't know what it is, to suddenly stand for something."

"Nathan Solomon, ex-child of the universe, more recently of the Front Populaire," Jacques toasted.

"I am going to become a citizen!" Nathan said excitedly. "A citizen, Jacques! Belonging to France."

"Finish that wine, Citizen Solomon," Jacques ordered. "This is a great honor for France. We will have to celebrate with a party for you in the suite tonight."

Next morning Nathan was at the office of the Alien Department at half past eight in the morning. At nine, it was unlocked by an officious little man with dirty spats. At nine-five, the little man took notice of Nathan, and explained that Monsieur l'Inspecteur had not yet arrived. At nine-thirty, Monsieur l'Inspecteur arrived, reading a newspaper as he walked.

"I want to take out my citizenship papers," Nathan told him breathlessly.

The inspector nodded. He did not throw his arms around him like Jacques, and propose a toast. He did not seem to realize that this was new life. Nathan reborn, a friend of the State. And for Nathan, flushed with new faith, it was impossible to realize that his political baptism was just so much red tape to the inspector, just so much work to be done before going home to his wife's good cooking.

"Don't you understand?" Nathan asked again. "I have decided to become a citizen. I want to take out papers."

"Yes, yes," said the inspector. "Let me see your credentials."

"Here is my passport," Nathan said busily, fishing out a greasy, torn document. "This is my birth certificate."

"And your five-year residence card?" asked the inspector, without looking up.

"Five-year what?" asked Nathan.

"Residence card, residence card," said the inspector

grouchily. "Proof that you have been a resident of France for the last five years."

Nathan felt small and Jewish and more natural. Behind him were Jacques and the Arc de Triomphe and the People. Ahead was silence, the lack of Irma, no paintings, no roots, no love. If Nathan had been a big man he would have gone out of there laughing, thinking this inspector is a good Christian who goes to church every Sunday and I am just a poor son of a bitch who happens to be like Christ, only I slap paint at a canvas instead of talk. But not being a big man like Christ, Michelangelo or Lenin, Nathan hung his head on his chest, like a pigeon with a broken neck, and he walked out of the office with funny jerky steps like a circus clown on stilts.

He walked through the bakery shop and M. Tandry said, "Come here, Nathan, and try this new pastry, still hot," but Nathan shook his head, the broken neck wobbling, and went up to the suite.

He told Jacques and Jacques was silent at first, and then smiled, saying five years in the suite goes by like this, and he drained his wine glass to illustrate.

"Five years is too long for me," Nathan told him.

"But where else can you go, Nathan?"

"Somewhere. Somewhere I can belong."

"But Nathan, you belong here with us now."

As Nathan watched his friend, it seemed to come to him, a new urge, where he must go, what he must do.

"I belong to Palestine," he said. "I am a lonely Jew. I want to belong. I want to feel enough a part of a country to paint it, as I tried to paint Poland and always failed."

"Why not Birobidjan?" Jacques suggested. "The Soviet Palestine, out of reach of Zionist hypocrisy."

"I must go to Palestine," Nathan said.

When he saw he had lost, Jacques threw himself into this as he did everything else. Jacques was a philosopher. That is, he could take corners on two wheels without turning over. When he saw he had lost, he wiped the wine from his mouth and said, "I will raise the money."

That night his suite was jammed with every comrade he knew.

"We all love France," Jacques began. "That is why we're willing to fight and die to put Hitler and the Fascists to rout."

It was so simple. Only a philosopher would dare to say such things. The applause was deafening. There was red smoke. But no laughter. And Nathan was outside all the smoke. He was a Jew, above the smoke, and somewhere beyond that smoke lay Palestine.

"Nathan Solomon is a martyr to progress," Jacques went on. "The Fascists ran him out of Poland. The French want to keep him in the waiting room for five years. He belongs where he can feel most at home. For Nathan it is Palestine. And I've called you here to help him go."

Jacques passed through the room collecting franc notes, and centimes until his big hands were full. Then he came over to Nathan, stuffed them in his pocket, poured him more red wine and bellowed a great toast.

"For people to hold up their heads."

Then the people laughed and cheered, and Nathan drank quietly, the pigeon-neck snapped, the Jew alone again.

Three days later the Front Populaire lost one of its members, Nathan Solomon. In his pocket was a ticket to Palestine via a small Italian steamer. In his pocket a few extra francs Jacques had given him. In his pocket a passport to Palestine, open sesame, Nathan's heart stamped neatly on a greasy page.

He boarded the *Venus de Milo* just before dawn, clomping across the dock slowly, while Jacques danced around him, a trifle drunk, a man to spit in the eye of Pan, an artist, a philosopher. Over Nathan's shoulder his easel was silhouetted against the gray light streaming through the clouds, like a constructivist stage set.

Twice the ship's whistle belched like a drunk turning over in his sleep. All aboard! The men embraced, knights of the all and the one, the joy and the pain of it, the Front Populaire and the Jew.

Nathan reached his bunk and looked around him in the dim light. He was trapped in a narrow stateroom where eight bunks were piled on each other like open coffins. He looked into the bunk of the one above him, where a man with long handlebar moustaches slept loudly and peacefully. The blanket was tucked neatly under the moustaches, and every now and then as it crept over them, they would twitch and struggle for air again like smothered cats. Across from him sat an enormous Negro. He was undressing, grunting as he took off his heavy shoes. All his consciousness was concentrated on this act, and he neither spoke nor looked at Nathan. Slowly Nathan undressed and crawled under damp sheets, pulling them over his head as he used to as a child in Minsk, this moment King of his Universe, the next moment so much dust twirling down into a deep black bin, smaller, smaller, until he finally fell asleep.

Breakfast was served for the twenty-seven third-class passengers at one long table. Opposite Nathan was another Jew, who sat down to it as if it were a banquet table. Mr. Brownstein from Brooklyn and next to him Sadie Brownstein, his wife, such a fine mother, and Julian their twelve-year-old, *epis,* and Annie, two and a half. Mr. Brownstein ate busily and rather loudly, only pausing occasionally to admonish his wife for his children's eating habits.

After breakfast, Brownstein and his Sadie whispered openly, their big eyes describing arcs around Nathan like watchtowers at sea. Finally Mr. Brownstein smiled and said, *"Ein Jude,* eh?"

Nathan extended his hand, not smiling like Mr. Brownstein, knowing he should like this comrade Brownstein, but finding something foreign in the man's eyes, something aggressive and sharp which set him apart from Polish Jews.

Brownstein was an American. He had the same stories to tell as Nathan, perhaps, being licked by little wops at school, being snowballed by hoodlums as he descended the El after a hot, tense day at the office. But there was something about democracy, Nathan thought, as he listened to Mr. Brownstein. Living in a democracy must be like sitting at the edge of the river with Irma. The confidence: being able to lift up your head and look the moon in the face. Even when Mr. Brownstein bitterly denied there was democracy in the States; where the yids couldn't work for Universal Electric or get to be president, he leaned over the table and spoke at Nathan and waved his arms, and puffed his cigar, and offered Nathan one, and grandly produced his business card like an American, a Walt Whitman democrat, something whole, a man with a vote, a man to stare you down, no Polish Jew.

"Why are you going to Palestine?" Nathan asked. "You speak loud enough to be heard in New York. Why do you need Palestine to amplify you into a man?"

"Sadie's old man," Brownstein sighed. "I close up a good business so we can see him for the last time. Cloak and suit . . . Sold it to my brother-in-law. For only half what it's worth."

Brownstein spoke so regretfully that Sadie looked at him reproachfully but sweetly, a Jewish wife with something to say, but knowing her place.

"Sol, you know Sam took it over just to help us, a fine, smart boy."

"Sadie's pop is a great old man," Sol Brownstein told Nathan, watching his wife for the desired effect. "Twenty-five years we save for this trip."

Twenty-five years, Nathan thought. In Minsk I wanted to go to Palestine for twenty-five thousand years, a year for every day that Momma cried, a year for every time Max coughs in Warsaw, a year for every stone they throw at old man Gutterman. And no cloak and suit store behind. Just an empty window and some old cheese on the sill. Just hate, twisting through the woodwork like worms.

"How do you like third class?" Brownstein was asking. "Sadie says, 'Sol, take your second-class tickets back. Down there it gives nicer people.' Just try to argue with your wife!"

And Sadie suddenly wipes the grease of third-class food from the corners of Annie's mouth, smiling because she has lost arguments to Sol for twenty-five years.

Sol was all for telling Nathan about his seven trips, all second class, across the Atlantic, but Nathan couldn't listen any more. It takes a Jacques to laugh with everybody, wanting to hear everybody, liking everybody. It takes a philosopher, a sense of humor. And Nathan could never be a philosopher. He was too lonely to be a philosopher. A philosopher can be alone, but he is never lonely. For he sees not only the people who avoid him, evade him, ignore him. He sees also the sky which roofs them all together and the earth which finally draws them all into it. He says we do not own this, it is only rented, leased for ninety-nine years and we all pay the same price. And this is funny, and he laughs, and then he cannot be lonely. For loneliness is minus, less than other people, behind the starting line, and laughter is plus, integration on a higher level, reaching for righteousness.

So Nathan said good night, very earnest and weary, feeling his body heavy and filling the corridor as he moved to his cabin, wondering if it would suddenly grow lighter as he stepped onto Palestine, like reaching the moon, where one step is a flight.

When he reached the stateroom the handlebar whiskers were already tucked snugly into bed, and the discordant vibrations emanating from the large nose above them indicated that their owner was slumbering like a baby, if somewhat more noisily. The big Negro wasn't sleeping. He was just pretending. He just didn't want to be bothered. As Nathan turned his face away from the one ventilator, he caught one Cyclopean eye staring at him. The man was on his guard against possible theft. Nathan tried to turn his gaze away from that eye. It followed him like a searchlight. He was like an escaped prisoner sighted against the prison wall, running madly for the darkness but always staring into the beam.

The room was hot, stuffy with bad air. It stank with the sweat of old clothes. It was full of evil. Evil thoughts smashing his temples. This black man did not trust him because he was a Jew. The Italian had not talked to him because he was a Jew. Even a black man, a strange, African black was better. It was horrible. Not a word, all the way from Havre. Stink and silence, broken only by his own coughing as his lungs threw back into his face the foul air.

Nathan grabbed the easel hanging from his bunk. He ran out into the corridor and up the hatchway to the small deck in the stern. A feeble light was burning. He set his easel and started to paint. The first thing he saw. The yellow light. The first thing he thought. Christ. Whom Christ had died for? For Paul Kazinski, the butcher boy who pulled old man Gutterman's beard, chanting, "You killed our Christ, you killed our Christ"? For Irma, the anti-Christ, who said faith is not enough, there is only struggle, class war for the right to live? For Nathan, who turned the other cheek until he spun around like a top?

That is what he began to paint, three Christs, three yellow Christs, burning like a light. And as he painted, Nathan thought: This I will paint as I feel, in turmoil, a yellow frenzy of doubt, yellow religion, yellow gold, yellow fire, yellow death. When I reach the promised land I will paint the sequel, in calm, cool colors, poised, rested, discovered.

Nathan did not realize that Mrs. Hazel MacKnowlton was looking down at him from the first-class deck until she called out. It was late at night and the woman had just slipped out from the cocktail lounge, partly because the mounting martinis had left her suddenly nauseous, partly because she had a reputation for being something of an adventurer. Mrs. MacKnowlton was on a round-the-world cruise and was always having adventures. In London she had escaped her guide and gained the top deck of a London omnibus, where she sat all afternoon, observing sufficiently to supply her with material for monologues for four dinners at the captain's table. In Prague she had walked the streets at night all by herself, until the increased tempo of masculine footsteps behind her drove her back to the metropolitan mediocrity of her hotel. Life aboard the *Venus* had been insufferably dull. The captain was a little black-bearded fellow who drank too much red wine at dinner, and had read too much of Garibaldi. The first mate was more distinguished, slender and handsome in his uniform, but, as he carefully explained to Mrs. MacKnowlton, he could not join her at the bar again as he had the first night because of his increasing and pressing duties. The passenger list, too, left much to be desired, and Mrs. MacKnowlton felt that she had no one but herself to blame for sailing on an obscure Italian scow instead of waiting for the *Roma.*

But this was a little better. Here it was, early morning, the Mediterranean, and perhaps an artist to be discovered, a poverty-stricken Italian workman who flares into genius by night. Here was something to make the folks in East Orange tell each other that Hazel simply must have an intuition about people, the way she seemed to get on with those artists and foreigners.

So Mrs. MacKnowlton called out in her best romanticism, and her best Italian, her cape blowing about her in the night wind. Oh, if she only had a picture of this to show the folks back home.

Nathan wheeled around abruptly, torn from his yellow light. He was slightly frightened, upset and surprised by this sudden intrusion. Mrs. MacKnowlton babbled on in her version of Italian. He looked up for a moment into this florid face nesting in a circle of furs. It was smiling down on him. Not snoring, or staring out of one eye, but smiling, glad to see him, a broad East Orange smile for a broad Minsk Jew. Nathan's first reaction was surprise, his second confusion, his third utter self-consciousness. He met the crisis by turning back to his easel as suddenly as he had left it.

Three Christs, three yellow Christs, three Edison Sons of God.

But Mrs. MacKnowlton was not only an adventurer, she was a persistent one. Now that she had her artist at bay she was not going to lose him. She ran back to the bar and pressed Mr. Benturini into service. Mr. Benturini was a good-natured American Italian who had made the mistake of smiling at Mrs. MacKnowlton as they went on board. She confessed to him that the artist she had discovered must speak some out-of-the-way dialect and asked him to venture forth with his more polished lingual weapon. So. Mr. Benturini joined her on the deck overlooking the steerage quarters, but his speech brought forth the same confused response from Nathan. He spoke in rapid Italian and Nathan only looked blankly at him, and turned to his canvas again.

So this is how it goes, thought Nathan. Always I am alone, alone or being chased. And now that I want to be alone, look, these people want to talk. No, it is too much, and Nathan shrugged his shoulders, thinking *Nu,* which is a profound thought and the nearest he ever came to being a philosopher.

But Mrs. MacKnowlton was not only a persistent adventurer. She was a positive turtle, the way she held on to Nathan. Back into the bar she went again. This time she selected Mr. Nussbaum as her champion. Mr. Nussbaum was the salesman for a Yiddish publishing house in New York. He was on his way to Palestine to bring the light to his people. Except for traveling expenses and a reasonable profit, it was a philanthropic mission. Mr. Nussbaum was also a linguist, speaking besides Yiddish broken English and a French he was just in the

progress of breaking. Mr. Nussbaum accompanied her, dignified and stately, to the deck, where he began impressively in
French, not anxious to be called in as a Yiddish interpreter.
But Nathan shrugged his shoulders at this, and Nussbaum
changed his gait, breaking into a cantering Yiddish. Mrs. Mac-
Knowlton could not help but be bitterly disappointed that this
artist was not a starving Italian or a Latin Quarter Frenchman,
but she consoled herself with the knowledge that after all there
were Menuhin and Mendelssohn and Einstein, and even if
they couldn't get into the Orange Country Club, you can't
have everything.

So she had Mr. Nussbaum ask Nathan if he would come to
her stateroom the next morning, and bring some of his work,
and Nathan nodded, thinking this is like Palestine already,
Nathan Solomon an Artist, a Jewish Artist in the shoes of the
Jew loafer.

Mr. Brownstein looked at Nathan's pictures rather doubtfully
next morning, nodding his head and trying to appear interested as Nathan brought out his dark Polish landscapes, his
mad yellows and greens, his splotchy portrait of Irma.

"This woman in the first class wants to see these?" he asked
meditatively.

Nathan nodded. Mr. Brownstein looked at the paintings
again. Not quite cloaks and suits, but still . . .

"If you are smart, this rich woman—she will buy, eh?"

Nathan shook his head. "Nobody likes my pictures, only
Irma, and she . . ."

"Mr. Solomon, excuse me, you know your business, but
confidence, it needs confidence. Now for ten percent . . ."

"Thank you, Mr. Brownstein. But paintings and suits—
not the same to me. If she feels them, she will buy. If she
doesn't . . ." He lifted his shoulders.

"A fine way to sell," commented Brownstein. "It gives me
goose flesh." And he washed his hands of the deal.

Mrs. MacKnowlton welcomed Nathan to her stateroom with open arms, like a mayor or a woman evangelist. It was a room as big as a barn, with chairs so clean he was afraid to soil them by sitting down. With her was Mr. Nussbaum, to act as interpreter, and seven or eight women selected for their aesthetic appreciation, their social standing, or their abject ignorance, in which case Mrs. MacKnowlton's knowledge of art would swell to Gargantuan proportions.

"Isn't it funny about people with artistic temperament," she began. "Me, for instance. I can always sense the presence of something creative, even if I haven't seen it. Last night I just didn't happen to wander out on the deck. Something in me *felt* your painting down there."

All the women agreed that this was certainly strange. They went from picture to picture, sighing and heaving. Wine was brought out, and its odor mingling with the cigarette smoke afforded the ladies a pleasant sensation of the salon.

And they turned their smiles on Nathan, like faucets, lip smiles, mouth smiles, condescension pouring into the sink and flooding the drain. Nathan saw that they were not outward, contact smiles but inverted, self-indulging, ego-sweetening smirks. He looked into their eyes, trying to find himself, the new friendship, the moral coitus we seek. But they were full and spilling over with their own image. And a Jew was not of them. Nathan was seen and admired and devoured like a surrealist canvas or a shapely woman who walks past a pool room. It is not enough to draw an occasional bucket from the well of loneliness. It is not enough to enjoy an occasional stretch and a chat after solitary confinement. This was not the laugh for the friend by the fire. It was the giggle for the chimpanzee in the zoo.

Nathan sat there very still, hating himself for not picking up his canvases and rushing back to Mr. Brownstein, who at least possessed the vulgar honesty to admit he thought they stank. Nathan looked at the blotched Irma, the dead Irma in which the life-colored vitality of the girl broke through here and there. She was looking up at them with her hard eyes, her cold black lips set in a twisted smile. She was hating these people, having no soft edges, never happy or fool enough to let them fool her. And suddenly Nathan turned her face to the wall, and Mrs. MacKnowlton smiled, remarking how interesting and impulsive these artists were.

With Irma gone, Nathan was completely alone in this room of pulpy flatterers, and there was no time for manners, though Mrs. MacKnowlton pleaded and Nathan promised to leave several pictures with her until they reached Jaffa, hoping he might sell one. He shuddered and ran out onto the cold deck, breathing the air deep, suddenly screaming to drive it deeper in his lungs, a berserk Jew, a bug of an artist, flapping his wings hideously to find a perch.

He didn't stop till he reached the prow, where, in the early morning light, he looked far ahead for the sight of land, Palestine, the promised land, the goal for the homeless gaze.

When the sun rose, he felt suddenly sticky and let down, and he stumbled into his bunk, pulling the damp covers over his head to hide from the light and the fear.

Nathan leaned on the rail as the ship shivered its way to mooring beside the swaying wharf in the harbor of Larnaca. The streets of the little town on the Isle of Cyprus seemed narrow and foreign and the swarthy little men who ran to catch the ship's ropes were like little black elves. There is always something about walking into a strange city that is unfriendly and sinister. But to look down into a city from deck rail forces one to a legless, godlike point of view. Nathan thought, Here are little dark men running, and the strange sounds, and new jobs to be done, and funny new little doors to enter, and all this has one meaning for them, meaning to last a lifetime, and I swoop over it, I fly, I am a bird so high over Warsaw I can't tell a stooped Jew from a low house.

The whistle blew. The water quickly spread between the ship and the wharf, like blood from a fresh wound. The desolate Larnaca wharf was dropping out of sight as if it were slowly sinking into the sea. Nathan still leaned on the railing, thinking that Larnaca was a tiny splinter being drawn slowly out of his world.

"Well, Mr. Solomon," said Brownstein at breakfast, "next stop is the homeland. Maybe if those Yids like art, we should set up shop together."

"You should come visit us when we get settled," said Sadie.

Nathan looked at their Julian, who was blowing at the hot coffee with such gusto that it was flying across the table at him like hot rain.

"Thank you. That is very kind."

"Oh, it is nothing," said Sadie, who had neglected to inform him just where in Palestine the Brownsteins could be found.

Nathan spent the day standing at the prow, watching the nose of the ship plough toward the homeland. The sea was rough, and he had to hold tightly to the railing as the deck seemed to soar toward the sky, and then, with an intoxicating tremble, hurl itself into the sea again. Nathan laughed into the wind. Every trip to the sky, every descent to the sea brought the homeland nearer. Nathan laughed as his stomach fell suddenly from under him and plunged into the sea. And he dove down after it, bringing it up with him and tossing it into the sky like a ball.

That night there was a knock on his stateroom door. Nathan sat up, dreaming he was knocking on the gates of the homeland, the homeland, and then he heard the handlebar whiskers snorting irritably at the interruption and the Negro rolling over like a walrus. He jumped out of his berth, stubbing his toe in the excitement, and opened the door.

It was Mr. Brownstein . . . He was so excited his usual volubility was concentrated in a few wild exclamations.

"Mr. Solomon, hurry, the inspectors, passports, you can see the lights!"

Nathan drew his trousers over his nightshirt and rushed out to join him.

Mr. Brownstein was right. In the dining saloon sleepy-faced officials were sitting behind tables ready to inspect the passports of those disembarking at Jaffa. While Mr. Brownstein was authoritatively pointing out the resemblance of Sadie, Julian and Anne to the passport pictures, Nathan ran out on deck. The ship was not more than half a mile from shore. Across that black expanse of water twinkled a few scattered lights. Jaffa. Gateway to Jerusalem. The gates of the homeland. Jaffa, Palestine's Cyclopean eye, winking at Nathan Solomon.

Nathan floated back to the dining hall and the row of officials. He floated up holding his passport out in front of him like a one-way ticket to heaven. As he reached the tables he noticed something that startled him. Mr. Brownstein ostentatiously drawing a wallet from his pocket and revealing to the officials a clump of green bills.

"Here is my forty pounds," said Mr. Brownstein. The officials checked his name.

"Well, Mr. Solomon," said Mr. Brownstein. "For a Jew this is a great day. My Sadie has been crying her eyes out, that's how happy she is."

Forty pounds? Nathan wanted to ask Mr. Brownstein why. But the official was already checking Nathan's credentials, and he was too timid to interrupt. He stood in front of the table wondering if he would ever be as confident and fitted-in as this inspector seemed. He wondered if this cocky, authoritative fellow could be a Jew like himself. But flashing through these worry-clouds like lightning was the ominous thought of that forty pounds.

The official looked at his passport and nodded. Everything seemed in order. He stamped the book with a flourish. Then he looked up at Nathan and asked, "And your forty pounds? Hurry up, man."

Nathan looked past him dumbly, as if motivated by the fantastic hope that the official would forget about it if he continued to ignore him.

Nathan looked at him stupidly.

"I do not understand. I have paid for my ticket."

"Listen, stupid, a fine Jew you are! You want to come in with empty pockets and live off the state? We can't afford that. No one can come in without forty pounds. Two hundred dollars."

"But I have my pictures. I can paint."

"Dumbhead, only half an hour this ship stops at Jaffa. And we should sit here and argue all night. Forty pounds."

"Forty pounds," said Nathan. "Six hundred zlotys. If a Jew in Poland could get that much money he would not have to come to Palestine."

"Forty pounds," said the official, "or you don't get off."

"Forty pounds?" Nathan asked, repeating the question like a record stuck in a groove.

He looked into the critical and slightly bloodshot eyes of the passport official. "You do not know how much I want to get into Palestine. The nights I spent dreaming of this, the days . . ."

"Maybe you should have spent more time gathering the money," joked the official, genuinely affected by Nathan's appeal, trying to appear the mechanical agent of the law he was paid to be.

"Half an hour," Nathan repeated, as if this time limit had suddenly registered. "Half an hour—wait, I will see. Wait for me," he pleaded, and he ran wildly to one of the stewards.

"Bring me to Mrs. MacKnowlton's cabin at once, up in first class. She will understand. She will let me in."

It was a little more adventure than Mrs. MacKnowlton had bargained for when Nathan pounded on her cabin door shortly before dawn, and she opened it to find a wild-eyed artist waving his canvases in her face.

"You must help me. You must buy these. My marvelous paintings. My great art. I have only half an hour."

She turned on her light, which she seldom did once she had taken off her switches for the night, and asked Nathan in. She could not understand a word.

The sight of Mrs. MacKnowlton without her makeup quieted Nathan somewhat, and when the steward brought Mr. Nussbaum to interpret again, Nathan was able to explain his difficulty more articulately. All his life, all his life he had wanted to go to Palestine, the one land where he would be free. And now, now that he was here, now that he had crossed every barrier, suddenly there was the greatest barrier of all, money, money, two hundred dollars of it piled high enough to wall him out of Palestine forever. But if only Mrs. MacKnowlton would buy his pictures, if only she would pay the small sum of forty pounds for five great masterpieces, he would forget all about what Irma would think of her. He would kiss her on both cheeks as the greatest philanthropist of all time.

Mrs. MacKnowlton bit her lip. Adventure is one thing and laying out two hundred dollars is another. Showing a cultural interest in obscure art is one thing and buying five unknown paintings is another.

Nathan read this in her face, and his blood seemed to stop circulating and stiffen like ice.

Mrs. MacKnowlton read this in his face. And she decided to become an adventuress, she decided to throw caution to the stormy Mediterranean winds.

"I'm sorry I can't afford these pictures," she told him. "But I can help you. I'll raise the money. I'll just wake everybody up I know and tell them I have to have it. I won't let them say no."

East Orange would never, never hear the end of this.

Nathan flew back to his little official.

"I will have it. In half an hour I will have it. Don't leave. Give me time."

"Shhh," said the official. "Don't shriek so loud, others are sleeping."

Mrs. MacKnowlton knocked methodically on the door of every passenger she knew. She knew now how Paul Revere must have felt. And Mr. Nussbaum, Mr. Benturini, the others, they could not help but be infected with Mrs. MacKnowlton's feeling. It was the germ of a real idea, something different, a real antitoxin, and they gave freely, until Mrs. MacKnowlton feverishly brushed the hair from her face and counted victoriously forty pounds.

In the classic manner, she called for a steward. "Tell Mr. Solomon in the third class I have succeeded, I will come right down."

There was just the right note of mystery.

The steward delivered the message to Nathan, and Nathan hugged him, and he wanted to hug the passport official too, but he edged away, saying cautiously, "You have ten more minutes. Then we must get off."

While Nathan was rejoicing, there was a knock on Mrs. MacKnowlton's door. She opened the door and found herself looking at the sturdy Roman features of the first mate. He was a very military fellow and saluted stiffly.

"Excuse me, madame, for disturbing you at this hour, but the Captain has heard of your—generosity to a Mr. Solomon. He regrets to inform you that he cannot allow such a collection as you have just made. He feels it would not—ah—not please the Fascisti."

This was more drama than Mrs. MacKnowlton had realized there was in the world before.

"But this poor man, I was only trying to help him get off the boat," she argued weakly.

"The Captain appreciates your kindness, but he feels it would set a—ah—dangerous precedent."

"Only five more minutes," said the official.

"Just wait, only wait, one more moment," Nathan pleaded.

Then a messboy brought him a second note from Mrs. Mac-Knowlton. He read it. And then he sat down and read it again. He crumpled it in his hand. And then he straightened it out and read it again.

"Don't wait," he said.

"I'm sorry," said the official.

"You can go now," Nathan said.

"Good luck," said the official. He put his hand on Nathan's bent shoulder. "Maybe soon I will see you again."

Nathan didn't answer.

Next morning the *Venus de Milo* drew anchor for its return trip. Nathan stood in the stern, watching the lights of Jaffa fade away like stars in the dawn. The homeland.

An Italian sailor came by, and stood by him a moment.

"Leaving Jaffa—a good thing—it means home to Naples soon again."

The last light was gone.

Breakfast was lonely without Mr. Brownstein. While he was eating silently, the chief steward entered.

"Mr. Solomon, your fare is only paid as far as Jaffa. I have orders to put you off at the first stop, Larnaca."

Nathan stopped eating, but he didn't look up.

"But you can't. I have no money. I know nobody there."

"I am sorry. There is nothing we can do."

"But this Larnaca—I never heard of it—it is a black dot—let me work my way back to Naples, anywhere."

"I am very sorry. That is impossible."

Nathan ran his hands over his face. Then he flung them to his side in anger at the futility of the gesture.

■

It was evening when the *Venus* reached Larnaca again. Nathan moved slowly down the gangplank, his bag in one hand, his paintings in the other and his easel slung across his back. Never changing his pace he walked to the end of the pier where he was directed to the immigration office.

Behind the pier he could see the narrow, dark streets, running off into the darkness.

The city seemed dark and shut to him; the whole world.

Someone asked him for his passport. He began, falteringly to explain. The man shook his head. He could not understand him. He went away to find an interpreter. Nathan waited. There was a stillness inside him, and a draining out. He could wait. He had time.

The interpreter came, another Jew.

"Where is your passport?"

Nathan gave it to him quietly, braced for the man's retort.

"But this says nothing about Cyprus! Why have you come here?"

Nathan shrugged his shoulders. "I don't know."

The interpreter looked at him more carefully. The man is a loon. He does not know the right answers. He is dangerous. The interpreter did not know how to handle this. He left abruptly to consult his superiors.

Nathan was alone. It was not possible. Here, exiled in the darkness of an island he had never known, walked Nathan Solomon, the lone Jew, artist of passivity, with a sickness for friendship, who wanted only to paint his Poland yellow and green. Who wanted only Irma, cheese for breakfast, and a place to paint.

The interpreter returned. This was a serious case. Nathan must return in the morning to consult the chief immigration official. He would decide. Perhaps they could keep him. Perhaps they would have to send him—somewhere.

Nathan said, "Where shall I sleep? I have no money. I have nothing."

"We will board you for the night."

The man pointed through the window to a house across the street.

Irma was far away. Poland was far away. Revolution was far away. Forty pounds was far away. Hope was far away.

It was all a maze of bewilderment and torturous uncertainty. For there is no oppression so great as loneliness. Wandering up a blind alley of the world, Nathan heard Irma speak: There is no freedom but the struggle's brotherhood. But he could not answer. His throat was silent with fear and doubt.

He would never know. He would never know.

The door of the immigration office closed behind him. Nathan stepped into the darkness of the narrow street. He was safe for a moment. Darkness was the only refuge now.

Then he reached the new door. His nails dug into his flesh. Then he knocked, a brush of his knuckles, ever so timidly.

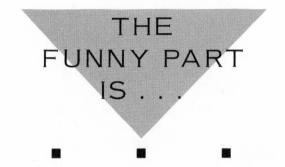

# THE FUNNY PART IS . . .

■       ■       ■

She was working behind a counter in her old man's diner in West Liberty, was where it all started. I had come into town with an alleged heavyweight by the name of Big Boy Price. Big Boy had looked so bad the referee had stopped the fight and called it no-contest, which meant we didn't even get our money. By the time I paid the training expenses, I was so flat it looked like I might even have to go to work for a living. Unless I rightaway found myself a meal ticket and I didn't expect to find any world-beaters in a one-mule town like West Liberty.

If I had to be stranded anywhere, though, West Liberty had its points. At least that's the way it looked to me the night I strolled into Foley's Diner and spotted Shirley. From that moment on I was a regular at Foley's. Talked to Shirley every chance I got. Even walked her home a couple of times. Never got to first base, though. But those first few weeks, I wasn't rushing things. I talked about New York City and Chicago,

■

about all the bigtime people I knew and the important money I had thrown around—oh, they didn't call me Windy Johnson for nothing—and I figured it was just a question of time until I wore down this little Oklahoma pigeon with my fancy patter and my big city ways. At least it looked like I had the field pretty much to myself. I didn't see anything in pants in West Liberty that was any competition.

To make it look like even more of a cinch, I talked Indian Joe Wood, the toughest middleweight in Oklahoma, into signing up with me, and in a couple of months or so I was back in the big money again. At least big money for West Liberty. I bought myself a yellow Chrysler roadster and I told Shirley she could drive it around all day while I was hanging around the gym, keeping an eye on Indian Joe. I figured she'd get so used to that Chrysler she'd have to move in with me to keep it in the family. She still had me at arm's length, you understand, but I'm a patient sort of a fellow, especially when it comes to Shirley. I figured she'd have to come around and it was just a question of time.

And I still think I would have been right, if it hadn't been for this no-goodnik Billy Bonnard. Billy the Kid, they called him. Every time I get to thinking how, if it hadn't been for me, this little louse Billy would never even have met Shirley, I get so tight inside, I need another drink.

Halfway between West Liberty and Oklagee there is a place called Dillon's Barn, where the amateurs beat each other's brains out every Friday night. They're called amateurs but they're really semi-pros because Fatso Dillon gives the winner of each fight an Elgin wrist watch which he buys back from the boy next day for twenty-five bucks. They're just punks, sixteen, seventeen years old, and they fight for blood, nothing fancy and everything goes. Well, one of the kids is a little baby-face who looks like he should be home doing his geography lessons instead of climbing into the ring at Dillon's to trade punches with a flat-nose who looks twice his age and has at least a ten-pound pull in the weights. Dillon never paid too much attention to how he matched 'em. As long as somebody came as close to getting killed as was within the law, Dillon and his customers were satisfied.

This Billy "The Kid" Bonnard didn't even own a bathrobe. He just came into the ring with a torn hotel towel over his shoulders. His body looked scrawny and white and he had a face like a sweet little choirboy. I settled back in my seat to watch the slaughter.

But at the bell the choirboy rushed out of his corner like Stanley Ketchel, come back for a second try. His lips were pressed tight together, and with no blink to his eyes, the look on his face . . . The other guy was just big and wild and tough and The Kid moved around him with tantalizing grace. The Kid peppered the big guy with his left, threw a beautiful right, and brought his left up so fast you didn't even see it. The bum had to be dragged away like a dead horse. The Kid had skinny arms and not enough strength in his shoulders to look like that kind of a puncher. But he was lithe and wiry and he knew how to snap his punches in.

I hurried around to the dressing room to line him up before any of the other managers could get to him. "Kid," I said, "I'm Windy Johnson, manager of champions. You looked sensational tonight. I'm going to give you a big break and add you to my stable."

He was a good-looking kid all right but his lips were thin and there was a hardness in him that came through the baby face. My sweet talk didn't go to his head—he was ahead of me. "Why shouldn't I look sensational?" he said. "I'm good. I c'n beat tomato cans like that half-a-dozen at a time."

"Here's half a C," I said, handing him a crisp fifty. "That's an advance on our first fight. A year from now I'll have you in the big time."

"A year!" The Kid said. "I fuckin' oughta be there now."

That's the way The Kid was, cocky, impatient and not taking

anything from anybody. The day of his first pro fight, at the West Liberty Arena, I took him in the diner to buy him a couple of chops before he went back to the hotel to lie down. Shirley came over to take the order. "Kid," I said, "I want you to meet my girl."

"Hey, Windy," The Kid says, right in front of her, "you been holdin' out on me. Why din'tcha tell me you knew a beautiful broad like this? Scared I'd break trainin' or something?"

Now there wasn't a guy came into the diner who didn't give Shirley the eye or the line but one thing that stood out about her was the way she brushed them off. Most of the waitresses in the joints in West Liberty were the friendly type but Shirley was special. Shirley played harder to get than a first-division deb, but she always seemed to know how to let them off easy, unless she really went up against a fresh guy and then she could be mean as a mother dog. So I was ready to see her put this young punk in his place. But she didn't put. She even smiled as if she liked it. And she was the one who had been telling me she never let the customers flirt with her. Inconsistency, thy name is woman!

When Shirley came back with the check, The Kid said, "How'd ya like to come to the arena and see me knock somebody stiff tonight?"

"Stop wasting your breath," I said. "I been trying to take her to the fights for months. Shirley don't like the fights."

"I think maybe I'd like to go this time," Shirley said.

Billy looked over at me and laughed. "See that, Windy? She's got the hots for me!" He was really talking to Shirley.

"Well, you certainly have a high opinion of yourself," she said. But she said it kind of smilingly.

"Why not?" he said. "Ever since I was an eight-year-old kid peddlin' papers, the kids ran away from me and the broads ran to me."

Then he did something that showed he was just as nervy

with his hands as he was with his mouth. He reached out and patted her on her sweet little keister. Real familiar. I waited for Shirley to let him have one. Shirley just blushed and said, "Fresh!" And when she walked away, something told me she was walking for The Kid.

The opponent they put in there with Billy for his first pro fight wasn't a world-beater but he was a real club-fighter who could take a good punch, what they call a crowd-pleaser, which means he's the kind of pug who doesn't spare the blood, his or the other guy's. A target for The Kid's fast left hand, a sucker for the straight right, but plenty of competition for a boy with no professional experience. He liked to get inside and hold on with one hand and club with the other, strictly a saloon fighter, and in the first round The Kid was getting bloodied up a little bit because he wouldn't stay away and box the fella like I told him to.

He was a great little piece of fighting machinery, The Kid, but a know-it-all from way back and very slow to take advice. So he had to get his nose bloody and a red blotch over his kidneys before he began to stay away and make the guy fight *his* fight the way I wanted him to in the beginning. After that it was all ours and The Kid got a nice hand when he left the ring. He looked around for Shirley and blew her a kiss. My girl, and the first day he meets her he's moving in!

"How you feeling, Kid?" I asked him when he came out of the shower.

"Like a million," he said. "That bum never hurt me."

"That side of yours looks like a slice of beef," I said. "A clown like that shouldn't lay a glove on you. Next time do what I tell you."

"I c'n take care of myself," The Kid said.

"Here's your purse," I said. "All I'm keeping is the fifty you owe me. The rest is all yours."

I always do that with my boys when I'm starting them out. Psychology. Makes them feel they're tied up with a square shooter. When they get in the big bucks is time enough to split it down the middle.

"Look, Kid, I figure we're going to be together a long time, so don't try to impress me with how tough you are. Save all your fighting for the ring. Now get dressed and go on back to the hotel and get a good night's sleep."

"Fuck sleep," The Kid said. "I ain't had a glass o' beer all the time I been training. I'm going out and grab some fun. I got a heavy date."

Why is it that the guys with no talent always obey me like I'm their father? And the kids like Billy with something special on the ball are always trouble?

"Listen, Kid," I said. "I been in this racket since you could chin yourself on a bar rail. And one thing I know, fighting and night life don't go, especially when the latter involves the mouse department. So as your manager, I'm telling you to get yourself over to the hotel and start pounding your ear."

"Yeah," he said, not looking so handsome when he was talking through his teeth, "so you c'n be sure I'm not making it with Shirley."

"What's Shirley got to do with it?"

"Shirley's going to the Legion dance with me over to Oklagee," The Kid said.

"Lovely," I said. "I loan you dough. I get you a semi for your first pro fight. And how do you show your gratitude?"

It was hard to figure. I knew for a fact that Shirley never liked to go over to Oklagee. She thought the boys were too fresh and tough over there. And here she was going with the freshest and toughest of them all. It was a terrible blow to my pride. I would have thought a girl like Shirley would have had more sense than to give me the air for a little pug-nosed brat who happened to have a nice pair of shoulders and a waist that tapered down like a ballet dancer's.

When I was leaving the stadium, I saw them at the curb together. He was helping her onto the back of a shiny silver motorcycle. I went over to them and said, "Kid, you got a big career ahead of you. You oughta know better than to take chances riding around on one of those things."

"Get out of our way," The Kid said. "We're late."

"The Kid's a screwball," I said. "He's just as liable to wrap you and this scooter around a tree."

"Billy is the best motorcycle rider in the country," Shirley said. "He won a big silver cup at the fair last year."

She had known him less than one day and already he had her sounding like him.

"I'll bet he stole it," I said. But the words were blown back in my face by the blast-off.

In those next few days they became the talk of West Liberty. They'd go roaring up and down the street on that damned motorcycle, Shirley holding on for dear life with her dark red hair flying out behind her. If Billy hadn't been the best prospect I had run across in a flock of Sundays, I would have washed my hands of both of them right there. But Billy looked like an A-1 meal ticket, and that's one thing a manager just can't afford to turn down.

What I did do, though, for Shirley's benefit, was to try to break up this thing with The Kid before it got any more serious. I did a little checking around and what I found out about Billy was enough to discourage any girl. At least that's the way it sounded to me. So the next day, while The Kid was doing his roadwork with his sparring partners, I slipped into the diner for a heart-to-heart with Shirley to set her straight.

"Look, honey," I said, "it's not just because I got the old torch out for you that I'm telling you this. It's for your own good. I've been getting a line on this Romeo of yours. He's got a bad rep. Did you know he put in sixteen months in the work farm for stealing a motorcycle? He's a little hipped on motorcycles. He even went over the wall once and stole another motorcycle and they had to bring him back. He was head of a gang of toughs and sneak-thieves in Oklagee. A real Hell's Angel. A real no-good."

"Poor Billy," Shirley said. "He's had a very hard life. His

mother died when he was five and his old man went off and left him. He never had anyone to tell him what was right. All he needs is someone to take care of him."

So you see what I was up against? Practically a criminal we've got on our hands, and all Shirley is thinking about is being a mother to him.

I will say one thing for Billy, though it hurts me to admit it. Although around the gym or with the fellas there was nobody meaner—jumping all the time and full of p. and v.—when he was with Shirley even his face seemed different. The way he looked at her. I wouldn't have thought there was that much feeling in him.

"It's because he doesn't feel inferior with me," Shirley tried to explain it. "I guess he grew up hating kids because they had mothers and fathers looking after them. With me, because he's sure of me, his real self begins to come out."

Well, frankly, I wouldn't know about all that shrink talk. How those dolls can dress it up when they fall but good!

Billy won his second pro fight just as easy as his first and this time we had three hundred dollars for our five minutes' work. With a few bucks in his pocket, things sort of went to his head because all of a sudden he asked me if I would be willing to stand up for him in case he and Shirley got hitched in the near future.

"Don't be stupid," I said. "Shirley has got too much brains to change her name to Mrs. Bonnard. And anyway, you haven't heard the last word from her old man."

I felt pretty confident that was one hurdle too many, even for my irrepressible little battler. Shirley's old man was rough-and-tumble, a bartender at a hangout for truck drivers, and from what she had told me, he had fairly definite ideas as to the qualifications of anyone aspiring to his daughter's hand. She had invited me home for dinner several times, but I hadn't felt quite up to coping with him. So I had no doubts as to just what sort of a reception The Kid would get if he actually popped the question to the head of the house.

Two days before The Kid's next fight, I had my answer, expressed in somewhat more violent terms than I would have liked. Billy showed up for his workout with a beautiful shiner. "What did you do, fall off your motorcycle?" I wanted to know.

"Naw, I got it from Shirley's old man," The Kid said.

"Don't tell me you had a fight with him." I was always warning Billy never to get in any fights that weren't for dough. Why take the chance of breaking your hand on an amateur? And getting busted? "I'm surprised at you fighting a man his age," I said.

"He c'n still hit you a pretty good punch," Billy said. "When I told him Shirley and me was thinkin' of gettin' hitched, he said no daughter of his was going to marry a lousy pug that had done time. Nobody can talk to me like that, not even Shirley's old man. So I poked him in the kisser. He takes a pretty good punch, too."

I figured that was curtains for Billy as far as Shirley was concerned, that she had seen him at last for what he was, a fresh-faced little roughneck with no respect for anybody or anything. But next day when I dropped into the diner to see how she was taking it, Shirley was on Billy's side stronger than ever. "I don't blame Billy," she said. "That was a terrible thing my father said to him. You see, all his life Billy's been kicked around. He never had a decent home. So he's naturally hyper-sensitive. You have to understand him."

Well maybe Shirley knew a little more about him than I did, but The Kid struck me as being about as sensitive as a slab of reinforced concrete. When a girl like Shirley goes, though, baby, she *goes*. No ifs, ands or buts. I found that out to my sorrow the following day.

The Kid won his first main event that night, catching a ten-year veteran in a flurry in the first round and putting him away in a minute and a half. When I paid Billy off, he and Shirley went roaring out into the night on the shiny silver motorcycle he had made a down payment on after his last fight.

I didn't think things were any crazier than usual, until around three in the morning when Shirley's old man called me, mad as a nest of hornets. It seems Shirley hadn't come home at all. It looked like she'd run off with my Kid. And in the morning, when they still hadn't been heard from, it was all too clear that that's exactly what had happened.

It was bad enough when I thought about Shirley. But what really hurt was that The Kid had run out on me, too. I had him signed for another main go that following Friday with a jump to five hundred but he didn't even bother to let me in on his plans. The next thing I heard he was fighting out of Oklahoma City for "Larceny Joe" Banfield, an old-time bandit disguised as a fight manager. It didn't surprise me, a couple of weeks later, when I heard that Joe had run out on The Kid, copping the last purse and leaving The Kid stranded. Well, it served Billy right, I thought, for running out on a square-shooter who was ready to split everything down the middle with him. But I was kind of worried about Shirley. It couldn't be much fun being stranded in a strange town with a wild man like Billy Bonnard.

I didn't have anything better to do so I decided I'd get myself over to O.C. and see if I couldn't talk some sense into Shirley, maybe even get her to throw in the towel and come back to West Liberty. When I picked up the papers in town the morning I got in, I got the surprise of my life. That night Kid Bonnard was meeting none other than Monk Wilson, the welterweight champ of the Middle West. That was an overmatch if I ever heard one. The Kid was a promising newcomer all right but he needed to be brought along real careful for at least a year before he could even belong in the same ring with Wilson.

I called all the hotels in town before I finally tracked them down at a ten-dollar-a-day flea-bag on the wrong side of town. I hustled right over there and found Shirley alone in a crummy little inside room that had nothing in it but an old brass bed.

There wasn't even a suitcase in the place. They had hocked that, along with everything else, when Larceny Joe took a powder on them. Shirley looked at least two years older than when I had seen her the month before. There were rings under her eyes and that beautiful young puss was full of troubles. For the last three days, she said, breakfast, lunch and supper had been donuts and coffee.

"Shirley," I said, "here's enough money to get you back to West Liberty." I held out fifty bucks. "Why don't you call it quits before this crazy kid wrecks your life along with his?"

All Shirley said was "I've got to stay with Billy. I'm married to Billy."

They were going to be all right, she was sure, after the Wilson fight. That would make Billy the biggest drawing card in the state and they'd have enough money to get their things back out of hock.

"How long are you going to keep on letting The Kid sell you a bill of goods?" I wanted to know. "Billy is a comer but he isn't good enough to stay in there with Monk Wilson. A couple of matches like this and Billy will be a has-been before he ever gets started."

"I wish you'd handle him again, Windy," Shirley said.

"Yeah, I owe him a lot," I said. "First he runs off with my girl, then he jumps to another manager and leaves me holding the bag. I should do him a favor!"

Outside we could hear a racket that sounded as if an airplane was coming right through the room. Shirley jumped up and instinctively her hand went up to adjust her hair. "That's Billy-baby," she said.

"You mean he's still got that friggin' motorcycle?" I said. "He'll hock your watch and your clothes and let you live on doughnuts but he won't give up that motorcycle."

"It'd break his spirit if he lost that motorcycle," Shirley said.

"How about your spirit?" I said.

"I love Billy," Shirley said, as if that explained everything.

The Kid came bouncing in as cocky as if he were already champion of the world, instead of a ten-to-one short-ender who couldn't buy his way into a pay-phone booth. "Hello, Windy old cock," he greeted me, just as if he were still in my stable and nothing had ever happened.

Well, I guess I'll always be a sucker for anything Shirley asked me, so I swallowed my pride like a plug of chewing tobacco and handled The Kid's corner that night. She was right there in the third row and the expression on her face was, well, there ought to be a law against a nice girl loving a bum that much.

As soon as the gong sounded, I knew Shirley should have been back in the hotel. The Kid came out swinging the way he always did, but Wilson knew too much for him. Wilson just sidestepped calmly and clipped Billy in the mouth. From the moment that punch connected, the Kid was fighting on instinct. His punches were wild and Wilson wasn't missing. I thought the round was never going to end. There was a bad gash in Billy's lip and his face was ashen. He was out on his feet at the bell.

I looked down at Shirley. She was holding her face in her hands. It's a tough assignment being married to a fighter, especially when he's a wise guy who wins a couple of easy ones and thinks he's ready for fighters like Monk Wilson.

"Kid," I said to Billy as I rubbed ice at the back of his head and dropped some ice cubes down into his balls to bring him around, "There's no percentage taking this kind of licking from Wilson. Lemme throw in the towel. A year from now when you know more you'll be ready for him."

The Kid shook his head and mumbled through his cut lip. "I gotta win this one. I bet my whole purse on myself at five to one. Five G's if I win and we can't buy our way outa the hotel if I lose."

Somehow he managed to come out for the second round. Wilson kept working on that lip. All the color was gone from

Shirley's face. It looked like both sides of the Bonnard family were needing smelling salts. And all the ringsiders around here were egging Wilson on to "work on that mouth." I don't see how she stood it. How either of them stood it. The Kid was down three times that round. But he kept getting up. When God put him together he must have run out of brains so he figured he'd make up for it with guts.

These days, in Vegas or the Garden, they'd stop a fight as bloodily one-sided as that, with their three-knock-down rule, et cetera, but in O.C. they played rough. Wilson kept piling it onto Billy for five terrible rounds. The Kid was down so many times I began to lose track. I don't know which of them was taking a worse beating, him or Shirley. I could see her flinch every time another punch cut into that torn mouth.

In the corner at the end of the fifth I begged him to let me throw in the towel. I'm a pretty good cut-man but this was too deep. His lip was pouring blood and both eyes were almost closed. But he wouldn't let me stop the fight. "I'm OK," he whispered, "but get Shirley out. I don't want her to see no more."

I went over and gave her The Kid's message. Her eyes were all red and runny. But she did as she was told.

The sixth round had just begun when Wilson hit Billy in the mouth again and he collapsed. He lay perfectly still. Monk did a victory dance in the opposite corner. A wave to a friend said, It's all over. I'll never understand how Billy did it—he seemed too far gone even to be able to hear the count—but at *eight* he suddenly rolled over and onto one knee and at *nine* he was back on his feet. Wilson was so surprised that he rushed in wildly to finish it with one punch. He wasn't even bothering to protect himself. There must have been some sixth sense hidden in the fog of The Kid's brain that told him what to do. Suddenly he put everything he had behind a right uppercut. It caught Wilson right under the chin and he started backward and The Kid hooked to the jaw and Monk fell forward and didn't move again until they were dragging him back to his corner.

Billy had to have eight stitches taken in his lip, one eye had to be lanced to reduce the swelling and a bone was broken in his left hand. But he and Shirley had their five thousand bucks and they were going to celebrate. The doc had told him he should stay in bed for at least three days but at four o'clock that morning he and Shirley were at the Kit Kat Klub on their third bottle of champagne. But they didn't need the wine to get a lift. They were both higher than a kite, just from love, exhaustion, and all that quick money after going in hock.

The three of us barnstormed our way east after that. The Kid was piling up an impressive winning streak and getting a national reputation. He accepted his growing fame just the way he had always accepted Shirley, strictly for granted. Of course he loved her in his own way, but it was a pretty brusque, one-sided, more-taking-than-giving way. At least that's how it seemed to me, watching from outside the ropes. Shirley would tell it different.

I finally booked him into the bigtime, on cable from Trump's Plaza, where the Kid became an overnight sensation by knocking out LeRoi Adams, who had lost a split decision to the champion. Billy still didn't know much more about boxing than when he left West Liberty but his speed, ferocity and punching power had simply overwhelmed Adams. A string of consistent wins on cable and Billy was a hot ticket, the Number 1 contender for the title. The Kid had already pocketed a coupla hundred grand for his end and he and Shirley were living it up in a penthouse on top of a class hotel on Central Park South. The Kid had a closet full of sharp five-, six-hundred-dollar suits and Shirley had a mink coat and everything that goes with it and looked like a million bucks. The only thing they didn't have was anything with four wheels. Believe it or not, the Kid was still faithful to his motorcycles. He had a new, shiny, custom-made silver Yamaha, and emblazoned on one side of it was BILLY THE KID and on the other, THE KO KING FROM OK. It was really something to see Billy on that motorcycle streaking through rush-hour traffic with Shirley behind him and holding on tight, her wonderful red hair blowing wildly in the wind. For a while there they were on the Manhattan merry-go-round and grabbing all the rings.

Then The Kid took the welterweight title from Ernie La Plante and things began to happen. A couple of sharpshooters from the casinos, Teddy Moran and Darney Fay, started wining and dining him and before I knew what had happened they had convinced him that I wasn't a big enough managerial gun to handle a champion. So after working him all the way to the top, I had to sell out to a couple of con men for a fraction of what I figured to make with the title. I thought I had a case against The Kid, but mine was small-claims stuff after I heard Shirley's. The night Billy successfully defended his championship for the first time she called me at my hotel around three o'clock in the morning. At first I thought she was trying to get me to come out and meet them somewhere and bury the hatchet. But instead she wanted me to come up to the apartment. And from the sound of her voice, I could tell something was wrong. When I got up there, I found her all alone. Her eyes looked as if she had been crying so long she had run out of tears. She had watched the fight on the TV, she said, for ever since that tough one in O.C. she had stayed away from ringside. When Billy won, she got all dolled up because he always liked to go out night-clubbing after polishing off an opponent. But this time Billy hadn't shown up.

That was the first time it happened. I wish I could say, for Shirley's sake, that it was the last. But Billy had a big year that year, knocking off the three leading contenders and after every spectacular win he could be found at a front table at the Waikiki Club, an expensive trap his new managers owned a piece of. Those two grifters also saw to it that he became acquainted with the ladies of the chorus. I guess it was just a case of too much happening all at once. Overnight a small-town punk was the Big Town's hero. His paynight for the last closed circuit was a million six. You need something special to take seven-figure money in stride.

The third time it happened I sat it out with Shirley. "Why don't you divorce the bum?" I said. "You've got too much on the ball to let this little son-of-a-bitch kick you around like this."

But Shirley shook her head just the way I had seen before, in West Liberty, Oklahoma City and points east. "No, Windy, that's not what I want," she said. "I've got to stay with Billy."

Well, there's only been one fighter who could hit the late spots and keep on winning, and Kid Bonnard was good but he wasn't Harry Greb. His fourth time out after winning the title he ran into a tartar in the person of José Ribera, a young, tough Mexican who had been doing his training on Fourteenth Street while Billy was doing his in the discos. The Kid had never taken my advice to master the finer points of the manly art and up till this night youth and speed and strength and a murderous left hook had carried him through. But some of Billy's zip had obviously been left behind in the Waikiki. By the end of the third round Ribera was giving The Kid the same kind of treatment Monk Wilson had handed him back in O.C. Only this time Billy had nothing left for an emergency. Somehow he managed to go the distance but he was out on his feet at the final bell.

No matter how many marks I had against him, it was kind of tough to have to watch The Kid slide off the stool onto the canvas after the ref raised Ribera's hand. There was so much pride in him, so much cockiness and bounce that it just didn't seem right to see him lying there while Ribera's handlers carried the new champion around the ring on their shoulders. Billy's left foot was shaking a little bit. I always hated that.

I went back to the dressing room to see if there was anything I could do. The Kid had one eye shut tight and an egg-shaped swelling over the other one. He was sitting on the rubbing table with his head bent low, a trainer pressing ice against the egg. Moran and Fay were telling him what a bum he was. They had nothing to worry about because the way they had it rigged, they would own a piece of Ribera if he won the title.

The Kid was in no mood for the Waikiki that night. "Where you wanna go?" I said. "Where d'ya think?" he said. "Back to Shirley's." When she took him into her arms, The Kid began to cry. She put him to bed and put cold compresses on his head to reduce the swelling. When I dropped around the next night to see how everything was getting along, The Kid was still in bed and Shirley was clucking around him like a contented hen. "Windy," The Kid said, "Shirley wants me to go back with you again. How about getting me a rematch with Ribera? I want to win my title back."

Well, The Kid had run out on me twice, but if that's what Shirley wanted, I figured I'd give it one more shot. So I lined up a couple of tune-ups with tomato-cans Billy could knock over without working up a sweat, even a Billy who had lost a step or two. I saw how those bums could drop a right hand on The Kid because he wasn't moving his head to the right when he jabbed. And when I yelled at him what he was doing wrong, instead of learning, all he did was get mad. But the last thing to go is the punch, and Billy had a left hook in a class with Raging Bull Jake LaMotta's, if you go back that far. That, and instinctively knowing how to finish opponents once he had them hurt, put KO's in his record that made up for the lack of finesse. A banger from the old school is what he was. A dancing master, a Sugar Ray Leonard, forget it.

Anyway, I finally signed the Ribera rematch, for a bundle. Big press conference at the Trump Plaza and all the honchos from HBO talking about the ratings and somehow Don King is in the picture too, calling it The Battle of the Little Giants. I don't let on, but I'm a little excited too, because in all the years I knocked around this dirty business, I never had a champion before. A couple of hopefuls looked as if I might be able to build them into contenders, into the elusive come-and-go of the top ten. But I never got them up to the level every manager dreams of—managing a champion of the world.

And now that I had the tiger I had been looking for all my life, I had him by the tail, or he had me. This fight with José (Little Marvelous) Ribera was the most important in his life. So did that mean he was in the gym every day working his heart out with the best Ribera-like sparring partners I could find for him at a hundred bucks a day? Half the time Billy didn't show up, and when he was late and I chewed him out, he'd say, "What's the big deal? I'll make the weight easy. That Ribera's a bum. Last time he ran like a thief and stole the fight. This time I'll cut the ring off, bull him into a corner and beat his brains out."

"Vegas has it almost three to one for Ribera, and the writers at your workouts are saying you look like you're in slo-mo."

"Fuck the writers. I beat Ribera the first time. I was robbed."

"Well, this is next time, Billy. And this Ribera is working like a son-of-a-bitch. Like his life depends on it. Which it does."

"Go over to Gallagher's, have yourself a T-bone and three or four belts, then a nice relaxing blow-job, stop worrying about Ribera, relax a little."

"In other words train like you've been training," I said.

"Look, Windy, don't be a pain in the ass. Did you see the look on Ribera the first time I gave him that shot to the body?" He threw a furious left hook that stopped just half an inch away from my belt.

"Yeah, I saw it," I said. "And I saw the second shot, and the third one. So what happens? Ribera gets smart, keeps circling away from the left and cops the decision."

"Robbed," Billy said. "Maybe fixed."

"Well, they won't have to fix this one," I said. "You're doing a pretty good job fixing yourself."

It was even worse than I thought. That night Shirley called me and said it was almost midnight and Billy wasn't home yet. Would I mind tracking him down for her?

Some tracking down. I cabbed right over to the Waikiki and there was our boy, living it up with a couple of hookers and the free-loaders for whom fighters like Billy have a fatal attraction, and vice versa.

"Come on, Billy, you're comin' home to Momma."

"In a pig's ass," said Billy.

I put my hand on his shoulder. "Come on, Billy, I thought you only tied one on *after* the fight—when you won."

I tried to pull him away from the table. One side of me wanted to leave him there and try to spring Shirley from this little son-of-a-bitch, but the other side was a manager who saw his championship slipping away.

I grabbed him and pulled him harder. His new pals were getting up. Waiters were coming over. A mess.

"Don't fuck with me, Windy. Go get a blow-job like I told you. Ribera is nothing. Bums I knocked out in O.C. could lick Ribera."

"Goddamn it, Billy, you're my one shot at a title, all my life the first shot and you're blowing it, baby, you're blowing it!"

I pulled him to his feet and he pulled back, then before I knew it I slapped him and he went crazy and threw a punch for real, only I know a little boxing and I slipped it, just like I tried to teach him, and he hit a pillar behind him, and I could see the pain go from his knuckles up his arm to his shoulder.

Next morning the left hand, the one I lovingly called "Jakey" for Jake LaMotta, is so swollen it looks like a sixteen-ouncer for the amateurs.

I go to the boxing mavens of HBO and plead my case, and try to get help from Don King, who drowns me in words of four and five syllables which all add up to "No way." It's not like the old days when an injury is an injury and you get the postponement. This is show business, showbiz with blood, but still show business. There have been promos for weeks on TV across the country, and it's in *TV Guide,* and there are advertisers to worry about, it's like a big TV special, only it's a live fight.

So there I was, going down the aisle to the ring in Convention Hall, which should have been one of the highlights of my career, and now it felt more like I was escorting myself to my own execution. And what hurt the most was here I was with the first world champion I ever had, and also the first kid I handled in all my years I ever had to fight physically, and then sucker him into breaking the hand he may have been able to stop Ribera with, even if he has trained with all the dedication of a Harry Greb or a Maxie Baer.

Comes round one, Ribera is doing a number on The Kid, until twenty seconds before the bell, when the Mexican flash gets careless, and Billy lets the left go, *whack!* I can feel the pain shooting all the way up Billy's arm, to his shoulder and into his brain. But Ribera feels the pain too, he's down on all fours, with a silly grin on his face. He's up at *nine,* barely, and has enough ring-smarts left to grab Billy and tie him up, and the ref is pushing his way between them when the bell gives Ribera a minute's rest.

That's all he needs, because Billy only had that one shot with his left, he's resting it against his chest in round two, helpless now, like going into battle without a gun. He's got a nasty cut over his left eye and his left hand is like a dead cat lying there on his knee and he's already out of gas from not enough road work and too much Waikiki.

"I'm stopping the fight," I told him. "Say you broke your hand on his head in round one. Save a little face."

"You stop this fight, I'll finish what I started in that joint." I could barely make out what Billy was saying. I used all of

Angelo Dundee's tricks and a few of my own to close the cut,
and it felt like thirty seconds instead of a full minute when the
bell sent Billy back to the slaughter. Ribera knew about the left
hand now, and he could see how The Kid was trying to
breathe through his nose. He caught him in a five-six-seven
combination, and Billy's mouthpiece went flying, and then
Ribera was all over him, and there was The Kid knocked cold
for the first time in his life. The referee counted to ten, a
number I never bet, on horses or casinos, and when we lifted
Billy up he didn't know the fight was over and tore after
Ribera, who tried to give him the winner's consolation hug
and almost got kneed in the balls for his troubles.

In the dressing room I brought him back to his lovable self
with smelling salts, and then the doc sewed up the gashes over
both eyes. What a mess. His jaw was swollen and his ego was
shrunk.

"Well, Kid," I couldn't resist saying because I really wanted
to kill him, "maybe we'll hit the Waikiki, cheer you up a
little."

The Kid made a face when they sewed him up, and a little
moan went out of him when the doc barely touched the swollen left hand. When he heard what I said he didn't think it was
funny. "I go home to Shirley."

The Kid was over the peak now and going down fast. I got
him the best bone doctor for his hand, and three months' rest,
but he broke it again the first time he threw it for real. Looks
like I had really fixed him, or he fixed himself, that last night
in the Waikiki. But the Kid found another doctor, and tried
again. He couldn't believe it was over. They never do. He
took some awful pastings while we tried to convince him that
it was time to rack up. But every time he got beat he'd go right
home to Shirley and she'd patch him up, make him comfortable, fuss over him and nurse him back to health.

When Billy finally hung up the gloves, back in O.C., after
some new black kid out of the amateurs left him for dead, they

decided to settle down there. The Kid must be crowding thirty now but he still rides that motorcycle. Actually, if you ask me, he's living off Shirley, but to hear her tell it he's developing a couple of comers who are about to make them a million bucks. Well, maybe so. When you've got that much faith and heart, I guess anything can happen. But talking to Billy, I could see his speech was a little funny. Made you wonder how he'll be five years down the road.

The other day I dropped over to the restaurant where she's a waitress again. "Hi, Shirley," I said. "How's every little thing?"

She wasn't a trim featherweight anymore, closer to super-lightweight, but I still had the hots for her.

"Just fine, Windy," she said. "You ought to come up and have dinner with Billy and me some night. We just moved into the cutest little apartment."

I knew what that meant. They had dropped down a peg to a one-room flat with kitchenette. I've got two or three pretty good prospects, including an honest-to-God white heavy-weight, which as you know is an endangered species. A white contender could put me back in the chips again, like I was with Billy the Kid. So if Shirley had stuck with me she'd have somebody looking out for her, instead of having to hustle for tips and handle the come-ons, living on lean street with a burned-out Billy Bonnard.

But the funny part of the whole deal is, even if I figure she's winding up with a loser, who can only get worse as the years roll by, and the brain damage really getting to him by age forty—in my daydreams I see her pushing him in a wheelchair and he's still giving her a hard time—but she'll never see it that way. The funny part is, she's happy.

# THE HOWLING DOGS OF TAXCO

Worn out by story conferences in which he was invariably overruled by an overbearing producer he feared and needed, fed up with wrangling about money in his separation settlement with his second wife, Rhoda, weary of Hollywood Christmas parties, the inevitable New Year's Day hangover and even the Rose Bowl game (and the Rose Bowl traffic), Howie Steiner thought there must be a more imaginative, a purer way of celebrating the endless quest for peace on earth and a better tomorrow.

So, on the advice of Rhoda, who was proud of her modest collection of pre-Columbian art, he went down to Taxco, in the state of Guerrero, in the heart of Old Mexico, to a small hotel that opened on a garden near the plaza. This is more like it, he was thinking, as a waiter brought him a complimentary margarita in the patio. Away from the rat race. For Steiner it was love at first sight: the steep and narrow cobblestone streets, the tiny silver shops, the faded pastel stucco houses, the copper-skinned natives who made the *gringo* tourists look even pastier than they were, the small but ornate tree-lined plaza that separated Paco's Bar from the other landmark, the Santa Prisca Cathedral.

Sunset drew Steiner to the balcony of Paco's, to watch the light of the sun subtly changing against the rococo facade of the pink cathedral that seemed to sit in benign judgment on the town. Every night there was a *pasada,* a procession of candle-bearing singers who would call on their neighbors, singing a traditional Christmas hymn until admitted for a festive serving of tropical fruit, Oaxaca cheese, fresh bread and wine before going on to the next little house. Although Steiner was not a Christian, he had always been moved by the ceremony of Christmas. Now watching the *pasada* slowly ascend the ancient cobblestone steps, with its haunting Mexican carols and its candles flickering in the soft evening air, he felt he had discovered the heart of the true Christmas season.

One evening in the plaza Steiner was reading on a park bench when an urchin came up to him—maybe ten years old, ragged, barefoot, his skin the dark, unpolished bronze of the true Guerrero Indian. His eyes were deep brown, intense, so beautiful they seemed to have been painted by Diego Rivera. In his hand was a crude stone object, a caricature of a face with an intimidating nose and, in place of hair, what looked like corncobs rising from the top of its head.

"Meester," the boy said, "very old. I find in cave. Only five dollar."

Steiner turned the stone head around in his hands. He had been interested in archaeology ever since taking Archy I and II at N.Y.U. Especially Mexican archaeology. He had even flirted with the idea of going into archaeology, but an early marriage, a flair for writing and a chance opening through a friend from the N.Y.U. film school had brought him to Hollywood.

"Five dollars!" Steiner said, "Chico, you're a little thief."

He had almost memorized his small *Terry's Guide* dictionary.
*"Ladrón!"*

"Hokay," the barefoot salesman said with a practiced smile,
"two dollar."

"It's not worth twenty-five cents. *No vale nada.*"

The boy pleaded with his almost irresistible dark eyes, then
finally with a shrug moved on to another *gringo* prospect.
Steiner went back to his book—he was reading *Mexico South*
by the painter-illustrator and self-taught archaeologist Miguel
Covarrubias. The book drew Steiner into the vivid, visionary
world of the jaguar and the serpent, of the enlightened god
Quetzalcoatl, at once white and human, and the feathered
serpent; and his ferocious rival from the north, the blood-
thirsty invader Quitzilopoctli.

Steiner didn't see the urchin-"archeologist" again until
New Year's Eve. In Taxco the arrival of the New Year is
celebrated at a midnight mass in the cathedral. For hours
beforehand the ancient bells ring out. A thousand worshippers
are drawn to Santa Prisca. Those who can, crowd into the
large, bare hall, pushing as close as possible to the brilliant
altar. Those who can't, fill the huge open doorways and spill
out onto the steps, and into the plaza. At midnight they fall on
their knees and join the *padre* in prayer that they may live up
to the example of *El Cristo Rey* in the year to come. Then
fireworks shoot off into the sky and burst in joyous sound and
color over the cobblestones.

Steiner came out of Santa Prisca with a sense of exaltation,
of cleanliness, pleased that for the first time since he had left
New York for Hollywood he would face the New Year not
with a hangover but with a clear head and fresh eyes. At that
moment he felt a tugging at his sleeve. Steiner recognized the
earnest, brown face of the undersized vendor in pre-Columbian artifacts.

"Meester," he said, "I am your friend, Miguelito. At the
mass I feel very bad to cheat you. The *padre* tells us we must

start well the *año nuevo.* Tomorrow morning, if you will pay for the horses, I will take you twenty kilometers to cave of old Guerrero gods. No *turistos* ever see this. I will go into the cave with you, and we will see what we can find, hokay?''

How could Steiner, how could anyone drawn to Mexican archaeology, refuse?

That night Steiner heard again the choral screams that had awakened him the first night, and that had been explained by the night clerk with a casual shrug. "Oh, those are only our dogs, *señor,* we call them the howling dogs of Taxco. They are very hungry and up in the mountains they hunt in packs, like wolves. The nights are so quiet that we hear them miles away."

The howling dogs of Taxco . . . Steiner could picture them up there, baying at some invisible prey. The sound was unlike anything he had heard, but after a while he grew used to it, accepted it as part of the night life of Taxco, and went back to sleep.

Next morning at dawn Miguelito was waiting for him with two very small horses. In the fine, early-morning air they galloped down the high ground from Taxco and out into the countryside to a village, a *poblado* of half a dozen thatch-roofed huts. Beyond them, on a stony hillside, they hitched their horses, and Miguelito led Steiner toward a narrow opening in the rocks. With a dramatic flick of his small flashlight, Miguelito beamed it into the darkness. God or Quetzalcoatl be praised, Steiner was thinking, Miguelito had brought him to his first archaeological cave.

There were the ancient stucco walls, the faded fresco, the steps leading from the entrance cave to the next chamber. There were indentations where idols had been placed more than a thousand years ago. They followed the path of the flashlight until the cave narrowed to a tunnel barely wide enough for Miguelito to squeeze through.

"I go in," Miguelito said. "Never go this far before."

"*Cuidado,* be careful," Steiner said. For some reason, perhaps because this place had a churchlike atmosphere, they both spoke in whispers. At least five minutes passed, possibly ten, while Steiner waited in the darkness. He heard some strange, scurrying sounds. Lizards, rats? He felt excited and a little frightened. At last he was being his own archaeologist, his own idol-hunter. Then, from inside, he heard a muffled cry. A few moments later, Miguelito appeared.

"Meester—look! Look, Meester!"

In Miguelito's hand was an idol, in the shape of a drinking vessel. The ears were handles. The face was that of an ancient warrior of Guerrero. It was chipped and cracked but intact. Miguelito wrapped it tenderly in a cloth he had brought, and back they rode, triumphantly, across the valleys and *barrancas* to Taxco.

In Steiner's room they bargained gingerly. "Five hundred pesos—forty bucks U.S.," Steiner opened. Miguelito shook his head. It was such a treasure he hated to part with it. Actually he should turn it over to the National Museum, which would probably give him two thousand pesos for it. Steiner raised his bid to one thousand—eighty dollars. They finally settled on one hundred even.

At lunch Steiner showed his prize to the plump, seedy-prosperous *patrón* of the hotel, who turned it over carefully in his hands and pronounced it old, very old. *Si, señor,* a very rare, very fine piece. *Muy antiguo. Muy preciosa.*

*Antiguo, preciosa* hummed in Steiner's mind all the way back to Los Angeles. He even showed it to Rhoda, the wife he was separated from but still saw occasionally, like a bad habit he couldn't break. Rhoda had once gone on a dig to Yucatán and so considered herself a pre-Columbian maven. She was taking extension courses at U.C.L.A. and knew practically everything. "I'd take it to Stendahl's," she suggested, "and have it appraised." Stendahl's was the gallery on La Cienega known for its pre-Columbian collection and expertise.

Stendahl fingered it carefully, held it up to the light, wet his finger and rubbed it—and, almost inaudibly, pronounced it worthless. A good fake—but still a fake.

Discouraged by his fiasco as a would-be collector of pre-Columbian art, Steiner stayed away from Taxco for several years. But finally, after finishing a screenplay that was actually going into production, he couldn't resist going back, and found himself caught up again in the appeal of the old church, the twisting cobblestone streets, the fawnlike Indian children, even the howling of the dog packs in the mountains.

Next morning in the plaza Steiner felt a polite tap on his shoulder and turned to face a slender young man dressed in powder-blue *guayabera,* pressed tan slacks and polished sandals, his black hair looped artfully over his forehead.

"Meester, you remember me? Here is Miguelito."

"Miguelito, get away from me. *Vayate!* You're a liar, a thief, a crook."

Miguelito tried again but Steiner left him at the foot of the steps leading up to Paco's. Next morning when Steiner came down for breakfast, Miguelito was waiting for him in the patio restaurant of the hotel. He had with him a brown gunny sack. He had something to show Steiner, he said, that was *muy importante, muy serioso.*

"Miguelito, you are ruining my trip," Steiner said. "I want to enjoy Taxco—without you. Now, *vayate,* beat it, get lost."

"Please, my friend, *por favor!*" The tears in Miguelito's eyes were genuine. "Last night, at the midnight mass for the New Year, I say, 'Miguelito, you are very bad. *Muy malo.* You lie. You cheat.'"

"It was after the other midnight mass that you cheated me," Steiner reminded him.

"Yes, I know," Miguelito confessed. "But this time I bring you something true. In fact it is something so special I cannot show it to you here in public."

Intrigued in spite of himself, Steiner took Miguelito back to his room again. The balcony opened on the great church. The bells were clanging. They always seemed to be clanging. Reverently, like a priest, Miguelito drew from the gunny sack a great head, exquisitely chiseled, the neck lean and tender, the hair a mass of curls that on closer inspection were sculptured serpents.

*"Mi gran amigo,"* Miguelito said, "this time I swear on my beloved mother and the sainted Virgin . . ."

"You lied to me twice," Steiner said.

*"Señor!"* Miguelito pleaded. "Would I lie to you a third time?"

"If you could get away with it—hell, yes! Go find yourself another *gringo* sucker. This town is full of them."

Miguelito left with his sack and his hurt dark eyes. Steiner decided he had had enough. He knew enough phonies in Hollywood. Who needed an Indian version in Taxco?

In the morning when he was checking out, the sleepy desk clerk reached down and handed him a gunny sack. There was a note pinned to it: *"Señor* Steiner—I am everything you say. *Muy malo.* A *ladrón!* But I wish you to take this with you as a gift to remember me in a better way. Your friend in truth, Miguelito."

Steiner left the sack on the floor near the desk but the clerk ran out to Steiner's rented car parked at the entrance. *"Señor, señor,* you forget thees." With the patience or stoicism he had admired in Mexican peons, Steiner managed to stuff the sack into his duffel bag.

Home from Mexico again, Steiner dutifully lugged the gunny sack to Stendahl's. This time Mr. Stendahl stared at it intensely for several minutes, and then asked for a few days to study it more thoroughly.

The next day Stendahl called Steiner at the studio, asking him how soon he could come to the gallery. Steiner had been

waiting for a call from his producer that he didn't really expect
to come through for days, and it was almost lunch time. Sensing something was up, he said he'd be over right away.

"Mr. Steiner," Stendahl greeted him, "you have brought us
a very, *very* important piece from the Rio de las Balsas area,
from the classic period of the little-known Guerrero culture.
It is almost too good to be true—the nose, so fine, so delicate,
should have broken off centuries ago. I have only seen a few
heads like this before, but never with all the serpent coils
intact. It is one of a kind. And belongs in a museum. Right now
I am ready to offer you one thousand dollars for it."

A museum! How could an amateur collector like Steiner
monopolize it? When Stendahl interpreted Steiner's shock as
hesitation, he quickly went up another two hundred and fifty
and Steiner took the money, thinking how it would help his
settlement problem with Rhoda. A few months later Steiner
heard that Stendahl had sold the piece for twenty-five hundred
dollars, and now he had no doubt but that one day it would
be worth twenty-five thousand.

The following Christmas, when Steiner returned to Taxco
again, and asked for Miguelito in the plaza, he was directed to
his new *casita,* a steep ten-minute climb up from the cathedral.
Steiner found him sitting in an elaborate wicker chair on his
freshly painted portico, which was full of flowering plants in
gasoline cans, and cages of small birds. He was reading a new
pamphlet from the National Museum on the classic culture of
Guerrero. He had grown a little moustache, wore real shoes
now, and looked every bit the *petit bourgeois* he was becoming.

A little brown urchin, who could have been Miguelito when
Steiner first met him, ran up with a fistful of pesos. "Here you
are, Don Miguel, I sell mine very quick." Miguelito counted
the money carefully and handed his young salesman his cut.
Meanwhile another Miguelito look-alike from five years back
ran out of the house with two grotesque clay heads that were

dead-ringers for the fakes Miguelito had palmed off on Steiner that first time.

"First try the steps of the church," Miguelito instructed, "and if that doesn't work, try Paco's Bar. Those *gringos borrachos* will never know the difference. And don't forget to say, 'I find this myself. *Mucho auténtico.* Only five dollar.' "

Steiner had been standing there watching him for a moment. When he saw his old customer, Miguelito jumped up to grab him in a warm *abrazo. "Señor* Stein-err!" he said. "Always I am hoping you come back."

"I see you are still up to your old tricks," Steiner said. "Only now you have become a big *comercio,* with your own sales force." Miguelito gave an exaggerated Guerrero shrug. "Remember what I say to you when I am still barefoot in the plaza? You are the colossus of the north. We are a very poor country. So we must do everything we can to get your dollars into our empty pockets."

"Miguelito, you don't have to apologize. You have a nice little business. Lots of our people are in the business of selling fakes, one way or another." He was thinking of his producer, and of half the people he knew in Hollywood.

Miguelito brought out his aged *tequila especiál* and poured generous shots for each of them. They touched their stubby glasses ceremoniously.

"Miguelito, this time it is my turn to feel guilty. This Christmas I've come back to tell you *I* have cheated *you."*

*"Mande?*—please?"

When Steiner told him of his profit at Stendahl's, Miguelito nodded, unsurprised.

"I knew it was *auténtico.* Of course I did not realize it was worth almost a million pesos, but I found it myself. In a new secret place down the River Balsas. *Un million pesos!"* Pleased with himself, he poured them each another *añejo.* "It's like hitting the *lotería."*

"Exactly," Steiner said. "In your country, with the peso constantly falling, a small fortune. And I feel it belongs to you. After all, you *gave* me that piece."

Miguelito nodded proudly. *"Si, como no?* I felt I owed it to you, *amigo."*

"But why—*why*—after cheating me twice?"

"My very good friend, this time I speak the truth. As you know, I was born here very poor. I walk barefoot on the cobblestones. I sleep like a dog on the floor. I see the rich *gringos* come to take pictures of us and look down on us, and I say to myself, Miguelito, you must find a way to—"

"—get our dollars out of our pockets and into yours—even if you have to lie and cheat?"

Miguelito gave that familiar shrug that bespoke the local philosophy. "You have heard the howling dogs of Taxco? When a dog is starving he will snap at your hands to get what he needs."

"So what changed you, Miguelito, from a little crook to an honest man?"

"Last year my Mami—who loves the Church even more than she loves me, her little Miguelito born like *Jesu Christo* without a father—she die. There is not even time to say good-bye. I feel very sad. I never go in the big church except maybe to find customers. But now I go in to make confession. I feel very bad for all my lies and cheats. I promise my mother and the Blessed Virgin I will do something to make up for all my *mentiras.* So when you come back for Christmas, the Holy Spirit moves me to give you free gratis no charge the *escultura classica* I discovered on my first expedition after I bury my mother in the little cemetery at the bottom of the hill."

Steiner offered to give him half the money from Stendahl but he refused. It was hard to believe.

"Not even the big archaeologists from the Museo Nacional know about my cave on the Balsas. And I have been very careful not to let my local competitors know where I am going.

So it makes me happy if you keep the money. Next week I will make another expedition. And maybe, God willing, I will find something else further back in the cave, even more valuable."

A few months later, home in West Los Angeles, Steiner was awakened by a phone call in the middle of the night. As he answered, he checked his watch, almost two o'clock! It was, most unexpectedly, Miguelito, and he sounded breathless. *"Hola, gran amigo,* here is your old *compañero* Miguel! I am just come back from a wonderful trip down the Rio Balsas. And *señor,* I have found something truly *fantástico.* You must think me *loco* to call at such an hour, but I could not wait until morning. This piece is so serious I will keep it for your eyes only."

"Where are you calling from, Paco's Bar?" At four o'clock in Taxco, his little archaeologist could only be calling from one too many *tequilas añejos.*

"No, no, I call from my house, in my *oficina.* I have my own telephone now. *Amigo mio,* would I call you at such an hour if this was not the discovery of a lifetime? You know, I have been studying with the masters at the *Museo.* I study Olmeca and Vera Cruz Classico and I learn all the periods of my own Guerrero. And tonight, what I bring back, believe me, *señor,* it is worth a special trip to Taxco."

Two days later Steiner was flying down to Mexico City and then speeding around the hairpin turns that took him past Cuernavaca and on to Taxco. Miguelito was waiting for him at their usual meeting place, the congenial balcony of Paco's overlooking the plaza. His moustache was fuller now, more authoritative, it seemed, and instead of the familiar native vest, he was wearing a proper city suit. Next time Steiner came, he speculated, the urchin he first met when he was running barefoot on the cobblestones would be mayor of Taxco, if not the local *presidente* of *Turismo.* He was on his way. Everything about him advertised his climb. Like the self-important way he said to Steiner, "First we will have a *copita* to celebrate the treasure. And then you will come with me to feast your eyes on it."

When they climbed the steep cobblestones to Miguelito's house, and while Steiner paused to catch his breath, his host disappeared into a deep rear closet. When he reappeared, he held an object wrapped in cloth, which he uncovered with deliberate ceremony.

Revealed to Steiner was the stone head of a jaguar, carved in worn brown stone, with fierce fangs, menacing square teeth, and gaping, heart-shaped holes for eyes. It was round as a pumpkin, and about six inches high and six across. Between the fangs a large, flat tongue extruded, lighter at the tip than in the middle. As an amateur, haphazard collector of pre-Columbian artifacts, Steiner had never seen anything like it.

"Pick it up," Miguelito said. "Hold it to the light." As Steiner did so, he was aware of the new professional tone. "It is a jaguar mask, brown marble, from a very early period in the culture of Guerrero. From the shape and the treatment, I would think it is definitely Olmeca. Certainly the Olmec influence. Although I must confess I have never seen bold square teeth like that in other Olmec pieces I have studied."

Steiner held it to the light of the sun in the doorway, slowly turning it over in his hands, reverently caressing its smooth brown contours, even its cracks and blemishes.

"Well, my old friend, what do you think now?"

Steiner could only shake his head in wonder. "A marble jaguar head all the way back to the Olmecs? It must be worth a fortune."

"In L.A. or New York, I would think at least five thousand dollars," Miguelito said matter-of-factly. "But for you, since I consider you my *patrón* who made me think seriously about my profession, I will let you have it for half."

Since in Mexico the bargaining spirit is the spice of life, Steiner said, "Even that is a little high for me. What about one thousand now? And another thousand next month, when my next payment is due from the studio?"

Miguelito nodded. "For you," he said. "But only for you would I part with such a treasure at less than half its true value."

Next day Steiner flew back to Los Angeles with his prize. He felt a little guilty about sneaking out an archaeological treasure. But he rationalized that he had already visited the enormous basement of the National Museum, where there were at least ten times the thousands of pieces in the public exhibitions above, so this venerable brown marble jaguar head would hardly be missed.

In Los Angeles Steiner showed it to a professor of archaeology at U.C.L.A. who marveled at his find and asked to put it on temporary exhibition at a pre-Columbian show he was organizing on campus. Before Steiner did that, he took it to Stendahl's, who were equally impressed, indeed offered him a handsome profit. But this piece, Steiner felt, was too precious for material gain.

Six months later, when his marble jaguar came back from the university, its heart-shaped eye spaces kept staring at him accusingly from its place of honor on the mantle in the living room, and its tongue in contrasting shades of brown marble seemed to be sticking out at him in a way that stirred his conscience. As an old friend of Mexico, as a lifelong *aficionado* of the Mexican spirit, did he deserve to hoard a treasure that belonged to the people of Mexico, no matter how cluttered with ancient artifacts was the basement of their Museo Nacional?

After wrestling with his conscience, Steiner decided to smuggle it back. As soon as he was settled in at his favorite old hotel in the burgeoning city, the unreconstructed sixteenth-century Cortez, he taxied to the National Museum and asked to see the director, the author of several scholarly works on pre-Columbian art.

The director, theatrically bearded but surprisingly youthful, thanked Steiner for bringing it to his attention, turned it over in his hands slowly, and then asked if he might keep it for a few days for his colleagues to examine more carefully.

When Steiner returned at the end of the week, the director of the *Museo* kept him waiting almost half an hour. Steiner didn't mind, as he was accustomed to the slower pace of Mexican life, and so he occupied himself with a new, illustrated booklet on the pre-Columbian art of Guerrero just published by the *Instituto.* The booklet opened with an introduction, in Spanish and English, by the director he was waiting to see. There was a full-page color plate of a jaguar head that seemed almost a twin of Steiner's. He was devouring the text with the enthusiasm of the dedicated amateur when the director called him into his office. The manner of the museum official was very quiet, very dry, very un-Mexican.

*"Señor,* we appreciate your honesty in offering us this piece. But unfortunately we have no interest in it. It is not *auténtico.* Not an original." As he saw the stricken expression on Steiner's face, he added, sympathetically, "I am afraid that you have been taken in, my friend."

"What? Not this time! I can't . . ."

"I understand," the director interrupted with a thin smile. "There are good fakes and bad fakes, and then there are fakes that are almost a work of genius."

"But still a fake?" Steiner said. The question mark hovered there for a moment, then quickly disappeared in resignation.

The director's nod was more like a shrug as he handed back to Steiner the beautiful brown marble jaguar mask. "You see," he took the trouble to explain, "today there is a new breed of what we call 'archaeological pirates.' They actually find real marble of the same age as the originals. And then they hire master craftsmen, sometimes the very same people we employ here to put together fragments of authentic pieces. So not even tests like carbon-1 4 will give them away. They are like brilliant copies of an Orozco or a Rivera. But copies just the same."

"A fake," Steiner repeated because he could think of nothing else to say. "Another fake."

"Still, it is a very nice souvenir of our Indian culture," the director tried to console him. "So take it home and enjoy it for what it is. An absolutely first-class reproduction."

As Steiner held it in his hands it seemed to have shrunk in size and weight.

"By the way, how did you happen to get it?" the director asked casually.

"From a dealer in Taxco," Steiner said. "Actually, a friend of mine. Miguel . . ."

"Miguel Delgado," the director said quickly.

"Oh, you know him?"

*"Como no?* He brought the piece here a year ago but we were on to him. Of all the archaeological pirates—and it's what you might call a 'growth industry'—your Señor Delgado is one of the most sophisticated. He knows everything there is to know about archaeology. As much as we do, really, everything except about telling the truth."

Steiner walked out into the hot sun of the *Museo* plaza in a daze. He had planned to drive on down to Taxco for the holidays and spend Christmas and New Year's in congenial celebration with his rags-to-riches *compañero* in archaeology, Miguelito. He had even thought of asking Rhoda down to join him for a possible reconciliation. But now he could hear her saying, "Why are you always such a patsy for these phonies? I could've told you you were being taken . . ." He could hear the self-righteous scolding and nagging, and the inevitable argument that drew them back to the most bitter of their differences.

So now he decided just to stay here alone in Mexico City, where the bogus Santa Claus of the north was moving in on the Three Kings. When he stopped to wonder at a porky Mexican, sweaty and uncomfortable in his heavy red Santa outfit, unconvincing white beard and incongruous red cap, waving dispiritedly from a new department-store show-window, Steiner felt like taking his brown marble jaguar head and hurling it through the glass.

But he restrained himself and retreated to the courtyard of the Hotel Cortez, where he drowned his archaeological blues in *tequila añejo,* thought about Miguelito's mother lying there in the hillside graveyard, spared the knowledge of how her piety was being used to lend credibility to her son's ingenious piracy, and consoled himself that at least one poor little mongrel bastard would never have to go barefoot on the cobblestones, or howl with the hungry dogs of Taxco.

# LETTER TO MACFADDEN

Mr. Bernarr Macfadden,
*Liberty* Magazine
U.S.A.

Cross my heart, Mister Macfadden, I would never think of bothering a busy important man like you if it wasn't for a good reason. No sir, I know a man like you who puts out all those magazines we public have been enjoying for the past twenty years or so (and I'm not saying that just so you will keep on reading this letter either) a high mucker-muck like you has his hands full all ready without listening to every tom dick and harry who thinks he wants to wash his dirty linen in public, like my wife Sarah always says.

But I'm no tom dick and harry, Mister Macfadden. I'm a man who happens to have good common ordinary old-fashioned American hog sense, and I still like to think I have some of the old ideals left even if the young fellows laugh nowadays when you talk about ideals only I'll bet they would be laughing out of the other side of their mouths if they only knew how things used to be in those days when a man wore his ideals proudly like he did his old derby instead of stuffing them in his pocket like these new fangled berets. And if a man hasn't got good American ideals in him why he might as well go back to somewheres where he belongs like Red Russia or some of those other places where I read in your magazine *Liberty* that the state runs everything and a man can't even spit without getting the written permission of some high and mighty dictator.

But as I was saying I would never think of writing this letter if it wasn't for the fact that I can't help feeling you and me have a lot in common even though we never met and you are a big shot and I'm just another of those people who can't seem to climb back on his feet yet though I'm not through trying by a long shot. And I'm not saying this just to pull your leg either because if you knew me you'd know I was never the kind to pull anybody's leg. What I always say is I can stand on my own two feet, thank you and when I want help from anybody I'll ask for it.

For instance when I was seventeen I thought it was about time I got a job and I went in to see Mr. Shumacher who owned the cigar store downtown and he asked me if I wanted him to give me a job. Give me a job nothing said I just like that, I want to earn this job, and would you believe it Mister Macfadden in four years I worked myself up to where I could buy that store from Mr. Shumacher. So I have a pretty good idea of what a man can do with ideals even if I did happen to buy that store in '07 right when the Panic was about to burst and the Banks had to call in their loan on the store but how was I to know that or Mr. Shumacher either for that matter. So you can see we are not so different after all and why I am writing you because you are a man after my own heart all right and every time I read *Liberty* I always turn to the editorials first, that page with your name signed at the bottom of it in big letters, right next to that full page ad of Plymouth "America's Best-Engineered Low-Price Car."

Every time I read those editorials I used to feel like writing in and telling you how they were just about the best thing I have ever read and I've read a lot of magazines in my time, *Physical Culture* when you first put that out and I was still young enough for that stuff, *Western Stories* and a lot more I could write down if I think a minute or two only I am anxious to finish this letter because it is not just a fan letter as I was starting to tell you but a sort of business letter, in fact a matter of life and death.

There was one editorial that I carried around with me for weeks and I showed it to all the young squirts down at the shop. I might as well tell you now that I was working in a glass factory up here in San Francisco. My job was to lug the boxes around when the glass is being shipped out, that is I worked in the shipping rooms, loading the trucks from the floor of the storeroom that opens up on the back alley, but I guess that wouldn't mean much to a man like you who is too busy with your writing and thinking and everything to bother much with wondering what goes on inside a big factory like the one I started to tell you about where I've been working. Of course this work was just temporary. I always was cut out for something better than manual work if I do say it myself and during this depression I have just sort of been marking time waiting to get on my feet again and start up my own business like I used to have before that oughty-seven crash.

But anyway this editorial was the goods. Most of the boys on the floor gave me the merry ha ha when I showed it to them and when I said that the dignity and good breeding of labor stand for something, they said ha ha it stands for plenty, pop. And Sarah, that's my wife, when I showed it to her she just kind of sniffed like she does when the ice melts because our icebox leaks and the milk gets scummy around the edges and then she has to boil it because Harry, my youngest kid who still lives with us, Harry has been learning in high school and he says the heat has got to be used to kill the microbes. But as I was saying this editorial of yours was all about Capital and Labor and it showed in the picture one man standing there dressed in a suit and a stiff white collar with a sort of kind face shaking hands with another fellow in overall pants and an open white shirt, a big bruiser with his sleeves rolled up, looking husky and happy and smiling. And they were shaking hands together, both smiling at each other like Teddy Roosevelt when he went off to fight the Spaniards or hunt elephants, and on one side of the picture was written in good-looking little white letters Capital and on the other side Labor. And then one side was a picture of swell buildings and gobs of swell looking smoke and on that side it said, "Together we stand, solid, substantial, a challenge to the world." And on the other side all the buildings were flattened out and it looked like hell itself has broke loose and a couple of gulls were flying around or maybe they were buzzards flying around like they were in that story "To the Last Ditch," one of your stories too I think which I will never forget because I was reading it when I was waiting in line for the job in this glass factory I told you about and I was just up to the part where the buzzards are swooping down on the cow-puncher after he has been shot bang by the Mexican horse thief when my turn comes and when I got the job I was so happy I ran all the way home and forgot all about the story and Sarah, that's my wife, could see in my face that I had got it and we didn't say anything we just danced around the room like a couple of kids because I had been sitting around for seven months and Harry had to quit school just when he was learning all about microbes and decimals and had been chosen the president of his class.

I don't know how I happen to tell you all about this except that I guess even though I never met you I feel like we were friends because of those wonderful editorials if you know what

I mean. This picture showed how if Labor and Capital would only stop doing each other dirt and just shake hands like they did in the picture we could have the greatest wealth in history and be a challenge to the whole world. I can still remember the words because I memorized them and as I think I told you before I have a memory that can't be beat and when I was a kid my ma used to say I probably would be a school teacher or a senator or something and then I had to quit school when Pa died and go to work selling papers. But I don't want to sound as if I'm complaining, Mister Macfadden. I guess we both know there is no school like the school of hard knocks. That newspaper vendoring was the best thing in the world to make me a serious and ambitious boy and to teach me to rely on my own initiative and maybe if it wasn't that I never would have got to be owner of that cigar store I used to own.

When I began this letter I told you I was writing it because it was a matter of life and death and now I suppose you are thinking humph it can't be so gol-darned important if he doesn't get to his point quicker than this. But the reason I am telling you the whole story is because the whole thing started pretty much on account of those ideas of cooperation and I thought if you found out what happened to me just because I tried to carry out what you said you would want to help me because it would really be helping to spread those ideas of yours, or I should say ours.

This editorial of yours kept eating into me and I swear sometimes I would wake up mumbling, "Divided we fall, bringing chaos, ruin, wreckage, to the homes of the nation," like it said over that picture of the flattened buildings and the seagulls or buzzards or whatever they were. And Sarah would just look at me as if I was crazy and ask me where in landsakes I was spouting all that nonsense from and I would say just off-hand like, Oh just a few lines from an editorial I was reading in *Liberty.* Then she would jump up and look straight into me and say Mister Macfadden don't care about you and

me, he's just saying that so he and his kind can keep you where
they want you, upside down on a hook with your blood dropping out drop by drop. (I hope you'll excuse me please for
putting this in the letter, Mister Macfadden, but that's exactly
what Sarah said and there was no telling her anything different.) Now Sarah is a fine woman and all that and she has
always been a good mother but she has got some mighty
curious ideas. She got them from her old man, I think, whom
I never have seen because they sent him to jail one time in a
strike before I ever started to court Sarah. It was the railroad
strike back in '87 and when it was all over he couldn't get his
job back and he always went around talking about how the
capitalists and the working men would struggle until the workers finally got what they deserved and he got worse and worse
and finally he must have done something awful bad because
he never did get out and every time I try to ask Sarah about
it she just walks away and Harry says why don't you leave her
alone Pop and pretty soon she comes back with her eyes all red
and she doesn't say nothing only she yells at Emmie's kids if
they bounce a ball against the wall and then if she goes to bed
and Harry comes in late she yells at him for waking her up and
now just this week Harry's taken to staying out all night and
when I want to know where he went he says don't bother me
Pa you haven't got room for me anyway with you and Mom
fighting and that kid in the same room bawling. Emmie's kids
moved in last month. Emmie is my youngest daughter. She's
married to a nice young fellow who used to be a ripper in a
slaughter house but now somebody has invented a machine to
do that so I guess Emmie had to move her kids in with us.

So you see I know what it is when someone like Sarah's old
man doesn't understand your ideas. So there's just no use
trying to explain what you meant to Sarah because she
wouldn't be able to understand either. Sarah is a good deal
younger than me too so maybe that explains it. I am beginning
to think you have to come from our generation to really see

things. It seems to me the older Americans should try to get together on a plan of their own. My gosh, that wouldn't be a bad idea for one of your editorials, Mister Macfadden.

But as I was saying this editorial begins to sink into me and every time I get a few minutes I take it out and read it, and the more I read it the more I see that all these young men working down there on the floor have been making a bad mistake, trying to start a union and cause trouble just at a time like this when business is so bad that if we don't pull together we might have the whole damn boat sink right out from under us and pretty soon while we are swimming around some Jap boat will pick us up, and that will be the end of America. The trouble with these youngsters is they don't know how close the country is to going on the rocks and if they did they would shut up with all this talk about fighting the factory owner and they would see that unless we all pull together with smart men, like you for instance Mister Macfadden, the men who know what they are doing, why there won't be any wages to increase, there just won't be any wages at all and how would they like that I wonder.

Now right off I might as well tell you that I never was so good at ideas like this because I think I told you I never got a chance to finish school but I can tell a good idea when I see one thank you and when I do I don't like to just talk about it, like Sarah does with her ideas about the workingmen having the power to stop the whole government from working and then making the men who run the whole shebang give in. All I say then is well Mrs. Bolsheviki it's a good thing Mr. Green is president of the A. F. of L. instead of you because he knows what he is doing and is smart enough not to get the big shots sore at us little fellows, like Mister Macfadden says. That is just what I say and I'll stand up for it here. I guess I've always been the sort of man who doesn't care if anyone agrees with me or not. I guess you can't really blame Sarah so much because she has never got much out of life and after her Pa got sent up she

had to go to work ten hours a day and then after I lost my store
why she had to go to work again because kids had come and
I was a little down on my luck and now she has to cook for
Emmie's kids too and sometimes, I hate to say this, but sometimes I think the heat has kind of gone to her head, because
that shop is down in the cellar and when you are down there
all day and come out to go home the air from the Bay cuts your
breath like a sharp knife and your hot face cools off as fast as
those can-can girls are said to when they find out you are
broke, and then coming indoors again and standing in front of
that hot stove—well you see what it can do Mister Macfadden,
and so I try to be patient with her and I just laugh off her
radical ideas.

Well sir I keep thinking about this idea of cooperation and
being a sort of man of action I decide to start right in because
it is never too late and I noticed in the paper just today that
Henry Ford was congratulating some employee of his that was
sixty-six years old and had just been given another raise. So
yesterday morning I didn't go down to the floor and start
loading at nine like I've been doing for the past five months.
No sir, I went right up to the superintendent's office and there
was a lady sitting at a desk there nice and cool and her talk was
just as cool as she was saying Whom do you wish to see and
Have you an appointment and I got so excited I couldn't
answer right off but just kept looking at her until I guess she
thought I was just some crazy fool that had no business in the
office at all but then all of a sudden I was saying I'm Mr. Fulton
and I must see Mr. Nelson at once and I guess I must have said
it like I meant it and if I do say it I have always been able to
rise to situations like this. I have always known that this is the
place I should have, making contacts and being in offices
where I could use my brains and leave jobs like the one on the
loading floor to someone who hasn't got the same ideals that
I have. I guess that explains why I am able to grasp those ideas
of yours in those editorials. So maybe this whole thing I am
telling you about happened for the best after all.

Now I'm coming to the life and death part, Mister Macfadden. Ever since I lost my store I was waiting for a chance to walk into an office like Mr. Nelson's with a good idea, and finally this was it. And I suppose that now that the whole thing is over and I am writing you like this you must think I am sore because in a way it *was* your fault, advising me to cooperate and then having all this happen. You must think I am just writing because I think you owe me something for making all this happen. No sir, Mister Macfadden, I am just writing because here is a slick chance for you to really make those ideas of yours work, and I know that you would not want to pass up a good chance like this. So I will try to tell what did happen when I saw Mr. Nelson, just kind of sum up and then we can maybe get together on what is to be done.

I walked into Mr. Nelson's office like I was floating and my voice sounded so loud I couldn't believe it was me and it got louder and louder like it was coming through one of those big loud speakers on a truck coming towards me. Mister Nelson, I said, my name is Fulton and I work down in the warehouse department. Why come right in sir said Mr. Nelson, smiling with lots of teeth, what can I do for you, and I began to feel all warm inside like I do when I look over your editorial. Well, well, that's kind of you, that's certainly mighty kind of you, I answered, trying to think how to begin, and we both stopped, feeling awkward. Then suddenly I blurted out, Mister Nelson I came up here today because I can think of a lot of improvements I believe you should hear about. What's the matter, Fulton, what's the matter, any complaints? Mr. Nelson snapped before I could go any further. I felt a large lump pump up in my throat. I saw his fingers beating on that long shiny desk and I knew I had to talk fast because I certainly didn't want him to think I was just complaining because that wouldn't be very good cooperation would it. Well you see Mister Nelson, I said after a long time, I've been reading a fine editorial by Mister Macfadden, maybe you read it in *Liberty,* and it was all about cooperation between Labor and Capital and how they could build a solid nation if they only worked hand in hand like it showed them in the picture.

You work on the shipping room floor don't you said Mr. Nelson and there was something about the way he looked at his watch I didn't like and he didn't smile any more and come up and shake hands with me like you showed that boss doing in the picture of yours, so I guess I kind of lost my head and all those good ideas I had been thinking about all the time like having a joint board of picked workers and the heads of the factory meet once a week to get better cooperation and a few other good ideas I had for saving time, etc. I can't think of now because of all the things that have happened, well anyway all these ideas just got stuck inside me and wouldn't come out. I must have even said "Divided we fall" again because I can still hear Mr. Nelson barking You have just finished saying that Mister Fulton and now if you have nothing further to say, I'm a very busy man.

Then I was walking past the neat cool lady again, only I don't seem to remember if I walked or ran, and I guess Mr. Nelson must have thought I was drunk, at least that is what the fellows on the floor around me said and at first I thought they were kidding because they always joke with me and call me Grandpop. Then I got my notice and I was through. That is a laugh isn't it, getting canned for trying to do a little more than the next fellow and use my head and take a real interest in the organization? It certainly is, Mister Macfadden if it wasn't for what I am going to tell you now, although one thing about me is that I can always see the humor in things and my Ma used to say Bill (that's me) will be laughing at his own funeral.

Gosh, Mister Macfadden, this is what I want to ask you, this is the matter of life and death I am coming to now.

Gosh, I know you are a very busy man but I wouldn't think of writing if I couldn't see how you are really a friend of Labor (the right kind of Labor at least) and want to give everybody who is a Real American like me a square deal so they can get into offices like Mr. Nelson's where they belong.

But when I told Sarah what happened she kind of gave a little scream, only it stopped right away, and then her face puffed all up but she didn't say nothing, she didn't bawl me out but I almost wish she did, and this is the third day and she still hasn't opened her mouth and nobody says anything and even Emmie's baby seems to know something is wrong and stopped bawling and I couldn't stand it any longer I just can't so I am writing this because I know you will help me get that job back when you find out that the only reason I lost it was because I thought that editorial you wrote was so fine. My address is 1658½ Embarcadero. I will be waiting anxiously for your answer.

Yours for Cooperation and a Greater America,

William Fulton

# HOLLYWOOD VERSUS CHRIS SAMUELS, AGE NINE

■        ■        ■

Chris Samuels, nine years old and not particularly big for his age either, was writing a poem. Bicycling home from school, even while he was riding no-hands, Chris was composing a poem about motherhood. "Mother mine so good and true . . ." is the way it started. Pumping home through the sunlight of Wilshire Boulevard, turning left into Windsor Square with its rows of date palms and box hedges—fashionable then, in the early 1920's—he went on composing.

The poem was nearly complete by the time he pedaled up the driveway of the Samuelses' relatively modest mansion. It rhymed and had a beautiful sound to it when he said it out loud. It gave him a feeling that was unlike anything he could remember.

As soon as he had finished his milk and graham crackers he hurried to a special place to write down his poem. This hideaway was under the piano in the living room, as far back under the piano and into the corner as he could crawl. There he felt

■

safe, alone and cozy, a feeling summed up in his own word *guzzy.* He liked the idea that nobody knew where to find him. What made it even more exciting was that his mother had warned him not to go into the living room unless a grownup was there. That was because of all the breakable valuables around. One of Mrs. Samuels's talents was interior decorating; the living room was full of precious hazards in Bristol glass and Staffordshire china.

Under the piano Chris worked hard on his poem. First he wrote it down and then he thought of some better words to put into it and he did some erasing. Then he made a clean new copy, but soon that became smudged. Finally he made a nice, neat, finished copy with the fanciest writing he could do.

Chris had been working so hard that he did not hear his mother come into the living room. She was a pretty woman whose sturdy peasant origin had been modified by a wistful preoccupation with refinement, a consistent devotion to self-improvement. She had gone forward from Coué to Brill, she attended regular classes in psychology at the university and she was the founder of a local child-study group. A procession of visiting lecturers had bent a knee to her tea table. She was busy improving her mind and Chris's mind and all the minds she could get hold of.

She had come into the living room to "steal a cigarette." The coy sense of admitting the vice was a throwback to Victorian restrictions only recently lifted, even here in Hollywood. As she sneaked a cigarette from the palm of a glass hand she noticed Chris's feet under the piano.

"Chrissy, I've been looking all over for you."

"I've been in here, Mom."

"How many times must I tell you not to come into the living room when no one is here?"

"I wrote a poem, Mom. It's a poem for you."

Her pleasure at this artistic development overcame her anger at disobedience.

"Why, Chris, how nice! Will you read it to me?"

Chris crawled out from under the piano and straightened himself as he did at school when he was called on to recite. He read his poem with proud emphasis on every syllable. It contained six unabashed couplets in praise of his mother and of motherhood in general. Before he was halfway through, Mrs. Samuels's eyes had become soft and shiny.

When Chris finished he looked into his mother's eyes and there was a long and delicious pause. Then she said: "Chrissy, did you write that? Did you *really* write that?"

"Yes, Mother."

"Why—why I think it's beautiful."

She put her arms out and Chris went to her for an intimate celebration of hugging and kissing.

"Simply bea*u*tiful," she said, dabbing at her eyes. "Why, I had no idea—simply no *idea* you could write a poem like that. Such a beautiful poem!"

She took the sheet of paper from Chris and read it to herself, shaking her head in awe at this sign of genius in her own flesh and blood.

"Chris, I'm going to save this. When you're a famous, grownup writer I will always remember hearing your first poem."

"Is Daddy coming home for dinner?"

"I imagine so. He hasn't called."

"I want Daddy to read it too."

"Oh, you must read it to Daddy. Daddy will be so proud of his little writer."

"Gee, I wish he could come home early."

His father was the head of a motion-picture studio. The kids at school told Chris they wished their fathers could be the big cheese of a Hollywood studio because then they could get to see free movies and meet all the movie stars. "Boy, would that be keen!" they said. Chris pretended that it was. He had never been able to tell them that it wasn't so keen having your father a famous motion-picture executive. For one thing, the hours were awful. Chris would go days and days without even seeing his father, who had to stay at the studio having conferences and running rushes until long after Chris's bedtime. And while the stars had always been nice to Chris, his low opinion of them was a mild reflection of his father's. According to Mr. Samuels, they were a selfish, ungrateful, stupid and difficult lot. Chris was used to hearing his father say, "To become a movie star you have to be a bitch and what kind of a man wants to be a movie actor except a damned jackass."

Chris respected his father and although—or perhaps because—he didn't see him as often as he wished, he was always eager for his father's approval of whatever he was doing. On the occasional Sunday when there were no dinner guests from the studio, his father would read aloud to him. Mr. Samuels admired Melville, Twain, Dickens, Conrad and Galsworthy. Chris almost fell asleep on Galsworthy but he liked *Omoo* and *Typee* and Huck Finn and *Youth;* and *The Old Curiosity Shop* made tears in his eyes. His father had started out as a writer. He had won a prize in a city short-story contest and then he had written scenarios for the early movies. Then he had worked his way up to being a producer and finally the head of the studio. Chris had heard the story several times from his mother. Although his father was a producer of silent pictures he liked to talk about the sound of words and Chris knew from his mother that "Daddy has excellent taste."

Now that he had written his first poem, Chris got all jumpy inside, wondering what his father would think of it. Would the poem make Daddy cry the way it had Mom? Maybe his father would give him a gold piece after reading it. He had a habit of keeping gold pieces to hand out on special occasions.

Chris didn't know what to do with himself while he waited for his father to come home. He went outside and watched his pigeons circle the house for a while, he played with his dog Bunk, and then he got into an argument with Julian, the boy next door. Julian was the son of another movie producer at a smaller studio.

Across the hedge Julian began a ritualistic debate.

"My father makes better pictures 'n your father makes."

"He does not."

"He does too."

"He does *not.*"

"Oh, yeah?"

"Yeah."

Sometimes they would elaborate this stylized dispute by challenging picture for picture, but this afternoon Chris's heart wasn't in it. With a token intraindustrial sneer, he broke it off and went into the house. He looked at his poem again and got his crayons out to frame it in a border of red and blue. If his father wanted to take it to the studio, to show it to his stars and directors, it had to look right.

He was just finishing it when he heard someone in the hall. "Dad?"

His mother called, "No, Chris, it's just a chauffeur dropping off a script."

Chris groaned. Chauffeurs were always dropping off scripts. Scripts that people, all sorts of people, were trying to sell to his father. "Chris, I'd love to go out and see your new squabs, but I promised someone I'd read this script right away," his father would say. When he saw a script Chris could almost smell the cigar smoke that curled around his father as he rapidly turned page after page. After the last page his father would almost always throw the script down and say, "Goddamn it, the lousiest script I ever read." Chris would wonder why his father kept on reading them if each one was worse than the one before.

Poem in hand, Chris sat in the living room, waiting for his father.

"Do you think Daddy will like my poem?" he said to his mother.

Her answer was what he wanted to hear: "Of course, he'll like it. It shows unusual talent. Chris, I can't tell you how proud I am."

"It was easy to do," Chris said. "Lots of times I make them up to myself when I'm falling asleep."

"I had no idea," his mother said. "You know, your father used to write poetry when he was a young man. I'll show you some of it, when you're a little older. It must run in the family."

"I am going to write a poem every single day until I grow up," Chris announced.

"Songs from the heartstrings of a little boy," his mother said softly. "Why, perhaps Father could have them published. Wouldn't that make a lovely title?"

"Oh, I wish Daddy would come home," Chris said.

"Poor Daddy has to work so hard at the studio."

"I wish he was in a regular business," Chris said. "Like Jimmy. Jimmy's father has a store on Pico and he comes home for dinner every single night."

"Your father is a very successful man. A very famous man."

"Gee, I know," Chris said sadly.

James, the butler, came in to announce dinner.

"We'll wait just a few more minutes," his mother said, "and then if Mr. Samuels isn't here we'll sit down without him, James."

"Darn it, I wish he didn't have to stay so late with those bitch movie stars," Chris said.

"Christopher!"

It wasn't his fault. He had heard his father come roaring in from the studio so often that he could never think of movie stars without putting the other word on in front. Stupid bitches—ungrateful bastards—in the Samuelses' home these were mild terms for movie stars.

"Well, Mom, you know what Daddy says."

His mother rose, smiling in a polite, lonely way. "I suppose

we might as well start. Your father may not be here for another
hour."

"He's gotta read my poem before I go to sleep, he's just
gotta."

"Now, Chris, I know how anxious you are, but you have to
be patient."

They went into the big dining room together. His father's
place was very empty at the head of the long mahogany table.

"I know what I'll do," Chris said. "I'll put my poem right
on his plate so it'll be the first thing he sees when he sits
down."

"My, you anxious authors," his mother said, smiling.

They were finishing the main course when they heard the
car roaring up the drive and then the heavy, hurried tread of
Sol Samuels's feet running up the steps to the porch. Then
there was a long, loud ring and James went quickly to the door.

"Hello, dear," his mother called. "You forgot your keys?"

"Flo, do you think I'd ring if I hadn't forgot my keys?" his
father shouted. He was a dynamic, ruddy-faced man in his
early forties, an age that would have made him a prodigy in
any business but this prodigy field he had chosen to pioneer.

"Sit down, dear, you must be tired," his mother said.

"First I've got to have a drink," his father said. His voice
carried to the dining room as he disappeared into the den. "Of
all the goddamn days, the idiots I have to put up with. An hour
ago Larry wants to walk off the picture, the part is only going
to make him the biggest thing in Hollywood and the damn
fool thinks he's miscast! Well, just let him try and walk out—
I'll suspend him, I'll run that ham out of the industry, the
ungrateful son of a bitch."

Sol Samuels had reappeared with a highball glass in his
hand. The jaw that was a favorite target for caricaturists was
thrust forward in characteristic defiance.

"And then Mary comes in weeping those goddamn phony
tears and says she doesn't want Joe on her next picture. Joe is

the one director in town who can hold her down and get a
performance out of her. But she wants some third-rate punk
she can push around. I know my little Mary. I should, I discovered the bitch, so—"

"Sol, will you please sit down and eat your dinner."

"Now, Flo, just let me have one more drink. My nerves are
jumping like sand fleas tonight."

Chris watched his father disappear again into the den. He
got up and went to his father's place and straightened the
poem a fraction of an inch. Then he went back to his seat. His
mother smiled at him. His father returned with a refill, paused
at his wife's chair to brush her cheek with a distracted kiss and
rustled Chris's hair as he strode to his place.

"What the hell is this?" he said, picking up the paper.

"Sol, Chris has written a poem," his mother said. "A beau tiful poem, Sol. I had no idea he could do anything like that.
He could hardly wait for you to—"

"All right, now let me read it," his father said.

There was a silence. It could not have been a long silence,
for it was not a long poem. But it was a terrible silence. His
mother kept looking at his father with a motherly smile, a kind
of tentative smile, waiting to share with him their mutual
pride. Chris kept his eyes on his father's face, waiting for the
praise and the gold piece.

After a few seconds his father put the poem down, drained
his highball glass, and said: "I think it's lousy."

Chris looked at his father, then at his mother, through a
glaze of tears.

"Sol, how could you? His first poem. After all, he's only
*nine.* And to use such a word. Such a tactless, cruel word.
What's happening to your judgment, Sol? Your—your per-
spective?"

Chris heard the fight as if from a great distance through a
roar of disappointment.

"Goddamn it, I believe in being honest about writing, anybody's writing, even Chrissy's writing. How the hell will he ever improve if you don't level with him?"

"But, Sol, do you really think it makes sense to talk to him as if he were a professional writer on your payroll?"

Sol Samuels tried, as he often did when his wife had him cornered, to make a joke of it.

"Look, Flo, I just got finished telling a team of two-thousand-a-week writers their stuff is lousy. I pay Chris only fifty cents a week, so who has a better right to tell him *his* stuff is lousy?"

Chris Samuels's pride was being rubbed into the word the way his pup Bunk had his nose rubbed into the spot on the carpet when he forgot to scratch on the door. His lips began to tremble and the color drained from his face. He hated his father, he hated the studio, he hated the scenarios, he hated the bitch movie stars, he hated the lousiness of lousy. To keep his father from hearing him give in to it, he ran from the table with his hands held over his mouth.

He held himself in until he was upstairs in his own bedroom with the door slammed behind him. He could still hear the angry voices of his father and mother. What frightened him now was not that his father was cruelly and stupidly wrong, but that he might be cruelly and terribly right.

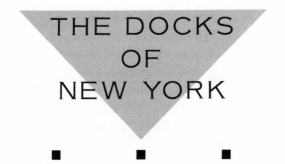

# THE DOCKS OF NEW YORK

The alarm was about to ring when Matt Gillis reached out his bearlike, heavy-muscled arm and shut it off. Habit. Half past six. Summer with the light streaming in around the patched window shades, and winter when half past six was black as midnight. Matt stretched his heavyweight, muscular body and groaned. Habit woke you up at half past six every morning, but habit didn't make you like it—not on these raw winter mornings when the wind blew in from the sea, whipping along the waterfront with an intensity it seemed to reserve for long-shoremen. He shivered in anticipation.

Matt listened to the wind howling through the narrow canyon of Eleventh Street and thought to himself. Another day, another icy-fingered, stinking day. He pushed one foot from under the covers to test the temperature, and then quickly withdrew it into the warmth of the double bed again. Cold. Damn that janitor, Lacey—the one they all called Rudolph because of his perpetually red nose. Never enough heat in the place. Well, the landlord was probably saying, what do they expect for twenty-five a month?

Matt rolled over heavily, ready for the move into his work clothes. "Matt?" his wife, Franny, murmured, feeling for him drowsily in the dark. "I'll get up; fix you some coffee."

"It's all right." His buxom Fran. Matt patted her. Her plump-pretty Irish face was still swollen with sleep. For a moment he remembered her as she had been fifteen years ago: the prettiest kid in the neighborhood—bright, flirty, sky-blue eyes and a pug nose, a little bit of a girl smothered in Matt's big arms, a child in the arms of a grizzly. Now she was plump all over, something like him on a smaller, softer scale, as if she had had to grow along his lines to keep him company.

"Matt, you don't mind me gettin' fat?" she had whispered to him one night in the wide, metal-frame bed after the kids finally had fallen asleep.

"Naw, you're still the best-lookin' woman in the neighborhood," Matt had said gallantly.

"At least you can always find me in the dark," Fran had giggled. They had got to laughing then, until Fran had to stop him because everything Matt did, he did big—laugh, fight, eat, drink, tell off the mob in the union. Even when he thought he was talking normally he shouted, he bellowed, so when he had chuckled there in the bed, the children—Tom and Mickey and Kate and Johnny and Peggy, the five they had had so far—had stirred in their beds and Fran had said, "Shhh, if the baby wakes up you'll be walkin' the floor with her."

Matt swung his long legs out of the bed and felt the cold touch of the linoleum. He sat there a moment in his long underwear, thinking—he wasn't sure of what; the day ahead, the days of his youth, the time his old man came home from the pier with three fingers off his right hand (copper sheeting—cut off at the knuckle nice and clean), and all those years the old man battled for his compensation. It was all the old man could talk about, finally, and got to be a joke—never to

Pop, but to Matt and his brothers when they were big enough to support him.

Big Matt sat there on the edge of the bed rubbing sleep out of his eyes, thinking, thinking, while his wife, warm, sweaty and full in her nightgown, half rose behind him and whispered, "Coffee? Let me get up and make you a cup of coffee." She wanted to say more; she wanted to say, "Look, Matt honey, I know what it is to go down there to the shape-up when the sun is still climbing up the backs of the buildings. I know what it is for you to stand there with three-four hundred other men and have the hiring boss, Fisheye Moran, look you over like you was so much meat in a butcher shop. I know what it is for you to go to work every morning like you had a job—only you haven't got a job unless Fisheye, the three-time loser put there by the Village mob, hands you a brass check." She wanted to say, "Yes, and I know what it is for you to be left standing in the street; I know what you feel when the hiring boss looks through you with those pale blue fisheyes that give him his name." *That's all today, come back tomorra.*

Matt was on his feet now, a burly bear in his long underwear, stretching and groaning to push himself awake. Fran started to get up, but he put his big hand on her shoulder and pushed her back into the warm bed. Well, all right. She was glad to give in. When could a body rest except these precious few minutes in the early morning? "You be careful now, Matt. You be careful. Don't get in no trouble."

Fran knew her Matt, the Irish-thick rebel of Local 474, one of the lionhearted—or foolhardy—handful who dared speak up against the Lippy Keegan mob, which had the longshore local in their pocket, and the loading racket, the lunch-hour gambling, and all the other sidelines that bring in a quick dollar on the docks. Lippy and his goons ran the neighborhood like storm troopers, and longshoremen who knew what was good for them went along with Keegan's boys and took what they could get. Matt was always trying to get others to back him up, but the fear was too deep. "Matt, I got me wife and kids to think about; leave me alone," they'd say, and push their thirty cents across the bar for another whiskey.

Matt tried to make as little noise as possible as he went down the creaky stairway. He closed the tenement door behind him and stood a moment in the clammy morning, feeling the weather. He zipped up his windbreaker and pulled his old cap down on his forehead. Then he drew his head down into the heavy collar, threw out his chest, and turned his face into the wind. It was a big, strong-boned, beefy face, with a heavy jaw and a broken nose, a face that had taken plenty. Over the years the Keegan boys had developed a begrudging respect for Matt. They had hit him with everything and he still kept coming on. The gift of getting up—that's what they called it on the waterfront.

Matt ducked into the Longdock Bar & Grill on the corner across the street from the pier. It was full of longshoremen grabbing a cup of coffee and maybe some ham and eggs before drifting over to the shape-up. There were men of all sizes and ages, with weatherbeaten faces like Matt's, many of them with flattened noses, trophies of battles on the docks and in the barrooms; here and there were ex-pugs with big-time memories: the cheers of friends and five hundred dollars for an eight-rounder. Threading through the dock workers was a busy little man whose name was Billy Morgan, though everybody called him J.P. because he was the moneylender for the mob. If you didn't work, J.P. was happy to lend you a deuce or half a bill, at ten percent a week. If you fell too far behind, J.P. whispered to Fisheye, and Fisheye threw you a couple of days' work until the loan was paid off. They had you coming and going, the mob. Matt looked at J.P. and turned away.

Over in the corner were a couple of Lippy's pistols, Specs Sinclair, a mild-looking, pasty-skinned man who didn't look like an enforcer but had maybe a dozen stiffs to his credit, and Feets McKenna, a squat muscle man who could rough-and-tumble with the best. Feets was sergeant-at-arms for the local. Specs, for whom signing his name was a lot of writing, was recording secretary. Matt looked straight at them to show he wasn't backing away, ever. Union officials. Only three-time losers need apply.

Matt pushed his way into the group at the short-order counter. They were men dressed like himself, in old trousers and flannel shirts, with old caps worn slightly askew in the old-country way. They all knew Matt and respected the way he stood up; but a stand-up guy, as they called him, was nobody you wanted to get close to. Not if you wanted to work and stay in one piece in Lippy Keegan's sector of the harbor.

Matt was waiting for his coffee when he felt a fist smash painfully into his side. He winced and started an automatic counter at whoever it was, and then he looked down and grinned. He should have known. It was Runt Nolan, whose hundred ring battles and twenty-five years of brawling on the docks were stamped into his flattened face. But a life of beatings had failed to deaden the twinkle in his eyes. Runt Nolan was always seeing the funny side, even when he was looking down the business end of a triggerboy's .38. Where other longshoremen turned away in fear from Lippy's pistoleros, Runt always seemed to take a perverse delight in baiting them. Sometimes they laughed him off and sometimes, if he went on provoking them—and longshoremen were watching to see if Runt could get away with it—they would oblige him with a blackjack or a piece of pipe. Runt had a head like a rock and more lives than a pair of cats, and the stories of his miraculous recoveries from these beatings had become a riverfront legend.

Once they had left him around the corner in the alley lying face down in his own blood, after enough blows on the noggin to crack the skull of a horse; and an hour later, when everyone figured he was on his way to the morgue, damned if he didn't stagger back into the Longdock and pound the bar for whiskey. "I should worry what they do to me, I'm on borried time," Runt Nolan liked to say.

Runt grinned when he saw Matt rub his side with mock resentment. "Mornin', Matt me lad, just wanted t' see if you was in condition."

"Don't be worryin' about my condition. One more like that and I'll stand you right on your head."

"Come on, you big blowhard, I'm ready for you." Runt fell into a fierce boxing stance and jabbed his small knuckle-broken left fist into Matt's face.

Matt got his coffee and a sinker and sat down at one of the small tables with Runt. Runt was rarely caught eating. He seemed to consider the need for solid food something of a disgrace, a sign of weakness. Whiskey and beer and maybe once a day a corned-beef sandwich—that was Runt's diet, and in the face of medical science it had kept him wiry and resilient at fifty-five.

"What kind of a boat we got today?" Matt asked. Runt lived in a two-dollar hotel above the Longdock Bar and he was usually up on his shipping news.

"Bananas," Runt said, drawing out the middle vowel in disgust.

"Bananas!" Matt groaned. Bananas meant plenty of shoulder work, toting the heavy stalks out of the hold. A banana carrier was nothing less than a human pack mule. There was only one good thing about bananas: The men who worked steady could afford to lay off bananas, and so there was always a need for extra hands. The docker who had no *in* with the hiring boss, and even the fellow who was on the outs with the Keegan mob, stood a chance of picking up a day on bananas.

By the time Matt and Runt reached the pier, ten minutes before the 7:30 whistle, there were already a couple of hundred men on hand, warming themselves around fires in metal barrels and shifting their feet to keep the numbness away. Some of them were hard-working men with families, professional longshoremen whose Ireland-born fathers had moved cargo before them. And some of them were only a peg above the bum, casuals who drifted in for a day now and then to keep themselves in drinking money. Some of them were big men with powerful chests, large, raw-faced men who looked like throwbacks to the days of bare-knuckle fights-to-a-finish. Some of them were surprisingly slight, wizen-faced men in cast-off clothing, the human flotsam of the waterfront.

Fisheye came out of the pier, flanked by a couple of the boys, "Flash" Gordon and "Blackie" McCook. There were about three hundred longshoremen waiting for jobs now. Obediently they formed themselves into a large horseshoe so Fisheye could look them over. Meat in a butcher shop. The men Fisheye wanted were the ones who worked. You kicked back part of your day's pay to Fisheye or did favors for Lippy if you wanted to work regular. You didn't have to have a record, but a couple of years in a respectable pen didn't do you any harm.

"I need two hundred banana carriers." Fisheye's hoarse voice seemed to take its pitch from the foghorns that barked along the Hudson. Jobs for two hundred men at a coveted $2.27 an hour. The three, maybe four hundred men eyed one another in listless rivalry. "You—and you—Pete—OK, Slim . . ." Fisheye was screening the men with a cold, hard look. Nearly twenty years ago a broken-down dock-worker had gone across the street from the shape-up. "No work?" the bartender had said, perfunctorily, and the old man had answered, "Nah, he just looked right through me with those fuckin' fisheyes of his." Fisheye—it had made the bartender laugh, and the name had stuck.

Anger felt cold and uncomfortable in Matt's stomach as he watched Fisheye pass out those precious tabs. He didn't mind seeing the older men go in, the ones he had shaped with for years, especially family men like himself. What gave him that hateful, icy feeling in his belly was seeing the young kids go

in ahead of him, new-generation hoodlums like the fresh-faced
Skelly kid who boasted of the little muscle jobs he did for
Lippy and the boys as his way of paying off for steady work.
Young Skelly had big ideas, they said around the bar. One of
these days he might be crowding Lippy himself. That's how it
went down here. "Peaches" Maloney had been Number
One—until Lippy dumped him into the gutter outside the
Longdock. Matt had seen them come and go. And all the time
he had stood up proud and hard while lesser men got the work
tabs and the gravy.

Fisheye almost had his two hundred men now. He put his
hand on Runt Nolan's shoulder. "All right, you little sawed-
off rat, go on in. But remember I'm doin' ya a favor. One word
out of line and I'll bounce ya off the ship."

Runt tightened his hands into fists, wanting to stand up and
speak his mind. But a day was a day and he hadn't worked
steady enough lately to keep himself in beers. He looked over
at Matt with a helpless defiance and went on into the pier.

Matt waited, thinking about Fran and the kids. And he
waited, thinking at Fisheye: It ain't right, it ain't right, a bum
like you havin' all this power. He couldn't keep it out of his
face. Fisheye flushed and glared back at him and picked men
all around Matt to round out his two hundred. He shoved
Matt's face in it by coming toward him as if he were going to
pick him and then reaching over his shoulder for Will Murphy,
a toothless old sauce-hound whom Matt could outwork five for
one. There never had been enough caution in Matt, and now
he felt himself trembling with anger. He was grabbing Fisheye
before he had time to think it out, holding the startled boss by
the thick lapels of his windbreaker.

"Listen to me, you fatheaded bum. If you don't put me on
today I'll break you in two. I got kids to feed. You hear me,
Fisheye?"

Fisheye pulled himself away and looked around for help.
Blackie and young Skelly moved in.

"Okay, boys," Fisheye said, when he saw they were there.

"I c'n handle this myself. This bigmouth is dumb, but he's not so dumb he wants to wind up in the river. Am I right, Matt me lad?"

In the river. A senseless body kicked off the stringpiece into the black and secretive river, while the city looked the other way. Cause of death: accidental drowning. Dozens and dozens of good men had been splashed into the dark river like so much garbage. Matt knew some of the widows who had stories to tell, if only someone would listen. In the river. Matt drew away from Fisheye. What was the use? Outnumbered and outgunned. But one of these days—went the dream—he and Runt would get some action in the local, some following; they'd call a real election and—

Behind Matt a big truck blasted its horn, ready to drive into the pier. Fisheye thumbed Matt to one side. "All right, get moving, you're blocking traffic, we got a ship to turn around." Matt spat into the gutter and walked away.

Back across the street in the Longdock, Matt sat with a beer in front of him, automatically watching the morning television: some good-looking, fast-talking dame selling something—yat-ta-ta yatta-ta yatta-ta. In the old days, at least you had peace and quiet in the Longdock until the boys with the work tabs came in for lunch. Matt walked up the riverfront to another gin mill and sat with another beer. Now and then a fellow like himself would drift in, on the outs with Lippy and open to Matt's arguments about getting up a petition to call an honest union election: About time we got the mob's foot off'n our necks; sure, they're tough, but if there's enough of us . . . it was the old dream of standing up like honest-to-God Americans instead of like oxen with rings in their noses.

Matt thought he was talking quiet but even his whisper had volume, and farther down the bar Feets and Specs were taking it in. They weren't frowning or threatening, but just looking, quietly drinking and taking it all in.

When Matt finished his beer and said see-ya-later, Specs and

Feets rose dutifully and followed him out. A liner going down-river let out a blast that swallowed up all the other sounds in the harbor. Matt didn't hear them approach until Feets had a hand on his shoulder. Feets was built something like Matt, round and hard. Specs was slight and not much to look at. He wore very thick glasses. He had shot the wrong fellow once. Lippy had told him to go out and buy a new pair of glasses and warned him not to slip up that way again.

"What d'ya say, Matt?" Feets asked, and from his tone no one could have thought them anything but friends.

"Hello, Feets, Specs," Matt said.

"Listen, Matt, we'd like to talk to you a minute," Feets said.

"Then talk," Matt said. "As long as it's only talk, go ahead."

"Why do you want to give us so much trouble?" Specs said—any defiance of power mystified him. "You should straighten yourself out, Matt. You'd be working three-four days a week if you just learned to keep that big yap of yours shut."

"I didn't know you were so worried about whether I worked or not."

"Matt, don't be such a thickheaded mick," Feets argued. "Why be agitatin' alla time? You ain't gonna get anywheres, that's for sure. All ya do is louse yourself up with Lippy."

Matt said something short and harsh about Lippy. Feets and Specs looked pained, as if Matt were acting in bad taste.

"I wish you wouldn't say stuff like that," Specs said. His face got very white when he was ready for action. On the water-front he had a reputation for enjoying the trigger-squeezing. "You keep saying that stuff and we'll have to do something about it. You know how Lippy is."

Matt thought a moment about the danger of saying what he wanted to say: Fran and the kids home waiting for money he'd have to borrow from the loan shark. Why look for trouble? Why buck for the bottom of the river? Was it fair to Fran? Why couldn't he be like so many other longshoremen—like Flanagan, who had no love for Lippy Keegan but went along to keep food on the table? Lippy ran the piers just like he owned them. You didn't have to like Lippy, but it sure made life simpler if he liked you.

Matt thought about all this, but he couldn't help himself. He was a self-respecting man, and it galled him that a pushy racketeer—a graduate of the old Arsenal Mob—and a couple of punks could call themselves a union. *I shouldn't say this*, Matt was thinking, and he was already saying it:

"Yeah, I know how Lippy is. Lippy is gonna get the surprise of his fuckin' life one of these days. Lippy is gonna find himself—"

"You dumb harp," Feets said. "You must like to get hit in the head."

"There's lots I like better," Matt admitted. "But I sure as hell won't back away from it."

Feets and Specs looked at each other and the glance said clearly: What are you going to do with a meathead like this? They shrugged and walked away from Matt, back to their places at the bar. Later in the day they would give Lippy a full account and find out the next move. This Matt Gillis was giving their boss a hard time. Everything would be lovely down here if it wasn't for this handful of talk-back guys. They leaned on the bar with a reassuring sense that they were on the side of peace and stability, that Matt Gillis was asking for trouble.

Matt met Runt in the Longdock around five-thirty. Runt was buying because he had the potatoes in his pocket. They talked about this petition they were getting up to call a regular meeting. Runt had been talking to a couple of old-timers in his hatch gang who were half scared to death and half ready to go along. And there were maybe half a dozen young fellows who had young ideas and no use for the old ways of buying jobs from Fisheye and coming on the double whenever Lippy whistled. Another round or two and it was suppertime.

"Have another ball, Matt. The money's burnin' a hole in me pocket."

"Thanks, Runt, but I gotta get home. The wife'll be hittin' me with a mop." This was a familiar, joking threat in the Gillis domain.

Matt wiped his mouth with his sleeve and rubbed his knuckles on Runt's head. "Now don't get in no arguments. You watch yourself now." It was bad business, Matt knew, bucking the mob and hitting the bottle at the same time. They could push you into the drink some night and who was to say you weren't dead drunk, just another "death by accidental drowning."

Matt was worried about Runt as he walked up the dark side street to his tenement. Runt took too many chances. Runt liked to say, "I had me fun and I drunk me fill. What've I got to lose?"

I better keep my eye on the little fella now that we're pushin' so hard for this up-and-up election, Matt was thinking, when he felt something solid whop him just behind the ear. The blow had force enough to drop a horse but Matt half turned, made a club of his right hand and was ready to wield it when the something solid whopped him again at the back of his head. He thought it was the kid, the Skelly punk, there with Feets, but he wasn't sure. It was dark and his head was coming apart. In a bad dream something was swinging at him on the ground—hobnailed shoes, the finishing touch. Feets, they called him. The darkness closed in over him like a black tarpaulin.

Everybody was talking at once and—was it time for him to get up and shape?—he was sprawled on the bed in his room. Go 'way, lemme sleep.

"Matt, listen, this is Doc Wolff." The small, lean-faced physician was being pushed and breathed on. "The rest of you go on, get out of here."

Half the tenement population was crowded into the Gillises' narrow flat. Mrs. Geraghty, who was always like that, took the kids up to eat at her place. Doc Wolff washed out the ugly wounds in Matt's scalp. Half the people in the neighborhood owed him money he would never see—or ask for. Some of the old-timers still owed his father, who insisted on practicing at seventy-five. Father and son had patched up plenty of wounds like these. They were specialists on blackjack, steel-pipe and gun-butt contusions. Jews in an Irish district, they never took sides, verbally, in the endless guerrilla war between the dock mob and the "insoigents." All they could do, when a long-shoreman got himself in a fix like this, was to overlook the bill. The Wolffs were still poor from too much overlooking.

"Is it serious, Doctor?"

"We'd better X-ray, to make sure it isn't a skull fracture. I'd like to keep him in St. Vincent's a couple of days."

It was no fracture, just a couple of six-inch gashes and a concussion—a neat professional job performed according to instructions. "Don't knock him out of the box for good. Just leave him so he'll have something to think about for a week or two."

On the second day Runt came up with a quart and the good news that the men on the dock were signing the petition. The topping of Matt had steamed them up, where Lippy had figured it would scare them off. Runt said he thought they had enough men, maybe a couple of dozen, to call a rank-and-file meeting.

Father Conley, a waterfront priest with savvy and guts, had offered the rectory library as a haven.

But that night Fran sat at the side of Matt's bed in the ward for a long talk-to. She had a plan. It had been on her mind for a long time. This was her moment to push it through. Her sister's husband worked for a storage company. The pay was good, the work was regular, and best of all there weren't any Lippy Keegans muscling you if you didn't play it their way.

This brother-in-law said there was an opening for Matt. He could come in on a temporary basis and maybe work his way into regular union membership if he liked it. The brother-in-law had a little pull in that direction.

"Please, Matt. Please." It was Fran's domestic logic against his bulldog gift of fighting back. If he was a loner like Runt Nolan, he could stand up to Lippy and Specs and Feets and young Skelly and the rest of that trash all he wanted. But was it fair to Fran and the kids to pass up a sure seventy-five dollars a week in order to go hungry and bloody on the piers?

"Why does it always have to be you that sticks his neck out? Next time it'll be worse. They'll . . ."

Yes, Matt knew. The river: Lippy Keegan's silent partner, the old North River, waiting for him in the dark.

"Okay, Franny," Matt was saying under his bandages. "Okay. Tell Denny"—that was the brother-in-law—"I'll take the job."

In the storage vaults it was nice and quiet. The men came right to work from their homes. There was none of that stopping in at the corner and shooting the breeze about ships coming in and where the jobs might be—no hit or miss. The men were different too: good steady workers who had been there for years, not looking for any excitement. It seemed funny to Matt not to be looking behind him to see if any of Lippy's boys were on his tail, funny to have money in his pockets without having to worry how he was going to pay it back to the loan sharks.

When Matt had been there three weeks, Fran went out and bought herself a new dress—the first new one in almost two years. And the following Sunday they went up to the park and had lunch at the cafeteria near the zoo—their first visit to a restaurant in Lord knows when. Fran put her hand in Matt's and said, "Oh, Matt, isn't this better? Isn't this how people are supposed to live?"

Matt said yeah, he guessed so. It was good to see Fran happy and relaxed, no longer worried about food on the table for the kids, or whether he'd get home in one piece. Only—he couldn't put it into words, but when he got back to work on the fifth floor of the huge storage building, he knew what was going to come over him.

And next day it did, stronger than at any time since he started. He wondered what Runt was doing, and Jocko and Luke and Timmy and the rest of the gang in the Longdock. He hadn't been in since the first week he started at the storage. The fellows had all asked him how he was feeling and how he liked the new job, but he felt something funny about them, as if they were saying, "Well, you finally let Lippy run you off the docks, huh, Matt?" "All that big talk about cleaning up the union and then you fold like an accordion, huh, Matt?" It was in their eyes—even Runt's.

"Well, I'm glad to see you got smart and put your hook away," Runt actually said. "Me, I'd do the same if I was a family man. But I always run too fast for the goils to catch me." Runt laughed and poked Matt lightly, but there was something about it wasn't the same.

Matt ran into Runt on the street a week or so later and asked him how everything was going. He had heard the neighborhood scuttlebutt about a new meeting coming up in the parish house. A government labor man was going to talk to them on how to get their rights. Father Conley had pulled in a trade-union lawyer for them and everything seemed to be moving ahead.

But Runt was secretive with Matt. Matt felt the brush; he was an outsider now. Runt had never said a word in criticism of Matt's withdrawal from the waterfront—just occasional cracks about fellows like himself who were too dumb to do anything else but stand their ground and fight it out. But it got under Matt's skin. He had the face of a bruiser, and inlanders would think of him as "tough-looking." But actually Matt was thin-skinned, emotional, hypersensitive. Runt wouldn't even tell him the date of the secret meeting, just asked him how he liked the storage job.

"It's a real good deal," Matt said. No seven-thirty shape-up. No muscle men masquerading as shop stewards. The same check every week. What more could he want?

What more than stacking cardboard containers in a long tunnel-like room illuminated by neon tubing? Matt wondered what there was about the waterfront. Why did men humiliate themselves by standing like cattle in the shape-up? What was so good about swinging a cargo hook—hoisting cement, copper ore, coffee, noxious cargoes that tickled your throat and maybe were slowly poisoning you?

But that didn't tell the whole story, Matt was thinking as he handled the storage containers automatically. There was the salt air; there were the ships coming in from Spain, from South America, Greece, all over the world. There was the way the river sparkled on a bright day. And there was the busy movement of the harbor: the sound of the ferries, the tugs, the barges, the freighters and the great luxury ladies with their autocratic noses in the air. There were the different kinds of cargoes to handle—furs, perfume, sardines, cognac—and who was to blame them if they got away with a bottle or two; it wasn't pilferage on the waterfront until you trucked it away. There was the teamwork of a good gang working the cargo from the hatch and over the deck to the pier; the winch men, the deck men, the hatch boss, the high-low drivers, everybody moving together to an unstated but strongly felt rhythm that could be thrown off if just one man in a twenty-three-man gang didn't know his job. And then there were the breaks for lunch—not cold sandwiches in a metal container, but a cut of hot roast beef in the bar across the street, with a cold beer to wash it down. And there was the talk of last night's fight or today's ball game or the latest cute trick pulled off by the longshore racketeers.

The waterfront: the violent, vivid, restless, corrupted, "we're-doin'-lovely" waterfront.

Matt felt that way for days and said nothing about it. He'd sit in the front room with his shoes off, drinking beer, reading the tabloids, and wondering until it ached him what Runt and the boys were up to.

One evening when he came home, Flanagan and Bennett and some of the other neighbors were busy talking on the steps. Matt heard. "Maybe he's just on one of his periodicals and he's sleeping it off somewheres." And, "He coulda shipped out somewhere. He used to be an A.B. and he's just ornery enough to do it." And Matt heard, "When he gets his load on, anything c'n happen. He could walk off the end of the pier into the river and think he was home in bed."

Runt Nolan! No hide nor hair of him in three days, Flanagan said. Matt ran upstairs to tell Fran. She saw the look in his eyes when he talked about Runt, who always said he was "on borried time." "Now, Matt, no use getting yourself excited. Wait and see. Now, Matt." She saw the look in his eyes was the old look, before he settled for the cozy inland job with the storage company.

He paced up and down, but the children got on his nerves and he went over to talk to Father Conley. The father was just as worried as Matt. Specs had been warning Runt not to hold any more meetings in the rectory. Specs had told Runt to take it easy for his own good.

Matt went home after a while but he couldn't sleep. At one-thirty in the morning he put his clothes back on and went down to the Longdock. What's the story, any news of Runt?

Nine days later there was news of Runt. The police department had made contact with Runt, by means of a grappling hook probing the soft, rotten bottom of the river. Runt wasn't "on borried time" any more. He had paid back every minute of it. Cause of death: accidental drowning. On the night of his disappearance, Runt had been seen wandering the gin mills in a state of inebriation. In other words, bagged. There were no marks of violence on Runt. How could anyone prove he hadn't slipped. The good old North River, Lippy's silent partner, had done it again.

It was a good funeral. Everybody in the neighborhood was there—even Lippy Keegan, and Specs and Skelly and the rest of the boys. After the Mass, Father Conley came out on the sidewalk, and Matt and some of the others who were closest to Runt gathered around to hear what the father had to say.

They had seen the father steamed before but never like this. "Accident my eye," he said. "If they think we're going to take this lying down, they're dumber than I think they are."

"What can we do, Father?"

Everybody looked around. It was Flanagan, who had come up behind Matt; Flanagan, who always played it very cozy with the Keegans. But like most of the others, he had liked having Runt around—that cocky little bantam. The Longdock wouldn't be the same without him. It looked like Runt, at the bottom of the river, had done more damage to Lippy than when he was around the docks shooting off his mouth.

Father Conley said, "We're going to keep this case alive. We'll question every single person who talked to Runt the day they hit him in the head. We'll keep needling the police for action. Keegan hasn't heard the end of Runt Nolan."

"Now's the time to put somebody up to run for president against Lippy," the Bennett kid said.

Everybody looked at Matt. Matt looked down at his uncomfortable black shoes. He would have given anything to have been with Runt the night Keegan's cowboys caught up with the little guy.

"That's right, keep pressing them," Father Conley said. "Maybe they don't know it yet, but times are changing. One of these days you're going to knock them out of the box for good." He looked at Matt and said, "I can help you. But I can't do it for you. It takes leadership."

Matt looked down at the sidewalk. He always felt strange

in his dark blue suit. He looked over at Fran, talking with some of the other wives. In his mind, Fran and the storage company and the welfare of the kids were all churning around with Runt and what Father Conley was saying and the faces of these dock workers looking at him and waiting for him . . .

The morning after the funeral Matt's alarm clock split the silence at six-thirty. Matt swung his legs over the side of the bed. Fran stirred behind him. "I'll get up make you some coffee." She sat up and they looked at each other.

"I'm sorry, Fran, I—"

"Don't be," she said.

Even before what happened to Runt, she had felt it coming. And on the way home from church he had said, "All the fellers liked Runt. There'll be hell to pay. Now's the time to get 'em movin' in the right direction."

Fran, sitting up in bed behind him, said, "Don't get in no more trouble than you can help, Matt."

Matt stood up and stretched, groaned, and reached for his pants. "Don't worry, I'm gonna watch myself, I ain't gonna take no crazy chances like Runt, Lord-'ve-mercy-on-'im."

She wasn't even disappointed about the storage job. A storage man is a storage man, a longshoreman is a longshoreman. In the deepest part of her mind she had known that all along.

"I'll get up make you some coffee," she said again, as she had a thousand times before, as she would—if he was lucky—a thousand times again.

For a moment he roughed her up affectionately. "You're gettin' fat, honey." Then he was pulling his wool checkerboard shirt on over his long underwear. If there was enough work, Fisheye was liable to pick him, just to make it look good in case there was an investigation.

The cargo hook felt good in his belt. He zipped up his windbreaker, told Fran not to worry, set his cap at the old-country angle, and tried not to make too much noise on the creaky stairway as he made his way down through the sleeping tenement.

Flanagan was coming out of his door as Matt reached the bottom landing. The old docker was yawning and rubbing sleep out of his eyes but he grinned when he saw who it was.

"Matt, me lad, we'll be needin' ya, that's for sure."

We. It had taken Flanagan a long time to get his mouth around that *we*. There wasn't any *we* over at the storage company. Matt nodded to Flanagan, a little embarrassed, and fussed with his cap like a pitcher.

"Once a stand-up guy, always a stand-up guy, huh, Matt?"

Matt grunted. He didn't want them to make too much of a deal out of it. Matt felt better when he got outside and the wind came blowing into his face. It felt good—like the cargo hook on his hip, familiar and good.

As they reached the corner, facing the elevated railroad tracks that ran along the river, two figures came up from a basement—Specs Sinclair and young Skelly. Specs had a bad cold. He was a sinus sufferer in the wintertime. He wished he was down in Miami scoring on the horses.

"So you want more?" he said to Matt, daubing his nose with a damp handkerchief. "We run you out of here once but you ain't satisfied. What's a matter, you lookin' to wear cement shoes?"

Matt gazed at him and felt pleased and excited that he was back with this old hoodlum Sinclair and this punk Skelly. They were like old friends in reverse.

"Quit racing your motor," Matt said. "It ain't gonna be so easy this time. None of us is gonna go wanderin' around alone half-gassed like Runt Nolan. We're stickin' together now. And Father Conley's got the newspapers watchin'. You hit me in the head and next thing you know they'll hit you with ten thousand volts."

Specs looked at Skelly. Everything was getting a little out of hand, there was no doubt about it. In the old days you could knock off an old bum like Nolan and that was the end of it. This Matt Gillis, why didn't he stay in cold storage? For the first time in his life Specs worried whether Lippy Keegan would know the next move.

Matt crossed the street and pushed open the door of the Longdock. Everybody knew he was back. Everybody was going to be watching him. He wished Runt would come over and stick him in the side with a left hand. He knew it wasn't very likely, but, as a boilermaker was set in front of him, it made him feel better to wonder if that scrappy little son-of-a-gun was going to be watching too.

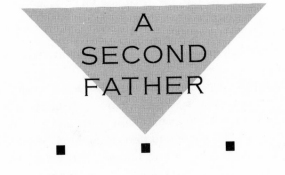

# A SECOND FATHER

Mrs. Samuels was interviewing a new chauffeur when Chris came in from school.

"Hello, Mommy." He kissed her, dutifully, on the cheek and she cuddled him a moment, asking him the automatic question, How was school today? Then she told him to run along and play, she was very busy now.

"Is Daddy going to take me to the ball game tonight?"

His mother smiled politely at the applicant chauffeur to forgive the interruption.

To Chris she said: "I'm sure Daddy will do his best, dear."

"Well, he promised . . ."

"Yes, I know, but—" Chris's father was the head of a film studio, a job that seemed to consist of an endless series of "conferences" running on into the night. He was always promising Chris things that had to be called off at the last minute because he was "tied up." Mrs. Samuels did her best to explain this to Chris but it was difficult for Chris to understand. Why couldn't his Dad simply say, "Look, people, I have to end this conference in ten minutes. I have a date to take my son to Gilmore Stadium." Why couldn't it be as simple as that?

"But he did promise," Chris said again.

"Chris, I'm busy now."

"You like ball games, sonny?" asked the man talking to his mother.

Chris turned and looked at him. He was a square-jawed, ruddy-complexioned, well-built fellow with black curly hair. He was smiling at Chris an unusually warm and winning smile that immediately communicated something important to Chris. The man likes me, he thought. Grownups from the picture studio were always telling Chris what a wonderful man his father was and how they hoped Chris would grow up to be just like him. Usually they said this with a little, fond pat on Chris's shoulder, but the ten-year-old boy was never completely sure they liked him.

"Chris loves to go with his father to fights and ball games," his mother answered for him. "Of course his father is terribly busy, so—"

"When I was a kid I used to watch 'em play almost every day," said the stranger who liked Chris. "Of course I never had money for a ticket. I got awfully good at climbing those telephone poles."

He laughed easily, the skin crinkling around his eyes in straight lines like the sun rays in Chris's drawings. Chris always felt like laughing when other people laughed. Chris's mother smiled indulgently, something in her manner saying, And now let us get back to business.

"You say you have no references here in Los Angeles?"

"No, ma'am. I've been with a family in Westchester, New York, for the past three years, ma'am. I did all their driving and filled in as a butler for their parties. I even used to give Mr. Hawthorne a rubdown on Saturdays. I've been a physical education instructor." Then he turned toward Chris and said for his benefit, "I even did a little professional boxing when I was a kid."

Chris noticed that the man's nose was slightly dented about two thirds down the bridge. Chris liked the way it looked. It made the man look tough and formidable and yet he was handsome and had a nice smile.

"What's your name?" Chris asked the man suddenly.

"James," the man said, "James H. Campbell. H for Hercules. I weighed fourteen and a half pounds when I was born."

"Are you going to be our new chauffeur?"

James smiled. "That's up to your mother, young man."

"I hope so," Chris said.

The chauffeur grinned. "Thank you." He turned to Mrs. Samuels. "I like kids. We always get along fine."

Chris went over to his mother. "You are going to make him our new chauffeur, aren't you, Mommy?"

Mrs. Samuels's expression was one of gracious embarrassment.

"Now, Chris, will you please go out and play and let me finish this interview."

That evening, as Chris had feared, his father called from the studio just before dinner to say how sorry he was that the *Catherine the Great* script had hit a snag and it looked as if he was going to be tied up with the writers for hours. They were blocking out an entirely new final sequence. He hated to disappoint Chris about the ball game but he would take him to the next L. A.-Hollywood game a week from Saturday. That was a promise.

Chris went up to his room and slammed the door. It wasn't fair. He went back to the door, opened it and slammed it again. When he heard his mother coming he threw himself on his bed and started to cry loudly. His mother was not sure whether to scold him for slamming the door or sympathize with him in his disappointment.

"Chrissy, you mustn't give in to your temper like that.

Daddy works very hard for you. He can't help it if he has to work so hard."

Chris gulped back his sobs.

"Is James coming back, Mommy?"

"James?"

"The new chauffeur you were talking to."

"Oh, the chauffeur. Well, I don't know. I also talked to a Japanese boy."

"Please, Mommy. I want James."

Mrs. Samuels looked at her only son, a tow-haired, rather frail child who, in the opinion of his father, needed to be toughened up. One trouble was that Sol Samuels was much too busy to do anything about it and Alma Samuels liked his being "poetic" and soulful. She was always saying how sensitive he was.

"Chris, if James doesn't work out, well, I don't like to see you disappointed."

"Oh, Mom, I know he will. I just know it."

Sol really should make a little more of an effort when he promises him these baseball games, Mrs. Samuels was thinking. "All right," she said. "We'll try him. Just *try* him, you understand." She fondled the back of Chris's head. "Wait 'til I tell your father that you're hiring the chauffeurs now."

James moved into the chauffeur's room above the garage that Sunday evening. Next morning Chris was up especially early so he'd have a chance to talk to James before school. One trouble with his father was that he never got up until after Chris had gone to school. That way days, even whole weeks, would go by without their seeing each other. Mrs. Samuels was always explaining how sorry he felt about this and Chris was always saying that he understood. "He does understand," his mother would say proudly. "He's more understanding than a lot of grownups I know." Such praise made Chris uncomfortable and he didn't know why.

On Monday morning Chris bolted his breakfast so recklessly

that Winnie, the maid, warned him against indigestion. Chris gulped down his milk ("so you'll have nice strong bones") and hurried out to the garage. James was already at work, stripped to his undershirt, washing the town car.

"Hi, Chris," James said, as he hosed down the glossy maroon hood of the long custom-made Lincoln.

Chris liked the way the new chauffeur called him Chris right away. Not *sonny* or *lad* or *buster* or any of those drippy names the others had used. Chris stood as close as he could to James without getting wet, and watched in fascination the way the colored pictures on the chauffeur's arm rippled into life as he worked his muscles. On his left arm was a a young, full-breasted woman without any clothes on, identified in purple letters as Jo-Ann. On his right arm was an American flag and curving around it in fancy letters: M-O-T-H-E-R. Chris had never seen anything like that before. Everything about this chauffeur was big and strong and different.

"You've got pictures on your arm," Chris said.

James raised his hand modestly to shield the figure of Jo-Ann.

"That's right. I've had 'em on so long I forgot all about 'em."

"Don't they come off when you take a bath?"

James explained the principle of tattooing to Chris.

"Little needles? Don't they hurt a lot?"

"Sure they do. But we just grit our teeth and take it like a man. I'll bet you don't cry when you get hurt, do you, Chris?"

Chris had a tendency to cry more than he should at going-on-eleven. ("I don't know why he should be such a nervous child," his mother would say.) But now he said, "I hardly ever cry."

"That's a boy," said James. "Here, hold this hose a minute. I'll go put my shirt on."

No one had ever asked Chris to help wash the cars before. It is hard to explain how important you can feel when you aren't quite eleven and are trusted to hold a hose in your hand. If you stand too close to the car the water bounces back and splatters you. If you hold the hose too high the stream of water misses the car entirely and soaks the roadster and the tools in the garage. You have to do it just right.

In a few moments James was back with his uniform jacket on. It buttoned tight at the neckline like a Marine dress uniform and James wore it very well. "Thanks, Chris," he said, taking the hose, "you did a nice job. Now you can turn the water off."

Chris hastened to obey. James winked at him. "I can see you're going to be a big help to me."

"I'll help you wash the cars every day," Chris said proudly.

One of the big problems in Chris's life was having to be driven to school in the town car. Sol Samuels, in a burst of democratic expression, had insisted that Chris go to the large public school bridging the exclusive Windsor Square section and the plebeian neighborhoods toward Western Avenue. The school reflected southern California's cultural overlapping, for there were Mexicans, Japanese and Negroes as well as white children whose fathers were not heads or even assistant heads of movie studios. "I don't want Chris to get any false ideas about people," Mr. Samuels would lecture. "After all we came from New York's Lower East Side. Our parents were driven out of Europe. And I try to make pictures for average people, that everybody can enjoy. I never want Chris to grow up a snob, and the best way to check that is to keep him in touch with the people."

A noble speech, but, as in many of us, there were inconsistencies in Sol Samuels. On the wave of a magnificent bonus from the company, following a particularly profitable series of pictures, he had brought home the most remarkable automobile Chris had ever seen. Instead of having a long, sleek body like any ordinary expensive limousine, this one had a body like an old-fashioned royal coach crisscrossed in gold petit point.

It was an authentic eighteenth-century coach down to the smallest detail, with elaborate coach lights in gold, and gold-plated door handles. The chauffeur sat out in front under a canopy like a coachman. There was no worse torture, in Chris's mind, than being driven to school in that outlandish car. The only way he could manage it at all was to flatten himself on the floor so no one could see him through the small oval side windows. Then he would insist on stopping down the block and across the street from the school entrance. There he would crawl out onto the sidewalk on his hands and knees, like a soldier in enemy country, then jump up suddenly and quickly walk away from the motorized monstrosity, as if he and it were total strangers.

James didn't understand what Chris was doing that first morning when he saw him pressing himself against the floor of the coach. He laughed when Chris tried to explain it to him. "If I had a buggy like this I'd be proud of it," he said. "Your old man made all this money because he had brains. Why should you be ashamed of that?"

It had something to do with not wanting to be special, Chris knew, but he couldn't explain it very well. On the way home James got him to come up and join him on the driver's seat, once they were far enough away from school for Chris to feel relatively safe. Chris told James how he had been teased about the car. A Mexican boy who was the best fighter in the class had called him "Meester Reech Beech." Had Chris told him to shut up and mind his own beeswax? James wanted to know. The possibility of such defiance was scary to Chris. Iggy Gonzalez was the human embodiment of danger and fierceness. He was a dark, wiry boy a year or so older than the other fifth graders. And his brother Chucho was the amateur feather-weight champion of greater Los Angeles. Chris could think of nothing more frightening than being forced into physical combat with Iggy Gonzalez.

James looked Chris over carefully. Chris had thin, long arms and legs. "Growing out of himself," he had heard his mother describe it.

"Ever have any boxing lessons?" James asked.

No, Chris had gone to the Legion fights with his father, but he had never tried it himself.

"I fought a couple of semi-windups in the Legion seven, eight years ago," James said. "I was runner-up to the champ of the Pacific Fleet when I was in the Navy, where I picked up the tattoos. How about you and me putting on the gloves? I'll show you a few things that'll knock Gonzalez's head off. Then you can sit up here in front with me right up to the school door. And if anyone kids you, you tell 'em to shut up or else. Isn't that better than hiding on the floor?"

The way James said it suddenly made it sound possible. Driving home under the canopy with this formidable James at his side, Chris let his mind explore heroic possibilities. His new, powerful self was flailing away at Iggy Gonzalez until the bigger boy slumped down at Chris's feet. "You ween—I geev up—I have meet my master," his former tormentor sobbed. With faultless magnanimity, Chris knelt beside his fallen foe to administer first aid. "Come on, I'll drive you home in the car. You'll be OK after you rest up. You're a good man, Iggy, as brave as I ever fought."

The town car was pulling to the curb on Larchmont. "I'm going to stop in here right now and get you some boxing gloves," James was saying. "We'll start the first lesson this afternoon."

They squared off on the back lawn near the garage, James with a pair of huge, greasy, worn gloves and Chris with a little pair in shiny red leather. Chris was stiff with fear at the strangeness of it and James did his best to show him how to relax and how to place his feet so he'd be in balance and able to move back and forth like a dancer. He told Chris to hit him in the belly as hard as he could and Chris enjoyed hitting with all his might. James told him to turn his left toe in a little and to pivot

on the right foot—"now with your body behind it"—smack!—
"that's better!" Chris was enjoying the sensation of sweat oil-
ing his body. If he kept this up he was going to have a big chest
and a hard, tight stomach like James. Wham-bang, wham-*bang*.
"Hey, that's pretty good! I could really feel that one."

In his going-on-eleven years, Chris could not remember
hearing anything that made him feel so alive. He listened
devoutly, desperately anxious to please, as James drew him
into a new world where belligerence was fascinatingly linked
to skill. Chris found, under James's tutelage, that he could pull
his head back a few inches to avoid a punch, or deflect it with
his glove. "The first thing to learn is how not to get hit." James
dramatized his lesson with stirring accounts of his Navy bouts:
like the time he forgot to duck and the Navy middleweight
champ Jocko Kennedy knocked him cold with a haymaking
right. "I was out for ten minutes. They thought I was dead.
They say you hear birdies but it's a funny thing—I heard
telephone wires. You know how you hear them buzzing sometimes in the country?"

James had just told him he had had enough for a while and
Chris was stretched out on the grass, listening. He had never
heard anyone tell such wonderful stories. He was looking up
into James's face as the chauffeur told him of his determination
to fight Kennedy again. James's shipmates had lost their
month's pay on him and he felt he owed it to them to turn the
tables on Kennedy. On shipboard, all the way from San Diego
to the Philippines, James practiced how to duck under that
haymaker right, and then to bob up quickly with a left hook
of his own. Day after day in the hot sun of the Oriental seas
James fought his imaginary battle with the fearsome Jocko
Kennedy. It was like fighting Iggy Gonzalez, Chris was thinking. Was there anything more exciting in the whole world than
to choose the one person you are most afraid of and then to
devote yourself to a long-range careful plan for licking him?
Chris lived through the days when James was preparing him-

self for his ordeal. The plan was to challenge Jocko formally to a rematch when the Pacific Fleet assembled in Manila Bay.

Chris was sitting up now with his arms clasped around his bony knees. His gentle face was set in an unusually serious and manly expression, as if his vicarious sharing of the chauffeur's experiences had already cut him off from his sheltered child's world.

"We better not get too cooled off," James interrupted himself. "Let's go one more round and I'll finish the story."

"Oh please, please finish it," Chris begged. He was sailing into Manila Bay, ready for Jocko Kennedy. On Sundays his father had read him Dickens and James Fenimore Cooper and it had been rather pleasant. But this wasn't listening to a story, it was being inside a story. He and James on one side and Jocko and Iggy on the other. Chris was in training to duck Gonzalez's fiercest blows. Oh, he had to beat him, he had to, in this grudge match in Manila Bay!

"James, please, finish about you and Jocko." Wham-*bang*— inexplicably Chris pistoned his small fists into the air. With his newfound feeling of power came a new kind of laugh.

"Well, the night we hit Manila we all got shore leave. And you know how the sailors are, a lot of young punks who don't know any better, they hit the bars pretty hard. Around one o'clock in the morning I was in some dive called the Yellow Dragon feeling pretty good. There was an argument in the other corner, some loudmouth getting fresh with one of the Filipino barmaids and I look over and see my old friend Jocko Kennedy. I say, 'Pipe down, Jocko, ye're rockin' the boat," something like that. This Jocko, he bellows like a bull. Twenty Shore Police can't hold him when he's boozed up. I see him coming at me with a bottle. My shipmates, they say to me, 'Let's powder out of here, Jimmy, that Jocko's the toughest rough-and-tumble fighter in the Navy.' All those months I been practicing to meet him in the ring where I c'n use my footwork and science, not in a dim-lit bar with a bottle. But

I tell my pals, 'You clear out if you want to. I ain't afraid of no man, bottle or no bottle.' The boys back away to give me fighting room. Jocko comes at me swinging the bottle at my head. I do just what I been practicing on shipboard. I duck and then bob up quick and put everything I have into a left hook to the jaw. I follow it up with a right cross as he's going down. Jocko Kennedy is through for the night. His jaw is broken and he's still in sick bay when his ship pulls out."

There was a long, delicious silence as Chris saw himself in the smoky haze of the Yellow Dragon looking on in nonchalant curiosity as Iggy Gonzalez was being carried out with a slack and bloody jaw.

"OK, now let's work one more round," James said and Chris jumped up and assumed the stance his mentor had taught him. "That's it, now tuck your chin in a little more, now move around and jab, snap it out, snap, snap!" Chris was feeling light on his feet and formidable. Someday he would have colored pictures on his arms and know how to do as many things as James.

Mrs. Samuels came out to find the new chauffeur and was surprised to find him sparring with her little boy. "Why, Chris, where did you get the gloves?"

Chris stopped, panting and sweating proudly. "Jimmy got them for me, Mom."

"Who?"

"Jimmy." He nodded toward his friend.

"Oh. James?" Mrs. Samuels looked at the chauffeur. "I'll have Mr. Samuels reimburse you for that."

"It's my pleasure, Mrs. Samuels," James said. "It's my present to him."

"But—you hardly know him," Mrs. Samuels said.

"I wouldn't say that. We're pretty good pals already, aren't we, Chris?"

"He used to be a real fighter, Mom. He's been teaching me a lot of keen stuff. Look—watch me, watch me, Mom!"

Chris began swarming all over James, fearlessly, as James let the small punches through his guard.

"You've got a wonderful little boy here, Mrs. Samuels."

"Yes. Thank you," Mrs. Samuels said. She didn't know why the sight of them sporting like this should disturb her even mildly. Was it because it pointed up some failure on Sol's part? Or because there was a certain roughneck quality in James, under the careful chauffeur manners, that could coarsen Chris if their relationship grew too close?

"James, I'd like you to have the car out in front in fifteen minutes," Mrs. Samuels said.

"Very good, madam," James said.

"Chris, you look terribly overheated. Don't you think you should go in and take a nice cool shower?"

His mother was forever telling him things in the form of questions.

"I want to stay out here with James," Chris said.

His mother stared at him. She had never heard her son speak so positively, almost rudely, before.

As Mrs. Samuels returned to the house, James looked over at Chris and winked. Chris grinned. Their wink. The beginning of an entirely new experience, of an intimacy outside of and even opposed to his mother and father.

All through his school days Chris looked forward to his boxing lesson with James. In two weeks it had become a ritual, the sparring punctuated by talks on the grass between rounds, the valorous accounts of James's fistic jousts that had begun to crowd out of Chris's mind the gallant battles of Sir Lancelot and Sir Galahad. And then there were the glorious stories of the sea, when James had hung on to the wheel of a sinking destroyer, or had to dive into the shark-infested waters of the South Pacific to save an exhausted shipmate.

When Chris's father did break away from the studio ("I'll try to break away in time," was the phrase he always used) his description of the more harrowing events of the day was frequently interrupted now by Chris's boastful reference to some singular deed of James's. "James was the best fighter in the whole Pacific Fleet, Dad," Chris would say suddenly, interrupting his parents' familiar conversation to speak his mind on a subject that seemed to him of far greater importance than all this talk-talk about making pictures.

One evening after dinner Chris's father apologized for his delinquencies as a parent and offered to make atonement by taking up Melville's *Typee* where they had left off nearly four weeks before. To his surprise, Chris said he had promised to meet "Jimmy" after dinner—Jimmy had something in his room he had promised to show Chris. Chris hurried off from the dinner table as soon as he was excused.

"What is this *Jimmy* business?" Sol Samuels wanted to know.

"Chris is simply wild about James," Mrs. Samuels explained. "I don't remember ever seeing him like this before."

Mr. Samuels frowned. "I wonder if it's a good idea, letting him get this chummy with that fellow. After all, we don't know very much about him."

"I wouldn't worry too much," Mrs. Samuels said. "He seems to adore Chris. And he's all the things a boy would idolize—a sailor and a fighter and—" She saw a suggestion of regret or jealousy come into her husband's eyes for a moment and she quickly added, "I'm afraid he's at an age when being an ex-fighter or even having a spectacular tattoo seems a little more important than merely being the head of a movie studio."

Sol Samuels nodded, absently, and then he sighed with an exaggerated intake of breath. "God, I had a helluva day. That Gloria may bring in millions at the box office but she takes every dollar of it out of my hide."

"Those stupid, temperamental girls," Mrs. Samuels sympathized, shaking her head at a whole generation of glamorous ladies who fought each other tooth and nail for larger dressing rooms, more close-ups and better billing.

The chauffeur's room above the garage was rather small and unprepossessing but Chris entered it with a sense of wonder. It supposed a new sense of intimacy with his big friend, of entering into an almost forbidden world of adults and their strange, secret ways. Over the chauffeur's bed were three pictures of young women, two of them in bathing suits and one of them almost naked.

"That middle one is my sweetie," James said. "She works in the movies once in a while. She's an extra girl. Maybe one of these days your old man will give her a screen test."

"I hate girls," Chris said.

"Just wait about five more years," James said.

"Oh boy, a gun," Chris said, seeing a rifle set on pegs above the door.

"That's my deer-hunting rifle," James said. "One of these days I'll take you up in the Sierras and we'll get ourselves a twelve-point buck."

"Can I hold it, Jimmy, please?" Chris begged.

"I don't know if your mother 'n' father'd like it."

"I won't tell them if you won't."

James grinned and roughed up Chris's curly yellow-brown hair.

"You're a rascal. OK. It'll be our secret."

He took the rifle down from the wall, checking it to make sure it was safe, and handed it to Chris. Chris held it up and made the expert ricochet sound that has replaced in young vocabularies the old fashioned *bang-bang.* Then James set it back on its pegs again. Chris's mother and father hated guns and wouldn't have one in the house.

"When I'm big will you teach me how to shoot it, Jimmy?"

"Sure, Chris, you just stick with me and I'll teach you everything I know. And one of these days when you're a big famous movie producer like your father I'll be your assistant, how about that?"

Chris frowned slightly because everybody from the studio

was always telling him he'd be a famous producer like his father one of these days. The people who told him that were his father's friends and not his friends and it worried him that Jimmy, his own private grown-up friend, should mention the studio like the others.

"I don't want to be a producer. I want to be an explorer and an archaeologist."

"An archaeologist? Hey, what's that?"

"You dig up old cities that are all covered over with grass and trees. Pyramids and stuff like that."

"Like digging for buried treasure, huh? Well, you're going to make a bundle, whatever you do. You're a smart kid."

"Have you got any more guns?"

James laughed at him and jabbed him lightly, playfully, on the jaw.

"What are you, the house dick around here? Come on, now, don't be so nosy."

"Chri-is, oh Chris-sy-boy," his mother's voice, plaintive but persistent, spanned the mysterious gulf between the main house and the chauffeur's quarters.

"Now, remember, fella," James said, "don't tell your old lady I let you handle a gun." He winked toward the bathing-suit pictures over his bed. "And I wouldn't mention the cheesecake to her either. I don't want her to think I'm leading you astray."

Chris did not entirely understand the chauffeur's meaning but he did appreciate the fact that they now shared certain rather delicious secrets together.

"I won't tell, Jimmy," he said solemnly, "I swear I won't tell."

"Attaboy. Hit the sack now. You got to get lots of sleep if you want to grow big and strong like your Uncle Jimmy."

"I'm going to be in the Navy and have pictures all over my arm," Chris said happily, as he ran to obey his mother's now slightly more impatient call.

The next afternoon when James picked Chris up in front of
the school in the hateful gold petit-point town car, the nemesis
Iggy Gonzalez was watching disdainfully. James was resplen-
dent in his dark maroon uniform.

"Jeez, get a load of the little prince," Iggy said. He was a
tough, young American with only the faintest echo of a Mexican accent.

Chris was hating the car and Iggy Gonzalez and all the
moving-picture money that wasn't his fault.

"Hey, stuck-up, what you got that guy in uniform for? So
you don't get your block knocked off?"

A few of Iggy's admirers laughed. Iggy had wiry brown
arms and a cocky way of walking, as if he was already a winning
prizefighter like his big brother Chucho. Iggy came closer,
charging the atmosphere with his schoolboy snarls. Chris was
ready to duck into the safety of the coach when James said,
"Go ahead. Stand up to him. Left hand in his face like I showed
you."

Chris was terribly afraid of Iggy Gonzalez but he was even
more afraid to be a coward in the eyes of his benefactor Jimmy.
Visibly trembling and embarrassingly close to tears, he did as
the chauffeur told him. The two boys circled each other with
intense concentration, Chris moving jerkily in his fear, Iggy
feeling his man out coolly as befitted a veteran of these school-
yard bouts. Then he rushed at Chris, but Chris, to his own
surprise, put into practice the cleverness James had been teaching him. He drew back quickly and stepped neatly to one side
and Iggy went rushing foolishly by him like a little bull. Iggy
cursed and came charging in again. Chris put out his left hand
and Iggy ran into it. His nose began to bleed. Iggy's rooters
called out, "Come on, Ig, he can't fight, knockum down. Hit
'im on his Jew nose!" They were vicious cries and made Chris
panicky. But he kept pushing his left in the dark sweaty face
coming at him, as James had tutored him. Iggy was breathing
hard like a little bull through his soggy nose. He knocked

Chris's surprising left hand away and swung on him with his hard wild right. Chris cringed and ducked, both automatically and in fear, and they fell into each other, the clinch deteriorating into a stand-up wrestle. They teetered and fell to the ground, grabbing frantically at each other, Chris on the verge of hysterical sobbing and fighting with the survival strength of some small cornered animal. Iggy was working his hard, bony knees into Chris's neck when James decided this was the strategic moment to extricate his charge with honor.

"OK, kids, good fight, let's call it a draw," he said and he pulled them apart. Iggy had not expected any resistance from Chris. He stared at him with sullen respect. Chris was still trembling inside and giddy with relief at having the ordeal behind him, this thing he had dreaded from the time he was eight.

"Come on," James said to Iggy. "Hop in. I'll blow both you champs to a soda."

It was a master stroke. Secretly, for a long time, Iggy Gonzalez had been wishing for a ride in the gold petit-point coach, and once he accepted he could hardly heckle Chris about it again.

Chris felt even closer to James after that. He'd be in James's room almost every evening after dinner, and occasionally James would even be invited to Chris's room, to examine the rock collection or to talk over some secret plans that Chris enjoyed being mysterious about in front of his parents.

Sol Samuels still had doubts about the wisdom of allowing so close a relationship but Mrs. Samuels said she had to admit that Chris was a good deal more manly than he had been before James came into his life. "Really, James has done wonders for him, Sol. I wouldn't say he's the best chauffeur we ever had, but he's almost like a second father to Chris."

A few weeks after school let out for the summer there was a company convention in Chicago and the Samuelses planned to be away for five or six days. They were going to take Chris along, and Winnie to care for him. But when Chris heard about it he said, Gee whiz what fun would that be, he'd rather stay home with James. "We thought this would be a good time to give James his week's vacation," Mrs. Samuels said. This conversation was held in the yard and James happened to overhear it. After lunch he came in and asked Mrs. Samuels if he could talk to her.

"Mrs. Samuels, I've been thinking what to do with my week. I thought I'd pack into the Sierras with a gun and some fishing tackle and sleep out of doors."

"That sounds very nice," Mrs. Samuels said stiffly.

"What I was thinkin' was maybe you'd let me take Chris along with me."

"Well, I really don't know what to say. I'd have to talk to his father. Are you sure you'd like a little boy along on your vacation?"

"He's real good company, you'd be surprised," James said, unaware of all that he was saying.

Late that night, after Sol Samuels had had a particularly prolonged wrangle with a doll-faced star who was tough as snakehide, he and Mrs. Samuels discussed James's invitation.

"But, Alma, darling, I tell you we don't know the fella. After all, we simply brought him in off the streets."

"He had beautiful references from Westchester."

"Those people never answered, Alma. Maybe they don't even exist."

"Any man who loves children so much," Mrs. Samuels said vaguely.

Sol Samuels still had his doubts. Alma answered him with the old argument that he spoke out of jealousy and guilt for not spending more time with his only son. It was a slightly unfair if rather unanswerable kind of reasoning and finally Sol threw up his hands. "All right, dear, all *right*. Now I've got to work on my speech for the convention."

The trip into the mountains with James was Chris's version

of going to heaven. There was a bigness, an importance about the way he felt that was more than his word *keen* could ever suggest. It was dry and hot under the summer sun. They climbed and suffered manfully. Then they would come upon a stream, with a natural pool three or four feet deep and they would stretch out alongside it and lower their mouths to the surface of the cool water. Chris saw beguiling shadows under a trickling waterfall and cried out, "Look, Jimmy, look!" James laughed as the sub-limit trout darted out of sight. "Next time whisper," he said. "We'll drop a fly on their noses and see if they're hungry."

Later in the day they found a real trout pool and they rolled up their pants and stood in the melted-snow water up to their knees. Chris got his line badly tangled in the underbrush and had no luck but James finally brought one to the net, about ten inches long and so lively that it kept flopping in the basket that Chris was allowed to hold. It made his heart pound with joy and excitement and some sort of fatalistic sorrow as he heard the flip-flopping get stronger and stronger, and then begin to slow down and weaken. There was a long silence, perhaps two minutes, and Chris raised the lid and peeked in to see if the fish was dead. It jumped toward the light and Chris slammed the lid down just in time. James managed to net another one about the same size, just as the sun was ducking down behind the folding range. Then came the best fun of all, starting the fire and frying the fish.

Chris would never eat fish for his mother or Winnie, but James's fish were different. He ate his whole portion, with fried potatoes that he had sliced himself and that James had taught him how to cook. Then he threw the remains into the fire and watched the paper plate flame up and twist into ashes. They sat around the fire talking, James with a pipe in his mouth exhaling little clouds of smoke into the still night air. Chris liked the smell of it. So much sweeter than his father's stinky old cigars. Chris asked James to tell him all over again about his fight with Jocko Kennedy in the Yellow Dragon in Manila. Later they talked about the woods and Chris thought it would be fun to live up here the rest of his life, being a mountain ranger and putting out forest fires and catching bandits and things like that. James laughed and said that was only because Chris was still very young. The day would come when he would be happy to take over his father's studio and have some oomphy red-headed star for his girlfriend. And James would come to the studio gate and Mr. Bigshot Chris Samuels wouldn't even let him in.

Oh, no, no, that would never happen, Chris cried, and he wished inside of him that James would forget about the studio and how rich or important his father was, or that he was going to be. He didn't want his father and the studio along on this trip. This was to be just Jimmy and Chris camping out in the mountains. Maybe they could find gold together and set up a mine and be partners for life. How much more fun that would be than any old studio.

After a while Chris got very sleepy from looking into the fire and James told him it was time to crawl into their pup tent. While Chris was lying in there thinking about the day, suddenly it began to thunder. The sound of it seemed to roll along the mountain slope and fall away into the valley below. Then lightning struck as if it were hop-skipping from scrub pine to pine around the tent. Chris would have been very scared if James hadn't been there. But James was there. He had moved into the tent and was squatting by the entrance flap looking out at the summer storm. Chris was sure James would know what to do in any emergency. Muscle-weary, but pleasantly so, he drifted off into visions of heroic comradeship, prospecting in Arizona where a bad man jumps them to steal their claim but he and Jimmy fight back like wildcats *You thought we didn't know how to box, huh? This'll teach you* flying together in a Navy PBY forced down in enemy waters and sailing their little rubber lifeboat into a desert island cove where fish were jumping all around them *Good boy Chris pull 'im in this'll keep us going 'til the search plane spots us. . . .* How long Chris had been sleeping he had no idea but suddenly he was awake again and for a funny moment he thought he was home in his own familiar bed. Winnie must be running a bath for him. He stretched out his hand and felt the dark canvas of the tent. Oh, the sound of running water was the brook outside. But what was this dark form kneeling over him? Half awake he cried out his fear of it. "James?"

"Yeah."

He felt better. But what was Jimmy doing so close to him, and looking down into his face while he slept? And what did he have in his hand? Chris could feel it as he lifted his own hands instinctively. A rope. "James?" Chris said again, in a quavering voice and after a moment or two he was reassured as the chauffeur's voice sounded more like him again. "It's OK, kid. It's me, kid."

"What are you doing with that rope?"

James cleared his throat and said, "It was getting kinda windy. I thought I'd go out and see if I can batten down the flaps."

Before Chris could answer, James was gone. It was spooky quiet and dark inside the tent. It shouldn't take Jimmy very long, Chris was thinking. Minutes passed. Chris huddled uneasily in the darkness. Why was it taking so long? Chris felt his way to the entrance flap and called "Jimmy, Jimmy!" There was no answer. "James! Jaaaaaa-mes . . . !" No answer. Chris crawled back under his covers and tried to think what to do. But the thinking got all jangled up in his head: too frightened to think. There was a cold clammy panic filling him up inside. He yelled JAMES so loud it strained his throat. Then he started to cry. He couldn't stop crying. It became a harsh hysterical rasping. Lost in the mountains, deserted and left to starve, like a scene from an old movie of his father's. Oh James, James, Jimmy, come back, come back, his mind begged the rainy out-of-doors. He lay still for a while, burrowing into his fear and then he heard the footsteps coming toward the tent and James was back.

"Hi, fella," he said, "afraid I wasn't coming back?"

Chris threw himself into the chauffeur's arms and tried, as James had taught him, not to cry.

"I walked back to the car to get a tarpaulin to throw over the tent," James explained. They had driven up the mountain as far as the dirt road would take them and then had walked in to find the campsite.

"Oh," Chris said. "That's OK, Jimmy."

He did wonder why James hadn't told him he was going but he didn't want to mention it for fear that James would say something that would make him ashamed.

The next morning was fine again because the sun was shining and Chris found some salamanders in the stream. At first he called them little alligators, but James, who seemed to know everything, explained to Chris that this was their full size, a kind of water lizard, and that you could pick them up without their biting you. Chris thought they were beautiful, with their shiny dark-green bodies decorated with bright-yellow spots. He was anxious to take some home with him. He got a milk bottle to carry them in. It was such fun to look at them through the glass. Watching their silent, dark green struggle in the bottle, he had almost forgotten the scare of the night before. He spent the whole morning chasing salamanders—"water dogs," James called them—and would have been happy to catch and play with them all day but when the sun was overhead James thought they ought to be getting on back to town. Chris had expected them to stay another night but James said he didn't want to keep Chris up here too long. And anyway he had someone he had to stop in and see on their way home.

Chris was sorry to be driving down the winding mountain road. Except for the scary part in the night, it was the keenest time he had ever had. He was ashamed of himself for letting James frighten him even for a minute. He held his two salamanders in the bottle on his lap and he asked James if they could come up again that summer and stay even longer. James said, Sure, sure they'd have lots of good times together, but he didn't seem quite as easy to talk to as he had been driving up, or fishing the pools, or around the fire. There seemed to be something on James's mind. They drove a long time in silence, with Chris trying to touch the water dogs through the mouth of the bottle.

When they got down into the valley and on into the neat little white bungalow section of north Hollywood, James said that the person he wanted to stop off and see was his sister. James honked the horn and she came out, a flashy, good-looking girl with orangey hair.

"Hello, you," she said to James and she made a little kissing sound with her mouth.

"We've been up in the mountains camping out," James said.

"Goody for you," the girl said.

Chris saw that the hand of the girl played with James's hand and that she seemed to arch and stretch against him like a cat he had once. And where had Chris seen her face before? Oh, now he remembered, on the wall over James's bed, the one looking over her shoulder with practically no clothes on. James hadn't said anything about her being his sister then.

"Here's a kid your father ought to put in pictures," James said. "She was Miss Spokane two years ago. Isn't she a dead-ringer for Betty Grable?"

Chris wished they hadn't hurried to come down from the mountain.

"He's cute," the girl said, tossing her orange hair toward Chris. Then she looked at James in a funny way. "You must have had fun up there."

"I caught a lot of salamanders," Chris said. "Look, I've got two of them here!"

"You should have been along," James said. "Did you ever sleep in a pup tent?"

"Christ, I've slept everywhere else," the girl said. She and

James looked at each other and laughed. Chris wished they would get this over with. It had been so nice up there, just the two of them, standing in the cold, clear water looking for trout.

"You get back in the car now, I'll be right with you," James said to Chris, noticing how he was staring. "I've got something private I want to tell my sister."

"Come back again, honey," the girl said, and then she looked at James in that same way again. "When you're a little bigger."

Chris didn't like them laughing together. This wasn't like James at all, his pal Jimmy who invited him to his room over the garage and taught him boxing and fishing and how to slice spuds. Chris watched critically as James walked the girl back to her door. He put his arm on her shoulder and she brushed up against him again. Chris saw James whisper something in her ear and she flung her head back in mock anger and slapped him hard but fondly on the seat of his pants. Chris wished James would cut all this stuff out and come back to him.

On the drive through Hollywood to the Samuelses' home James said, "Say, Chris, when your parents get back, we don't have to mention this little visit to see my sister, OK?"

Chris did not exactly understand.

"It'll just be our little secret, like letting you hold the gun. OK?"

That was OK with Chris. He was sure his mother and father had secrets they never told him. He looked at his salamanders through the milk-bottle glass.

"I'll fix you up a tank for them," James said.

"And when we go back to the mountains we can catch some more," Chris said, feeling better again.

"Sure, we'll go again. We're gonna have lots of fun. Just remember now, you forget all about that little visit to see my girl—my sister."

Chris had half forgotten it in his reverie of salamanders. He wished James wouldn't keep bringing it up. He didn't want it to be so much on James's mind. "Tell me a story about how you were in the Navy and a big storm came up and the captain got washed overboard and you had to save the ship," Chris said.

James laughed. "You already know it by heart. You just about told it right now."

"Please, Jimmy."

The rest of the way home James kept Chris entertained with this wild tale of the sea. Chris listened with his eyes staring wide, living it through again. By the time they turned up the Samuelses' driveway he seemed to have forgotten everything but the fun parts of the trip and he was anxious to ask his mother and father how soon they could go camping together again.

James sat with Chris as the boy slowly talked himself on into sleep that night, talking of all the new things they had seen on the trip and all the things there were to look forward to on their next adventure. Chris was very tired and sleepy from their energetic two days and couldn't keep his eyes open to talk to James as long as he wanted to.

James turned out the light and tiptoed out.

"He's dead tired, he wore himself out up there," James said to Winnie, the maid, as he passed through the kitchen.

"I'm glad he's back safe. Good night," Winnie said. She had been with the Samuelses a long time and did not like to see the new chauffeur going so familiarly through the house.

In the morning when Chris woke up the first thing he did was to see how his salamanders were, in the bottle. One of them was floating on the surface. He was dead. His color had sort of paled out and he wasn't nearly so dark and shiny as he had been. Chris thought of them scampering alive in the mountain stream. It made him sad to see his little water dog floating lifeless in the bottle. He wondered if it had suffered very much. And whether the one still alive felt very lonely without his friend.

When Chris came down for breakfast that morning he was

surprised to hear from Winnie that his parents had come home during the night. They had not been expected until that afternoon. He hurried up to see his mother, who was having breakfast in bed. His father was in the bathroom shaving. His mother kissed him and hugged him and said he looked tired and then before Chris could tell her about the camping and the storm that came up and the salamanders and everything, she asked him in a cross, serious way if he knew where James had gone last night. With a child's innocent intuition Chris thought of the lively orange-haired girl who had slapped James in such an intimate way. But he kept silent while his mother told him why they were so angry with James. They had wired James to meet them at the station. Apparently he did not get the wire because he had left the house at nine o'clock, without permission, and had stayed out all night. They had called him from the station around one A.M. and there had been no answer. To make matters worse, when they got home by taxi they found that James had taken the town car with him. Daddy was furious. He had a special phobia about chauffeurs who used the cars at night for their own private pleasures. Sol wanted to discharge James immediately.

"Oh, please, *please* don't let him go," Chris begged. Who else was there to sleep with him in a tent and help him catch salamanders and build a tank for them to live in?

Chris's father came out of the bathroom half dressed, half shaved and very angry. James would simply have to go, that was all there was to it. He was taking advantage of his friendship with Chris. Sol was sorry Chris had formed this attachment but he could no longer allow a child's temporary sentiments to protect an employee who was obviously irresponsible.

Chris knew his father when he got stubborn mad instead of the easygoing way he usually was. It made the boy panicky. His life before James now seemed terribly pale and dull. The things James had taught him. The things James had showed him he could do. These past few months for the first time he had things to talk about with other boys.

James was called in to the breakfast room while Mr. Samuels was having his coffee. James was extremely polite and subdued. Yes, sir. No, sir. If you'll let me try to explain, sir. He explained that while the Samuelses were away he had spent so much time with Chris that he had needed an evening off for his personal wants, a haircut, some shopping and the rest. It was wrong of him to keep the car out all night, he admitted, but he had been visiting some relatives and when he suddenly realized how late it was he had thought it would be more practical to sleep over and return early in the morning. He would never, never take the car without permission again. He was devoted to the family, adored young Chris and would never risk losing the job again. James said all this very well, with a certain glibness, although with a pained expression on his face that seemed to reflect a rather intense suffering for the sins he had committed. In fact, his tone was not unlike that of a repentant sinner at confessional, in one of Mr. Samuels's movies.

Sol Samuels was a stern grand inquisitor, Mrs. Samuels was as usual softening and Chris remained silent and begged his father with his eyes.

In the end, because Mr. Samuels's defenses always crumbled before the combined efforts of his wife and son, James was allowed to remain on probation. "The slightest little act of disobedience and that is the finish, final," Mr. Samuels intoned, gathering up the crumbs of his authority. "I am only tolerating you now because you seem to have made such a hit with Christopher."

"He is a wonderful boy, sir," James said soothingly.

Later that morning Chris helped James wash the car and then James said he was ready to fix up the tank for the surviving salamander. He seemed a good deal more quiet than usual. Evidently Mr. Samuels's lecture had brought him down considerably. He didn't play and tell stories as he had before. But Chris imagined it would take him a day or two to get over the scolding. Chris was the same way.

That afternoon Mrs. Samuels took Chris to a Disney picture. James dropped them off and was told to pick them up outside the theater at five o'clock. He wasn't there when they got out and they waited patiently for fifteen minutes or so as the streets were often jammed up at that hour. At five-thirty Mrs. Samuels called home. Why, James had left shortly after four, Winnie said. He had been working on Chris's salamander tank most of the afternoon. At a quarter to six Mrs. Samuels and Chris went home by cab. A number of police cars were in front of the house. In the maid's room Winnie was thrashing on her bed having hysterics. After Mrs. Samuels's call she had gone up to Chris's room to be sure James wasn't there. It was then she noticed that Chris's little cash-register bank was gone. It was always on the night table by his bed. Then something had made Winnie go to the drawer where Mrs. Samuels kept her jewels. They were gone. Then Winnie looked through Mr. Samuels's bureau. His diamond watch was missing, and his gold cuff links, and a sapphire ring and a lot of other expensive accessories. Winnie called Mr. Samuels and he said, "The skunk. Even takes the kid's nickels and dimes and that's the fellow who's so nuts about Chris I can't even fire him." He told Winnie to look for his wallet in the back of the little drawer where he kept his links and handkerchiefs. The wallet was supposedly hidden. There was seven hundred fifty dollars in cash. Winnie ran up and looked. No, Mr. Samuels, that's gone too! And your silk monogrammed shirts and your silk robe and oh, he just took everything, *everything*. . . . Mr. Samuels told her he was calling the police immediately and how in the hell could he take all that stuff with you in the house watching him, Winnie? Winnie sobbed and stammered as if it was she who had been caught doing this terrible deed. He—he was in and out of Chris's room all afternoon fixing up that tank.

He kept going in and out to the garage to get tools and things. I never dreamed, I didn't think—Oh, Mr. Samuels, I feel as if I am going to faint. . . .

"Don't faint. Wait for the police. Tell them exactly what happened. And be sure and tell them what James looked like. That son of a bitch. I'll be home as soon as possible."

Chris went up to his room without saying anything. James had not finished fixing up the tank for the salamander as he had promised. Now the poor salamander would probably die. He knew it would die. He wished he could go back to the mountains and put his shiny green water lizard back in its home stream. It made him feel nervous having to take care of the salamander without James. It didn't seem possible that he was never going to see him again. The change hadn't quite happened for him yet. James was still his friend and chum going to take him camping.

He knew what an ordeal it would be when his father came home. "Goddamn it, now will you believe me? He was nothing but a bum, a cheap crook. I hope this will teach you not to be so goddamn trusting of everybody."

Chris didn't come down for dinner that night. He couldn't bear to hear all that from his father. He wished James had finished the salamander tank for him. It would have helped him get over it to watch the salamander swimming around the salamander tank. The salamander wasn't moving around as fast as he was before. In the morning, he bet anything, the salamander would be a paler green and floating belly up in the bottle. He hadn't even had a chance to name him and now he didn't want to name him if he was going to die. He wondered where James was this minute. He wondered how James could stand being away from him. James had liked him so much. It was that darned girl, that crummy orange-headed sister of his. Or whatever she was.

Impulsively Chris went over to James's room and looked around. Yep, her picture was still there, over his bed. Winnie

always told him he'd catch cold if he stood around after a bath
without putting his pajamas on. He wondered how it happened that someone had taken her picture before she had a
chance to put all her clothes on. Chris thought about that first
time he had come up to James's room. It was something to
have a big friend of his own. It was something. Oh James James
Jimmy how could you, how could you take my eight dollars
and seventy-five cents I was saving up? I wanted to take it
down to the bank that keeps people's money and get a regular
bankbook like my father. Chris felt like crying. His nose felt
all itchy as if he was going to cry. Who would help him get
grown up now? Who would teach him how to handle the Iggy
Gonzalezes? He felt like crying but he didn't cry because his
friend James had taught him things. Taught him how to keep
his left hand out. Taught him not to cry. It didn't matter how
many dollars James had taken. James had taught him things he
would always remember.

Next afternoon there were big black headlines in the evening papers about the capture of James. He and his gun moll,
it said, a prostitute and part-time extra girl by the name of
Tommie King, had been apprehended in Calexico, near the
Mexican border. They had ditched the gold petit-point town
car and had stolen a Ford sedan. In the paper James talked a
lot about the robbery, almost as if it was one of his sea stories.
"It was the easiest job I ever pulled. I decided the first day to
use the kid. Rich kids are dumb. They're lonely, most of them,
and that makes 'em dumb. Suckers for the big-brother pitch.
This Samuels kid was as square as they come."

And then Chris read something that scared him so he felt his
heart might choke up and stop beating. "I took the kid up in
the mountains and started to tie him up and was going down
and call his old man in Chicago and tell him I wanted fifty G's
to bring the kid back in one piece. But a storm was blowing
up and I figured I'd have a hell of a time getting to a phone
and back again. So I gave it up. When I heard I might get fired

any minute, for taking off with the car for a night, I figured I better get mine quick while I still had a foot in the door. I pulled a gag about building a fish tank for the kid to . . ."

It was a neat plan, James had boasted, and only a lousy turn of luck kept them from getting deep into Mexico and living off the fat. A hick cop, running him down for speeding, spotted his puss from an old post-office picture wanting him for some job way back. James had posed as a butler-chauffeur and driven off like this in quite a few different states.

That night Chris had a terrible dream. He was tied to a tree in the mountains and it was raining, pouring salamanders, and James and that orange-haired sister or gun moll or whatever she was were on the front seat of the gold petit-point town-car coach driving straight at him. They were looking at each other and laughing and Chris let out a scream, a long, shrill, terrible scream.

Mr. Samuels came running in. He sat on the edge of Chris's bed. "Oh Daddy, Daddy," the child cried out. Mr. Samuels hugged him. He had not held his boy to him like this in a long time. Perhaps years. He had been too busy at the studio. Chris was surprised to find himself in the arms of his father. He had avoided his father because he was so afraid of being scolded about the way he had loved and trusted James. It was too much for him, too much, and he sobbed and bawled like a baby.

Sol Samuels felt guilty. Alma had just given him a good talking-to about his neglect of Chris and how this blow to the boy never would have happened if Chris hadn't been so terribly in need of a father image.

"Chris," Mr. Samuels said, "tomorrow I'm going to take the whole day off from the studio. In the afternoon we'll go to Gilmore's and see the ball game."

Chris coughed and said all right. But he still couldn't get out of his head how nice James had been to him. The nicest anyone had ever been. If only they hadn't had so many things that James wanted, Chris tried to figure it out, maybe everything would have worked out all right. He just couldn't believe everything James said in the papers. Any more than he believed every single bit of the rescue in shark-infested waters or the triumph over Jocko Kennedy in the Yellow Dragon.

He peered in at the milk bottle standing on the deep window sill where the tank was supposed to be. The salamander was beginning to float toward the top and wasn't working its arms and legs very much. Jimmy must have liked him a little bit. To do all these things with him. Chris squeezed hard to keep his eyes dry. Jimmy must have liked him just a little bit.

# THE RELUCTANT PILGRIM

All week long young Obidiah Flagg worked the little farm his pa owned in Nottin'hamshire, but come Saturday the old man would spell him so he could go to town where he was apprenticed to a master carpenter. Scrooby, just the merest spit of a town it was, only it had two churches instead of the usual one like any respectable town, and that's how Obidiah's troubles began.

Saturday nights after he got through working his trade, he'd sit himself down at the Sign of the Golden Cock and wet his whistle with a dram of ale. Only he never had more than a farthing or two, so moist is about all he could call it. But one fatal Saturday night he met up with a young friend of his from Austerfield in the next county, who was chock full of conviviality and generosity and general high spirits because he was celebrating the end of his apprenticeship.

Obidiah and his friend from Austerfield drank enough ale to float the county of Nottin'hamshire out to sea, and came morning, they felt as if they were floating right along with it. It seemed as if they hadn't been sitting there any time at all when the church bells began pounding in their ears and the sun shining into their eyes. "Hellsfire if it ain't time to keep our appertment wi' the Lawd," said Obidiah, feeling saintly and virtuouslike, the way only a man with one too many tucked under his belt can, and somehow he managed to find the entrance to the church on the corner, though it was circling around him so fast he had to make a leap for the doorway as it went by.

He dozed through the sermon as usual, waking up just in time to groan *Amen* with the rest of the flock, and thought no more about it till the middle of the week when his pa stopped him right in the middle of his milking and said, "Son, how come ye let ye'self get mixed up with this darn fool Seprytist crowd over t' Scrooby?"

"Seprytists?" said Obidiah. "I don't know what ye're talkin' about, Pa."

"Don't ye be addin' lyin' to yer other sins," Pa said, mad as a hornet. "I know where you was Sunday mornin', worshippin' in that infarnal Seprytist church they be fixin' t' run out o' town."

Then Obidiah got to thinking how it was a mite harder to fall asleep this time than usual on account of the preacher having some blood in his veins. And all of a sudden it smacked him in the face like the tail of his cow. "Moly Hoses!" Obidiah said. "The Devil take me if I didn' go and sit me down in the wrong church!"

"He'll take ye all right if ye keep on with yer heretical ways, an' no mistake," said Pa. "The Church o' England was good enough fer Great-grandpa, for Grampy Flagg 'n' fer me, so I reckon it's good enough fer you."

Well, Obidiah didn't think much about it at the time, but his pa's warning seemed to stick in his craw. Because next Sunday he couldn't seem to keep his shoes from leading him right back into that darn Separatist church. He couldn't exactly explain why. Just plain old-fashioned orneryness, maybe.

But once he got inside he had a terrible time getting his rest. When they all closed their eyes for the opening prayer, he was drifting off pretty good when he felt a tug on his sleeve and a girl sittin' next to him was waking him up.

"You mus'n' pray so long, Brother," she was saying to Obidiah. She was a big, strapping girl who looked as if the Lord started out to make a plough horse and then changed his mind halfway through. She had a large, always-smiling round face and big snowy white teeth the Lord was so proud of he stuck them out good and proper so everybody would be sure and see them.

She kept looking at Obidiah out of the corner of her eye now and then so he couldn't help but listen to what was going on. It seemed that the regular minister, Reverend Robinson, had been locked up in the gaol with the debtors and the pickpockets. And Deacon Brewster, a curly white-haired little fellow who had taken over the service for him, was all het up about how Reverend Robinson was a religious martyr like the early Christians and Joan of Arc and folks like that. " 'Tain't right fer one man to force his way o' worshippin' God on another," he was saying, "an' 'tain't right fer the Church to be messin' around with the State nuther." The way he looked on it, all people were equal before God, and that went fer His Majesty and the whole royal caboodle.

Well, those were strange idees, Obidiah was thinking to himself. He had never given the subject much thought before, but why should the good Lord specially care what kind of a house you choose to worship Him in, long as you keep Him in mind? Same as a brewery doesn't care what the shape of the mug is you drink their brew from, as long as you drink it down.

In the midst of all that heavy thinking, Obidiah must have dozed off again without knowing it, because all of a sudden he

was awakened with a terrible start when the front door burst
open and in ran a captain of the King's Rifles with a bunch of
redcoats with their muskets ready as if they were charging into
battle instead of church. This captain ran straight down the
aisle and up to the altar, grabbed Deacon Brewster by the
collar and shouted, "I arrest ye and yer flock, in th' name of
our most dread sovereign, James the First, King of England,
Scotland, Ireland an' etcetery an' etcetery!"

And the next thing Obidiah knew, they had flung him into
the gaolhouse, just as if he were one of those Separatists himself.

"Maybe this is the Lord's way of letting our reverend finish
the service," said Deacon Brewster, and they all fell on their
knees and swore to God that all the persecuting in the world
wouldn't stop them from worshipping Him the way their conscience told them to. Well, Obidiah liked to think of himself
as a stubborn cuss, but he could see right off he was just a reed
in the wind alongside of them.

"Mule-stubbornest critters I ever see in m' life," he thought
to himself.

After prayers he was sitting there in a corner, wishing he'd
have stayed put in the King's Church where he belonged,
when that big draft horse of a girl who was sitting next to him
in church come over and started up a conversation. It turned
out her name was Silence, but if that's what she stood for,
Obidiah decided, he'd hate to meet up with a biddy named
Talkative. Why, Silence could take a simple topic of conversation like " 'Tis a nice mornin'," and work it up into a regular
two-hour discourse.

"Well," she said, "I just had to come over and tell ye how
happy it makes me to see young fellers like yourself joining
our movement of their own free will."

"I'm feared ye be barkin' up the wrong tree, gal," said
Obidiah. "I ain't no Seprytist and I ain't j'inin' nothin' that's
goin' to get me into no trouble nuther."

"Seems kind o' late to be thinkin' on that," Silence said.

"Not to my way o' lookin' on it," said Obidiah. "Ye don't catch me on the same hook twice. If I ever git out o' here, I'm stayin' away from ye Seprytists like ye had the leprosy."

"I'm sorry to hear on't," said Silence, " 'cause we be fixin' to pick up and go to Holland, where they say we can worship Him as we've a mind to. I was kind of hopin' you'd be comin' along. A carpenter'd come in handy, like as not."

"Don't be wastin' yer breath," said Obidiah. "Who wants to live among all them Dutchmen, away over on t' other side o' the channel? No siree. Goin' t' town 'n' back is travelin' enough for me."

"Well," said Silence, "if ye don't have the true religion, it's no use trying to talk it into ye."

Only just like a woman, that's exactly what she proceeded to do until finally the gaoler came to his rescue by unlocking the gates and letting out all but the leaders who had to stand trial.

"Serves ye good and proper," said Obidiah's pa when he saw him come running home with his tail between his legs. "Nex' time mebbe ye'll listen to yer elders when they try to tell ye what's good fer ye and what ain't. I never thought I'd live to see the day when the Flagg family had to live down the name o' havin' a Purytin among 'em."

"The Reverend Robinson, he says he ain't ashamed o' bein' called Purytin," said Obidiah. "He says he'll bear the scorn of his enemies on his shoulders like it was a cloth o' gold. He says there'll come a time when to call a man a Purytin won't be name-callin' at all but a word to be proud on."

"Stuff 'n' nonsense," his pa said. "Wait a spell and see if this whole Seprytist business don't blow away quicker'n leaves in November."

Obidiah hated like thunder to give in to anybody, but he had to admit his old man was talking sense. Being a stubborn, independent cuss is all fine and dandy, he thought to himself, but when you have to go clear over to Holland to keep on being one, it seemed to him that's going a mite far.

So he kept his nose to the grindstone and did extra chores after dark to make up for the terrible disgrace Pa said he had brought down on the family name, and by the time Saturday comes around, he's forgotten all about those Separatists and the pickle they had gotten him into.

Innocent as a newborn lamb, he came whistling into the shop of Mr. Hatfield, with the proud sign MASTER CABINET MAKER & JOINER over the door, and what did he see but Bobby Bailey, the freckle-faced lad from the next farm, standing in his place and wearing his apron.

"Good mornin', Mister Hatfield," said Obidiah. "A regular squire you be comin', what with two 'prentices and all."

"Two?" said Mr. Hatfield, looking down at Obidiah over his bay window as if young Flagg was apprenticed to the Devil instead of him and had sprouted a red tail and a pair of horns. "Only one apprentice here, the way I look on't. One apprentice and one ex-apprentice."

"Ex-apprentice?" Obidiah said. "Are ye foolin', Mister Hatfield? Mean to say my work ain't been satisfac'ry?"

" 'Tain't yer work, lad," said Mr. Hatfield, fitting a seat onto the legs of a chair and talking to Obidiah over his shoulder. "It's yer persuasion. Two more gentlemen canceled their orders just this mornin'. 'Don' want t' contribute to the support o' no Separatist varmint,' says they. For myself, I don't care whether ye be a Separatist or a son o' Satan himself, 'long as you know the right way to drive a peg. But if it hurt m' trade, I got no choice but to cast ye off like a split board."

It was hard for Obidiah to believe folks would let their minds grow so narrow but there he was, tarred with the same brush as Reverend Robinson, Deacon Brewster and all the rest. And everywhere he went in Scrooby he heard the same thing. "Sorry. No job for a herytic. If our Church ain't good enough for ye, nuther is our money." He had never realized before how terribly set people were in their ways. But finally when Harry Muggridge, the tavern keeper who had drunk so much of his own ale he had begun to look like one of his barrels, when even he wouldn't take Obidiah on as an extra barkeep to help with the Saturday night brawlers, Obidiah got in such a temper he just stood right out in the middle of the square and hollered, "This country's goin t' the Devil, if ye should ask me. When a body that's willin' and able can't get work 'cuz he happened to walk into the wrong church by mistake, things've come to a fine howdy-do. And if the high and mighty Church o' England is afeared of a handful o' dissenters, mebbe it ain't so high 'n' mighty after all. The Seprytists, they got some pretty strange idees, but if ye think ye c'n kill an idee by gaolin' its believers or starvin' em out, well you got another think comin'. . . ."

Obidiah had never talked like that in his life before, and while he was standing there trying to catch his breath and lower the wick on his anger, who should come up to him but Silence. "Brave words, Obidiah, and I'm proud on ye," she said. "Mos' courageous speakin' I hear in this village in quite a spell."

"Wasn't makin' no speech," said Obidiah. "Jest a-tellin' Mister Muggridge what I think on him fer bein' sech a consarned narrer-minded critter what won' even throw a poor persecuted dawg a bone of a job."

"Now, mebbe that's the way you blew it in," Silence said, "but that sure ain't the way it come out. The way it come out, that's the most law-defyin' speechifyin' heered in Scrooby since I c'n remember. The author'ties'll run ye in by nightfall for bein' one o' the ringleaders, I do believe."

"Saints 'n' sinners!" he said. "Obidiah, ye sure have the knack o' gettin' ye'self into one buster of a pickle."

"Ye do wrong t' call it a pickle," said Silence.

"And what would ye call it?"

"I call it the glorious state o' the true religion o' free men."

"The true religion o' free men is all very well and good," said Obidiah. "But it's kind o' stretchin' things t' call ye'self a free man while ye're lookin' out through the bars o' the Scrooby gaol."

Then Miss Silence turned her honest face around one way and then the other, conspiratoriallike, and whispered in his ear, "We be fixin' to go a-pilgrimizin' any day now and ye best be comin' with us. We'll be meetin' in Deacon Brewster's house tonight after lamps're out for to make the plans."

"Ain't interested," said Obidiah.

But that night he was walking the streets of Scrooby feeling lower than the underparts of a worm when the lamplighters came around to snuff out the wicks. Well, what've I got to lose, he thought to himself, my goose is cooked in Scrooby anyhow. So he sneaked up to Deacon Brewster's and set himself down. Silence greeted him with her best smile, and kept smiling to herself like a Cheshire cat.

And that's now Obidiah came to shake the dust of dear old Nottin'hamshire from his boots and set up shop in Leyden away over yonder in the land of the Dutch.

The good people of Holland left the migrant Separatists alone. They didn't seem to care if this strange little group prayed forwards, backwards or upside down, as long as it paid its way and kept the peace. Nice little country, Holland, for the Dutch, Obidiah was thinking. But it doesn't matter how fine a house is, if a man's only visiting it, your host can say, "Make y'self to home," till he's blue in the face and you still can't get yourself to feel comfortable in it. A man's got to build a country around him like a house.

That little bug of restlessness was biting all the Separatists, that and the fact that not being able to talk the Dutch lingo made supporting themselves as difficult as squeezing sweat from a stone. There were only a few hundred of them but when they went down the list of countries and the tyrants that were heading them, it seemed as if Europe wasn't big enough for Separatists and tyrants, too.

Now, there was a man among them, Will Bradford, who could read as well as any priest. He read so well he'd even set himself down to reading a book for the sport of it when he hadn't got anything better to do. And one day he happened to pick up a pamphlet that a fellow named Captain Smith had written about the New World, and especially a little corner of it called Virginia, which from the sound of it was second only to Paradise itself. In fact, Bradford told them, Captain Smith had to lean over backwards not to put it the other way 'round.

So, after the usual arguments and procrastination, it was decided to part with every article of worldly goods they could spare, pool their money and buy a couple of boats to ferry them across to that Kingdom of Heaven on Earth. John Carver, Miles Standish and Deacon Brewster had a guinea or two, but the rest of them were just plain yeomen that hadn't had any land to yeo, and humble artisans as honest as they were poor. So all together they didn't have enough gold to buy any but the poorest excuses for ships that ever shivered in a gale, and one of them was hardly bigger than the little Dutch canalboats. The *Speedwell* it was called, though the fellow that named it—Obidiah grumbled—must have been quite a jokester. And the other one was only slightly larger, just a little old wine freighter it was, with the letters spelling out *MAY-FLOWER* nearly weathered off the stern, though it didn't exactly suggest a mayflower to the nose, with the hold still smelling of stale, sour grapes.

The two boats were hardly big enough to hold more than half the group between them, so the old and the sick had to stay behind and wait until the first group got themselves settled over there. When old Reverend Robinson saw he had to be left behind, he knelt down on the dock and prayed the Lord to keep watch over them. "These pilgrims be yer bravest soldiers," he said, "a little army flying yer banner that's going forth to conquer a new world with love and peace in their hearts, instead of force and hate." Then everyone cried "Amen!" and fell to hugging and kissing, God-blessing and bawling, such tearful goings-on Obidiah hoped never to see again.

But after all that leave-taking, they had to turn back and go through it all over again because the *Speedwell,* the one Obidiah was on, turned out to be just about as seaworthy as a sieve. They were hardly out of the harbor before it began to look as if they had more ocean inside the ship than they had out. So they had to put back to shore and lay over a couple of days to mend the leak and try again. But damn if she didn't spring another leak, bigger than the first, and Obidiah thought his back would break from helping to pump her out till they made it to shore.

Obidiah figured those forty souls on the *Speedwell* would be running out of enthusiasm for Virginia by now and content to wait behind with the old folks and the sick ones. But those pilgrims who piled off the *Speedwell* couldn't wait to join the others on the *Mayflower,* till that old scow looked as if she was going under right there in the harbor.

"No thank ye," said Obidiah, when he was invited to come aboard. "Sometime I get to wonderin' if I wasn't a mite crazy to leave home in the fust place. But I'd a sight ruther go on livin' here in Holland—least it's got *land* in it, and that's more'n ye're likely to see in that plaguey tub o' yourn."

Then John Carver spoke up in his deep organ voice, "This is just the Lord's way of testing us to see if we be strong enough to go out into the wilderness in His name and build a new world." And then he fixed his fiery eyes on Obidiah and said, "For those who've got the faith and strength of spirit, all aboard. For those that haven't, all ashore."

"It ain't so much strength o' spirit I be lackin'," said Obidiah. "It's strength o' stomach. I was feelin' the seasickness afore we even left the harbor. There ain't a sea on the globe my spirit don't hanker to sail, if my stomach could be left behind."

"Let this be a free assembly of free worshippers," said John Carver. "May your conscience be your guide."

Silence was waiting right behind him, and as Obidiah stood there trying to make up his mind, she didn't say anything, but two big tears fell from her eyes and went sliding down her rosy cheeks.

"Reckon that trip'll be trouble enough, without havin' no woman on my neck," Obidiah muttered, and started to turn away. Just then the skipper of the *Mayflower,* Captain Jones, came up and tapped him on the shoulder. "I hear ye be a carpenterin' man," he said. "Would ye mind comin' aboard a minute to tighten a beam supportin' the main deck that's worked itself loose?"

So Obidiah carried his tools into the ship and sweated and grunted the beam back into place again. But when Captain Jones was satisfied the job was done, it took a little time for Obidiah to get away from Silence, who still hadn't given up trying to talk him into coming along.

"Fer the last time, no!" he said when all of sudden he looked out the porthole. "Cap'n, Cap'n, there's been a terrible mistake," he hollered. "You forgot t' leave me off."

"Well, I swan!" said the captain. "I thought ye went ashore when ye got the job done."

"And if it ain't o' been for a woman's gab, so I would," said Obidiah. "But since I didn't, ye had better put her about, becuz I ain't a-goin' with ye."

"That seems to be a matter of opinion," said Captain Jones, quietly smiling down his beard. "Looks to me like you be, fer a fac'."

Then John Carver stepped forward. "Since this be the exodus of free men searching for a place to live and worship as they please, seems like a bad omen to begin the voyage by forcing a man to come with us against his will."

"I don't know much about omens and sech," said Captain Jones. "Tides 'n' currents is my business. I can think o' worse things 'n startin' a voyage on a bad omen. Startin' it wi' the tides ag'in ye, fer instance. And that's the way it'll be if we take this young feller back."

"Nevertheless," said John Carver, "our duty is clear. Even if it means waiting over till the morrow."

Well, Obidiah wasn't a superstitious fellow, but he couldn't help thinking how maybe the Lord meant for him to go along, on account of their needing a carpenter perhaps, or because they had so many pious, heaven-minded souls aboard, the Lord figured it might not be a bad idee to send a likker-drinking, cussword-using critter along with them so they could see how far they had come along the road to the Pearly Gates. "Well, 'long as I'm aboard," Obidiah shrugged, "I reckon I might as well take m' chances wi' the rest o' ye."

"Praise the Lord!" said Silence. "I knew His voice would speak through ye afore it was too late."

"He spoke through me *after* it was too late," Obidiah protested. "An' that's the only reason I'm aboard."

"Who are we to question the ways of the Lord?" said Silence, smiling that smile that brought sunlight to the cold, dark places of the old scow.

If John Carver had put his offer to Obidiah the morning after the first night, young Flagg would have jumped at the chance to go ashore. The whole flock of them, women, children and all, had to sleep in one big room with sand on the floor and a ceiling that was just high enough to give your head a good crack when you tried to straighten up. And as for ventilation, when Obidiah lay on his back in the wooden bunk with the cabin so black he couldn't see his hand in front of his nose, he said to himself, "Obidiah, now ye know what it feels like t' be lyin' in yer coffin six feet under the earth." And the next morning when they barely managed to stagger up to the deck, the sea rose up beneath them until as they looked across the bow, they seemed to be flying up into the angry sky, only to come crashing down into the valley between those giant waves.

They were a sick-looking bunch of believers that day, and the next night even the seamen had fear in their eyes, though rougher, fiercer-looking brutes Obidiah had never seen. And in language that made Silence and the other maids put their hands to their ears, they grumbled and groused that it made no sense to go any farther with the sea a raging hell. Aye, they even muttered threats as to how they'd deal with Cap'n Jones if he didn't see eye to eye with them and turn his leaky tub of a ship around.

A toss of the ship sent Obidiah rolling from his bunk and when he landed on his arm and was sure it was broken, he was so mad he hollered out before he knew what he was saying, "God damn us all to hell if I don't think them tars be right. We wuz all a pack o' blasted idiots to trust our lives to this rotten ol' scow in the fust place. But we be even bigger fools if we don' give up this infernal wild-goose chase afore it's too late."

Then John Carver spoke up and his voice was as deep and strong as the roar of the waves. "Obidiah," he said, "mind your tongue. We're not afraid to live and we're not afraid to die. The only thing we be afraid of is turning back, 'cause that would be a confession of weakness. And the Lord wants nothing but strong men for to build a New World."

"But all we got lef' fer victuals is the stale bread and salt beef we've been sharin' with the maggots," said Obidiah. "And the damned boat is groanin' like it wants to split in two."

"Our faith will hold it together," John Carver said.

"I'm a carpenter," said Obidiah. "An' I never j'ined two pieces o' wood wi' faith yet. Takes pegs an' screws, it does."

"The Lord doesn't need such tools," John Carver said.

"But mebbe we're out to sea so fur the Lord can't see

us," Obidiah argued. "Mebbe He figgers He's got enough to do just watchin' over the land, an' the sea c'n go to the Devil."

"Obidiah Flagg," said John Carver, in his steely voice, "that comes mighty close to heresy."

"Well, a man's got a right to his own opinion," Obidiah talked back. "And I say the New World is about as far off as m' marriage to Silence. And ye know how far that be."

"Obidiah Flagg," John Carver said, pointing a long, bony finger at his head, "as the elected leader of this expedition, I find you guilty of blaspheming and undermining confidence." He turned to the group's only military man. "Mister Standish, put this man in the brig."

So there he was, cooped up in the tiny brig, with his chin cracking against his knees every time another wave crashed against the hull. He was cursing the day he ever wandered into that little church of theirs back in Scrooby, and thinking how nice it would feel to be back in Nottin'hamshire in the field with his pa, when all of a sudden the sea started falling away from under them until he thought they were going to hit the bottom for sure. But just as suddenly the water came up to meet them again, and the ship shuddered in its tracks like a butchered cow, and there was a terrible sound like lightning, only it was coming from inside the ship, right over Obidiah's head and he was resigned that the end had come at last. And while he was squatting there with his eyes closed waiting for Judgment Day, Captain Standish came running with a lamp in his hand and started to set him free.

"So it's every man for himself?"

"No," said Standish, "the main beam is sprung again. The upper deck's nigh cavin' into our quarters. An' ye're the only man among us who c'n fix it."

So Obidiah got out his lever, his mallet and his big brace, and went to work on the beam. When the tossing of the boat made him hit his thumb a mean lick with the mallet, he cried out in pain, "Hellsfire!"

"Mind your blaspheming," warned John Carver, and Deacon Brewster and Will Bradford and all the others watching Obidiah work nodded in agreement.

When he got the beam set, Obidiah told them all to put their shoulders to it and push. "Heave, goddammit, heave!" he shouted, and John Carver looked up again. "I said mind your blaspheming. Ye be out of the brig on good behavior. I don't want to have to warn ye again."

"Well, gol darn it," said Obidiah, "I can't work without cussin'. Kind o' helps me to bear down on what I'm a-doin'. So it's up to ye to decide whether to let me go on fixin' this damn ship or see us all plunge to hell."

John Carver kind of hesitated a minute, looking to Deacon Brewster for advice. Then he said quietlike so that maybe God wouldn't be able to hear him, "Go on with yer fixin'."

So Obidiah went on cussing and working, working and cussing, and pretty soon he got the blasted beam back in place again. Then Captain Jones came down and asked if he would take a "look-see at the middle mast that's a-splitting at the base." Well, it wasn't exactly the job Obidiah was hankering for but there didn't seem any way of getting out of it, so he climbed to the outer deck. Soon as he set his foot outside, his legs blew up over his head like a suit of long underwear hung on a line on a windy day. He had all he could do to hold onto the rigging, to keep from flying off into the foaming sea. So Captain Jones had a couple of tars lash Obidiah to the mast while he mended it as best he could. But just when they were untying him a big wave came over the side that seemed to be looking for Obidiah in particular. Before he knew it, he was getting the first bath he had had since he left Holland, only the tub he was taking it in was a mite too big for comfort. But he reckoned he must be too ornery to die, because the next wave slapped him right against the side of the ship and he grabbed hold of the topsail halyard that was hanging down and rode along that way for a while with his head mostly under water till they fished him out with a boat hook.

He lay there on deck, with a bellyful of seawater, looking deader than a mackerel three days on the dock. And Deacon Brewster was all ready to give him the proper send-off for his trip to the Heavenly Gates. And way off in the distance some-whereas he could hear them saying the nice things they only say about you after you're gone. But as he was lying there a little voice inside him began to tell him what a damnfool time this would be to quit the journey just when he was getting kind of interested to see how it would come out. And then he knew he was out of his head for fair, because he got the crazy notion that if he didn't keep on living, this old ship of freedom would go to the bottom.

So right in the middle of the prayer Deacon Brewster was saying over him, he suddenly managed to sit up and say, "Hellsfire, will one o' ye stop prayin' for my departed soul long enough t' help a man up to his feet?"

"Hallelujah! Our Lord's performed a miracle and brought him back to us!" he heard a familiar voice cry out, and when he opened his eyes there were Silence's buck-teeth smiling down on him and her big, warm hands stroking his hair.

"Miracle my foot," Obidiah said. "Jes' took me a minute or two t' git me wind back, is all."

"Hallelujah!" Silence said again, rubbing her warmth back into his hands. "He's coming back to his old self again!"

"Which still leaves plenty of room for improvement," said John Carver, to which Deacon Brewster and Will Bradford and Miles Standish all solemnly agreed, though Captain Jones had to remind them to save their lectures for later, since right now, improvement or no improvement, they needed to dry off their carpenter and get him working to keep the old *Mayflower* rightside up.

All through the night the storm kept raging, but early next morning it let up a bit and John Carver called the weary flock together. Dignified and seriouslike, he said, "From the look of things, seaweed 'n' birds 'n' such, we're near a landing at last. But Captain Jones is now of a mind that we're a way off our course for Virginia. That means the Virginia charter that's supposed to govern us won't hold good any more. So Deacon Brewster and Will Bradford and I have taken the liberty of writing up our own. Subject to the approval, of course, of all here on board."

John Carver took a deep breath and began to read:

*"In the name of God, amen, we whose names are underwritten, the loyal subjects of our dread sovereign lord King James, etcetery and etcetery, having undertaken for the glory of God, and advancement of the Christian faith, and the honor of our King and country, a voyage to plant the first colony in the northern parts of Virginia, do by these presents, solemnly and mutually in the presence of God and one another, covenant and combine ourselves together into a civil body politic, for our better ordering and preservation, and further-ance of the ends aforesaid; and by virtue hereof do enact, constitute, and frame such just and equal laws, ordinances, acts, constitutions, and offices, from time to time, as shall be thought most meet and covenient for the general good of the colony; unto which we promise all due submission and obedience. In witness whereof we have here-unto subscribed our names at Cape Cod the eleventh of November.* Anno Domini, *1620.*"

Some spoke right up and said it was the most liberty-loving document in the history of Englishmen and were all for sign-ing it on the spot. Others wanted to hold off a bit and ask the meaning of this line or that.

"Moly Hoses!" said Obidiah when he got it digested. "What that's sayin' is that even though we still be subjec's o' the King, we got the right to make our own laws!"

"Aye, that it does," John Carver agreed, "and since it be our faith that all men are equal before God, why shouldn' it follow that all men be equal one with another?"

"Well, I dunno now," Obidiah said. "I never heered o' such a thing afore."

"There has to be a first time for everything," John Carver said.

"I'm not so sure," Obidiah objected. "Makin' our own laws. Sounds kind o' dangerous t' me. If we ain't got no royal commands, what's to stop one man from doin' jest as he pleases, murderin' us in our beds f' instance, or stealin' our land?"

"The rest of us," John Carver said, "the civil body politic, as it says right here in black and white."

"I dunno," Obidiah shook his head. "Guess there's no use my signin' it if I can't get m'self t' believin' in it. Don't see how ye c'n expect common ordinary folks like us to know how to rule each other."

"Don't say 'each other,' " John Carver said. "Say *ourselves.*"

"Seems like an awful lot to ask o' simple folk," said Obidiah.

Just then a great shout of joy broke over the ship, "Land! Land ho!" and everyone fell to hugging and kissing and laughing the way they thought they had forgotten how, and the sick jumped up out of their bunks and danced around, and folks that the voyage had made enemies out of got to smiling at each other and shaking hands and slapping each other on the back. And all of a sudden Obidiah got the spirit and ran up to John Carver and shouted, "Gimme that darn fool paper, Gov'nor, I'll sign 'er all right. Probably the damnfoolest notion that was ever thunk up, but I guess it won' hurt to give 'er a try."

Then he ran up on deck and sure enough, laying dead ahead, was the prettiest little bay he had ever seen, calm as beer in a barrel, with a narrow stretch of cape curving out to them as if it were the arm of the New World beckoning them to shore. And with all the husbands and wives standing there side by side, Silence ran up to Obidiah so happy she actually looked kind of pretty, and she said, "Obidiah, my betrothed, isn't that a joyful sight?"

"Betrothed?" said Obidiah. "That be no way for a decent gal to joke."

"Why, Obidiah," she said, "don't tell me you fergot your promise."

"Promise! What kind o' promise? I don't 'member no promise . . ."

"Why you mos' certainly did! I heard you with my own ears. Tellin' Gov'nor Carver our marriage 'd have to wait till we reached the New World."

"Never said no sech thing," said Obidiah.

"Oh, what's to become o' me?" she cried, and he could see the wet come to her eyes. "The shame of it, to be publicly spoken for in front of all them witnesses."

Then Obidiah thought back on it, as hard as he could, and he kind of remembered saying something to Gov'nor Carver about Silence in the heat of anger, but it wasn't exactly how she took it—the New World is about as far off as m' marriage to Silence, is how he recollected it.

But by this time Silence was bawling good and loud, and everybody was listening. "I suppose ye want to wait for one o' them nekkid little heathen gals, like John Smith did," she blubbered, and tears the size of sparrow eggs slid down her apple cheeks.

Obidiah was silent. There was no answer for that kind of an argument. And as he looked across the bay at the green coast waiting for them to settle it, he started thinking to himself, An empty log cabin'll be a lonely thing t' come home t' these cold winter nights. After a back-breakin' day in the field, a woman in th' doorway 'twill be a warmin' sight, like the fire blazin' in th' fireplace an' the steamin' bowl o' porridge hangin' over it. An' Silence may not be the purtiest gal in the world, nor the fanciest in her ways nuther, but she looks like she's built to the proportions o' this country, large 'n' sturdy 'n' fertile 'n' formidable to approach but with a lovin' nature underneath, like the snow out yonder that's a-coverin' the rich yieldin' earth.

So he took Silence's hand and put it in his, his head all full of the things they had been through. Only something told him this wasn't the end of all their troubles neither, it was just the beginning. For they say some men are born to trouble and some others inherit it. Well, if trouble was money, Obidiah Flagg would be a millionaire three times over, once for the trouble that was in him by nature and twice for the trouble he'd find on the way. Seems like every time freedom's in a scrap, the harder he'd try to stay out of it, the harder he'd fall kerplunk into the middle of it. And in case you haven't noticed, freedom and trouble grow close together on the same branch, just like roses and thorns. If you want the one, you've got to take your chances of pricking your fingers on the other.

"Silence," said Obidiah, as he lifted her out of the shallows and carried her ashore, "I'm mighty proud o' my foresight in choosin' to j'in the Pilgrims and come to Americy, if I do say so m'self."

"Choosin'!" Silence exclaimed. "Why, Obidiah Flagg, if I hadn't a-coaxed ye . . ."

"Coaxed!" said Obidiah. "Jest like a woman, ain't got no more memory'n a rabbit." Then he set her down easy on that old Plymouth Rock.

# COUNTER–INTELLIGENCE IN MEXICO CITY

■  ■  ■

"How much farther is it?" asked the younger one. His name was Chucho and he had never been to Mexico City before.

"Just a little ways now," said the older man. His name was Lupe and in his village he was considered widely traveled because he had been to the city several times before. "Just over the next hill. We will be there well before dark."

So they walked on, some fifteen miles farther. Their feet had almost worn through their ancient sandals, and their bodies were nearly bent in two under the load of melons they bore upon their backs. The melons were carried in enormous baskets lashed with thick ropes that looped around the belly of the baskets and then across a patch of sweat-stained leather on their foreheads.

Like other beasts of burden, they had fallen into a slow but rhythmic pace. By the time the sun was directly above them they had begun to grow weary, but after stopping by the side of the road to eat the tortillas and cold beans their women had

■

prepared for them in the village that morning, they had felt stronger. When they were less than ten miles from the capital, they quickened their pace a little so as to reach the city before dark. They were weary no longer. They were beyond weariness. Instead they moved in a kind of sleepwalking monotony, neither talking nor thinking.

It was not until they reached the ridge and looked down into the valley where the city awaited them that they became men again.

*"Por Dios!"* said Chucho. Through his mind passed many other words but he was not able to say the things he thought about the incredible geometric design of streets and buildings that stretched for miles below him.

"Wait until you are in it," said Lupe, smiling with the pride that seasoned tourists always take in guiding first-timers. "Wait until you see the long cars that roll along without horses to pull them. And the mountains of steel and glass they have built themselves to live in."

The road was downhill now and their worn-sandaled feet followed each other in more rapid succession. In less than two hours they were in the city. The streets were crowded with people who all seemed to be wearing twice as many clothes as they needed and who rushed along in a terrible hurry as if all of them had just been told that their mothers were dying.

The buildings were so high that Chucho, with the melons preventing him from standing straight, could not lift his eyes to see the tops of them. Ahead of him was a new one half completed, a towering skeleton of steel that rose twenty stories into the sky.

"And people are going to live in that?" said Chucho. "How do they manage to climb up into their homes?"

"I don't know," said Lupe. "That is something I have often wondered at. Maybe with a rope."

Though they had penetrated far into the city they did not stop to rest and set their loads down so they could straighten up for a moment. Perhaps they feared lest such weakness would lead them to abandon their bodies to exhaustion and they would fall unconscious on the pavement. Or, more likely, it did not enter their heads to stop until they reached their destination. So they kept on until they reached the *mercado público*. Chucho had seen the open market in Cuernavaca that stretched through half a dozen narrow streets, but this market was like a great city in itself. Hundreds of farmers from Amecameca and Toluca and Texcoco were lying asleep in back of their stands with their wives and half a dozen children, waiting for their customers to come in the morning.

Chucho and Lupe found a place to set down their loads, lay their heads among the melons, pulled their straw hats over their eyes and snored until the first rays of the sun woke them in the morning.

In the sunlight the place swarmed with children, flies and people of the city who had come to buy. Lupe and Chucho squatted all day in back of their melons, laughing to one another at the funny way the people of the city looked and talked. Their own speech, the Nahuatal language of the Aztecs that had come down to them through the years, tinkled along like the flow of a brook. They had heard Spanish spoken before, but they could not understand it. It sounded to them as if it were being spoken by someone who was very nervous and always stuttering.

The sun was just beginning to slip behind the man-made mountains when Chucho and Lupe sold their last melon. In the little pouch around Lupe's neck was more money than he had ever seen at one time in his life, forty-four hundred and two pesos and seventy centavos. In the pouch was also a strange shiny coin that neither Chucho nor Lupe had ever seen before. It had been given to them by a fat man with a very red face although he had not wanted to buy the melons which Chucho and Lupe had offered him.

"I just wanna get a picture of ya if you'll just hold still a second," he had said in a language which was neither as musical as Nahuatal nor as soft as Spanish.

A sophisticated Indian from Xochimilco in the next booth who spoke Spanish with a Nahuatal accent and was so worldly that he could cry out at the *gringos,* "Hey, Meester, 'allo, meester," explained the strange coin to Chucho and Lupe.

"The gods are smiling at you today," he said. "They have given you a *gringo tostón."*

"What is it worth in real money?" asked Lupe.

"In our money, at least *cien pesos.* Maybe more."

Lupe looked at the coin slyly. According to their custom, the forty-four hundred and two pesos were to be shared among the farmers in the village who had planted and harvested the melons together. But the *gringo* who had pointed his little black box with the bulging glass eye at them had not photographed all the villagers together. Chucho and Lupe alone had taken the risk in case the foreigner's little box had turned out to be a deadly weapon. So by every right the *gringo tostón* was theirs and theirs alone.

"I'll tell you what we'll do, *compañero,"* said Lupe, placing a conspiratorial arm around Chucho's shoulder and feeling a little drunk already with the power of the strange coin in his hand. "We will take this coin and place it on the bar of the nearest *cantina.* It has been a fine day and we have sold all our melons and now we will celebrate our good fortune. Then we will get a good night's sleep on a bench in the park and start back to our village in the morning."

The *cantina* was small and dark and crowded and reeked with the smell of stale clothing, bad breath and beverages whose odors were as strong as their effects. In the middle of the room the jukebox was playing a *ranchero* song at the top of its mechanical lungs. Half of the customers were helping the record along by singing in voices more voluminous than harmonious. The rest of the clientele was discussing serious matters in voices that had to be raised to ear-splitting shouts to be heard above the din. The name of the *cantina* was La Puerta del Sol, the gateway to the sun, and Lupe and Chucho were very happy to be there.

Near them at the bar was a heavy-set, ox-faced fellow who wore with considerable pride if not with any particular grace the uniform of the *policía* of Mexico City. His name was Rodolfo Gonzales and he was already on his third double *tequila añejo*. Officer Gonzales, an honest and conscientious defender of the law, nine times out of ten, was trying to drown his conscience. The day before, while he was on his beat directing traffic, he had apprehended a *norteamericano* driving a Mexican car without a license. The fine for this, Rodolfo had pointed out, was five hundred pesos. But the *americano* did not have that many pesos. He only had two hundred. And he was in such a hurry that he did not have time to accompany Rodolfo to the police station as Rodolfo requested. Would the officer be kind enough to take the two hundred and deposit it in the police station for him? the *gringo* had asked. After some persuasion, Officer Gonzales had agreed. And now a terrible thing had happened. Officer Gonzales had slipped the bills into his pocket and forgotten all about them. Now it was too late to rectify this lapse of memory and so there seemed nothing for him to do but invest the pesos in the kind of peace and forgetfulness that may be found at the bottom of a glass of *tequila añejo*.

This was not the only thing that occupied the mind of Officer Gonzales. Although it did not show in his face, the twin rats of ambition and envy were gnawing in his brain. Only that day his friend Armando García had been promoted from the rank of ordinary policeman to that of *sargento*. And all because Armando had caught two Arabs in a bar who turned out to be members of a terrorist ring. Rodolfo had joined the force several years before Armando and it hardly seemed just for him to go on wasting his talents directing traffic while his

friend Armando was promoted above him. He consoled himself with another *tequila*. He did not like to flatter himself but
he was a much more capable protector of the peace than his
friend Armando García. If only an opportunity like Armando's
would fall into his hands!

Further down the bar Chucho's and Lupe's *gringo tostón* had
dwindled to a fifth its original value. The other four-fifths had
been changed into a currency more easily negotiable if one
were negotiating as Chucho and Lupe were, with a glass in one
hand and a slice of *limón* in the other. Lupe and Chucho were
not drunk. If they were leaning on one another at a rather
precarious angle it was simply an expression of the deep camaraderie that one Indian feels for another after accompanying
him on a journey of many miles and sharing with him the sense
of accomplishment one gets from selling all his melons at city
prices.

They were discussing at this moment a subject of considerable importance, an issue, in fact, that was beginning to divide
their entire village. Was it true that Angel Chavez had had his
way with the supposedly virtuous Elena Cruz?

"Of course it is true," Chucho insisted. "Only a fool would
doubt it. In another eight months Elena Cruz will be fat as a
sow before slaughter, you wait and see."

"But what makes you so sure?" said Lupe, who was far more
indignant about this case than he usually was about such
things, perhaps because it was public knowledge in the village
that Lupe could never take his eyes off Elena, and that she had
slapped his face when he pinched her a little too intimately
during the last *fiesta*. "I suppose you were there when it happened? I suppose you saw it with your own eyes?"

"No, I did not see it with my own eyes," Chucho admitted.
"But it was described to me by Pablo Rojas who got it from
Juan Montoya who heard it from Jesus Tavarez whose aunt
Josefina does claim to have seen it with her own eyes."

Officer Gonzales did not let Chucho and Lupe know that he

was observing them, for that is not the way a smart detective works, but he was edging toward them along the bar. He was unable to speak Arabic but at least he was clever enough to try and catch a word here or there. And he was quite sure he had heard these two foreigners mention something about Salina Cruz. Salina Cruz was a little port on the west coast and he had been saying to his friend Armando García just the other day, "If those Arabs try to blow up an Israeli freighter, it will be either Mazatlán or Salina Cruz."

*Sargento* Armando García. Well, if these two little fellows turned out to be what he thought they were, he might get his promotion too. He ordered another drink and rolled the title around on his tongue. *Sargento Rodolfo Gonzales.* It sounded pretty good. "Have another drink, *Sargento?*" he said to himself. "Thank you, don't mind if I do. It's nice to have a chance to talk with you fellows with no stripes on your sleeves. Keeps me in touch with what the rank-and-file are thinking."

He bit into another *limón* to cool the flames of the *tequila* that leaped in his chest. *And once I'm a* sargento, *what's to stop me from becoming a lieutenant? Just get in with the right people and do my job well.*

He bit into another lemon. *Teniente Rodolfo Gonzales.* That would give *Sargento* Armando García something to worry about. "Well, García, I've been going over your record. I'm frank to tell you I'm disappointed in you. Being a *sargento* doesn't give you the right to loaf, you know. And I've been hearing things about *mordita.* As your old friend, but now your superior officer, I'm giving you a little warning to watch your step."

He had another drink and edged closer to his suspects. He couldn't understand a thing they were saying but they were still talking about Salina Cruz.

"I don't care what she told you when you tried to pinch her at the *fiesta,*" Chucho was saying. "Elena Cruz is not the innocent little flower she pretends to be."

"If you're saying I'm not as good a man as Angel Chavez," said Lupe, who was tottering precariously between conviviality and belligerence, "come out and say it to my face so we know where we stand."

*And once I'm a captain,* Officer Gonzales was thinking as he stared into his empty glass, *what is to prevent me from becoming Chief of Police? All I need to do is build up a following, promise to make the sergeants lieutenants and the lieutenants captains . . .*

The bartender filled his glass again. Rodolfo picked it up and smiled. *Among the notables at the president's palace for the Grito last night was Mexico's popular chief of police Gonzales . . .*

"I am not saying that you are not as much of a man as Angel Chavez," Chucho said tactfully, if somewhat inarticulately. "I am merely saying that you were more inclined to respect Elena Cruz's maidenhood than certain others I could mention."

*And once I am chief of police,* thought Officer Gonzales as he put his glass down, *then I am somebody. My hat is in the ring. I might run for governor. Or even presidente. After all, look at Cardenas and Camacho. They were just poor Indians who did not have even as much of a start as I have.*

Officer–Sergeant–Lieutenant–Captain–Chief-of-Police–Governor–President Gonzales had one more drink, straightened his uniform and staggered up to Chucho and Lupe with the dignity the moment demanded of him.

"In the name of the Republic of Mexico, I hereby place you under arrest," he said. Then with Chucho in one hand and Lupe in the other he marched them out of the Puerta del Sol.

That night Chucho and Lupe found themselves cooped up in a small damp cell in the city jail.

"I wonder what we have done to be treated like this?" said Chucho.

"Perhaps there is some law against speaking Nahuatal in the city of Mexico," suggested Lupe, who knew more about the ways of the world than his younger friend.

That night three unfriendly guards, two in uniform and one

skinny fellow with a skinny moustache and a skinny civilian suit came to Chucho's and Lupe's cell. The one in street clothes asked them if they were Arab terrorists. When the two melon-sellers shook their heads, because they did not understand the question, the skinny one nodded to the two burly uniforms, who began beating them, unemotionally, as if they were beating stubborn burros. Lupe and Chucho were too confused to cry out. They accepted the physical abuse just as the burros do—as part of the timeless process of life and death that begins with pain and ends in pain.

Finally, when the thin one and his two hard-bellied assistants could not beat a satisfactory answer out of Lupe and Chucho, they gave up in disgust and slammed the metal door behind them. Chucho and Lupe attended each other's cuts and bruises as best they could. Lupe had lost one of his front teeth. He didn't have too many to begin with, and it had been one of his favorites. Chucho found it for him on the stone floor of the cell, wiped the blood off it and handed it back to his companion. "Perhaps the *bruja* can put it back for you," Chucho tried to console him.

"If we ever get home," Lupe said. "If we ever get out of this crazy house."

"Is it possible that we are not allowed to sell our melons in the city without permission?" Chucho asked. His head was aching and a purple lump was swelling over his left eye where the biggest of the two uniforms had hit him and then hit him again with his huge right fist.

Lupe nodded, with his hand over his hurt mouth. "In the city, anything is possible. In our village we live by the old laws. We do not have to write them down. Everybody knows them. But the city is full of people who are strangers to each other, so they can keep changing the laws as they please."

Young Chucho's head was pounding in confusion. "To-night let us pray to our Lord Tepoztteco that they make a new law that will let us go home."

But the following night the skinny man in the skinny grey suit returned with the two brutes in uniform. Again the little plainclothesman urged Lupe and Chucho to confess the obvious, that they were Arab terrorists whose plans to sabotage an Israeli freighter had been overheard by Officer Gonzales. And when Lupe and Chucho shook their heads, not so much in denial as in inability to understand what these city devils were talking about, the beatings were even worse than the night before. Another tooth was gone from Lupe's modest but precious collection, and after the angry trio slammed the iron door behind them, Chucho was so dizzy he could not stand up. He sat on the hard bunk holding his swollen head and praying to Lord Tepotzteco louder than he had ever prayed before.

"Lupe, maybe they are going to kill us," Chucho moaned. "Maybe there is a new law in the city that they kill people from the mountains who come down to sell their melons in the public market of the capital."

Feeling the bloody spaces where his teeth had been, Lupe said nothing because he did not want to admit how little he knew about the ways of the *capitalinos* and that he knew no more than Chucho did as to what was going to happen next.

On their third night in this damp and smelly jail, Lupe and Chucho expected another visit from the skinny grey suit and the two sloppy uniforms, but to their surprise nobody came except an old guard who brought them a bowl of watery *tortilla* soup. By this time they had stopped asking questions of each other. They were like burros who endured beatings and indignities each day as if that were what they were born for.

On the morning of the fourth day two guards who did not beat them, but only shoved them along, brought Chucho and Lupe to an office where a spruced-up and eager Officer Gonzales was waiting to bring his spy ring before the police court. There he delivered the speech that he had rehearsed before the mirror in his room, complete with dramatic gestures and repeated references to Father Hidalgo, Benito Juarez and the Great Revolution of 1910.

"But these look like nothing more than a couple of little Indians from the mountains," said the judge, after allowing Gonzales to reach his eloquent peroration.

"That may be the way they are disguised, Your Honor," said Officer Gonzales. "But they didn't fool me for a minute. They were talking Arab and making plans to blow up a Jewish ship in Salina Cruz."

The judge frowned, and asked the prosecutor if a representative of one of the Arab embassies could be called as a witness to clarify the situation. But one was not so easily available. While Lupe and Chucho prayed and simply existed in their small cell, the judge was told that none of the Arab entities in the capital, neither Egypt nor Saudi Arabia nor even Yemen and Kuwait would send anyone to intercede for or against Lupe and Chucho. Apparently they all reasoned that if indeed the Mexican authorities had apprehended a pair of Arab agents, it would be wiser for them not to get involved. And if they should prove not to be Arab agents, or even Arabs, then it was clearly none of their business.

At the end of the week, when Lupe and Chucho were sick, but literally sick of tepid *tortilla* soup, and beginning to wonder if the fates had sentenced them to life imprisonment in this terrible place, they were suddenly brought back to the court again. Since no Arab official would come forward, the judge had subpoenaed a refugee from Iran who was a lecturer on Moslem culture at the University of Mexico.

While Officer Gonzales waited expectantly, the bearded Arab professor appeared. When he gave Lupe and Chucho the traditional Islamic greeting, they stared at him blankly. When he proceeded to ask them a series of questions in Arabic, they stared at him in total confusion. "Where does he come from?" they asked each other. It sounded neither Spanish nor *gringo*. "Maybe he speaks Mayan or Zapotecan," Lupe said. They had heard these languages from the south were very different from their own.

"Your Honor," said the expert on Islam from the university, "I have no idea what they are saying, but most definitely they are not speaking Arabic."

The judge gave Officer Gonzales a look and sent for an interpreter from the Instituto del Indios. The Indian interpreter questioned Lupe and Chucho in Mayan, Zapotecan, Tarascan, Mixtecan, and finally in Nahuatal.

"They are farmers from a village in the *municipio* of Tepotzlan," the interpreter explained. "I am happy to say that in the remote mountain villages of Morelos, Nahuatal is still a living language."

"Let them go free," the judge announced. "And Officer Gonzales, you will stand trial for false arrest."

When Chucho and Lupe reached their village that evening after their long climb home, they went immediately to the hut of Emilio Lopez, the *mayordomo* of their *barrio,* to report what had happened.

"We have sold all our melons, but alas we have nothing to show for it," Lupe said. "When we asked for the money they took from us in the jail, we were told their records showed we had no pesos in our pockets when the *policía* brought us in. Alas, it is not safe for any of us to go down into the city of Mexico ever again. It seems they have declared war on us. As soon as they hear us talking our own language, they drag us off to jail, beat us and rob us."

That same evening, after a five-minute trial, Officer Gonzales paced the dark and lonely streets of Villa Obregón, the quiet suburb to which he had been exiled. With the horselaugh of *Sargento* García still ringing in his ears, he was soberly meditating upon the evils of *tequila* and the injustice of the world.

# THE
# BARRACUDAS

The trim, sound, fifty-footer *Lorelei* was holding her own in the churning waters of the Gulf. Rolling from trough to trough, she creaked and groaned and refused to come apart at the seams. Gerald Millinder was watching his wife and the skipper. They're actually enjoying the storm, he was thinking. He tried not to seem alarmed.

Captain Alan Banks looked back over his shoulder to reassure him from the wheel. "Don't worry, sir, she's not splittin' in two. She's plenty of boat. I'll sneak her into the Marquesas Keys before sundown."

The skipper was lank and hard and the skin was weathered tight over the strong sculpturing of his face. Every move he made was capable, confident, almost cocky. Millinder, with his rather delicate face and a bicycle-tire of fat at the belt-line, was ready to hate him for his leanness and his grinning disregard— if not relish—of danger.

"Isn't Al wonderful?" Madge said.

Instead of answering, Millinder tried to smile for his wife. She was a strong, handsome woman of thirty who had had three children and eight demanding but not really unhappy years with Gerald. These she carried lightly, for she still bore a startling resemblance to the Wellesley lacrosse player who had made a lasting impression on some Smith and Barnard teams, and eventually on young Gerald Millinder.

In their cabin last night she had advanced the theory—with just a little too much enthusiasm, Millinder thought—that men like Al Banks were throwbacks to a more heroic and primitive age, of a breed with Eric the Red, Captain Morgan, Laffite and Bowie. "I wonder if modern women aren't getting a little tired of brainy men burdening their wives with their thorny intellectual problems," she had said, and then had caught herself, or rather, the pained look on her husband's face had caught her. Gerald had had a year of thorny intellectual problems and overwork. It was the first, faint rumblings of breakdown that had led to this cruise—doctor's orders:

"Gerald, there's nothing wrong with you but pressuritis. Too much of this tug of war between artistic conscience and family responsibility. The medicine for you is a month, well let's say at least two weeks, in a different world, some place that never heard of book-club demands and intellectual integrity and the strain and stress of creative work. You book fellows with your ulcers and your nervous breakdowns—the occupational disease of Homo Intellectualis."

"I can't help it, Lew, it's a terrible decision. A book club is offering me a hundred thousand dollars for the new book, but there's a catch in it. They're asking for certain changes I know in my heart I don't want to make. But taking a year out to write a novel can be pretty rough on a family. And seventy-five thousand is a helluva lot of money, more than I've made out of my last three books put together. I've got my kids to think about, and Madge . . ."

"I still say go away," his doctor had told him. "A week or

two in the sun. I can give you the address of a place I think you'll like on the Florida Keys. Don't worry about a thing but how good the fishing is. I know you'll say you can't afford it, but think of it as medicine, and saving hospital bills. Then come home, rested, with a clear mind, and make your decision."

So Millinder had splurged at Abercrombie's, bought himself a long peaked fishing cap and some jeans to knock around in and a light blue fishing jacket and here they were aboard the *Lorelei,* dutifully "getting away from it all," just as travel books and practical physicians advise. Only instead of sun there was wind, and instead of fish there were waves, and instead of the second-honeymoon closing of emotional ranks with Madge, there was—well, nothing that Millinder could give a name to, just a nagging interior itch of strain and suspicion. In all their eight years, there had been no real schism, or even any rows serious enough to survive a single good night's sleep. What they hoped to find a cure for here in the Gulf was their sense of mutual fatigue, of love's having been carried away in tiny pieces by problem ants. Although she had had her share of delicate invitations, Madge had always shied away from the more literal forms of infidelity. All she had felt was a kind of private sigh—Oh, maybe it would do her good to go to bed with some nice healthy male she hardly knew, someone who didn't get love all mixed up with writing problems and the ethics of art.

Someone, she had thought that morning—not seriously but merely as an example, as speculation—well, like this skipper, Al Banks, a natural, lean-bellied, firm-muscled man, a man who was hard because nature was hard, and who was direct because that's the way life had been before it got all mucked up with too much civilization: progressive schools and child psychology and her friends' accounts of their sessions with their analysts and prejudice and social obligations and to what extent Gerald should sacrifice his principles to the needs of his family—Oh, the sea was wonderful, let the wind blow hard in her face forever, let the boat roll, rise, drop, crash back into the sea, the foam-flecked, violent, primordial sea.

"Gerald—darling—are you all right?"

Madge was bending over him with a solicitousness that was faintly irritating. Damn it all, he wanted to be wanted—not mothered. He sat up straighter in the fishing chair into which he had retreated in hope that its exposed position in the stern might help to counter his panicky anticipation of seasickness.

". . . all right?" Her voice was part of the wind.

"Hell, yes." Gerald tried to give the words a hearty ring, as if in half-conscious imitation of Al Banks. "How much longer till we get there? The Marquesas?"

"Al says he'll sneak us in in about an hour and a half. He's going to try a little short cut into the lagoon. Says he's never done it before but he thinks he can feel his way."

Madge's face was shiny with spray and exhilaration. If only he could enjoy the violence of the weather. He wished she and Al Banks weren't so—

"Gerald, are you *sure* you're all right?"

"Yes. Yes. Hell, yes." He said it a little too sharply.

"You look a little green."

Well, he *felt* a little green. But, "I'm all right," he said. "Those Dramamines seem to be doing the trick."

"I feel wonderful," Madge said. "I love a stormy day like this." She turned her face into the wind and her long dark brown hair blew wildly. She was wearing shorts and a sweat shirt and Gerald admired her long muscular legs, with strong calves and a pleasing fullness at the thighs from lacrosse and lots of tennis and a fondness for walking. He wished he had a better figure. He had never been very good at outdoor games. He could never find time for them. He had been a quiet, serious kid with a compulsion to work a little harder than he had to. Breaking in as a radio writer the summer he left college, he had forced himself after a few strenuously profitable years to cross the bar into that world where one must play slave to his own Simon Legree: free-lance writing.

He had worked passionately, religiously, and in ten years there had been five novels, one of them a mild best-seller. Gerald Millinder had nine lines in *Who's Who in the East,* an honorary degree from his college, and a secure niche in the insecure bracket of "promising authors." But a pattern of all-night typing and an incapacity for recreation had left him jittery. There was a notebook full of ideas but little to draw on for physical confidence. He had driven himself—as everybody called it—to the point of exhaustion. Right now, for instance, his stomach awash with the sickening roll of the boat, he had only to think around the edges of his book-club dilemma and he could feel tears coming into his eyes. First little signpost of breakdown, his doctor had warned. Where did responsibility to conscience begin and to family welfare leave off? Hell, the complexities of modern life, the compromises it kept demanding of you. No wonder this was a field day for those modern witch doctors, the psychoanalysts. No wonder they call them shrinks. As our world expands, our ability to cope with it shrinks.

Al Banks was holding the *Lorelei'*s bow at right angles to the swollen waves, easing her down, into and through the sea aroused by winds blowing out of the north. Once in a while he threw his head back and sang in a not-bad voice a snatch of a chanty. The words were a lusty description of the buxom charms of willing maids, and he looked around roguishly to see if they were with him.

"Isn't he delicious?" Madge said. "He's been telling me the most marvelous stories. He sailed all through the Caribbean by himself in a twenty-foot yawl. He's brought alligators back alive from the Everglades. He's even been a harpooner on a whale boat. He's done everything."

"Mmmhmmm, I can imagine," Gerald mumbled. As far back as he could remember he had been tormented with a fear of doing things. Physical things. He was, he knew to his regret, a sorry example of the atrophied species *Homo sapiens megalopolis*—modern city man. He had used his right arm to push a pencil by the hour, to dial the telephone, to shake hands and hold narrow-stemmed glasses at cocktail parties, to keep a chain of cigarettes nervously alive in his mouth and to tip an endless line of cab drivers, waiters, hatcheck girls and doormen.

Madge patted him on the hand, rather patronizingly, he thought, and said, in the same way, "I love you." He answered with a weak nod. Why, at this moment, must she tell him that? Could it be a twitch of guilt for the attraction she was feeling toward the skipper? Gerald felt impatient with himself for admitting such a thought. He watched as Madge went forward and stood beside Al Banks at the wheel. She stood with her legs apart and braced and it was something to see her standing there without holding on to anything and yet not losing her balance as the deck of the *Lorelei* angled precariously back and forth. Once the water fell away from the hull and the boat plunged downward with a resounding crash that almost sent Madge reeling backwards. She and Al looked at each other and laughed together in such a way as to make Gerald think. Somehow they're going to find a way to have each other, these two strong, fresh-air, physical people. And in any other society but ours his kind of man would have won her. In our brainy, shut-in world, women fall in love with our prestige and our Early American houses and our private schools for the children, with our winter vacations, with our evenings of hi-fi culture, with our *minds*. Not that Madge would ever think of it that way. In fact, if she had been able to read his mind she would have been shocked and hurt, and probably angry. What he meant was that his intelligence and little niche of prestige had given him the power, the opportunity to attract a woman like Madge that he would never have had in a less mental, more primitive society.

He dozed off into a troubled dream too jumbled to unravel or interpret, the toned-down ending of the book they wanted him to change, falling overboard and drowning and his youngest girl sobbing and Captain Banks and Madge making love on the deck. Then he was falling again, over the side and into a swarm of man-eaters. At the last moment he managed to save himself by suddenly waking. An abrupt lurch had almost swung him out of his chair and he saw that Madge was at the wheel, heading into the waves as Al had shown her, doing fairly well although the pitching of the *Lorelei* was even more violent now.

Gerald felt as if his stomach was rolling up through his chest and into his mouth. Scraping the bottom of his strength and concentration, he fought down the impulse to purge himself of the impurities that were poisoning him. Hold me in, hold me together, oh Dramamine, he prayed, and he hated worse than the biliousness the sign of weakness in front of these two. Somehow, in the green turmoil it seemed as if the two strong ones standing upright were man and wife and he was the intruder, that despised outsider whose unwelcome presence makes a crowd.

Al Banks looked around at him and tried to cheer him up. "Nearly there, Mr. Millinder. Are you OK? How do you like my new mate?"

Madge was steering confidently and Al Banks, close behind her, was leaning over her shoulder to check the compass.

At what seemed to Gerald the last possible moment for survival, he was given a reprieve. Al Banks took over and was working his way into the channel. In a few minutes they were on the lee side of the island and the sea cradled them gently. The horizon had swallowed the sun and a curtain of mist, incredibly blue, hung over the lagoon. The only inhabitants of the island were a few herons who stared at them suspiciously. There was a small beach and Al Banks eased the *Lorelei* in as close as she would draw. After the anchor-splash there wasn't a sound in the lagoon. More closely viewed, it looked as if blue smoke were rising from the smooth dark surface. Fifty yards into the lagoon was a miniature island with a slender arm of sand curving into the water to form a natural pool.

Madge went back to join her husband in the stern. "Know what it reminds me of? That picture on our record album—*The Isle of the Dead.*"

"Half an hour more and you could have buried me there," Gerald said. He had held on and soon he would be all right. He unbuttoned his shirt to his waist, exposing his narrow chest and a soft white belly. He took a deep breath and thought about how the fishing would be tomorrow if the wind let up. He breathed deeply again, enjoying the fresh evening air cooling his throat.

"Madge, how about a drink? Then we'll go ashore and claim these islands in the name of the Authors League of America."

"I'd love a drink," Madge said.

He went below to dig out a bottle of fifteen-year-old rum picked up on the Keys. He took off his canvas shoes and his socks and rolled up the cuffs of his pants. He wondered if Al Banks knew what a lucky s.o.b. he was, no worries, no problems, except to match wits with the winds and the tides. He twisted the cork out of the bottle and gulped a mouthful. He felt a little giddy with recovered strength, an unfamiliar vigor.

He brought the bottle back with him. Madge was peeling off her sweat shirt. "Are you up to a swim?"

"Isn't it too late?"

"The water looks beautiful, Gerald. All velvety."

He took another swallow from the bottle and handed it to Madge.

"OK, I'm game."

His momentary euphoria flagged at the thought of having to explore the deceptive calm of these waters. But he had to keep up with Madge. With Madge and her Al Banks. He had to show them. He had to prove something to himself.

Madge put one leg over the railing, ready to dive. She paused a moment, to remember it. About twenty feet off the stern there was a splash, a momentary swirl from which a circle of ripples widened toward the boat.

Madge said, "Al, something broke out there."

Al Banks came aft and studied the dark water. He held a light rod with a steel jig. He cast well out into the lagoon and reeled in rapidly. He watched the water closely as the jig wiggled up to the stern. Following it in was a long, slender shadow that sensed the boat and knifed away.

"A scooter," Al Banks said. "The place is crawling with 'em."

"You mean barracuda?" asked Madge.

"Will they really attack you?" Gerald wanted to know.

The skipper laughed. "Let me have a shot of that painkiller and I'll tell you a little story."

He wiped his mouth with the back of his hand.

"'There's this fellow from Minneapolis, manufactures television aerials and stuff like that, who comes down every winter. Only has one arm. His left arm is off clean, just below the shoulder. When he hooks a fish, someone has to hold the rod for him while he reels in. Most people who come out with me, the last thing they want to hook into is a scooter, but not this joker. 'Al,' he says to me, 'all I want is to get me a barracuda.' Well, it's not much of an order down here in the Gulf. So we find him his barracuda and he reels 'im in and then when I swing 'im in over the stern this one-armed bastard from Minneapolis takes a club and beats the head of that scooter to jelly. Then he says, 'OK, Al, that's all the fishin' I want for t'day.' Every winter the same story. I never asked him about his arm and he didn't seem over-anxious to tell me, but last winter we got weathered in for a couple of days at the Dry Tortugas and he got himself pretty well whiskied up and this is what he tells me.

"About fifteen years ago he was fishing out here in the Gulf and something hit his line and took off in such a hurry that it jerked him clean overboard. He was under water fighting to get to the surface when something hit him like a buzz-saw. The skipper finally fished him out, but as for the arm, well by that time a thirty-pound barracuda was sitting down to a fancy dinner."

Al Banks laughed and helped himself to another swallow of rum. The laugh puzzled Millinder. It was not even a nervous laugh. He was just laughing because he felt good and because he didn't mind about the arm and because he liked to sit out there over a jug of rum and spin the evenings away.

"Then these scooters really are dangerous?" Gerald said.

"I wouldn't say so," Al Banks said cheerfully. "A thing like that happens, well, maybe once in a thousand times. I've been fishing these waters since I was a kid and I've yet to see a man bit. Maybe if the scooter is crazy hungry, or if you're wearing something bright like a wide gold ring that flashes in his eye he might decide to go for you. But if you feel like you want to swim I'd say go ahead. I don't think these scooters will give you any trouble."

"How about you, Captain? Would you go in?"

Gerald's question had a petulant edge. Al Banks grinned disarmingly.

"Me, I never go in. Not even a swimming pool. I'm strictly a boat man."

Madge stared down into the black velvet water that was dead quiet now. "I think it's getting pretty late anyway."

Gerald was grateful. He had not been able to stop thinking about the feeling of barracuda jaws ripping at his flesh. Unseen and unheard it was on you like *that* and there was your arm in its cold sharp mouth.

"It does look a little too dark," he said, as casually as possible, as if ten minutes earlier he would have been eager for the dip.

After dinner they sat up for a while drinking rum and listen-

ing to Al Banks's tall stories of fishing and exploits of the sea.
There was the time on a yawl when he was caught in a hurri-
cane that snapped his mast and swept him forty miles off his
course. And the time he was alone in a dinghy leaking faster
than he could bail and a twelve-foot shark came up alongside
to wait for him and he got rid of the thing by reaching his leg
over the side and kicking it right in the face. "I know it sounds
like a fish story, but Mister Shark took off and never came back
again."

"And you weren't frightened, Al?" Madge had been watching him with what Gerald described to himself as flattering
intensity.

"Why be frightened? If you live on the sea I figure she's
gonna get you sooner or later. So you might as well have fun
right up to the minute they deep-six you. And that I have,
Madge."

He had never used her name before and it sounded
strangely intimate. "Everything I do is fun because I don't do
nothin' I don't want to do. Maybe I do some things I shouldn't
oughta do—things the missus would tan my hide for if she
knew—" He winked in a way that was winning enough to
make Madge smile, though Gerald saw the gesture as overbearing and cheap. "Yes sir, what I always say is if you can't
always be right have fun going wrong. Let every man do what
he's man enough to do and if it hurts someone else that's his
tough luck."

The skipper was feeling his rum. Gerald noticed for the first
time how small his eyes were; the pupils had contracted until
they were the size of gunshot. Gerald didn't like the way Al
Banks kept looking at Madge as he talked. It struck him—he
was convincing himself as he thought about it—as a look of
frank appraisal, of open invitation.

Around ten o'clock Gerald began to feel drowsy. "Well, if
the weather is with us we ought to pull out of here by dawn.
What do you say we hit the sack?"

"I'm not sleepy yet," Madge said, "and it's turning out to be a beautiful night. I think I'll have another cigarette."

Gerald felt awkward. He wasn't sure whether he should turn in alone or sit it out with Madge and the skipper. After a few minutes of forced conversation, he went below. Madge came down more than half an hour later. He had looked forward to this, hopefully, as a romantic night on the water, as a special adventure for them, and now it was more like the tension they had had before they left Westport. For no objective reason and almost without any exchange of words, a space had moved between them. Gerald made a furtive move toward her, at once appeasing and possessive, and she turned toward the edge of the bunk until her back made a wall against him.

He said something to her, almost in a whisper, and she said no, she was too tired.

"You weren't too tired to stay up on deck for an hour."

"Gerald, *please,* if you mean what I'm afraid you mean—"

"I don't mean anything. I just wondered."

"Just wondered what I was doing up there with him for twenty-five minutes."

"You don't have to put it that way."

"Oh, yes I do. I have to put it exactly that way. I could see the looks. I could feel the righteous suspicion. For God's sake, Gerald, I hardly know the man. If I was the sort of woman who—"

Finding herself caught up in the clichés of domestic strife, defending herself where there was no act, no case that needed defending, she lapsed into a resentful silence, first pretending sleep and then with healthy insensitivity actually slipping off into a deep, restful slumber. Gerald Millinder lay awake with his nerves and his fears, wondering if this was how a marriage dissolves, worrying about his children and the money-making changes that would weaken his book and the man from Minneapolis who had left his arm in the hungry jaws of the thirty-pound barracuda.

When they moved out of the lagoon at dawn the sea was almost as quiet outside the atoll as within.

"We'll catch fish this morning," Al Banks called to them.

But after trolling for nearly an hour all they had were some barracuda, around five pounds apiece. Al would lower them into the fish box with the hook still in their mouths and slam the lid down on their heads to hold them so as to get the hook out without taking a chance of their catching him with their sharp teeth.

"Nasty things," Madge said.

"I call 'em the rats of the sea," Al Banks told her as he threw back a dead one.

"But you still don't think they'd bother us?" Gerald said.

The skipper shrugged. "Like rats. If they're cornered or hungry. But around here there's plenty of small stuff for them. From sardine to shrimp. They ought to be satisfied."

"Before I took any chances with them I'd want to know for sure," Gerald said. "I'd just as soon not serve myself up as an extra little snack for some gluttonous barracuda."

"What do you want to bet you could swim completely around this boat right now," Al Banks said, "and come out the same way you went in?"

"Thank you, no—" Gerald started to say, and then his rod dipped suddenly under pressure of a solid strike and he had to attend to business. As he reeled it toward the boat they could see it was another barracuda. "Just another small one," Gerald was saying and then something hard hit his line and the line went slack. All he pulled in was the head of a barracuda. The body had been severed as cleanly as if a fishmonger had whacked it off with a sharp cleaver. The decapitated head was still alive.

"Ugh," Madge said.

"Another scooter went for him," Al Banks explained. "They'll do that sometimes."

"Nice fellers," Gerald said.

They cruised north for a few miles and then turned west for

another half hour. Except for one small bonito, it was the same story.

"Looks like barracuda day," Al Banks said. His business was to find game fish and he always felt increasingly fidgety and mean when this kind of fishing went on too long.

Finally, after Madge had pulled in another scooter she said, "Why don't we go in toward shore again and do some bottom fishing? We can catch some grouper and yellowtail. At least we'll have fresh fish for lunch."

Al Banks despised bottom fishing and he never ate fish when he could help it, but it was their hundred bucks. He worked in toward shore and fussed about until he found a good place to drop anchor.

Gerald didn't feel like fishing on the bottom for small stuff. He wanted action, sport, heroics, the things he had been missing all his life with his nose to the typewriter. But there wasn't anything else to do and he'd just get more restless watching Madge and thinking too much, so he dropped a line over too.

They caught a couple of fair-sized groupers and some grunts. The skipper's silence as he handled the fish for them seemed contagious. Al Banks was thinking about dolphin and sailfish and wahoo; Gerald Millinder was wondering how long this state of things would go on between him and Madge, and whether he was hopelessly ineffectual for not being able to make up his mind once and for all about the book ending. Madge was wishing there was something she could do to keep Gerald from getting so moody. She had hoped this fishing trip would help but it was turning out to be a mess.

In the silence, suddenly, they heard a splash a hundred yards or so off their bow. Al Banks turned his head quickly, with the sense of excitement real fishermen never lose. He was tired of this lazy, hand-line stuff and there was something about this joker Millinder that made him want to nudge the writer into action.

"There's something out there. Let's make one more pass at

'em before chow. Maybe we c'n catch ourselves an amberjack. Reel in your lines."

Half drowsing in the sun and looking on indifferently as a gray snapper teased his bait, Gerald Millinder was looking up from his desk, home in Westport, as Madge came in with the day's mail.

—Madge, the book club called today. They'll take the book.

—Gerald! That's wonderful!

—A hundred thousand dollars.

Madge hugged him. The book had taken longer to write than he had figured and the publisher's advance hadn't quite seen him through it. They had had to borrow on their insurance. And if the book should only sell five or six thousand copies, like the last one . . . Madge had been worried, more than she had let him see.

—A hundred thousand! We'll put half of it away for the children's education.

That had been one of the things worrying them.

—Only wait a minute. There's a catch in it, Madge.

—Oh?

—Yes, they want me to change the ending.

He had tried to make it sound casual, but it went to the heart of what he was trying to do. Eight years ago he had quit a thirty-thousand-a-year radio job to write as he pleased, to be his own man. The last fortress of individual enterprise, he had half-kiddingly called his study. Change the ending. Lord, the nights he had worked on that ending until he was satisfied that it said what he most deeply wanted it to say. And now they wanted to soften it, tone it down. It was too grim they said, too defiant. They weren't exactly asking for a happy ending, but . . .

Promptly, characteristically, Madge had said—If I were you, Gerald, I wouldn't do it.

And Gerald, troubled, torn—Madge, I don't know, we need that money like crazy. And is it fair to the kids, is the ending, any ending, that important? Is there any reason why they should be penalized for my artistic purity? Or maybe the book-club people are right. It isn't a bad ending they're suggesting. Not a too-convenient Hollywood ending or anything like that. Just a little less shocking, a little less—well, they think I go too far.

—I wish I could help you, Madge had said.—But you'll have to do what you have to do.

You have to do what you *have* to do.

"—all lines in the boat."

The sound of the motor and the sense of forward motion in the *Lorelei* brought him back from the bends of Westport to the blue-green quiet of the Gulf. The doctor was right—rest, relax, breathe deep, fish . . .

From the stern came an unfamiliar grinding sound and then, over his shoulder, snapping Gerald Millinder back to here and now, he heard a brief, vivid oath from Al Banks.

"God damn it, didn't you hear me tell you three times to get your goddamn lines into the boat?"

Gerald drew on his line and realized for the first time that it was taut, held firm, and being pulled out of his hand by something unyielding beneath the water. For a moment he thought he must have hooked a big one, a jewfish perhaps, and then he heard Banks cussing—

"God damn it, you got your line fouled in her goddamn propeller."

In a blaze of profanity, the skipper shut off the goddamn motor before the line could work its way right into the goddamn propeller shaft.

Shaken, and hating Banks, the *Lorelei,* fishing and primitive life in general, Gerald leaned over the railing and peered helplessly down at the fouled propeller. A few feet below the surface there were three barracuda, lying side by side, attracted by the bait on the line wound around the propeller.

The skipper stood right behind him. "Are you a pretty good swimmer?"

Gerald looked up into the hard, leathery face. "What—what are you talking about?"

"I'm talking about your line fouling up my propeller. Someone's gonna have to go over the side and work it clear."

"Can't we just leave it there and go on?"

"And grind your fucking line into my propeller shaft? Sorry, Mister, not on my boat."

The skipper stared at Gerald Millinder and Gerald looked down at the deck and then at the water and then at the skipper again and then at Madge. She was standing there watching them with a stiff, uncertain expression on her face. I know what she's thinking, Gerald tortured himself, that I'm afraid, that I'm not a whole man, that I'm not a positive male animal like Al Banks.

He leaned over the railing and cupped his hands around his eyes to study the barracuda. They were waiting, motionless, three of them, three big ones. He could feel their teeth ripping into the socket of his arm. He placed his other hand on that arm as if to hold it to him.

"The barracuda?" he said, with hardly any breath in his voice.

"They won't bother anybody. But just to make sure I'll break out my .22. The water's clear enough for me to see 'em and I can scare 'em off if they get frisky."

Nothing is simple any more, Gerald Millinder was thinking. Not even fishing. Problems of decision. Of courage and risk.

Al Banks was standing there waiting for him to act. The barracuda were down there waiting for him to act. Madge was watching him with a questioning look on her face.

If I can only disconnect my intelligence, Gerald was thinking. If I can find a way to black out this imagination. That's what makes these fearless heroes. A numbness. An ignition key for switching off the imagination.

He looked down into the water and tried. He closed his eyes and tried. And in the sun-struck darkness behind his eyes, he was seized with a strange discovery. He *wanted* to dive in.

He was excited with the feeling of wanting to be down there among the hard, swift, violent barracuda. He was crazy eager to plunge into fear and bloody danger and then to emerge heroic, exalted, primevally and finally *alive.*

"All right," he said, "get me some goggles," and this was not Walter Mitty living the *coeur de lion* dream of the faint-hearted, this was incredibly Gerald Millinder himself, stripping down to his swim-trunks in a daze of heroism, moving toward danger with mechanical will, suspended between the twin exhilarations of impetus and triumph.

While he paused at the railing, Madge was conscious of his bony knees, his undeveloped chest, the incipient pouch, the familiar ineffectuality of his physique.

"I think you're a heartless son-of-a-bitch," Madge said to Al Banks. Her husband had never heard her use that term before.

"Gerald, you're not going in. I'm not going to let him do this to you. It isn't heroic, it's crazy, senseless."

Millinder hesitated, caught between the two worlds.

Madge was telling the impassive face of Al Banks, "I don't care about your precious propeller. If he has to, he'll buy you a new propeller. But he's not going into that water. It isn't worth it. His courage—it's a different kind—you wouldn't understand. He's not going to have to prove it in your stupid, ridiculous, animal way."

"Madge, I said I would, and I feel I—"

"Listen, we have three children, and your work and—you're trying to be brave where it's a lot harder to be brave, and where it counts, for you. If you do this—this idiotic thing—I won't be proud of you. I'll think you're as big a fool as—as *he* is for egging you into it."

Al Banks was never a man for argument. Either do it or get off the pot was his philosophy. Now he came over and said:

"Tell you what I'll do with you. I'll sneak her slowly back into the lagoon. She only draws two and a half feet and I can practically lay her stern on the beach. Then I can cut the line out."

"Take her into shallow water and I'll get the damn line myself," Gerald said.

So that's the way it was compromised. Millinder put on the goggles and held himself under the boat a minute or so at a time and finally worked his line free. There was still some slight danger from barracuda—if indeed barracuda are dangerous—but not much. Millinder felt somewhat exhilarated but not as much as if he had accomplished the feat in deep water. Al Banks felt justified but not as much as if he had been able to prove to Millinder that the fear of barracuda was mostly in his mind. Madge felt satisfied with having put an end to daredevil foolishness but not as much as if she had been able to get Gerald not to go into the water at all.

Between the Millinders and Al Banks almost nothing was said as he took the *Lorelei* back across the straits. Two worlds had collided and held each other fast for a moment, and then each had shaken the other off and backed away to resume its own course.

Sitting with Madge in the stern on the way in, Gerald was thinking of the barracudas lurking beneath the surface of his creative life. Let me dive down among the waiting shadows and realities. Let me dive down.

And then, so clearly it startled him, his decision was in his mind. "Madge," he said, "I just decided. I've got to keep that book my way. To hell with the money."

Madge let her hand rest on his.

"Good. It's your book. The best so far."

"If it could just make that damn best-seller list."

"We'll manage. I'm glad you decided. Now try to put it out of your mind. Let's enjoy the day."

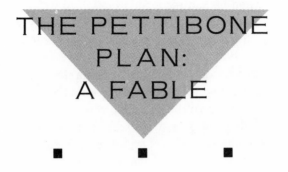

# THE PETTIBONE
# PLAN:
# A FABLE

■   ■   ■

The old man, hatless, coatless, was walking solemnly up the desolate highway between the ocean and the mountains. The raw, stiff California night wind ripped around him from the sea, blowing his faded yellow beard wildly about.

Now and then as specks of lights in the distance became great blinding headlights looming up, he would hold out to them a sun-leathered, weather-twisted hand, letting it fall slowly, not angrily, as the cars sped on by, racing for cities, afraid of the open darkness and the strange figures of the night trudging through.

After the cars rushed past, the old man would resume his steady pace, watching the tiny rear lights twist through the passes and over the hills like red fireflies. He was able to watch them disappear with little sense of bitterness and less of hate, for the old man had walked across America for ten years now, until he felt that he had walked all the evil out of him; in his

■

mind, at last, there was understanding, and his heart was full of love.

Then, when he had reconciled himself to walking through the night until his bones grew so weary that they would not know the difference between a feather bed and a clump of rocks by the side of the road, a car stopped for him.

It was an old rattletrap Ford, driven by a clean-faced country kid who was taking his girlfriend for a ride along the ocean.

"Pretty cold for an old coot like you to be out walkin'."

"Just a little wind. I'm used to the cold," the old man said.

"You can climb in back if you want," the kid offered.

"God bless you," the old man said. "It's only the old jalopies that'll stop for you."

The old car vibrated along peacefully, except when the wind gusted so violently it blew it two or three feet across the road. The kid sized up the old man through the mirror. His clothes were wrinkled and badly worn, but there was something in the way the old man wore them that kept them from looking sloppy. His old blue suit looked as if once it might have been fashionable. And when the wind blew his handsome yellow beard away from the face, the youth saw that he was wearing a tie.

"You don't look like an ordinary hobo," the kid said.

"There's no such thing as an ordinary hobo, son," the old man said. "In these last ten years it's been my privilege to reside in some of the best-known jungles in the nation. I've met hoboes of all ages, sizes and dispositions. And there wasn't an ordinary one in the lot. There couldn't be. Because it isn't ordinary for human beings to roam the earth hunting their food and shelter like wild animals, is it, son?"

The old man's voice was gentle and the kid was curious. So they talked as they drove along the beautiful California coast north of Santa Barbara, the girl silent, half asleep as she nestled under the young man's shoulder.

"I forgot to ask you," said the kid. "Where you headin'?"

"Nowhere," the old man said.

"No particular place you want to be tomorrow?"

"Yes, there is, but anyplace you drop me will probably do."

"That don't exactly make sense."

"Excuse me," the old man said. "I don't mean to confuse you. I meant that any of the little valleys off the ocean will suit me fine."

"What's in the valleys?" the young man asked.

"Flowers," said the old man. "Wildflowers. I always hunt for them. Seeds and bulbs. This is fine country for them."

"Sort of a hobby with you, huh?" the young man asked, thinking, *I hope I haven't picked up a crazy. Pa always told me not to stop for strangers. . . .*

"No, not a hobby," the old man said. "It's my life's work. I just gather all the different kinds of wildflowers—seeds and bulbs—I can find as I go along. Now and then I sell a couple in the cities. Other times I just plant them where I think they'll look nice."

*Anyway, he sounds harmless,* the kid thought. *Gee, I hope he is harmless. . . .* "How long you been at this wildflower stuff?" he asked.

"Since October 1929," the old man answered.

"What made ja start then?" the youth asked.

"It's a long story, son," the old man said. "But I never get tired of hearing it myself. You care to know it?"

*Better not stand in his way,* the young man thought. *Guess it's safer if I let him have his way. He looks harmless enough but you can't always tell by looks. . . .*

"Before 1929 I was a stockbroker on Wall Street. I made money for people who didn't have the slightest idea what made one stock go up and another go down. I didn't have too much idea myself but I was very proud of my profession, pleased that I had chosen a respectable calling. I always felt so dignified of a Sunday afternoon strolling down Fifth Avenue in my walking suit. Dignity, son, is very important. And suddenly all in one week I saw my profession lose its dignity. I saw respectable citizens go into the men's room and blow their brains out. On the following Sunday I saw my partner, dressed in a dignified afternoon cutaway just like me, walk out of his penthouse window. He flopped over and over in the air like a scarecrow. I assure you he didn't look dignified in the least. So I made up my mind that if I was to regain my dignity I could not do it by returning to the Stock Exchange or following my partner out the window. So I simply started walking. In search of dignity, and I've stopped to pick wildflowers on the way."

The young man was glad when he came to his turnoff in the road. "Sorry to put you out," he said, "but this is the end of the line."

"Let me give you a little something for your kindness," said the old man. He reached into one of the burlap sacks he was carrying. "I picked these up Vermont way last spring," he said, handing the youth a little paper bag. "If you water them well they will grow up into lady's slippers. You might like them for your garden."

"Thanks, Mr. . . ."

"Pettibone," said the old man as he stepped out onto the road again. "When your lady's slippers bloom, just think of Mr. Pettibone, the flower man."

The rattletrap Ford turned away and Mr. Pettibone was alone again. The wind was blowing so hard now that it was easier to keep going than try to sleep. As he walked he saw a great white city rising in front of him just beyond the shore. At first he thought he must be dreaming, for often in these all-night stretches his mind would drift off while his body, needing little conscious guidance, would plod on. But as he came closer the buildings grew three-dimensional, one huge structure surrounded by rows and rows of little houses below, suggesting a feudal town. And covering the roofs, covering the sides, covering the ground around them, covering the telephone wires and filling the air were millions of little chalky flakes, which Mr. Pettibone, if he did not know the mildness of California autumns, would have taken for snow.

Here and there through the chalky haze Mr. Pettibone saw a light flickering, so he kept on until the chalk flakes were flailing around him, stinging his eyes and almost blinding him. Then as he stared up at the huge lettering on the sign of the large building he discovered what the flakes were. Cement. Here in this desolate rocky country with the ocean beating up just below he had stumbled onto a cement factory and all the little houses surrounding it were the workers' homes, for the factory was so far removed from any cities that mill and mill workers had to form a complete and self-sufficient city unto themselves.

The wind flinging the cement dust around had punished Mr. Pettibone so severely around the eyes that he gave up all thought of going on, and groped his way toward the nearest light.

He knocked several times before a woman's voice answered just behind the door.

"What are you up to this time o' night?"

"I've traveled all day by foot and I'm weary. Could you put me up for the night?" Mr. Pettibone said softly.

"Sorry, old man, never take in strangers."

"My name is Mr. Pettibone. Now tell me yours and we won't be strangers. My eyes are full of cement dust."

The woman behind the door understood cement dust. It had been in her eyes and her food and her mind for a long time. And the old man's voice sounded nice and gentle. She set the door ajar.

"Well," she said, "our name is Evans. I suppose it won't hurt if you sleep in the kitchen."

Next morning Mr. Pettibone rose very early and walked around the town. It was the drabbest little place Mr. Pettibone had ever seen. All the houses were the same, looking like nothing but rows and rows of matchboxes. There was only one color in the town, the color of the cement dust. Mr. Pettibone could hardly tell where the ground left off and the house began, where the house left off and the sky began.

Nor was there any relief when he returned to the Evanses' house for breakfast. The three rooms were plain and un-adorned, absolutely empty and colorless. There were no curtains on the windows, no rugs on the floor. And Mr. Pettibone was shocked to see that the inhabitants seemed to reflect the drabness of their surroundings. Mr. Evans, for instance, might have been a fine respectable figure of a man, with bushy eyebrows, dimpled cheeks, handsome shoulders and a good, strong jaw, but it was impossible to really see his face because it was so speckled with cement dust. Mr. Pettibone felt as if he were looking at Mr. Evans through gauze. And Mrs. Evans was just as bad. You couldn't actually see the specks on her face, but her whole complexion was grey, her hair and her eyes and her skin, so that Mr. Pettibone had to observe to himself that she looked like a drawing done in white chalk. And the two children, little Marilyn and the baby, Peter, Mr. Pettibone felt, were the saddest of all because they still had a little youthful flush to their cheeks, but it looked like the sun trying to peek through on a cloudy day. They had not yet been consumed by cement dust but they were on their way. The frugal morning meal was eaten in silence, butter and bread and cocoa made with water. Finally Mr. Evans kissed his family perfunctorily, shook Mr. Pettibone's hand halfheartedly and said in a mono-tone, "Guess I'll be back for lunch."

Mr. Pettibone looked after him thoughtfully, and then he said to Mrs. Evans as he helped her clear the table, "I feel very sorry for your husband. There's precious little dignity around his home."

"Dignity," Mrs. Evans scoffed. "There's plenty more important things we need around here besides dignity."

"Excuse me for disagreeing," said Mr. Pettibone. "I know from experience. Once you get dignity, half the battle is over."

"It's no use trying to get anything around here," Mrs. Evans said as she piled the dishes in the sink. "We've given up trying a long time ago. When I was still a young girl I had hopes. But we've got cement dust in our children's blood now."

Mr. Pettibone looked around at the solitary greyness. "I think I know how to bring a little color to this place," he said. "A bit of dignity as well, perhaps."

He's cracked, she thought calmly, but at least he's different, I'll say that for him. He's something to break the monotony of a lonely grey morning, he is.

"I think I know a way," Mr. Pettibone said. "It won't take very long. Would you mind if I try?"

"Just make yourself to home," she said. "You can't make things any worse."

So Mr. Pettibone puttered around the place until he found a hammer and some nails and some loose shingles and then he set himself down on the front steps, sneezing now and then when the dust got too far up his nose, but looking quite contented as he kept on hammering away.

Once Mrs. Evans stopped in the middle of her washing and said, "Just whatever are you making, Mr. Pettibone?" But the old man simply smiled to himself and shook his head, "You'll see. You'll find out in time. Wait till you see what a change it makes."

Later in the morning, when Mr. Pettibone had several rectangular boxes lined up in front of him, a company superintendent came by.

"Who are you?" he asked brusquely.

"My name is Pettibone."

"We don't like strangers around here."

"But I'm not a stranger. I'm a friend of the Evanses."

"Where's your home?"

"I haven't got a home."

"No home, eh?" The superintendent frowned. He didn't like this. He had orders not to let suspicious-looking characters loiter about.

"Not from the union, are ya?" he asked. He had orders to keep a sharp eye out for labor organizers.

"No," Mr. Pettibone answered. "I'm just the flower man."

"Well," the superintendent growled. "Just don't try any funny business. I've got my eye on you."

"Please don't upset yourself on my account," said Mr. Pettibone.

By the time Mr. Evans came home for lunch, Mr. Pettibone had completed his morning's chore. He had finished making four oblong boxes, which he was painting white with red borders.

"Those are your flower boxes," he explained as he began to nail them just outside the windows. "Now, if you don't mind, I will take the children out beyond the dust line, and we'll gather up enough good earth to plant the flowers in."

So Mr. Pettibone took Marilyn by one hand and Peter by the other and they walked far, far beyond the dust area, until they were out into the sunshine again. There little Marilyn pointed toward the hills and said, "They had a big fire over there last year." And Mr. Pettibone said, "Then we are in luck, Marilyn, because wildflowers always grow best after there's been a forest fire because then the sun can reach the little seeds and bulbs that the big trees always hide."

They found wild poppies, big fat orange ones, and tulips, yellow and deep red, and Mr. Pettibone showed them how to lift them gently out of the ground, with enough of their own earth around them to make them feel at home. Then they filled the sack they had brought with the fine warm soil and started back.

When they reached the little house, Mr. Pettibone worked furiously until dark, filling the flower boxes with dirt, tenderly transplanting the flowers from the neighboring hills, and planting among them some of the violet seeds and lupines he had been carrying with him.

The next morning he gathered his things together and

began to say good-bye, but Mrs. Evans said, "Where are you rushing off to? Why don't you stay and see if the flowers grow?" And so Mr. Pettibone stayed, nursing his poppies and tulips and violets and lupines, even though the superintendent growled as he passed him now and then, "This is most irregular, don't try any funny business, it's against orders."

Soon Mr. Pettibone's labors began to take root. There was great excitement in the Evans household as the bulbs began to burst through and the boxes were filled with the tiny green stems struggling up toward the sun. Marilyn and Peter fought for the honor of watering them, and Mr. and Mrs. Evans were very pleased when Mr. Pettibone counseled them to take turns. And even Mr. Evans, who was always lazy about the house and apt to bark at his wife in his discouragement, began to sneak out and water them himself, and when Mrs. Evans caught him at it red-handed he broke down and confessed, "I suppose it does give a man something to come home to, seeing his own flowers come up that way." And Mr. Pettibone straightened his faded yellow beard with pride and said, "You see, that is what I mean by dignity, having something in life to be proud of, not stuffed-shirt, three-piece-suit dignity, but simple, earthy dignity, the dignity of your own flower boxes and gardens."

So the Evanses began to have color in their lives for the first time. Mrs. Evans would call to her neighbors to ask how they liked her red-and-white flower boxes, "Don't they set the house off pretty, though?" and Marilyn brought her teacher a lovely yellow tulip, saying "I picked it out of my own garden," and even Mr. Evans, though he never said much about it, when he was at his work with that sickening cement dust flying all around would think of the fat poppies and the brilliant tulips and the cute dog's-tooth violets and he'd have to smile, even though he smiled through closed lips so the dust wouldn't go down his throat.

It wasn't long before all the wives were telling their husbands about the Evanses' flower boxes, and after that the men started going by the Evanses' house on their way to work mornings. And finally the first couple came to call on the Evanses after supper, to find out all about the flower boxes and where the soil came from and where they got the flowers, and Mr. Pettibone got his burlap bag out again, and carefully handed out the seeds and bulbs they needed, and promised to keep an eye on their flower boxes, too.

Then another couple came, and another, and pretty soon, the drab cement town was speckled with flower boxes, all in different colors, and everyone told everyone else what a difference it made in the atmosphere of the place, and Mr. Pettibone became quite the town hero, everybody nodding to him friendly and pleased as he went by, saying, "Good morning, Mr. Pettibone, you haven't seen my tulip bulbs in two days—they've begun to sprout already," or, "Good evening, Mr. Pettibone, would you like to take a hike in the hills with us, Sunday? We thought we'd look for purple tulips." And even the superintendent who had been so suspicious would say, "Howdy," as Mr. Pettibone went by, thinking, *Not a bad idea, having him around after all. He's made 'em a darn sight more content than I've ever seen 'em before.*

One evening when Mr. Pettibone returned home to the Evanses' after his sunset walk, he found Mr. Evans digging up the ground in front of his house with a shovel.

"I should think you had enough work for one day, Mr. Evans," said Mr. Pettibone. "What are you doing with that shovel?"

And Mr. Evans, hardly pausing between shovelfuls, said, "Those flower boxes are nice enough for the women, Mr. Pettibone. But I've decided to make myself a regular garden."

"A wonderful idea, Mr. Evans," Mr. Pettibone said. "I had thought of suggesting it myself, but I don't like to seem to be forcing things on folks."

Then Mr. Evans stared down at his shovel without quite

knowing how to go on. "And Mr. Pettibone, I don't want to hurt your feelings—but would you mind letting me make this garden entirely by myself? It'll sort of give me a feeling of, well, of . . ."

"Of dignity," said Mr. Pettibone with a smile that his wide yellow beard hid completely. "Of course, Mr. Evans. I understand perfectly."

And so Mr. Evans worked on his garden every day, a few minutes in the morning before breakfast, and every evening from the time he knocked off work until the sun went down. And soon the green sprigs of Mr. Pettibone's wildflowers began to rise in neat little rows.

After that it seemed to occur to practically every other man in the cement town that life without a little garden of one's own to cultivate meant very little. Men who usually lolled about the house all day Sunday would be out from morning to night, lugging fresh earth down from the hills, exchanging tips on how best to plant Mr. Pettibone's seeds, digging down into their front yards as deep as possible to avoid the layer on layer of cement.

Soon the whole town was quilted with little green squares and Mr. Pettibone was busier than ever, walking among the plots, stroking his faded yellow beard thoughtfully as he passed judgment. "Not a very straight row, is it, Mr. Lewis?" or "Better get after those big weeds, Mr. Olivante, they'll drink up all the water."

But Mr. Pettibone's flowers had a much greater enemy than crude care or weeds. Mr. Evans was one of the first victims. One evening when Mr. Pettibone came back from his walk, Mr. Evans held out to him a limp, dead flower. It was one of the original wild tulips Mr. Pettibone had planted in the flower box. Mr. Pettibone examined its head closely and then let it drop back like a corpse over Mr. Evans's hand.

"I've been afraid of this for a long time," he said, turning away from the dead flower.

"Is it . . . bad?" Mr. Evans asked anxiously.

Mr. Pettibone nodded. "It's the dust from the cement, my son."

Mr. Evans's fists clenched hard till the bones showed white through the tough skin. "Cement dust! It shortens our lives. It chokes our kids. And now—it even kills our gardens!"

"Please, Mr. Evans," Mr. Pettibone pleaded. "I don't believe in hate. Perhaps if we can obtain some fine netting, we can still save the flowers."

But it soon appeared that there was not nearly enough fine netting in town to save the flowers. The cement-dust blight was spreading through the gardens. Fresh winds were smothering the sprouting plants in chalky dust. And finally one night the wind stormed up from the sea, making the night white with the flying dust, and in the morning when the men hurried out to look, their gardens had completely disappeared under layers of cement dust.

Mr. Pettibone wandered among the ruins. In their homes, the women did their washing with blank faces. In the factory, the men walked mechanically. When the Evans children saw the wasteland outside their house they began to cry, and then they ran to ask Mr. Pettibone, "Why are all our pretty flowers gone?" And Mr. Pettibone wished to say something encouraging, but all he could do was shake his head.

That evening when Mr. Evans came home, Mr. Pettibone was surprised to find ten other men crowding in behind him. They all had the same serious face on, as if they were all possessed with the same idea.

"Put supper off a bit, Mother," Mr. Evans said. "We have more important matters to settle here tonight."

Then Mr. Evans turned to Mr. Pettibone. "This here is the Committee," he explained. "All the boys thought you ought to be in on it, inasmuch as you got us started."

"Got you started?" Mr. Pettibone said, a little frightened. "On what?"

"You know," Mr. Evans said. "I can't exactly put it into

words. I mean that dignity stuff. The boys know what I mean. Dignity. Those gardens you got us started with gave us a taste of it. But just when it seems like we're getting a little joy out of life, a little patch of color for our womenfolk, look what happens, the damned cement dust rolls over us like a tidal wave."

Then Mr. Olivante took the floor, his Italian blood darkening his dusty complexion. "Mr. Evans he speak the truth. Already ten years ago we should have stood on our feet like men and let them know we will not bury our lives in cement dust. We should have the right to breathe the beautiful California air that reminds me so much of my lovely Sicily."

And Mr. Lewis, usually so meek and quiet, slapped Mr. Olivante on the back, and pounded his small fist on the table and declared very solemnly, "The old man here has shown us the way. Now it's our turn to get things done. What do you say, boys? Let's recommend that we make no more cement till they promise to move our houses out into the open air."

Then there was a general hullabaloo, the making of motions, the swift seconding, everyone bursting with new ideas, as if the dam of resignation was suddenly broken after all these years, and all the old suppressed resentments were pouring over. One man said that the subject of flower boxes reminded him that none of the houses had enough windows, and another pointed out that the reason they had so little room for their gardens was that all the little houses were too close together, and that reminded someone else that for the amount taken out of their paycheck for rent the houses should be bigger than three rooms, and pretty soon they were all talking at once, making more excitement than this little town had ever had before, and Mr. Pettibone just stood aside and watched, blinking with amazement at what his handful of seeds and bulbs had set off. Finally, after several hours of talk and plans, resolutions and new hope, Mr. Evans turned to him and said, "Well, Mr. Pettibone, what do you think of it?"

And Mr. Pettibone answered promptly, "I couldn't exactly

follow all the details, but I know one thing—if they build your houses on the mountainside where that forest fire was last year you'll have the finest wildflowers you ever saw."

This seemed to please the men and they ended the evening with three rousing cheers for Mr. Pettibone, which left the old man very flustered, and incidentally awakened the superintendent.

As if it wasn't bad enough to upset the superintendent's sleep, the Committee started the next morning off disastrously for that official by informing him of their determination to hold out for what they called the Pettibone Plan, and by assuring him that it had the backing of the entire community.

When the superintendent reported this in turn to the general manager, his superior turned on him irritably.

"You're some superintendent, letting an agitator like this Pettibone get a foothold in our town."

"I figured him for trouble the minute I saw him," the superintendent insisted. "But then when I talked to him he just seemed to be a harmless old man hipped on flowers."

"Flowers!" the manager scoffed. "He was just playing dumb—probably their new tactic!"

"I'll know better next time," the superintendent assured him.

For days the general manager argued and haggled with Evans and his men but they wouldn't give in. They insisted that Pettibone's flower boxes had shown them the way and that they'd never turn back on the road to dignity.

Finally, weary and frightened, the general manager came to the superintendent and said, "It's no use. We aren't going to get anywhere until we get rid of Pettibone. See what you can do about him."

When Mr. Pettibone heard that the superintendent was coming for him, he said he would be very glad to see him and tell him how he happened to have so much success with the flower boxes. But when the superintendent reached the Evans house he found the door blocked by two of the biggest men in the plant. They explained that the Committee had appointed them Mr. Pettibone's special bodyguards and nobody was going to see him.

The general manager heard all this in thoughtful silence. At last he said resignedly, "Maybe this is the best way out. Rebuilding their houses out on the hillside is the least of our worries. And perhaps it will be healthier for the men at that. But this man Pettibone is something else again. It seems obvious to me that as long as he stays on here there can be no peace. So go back and tell them that we'll do everything they say on one condition—that Pettibone leaves town."

When the men heard the condition on which their wishes had been granted, they were reluctant to accept. "We've all gotten pretty fond of you, Mr. Pettibone," Mr. Evans admitted. "And anyway, once we're living out on that hillside, it's going to be pretty hard to plan those big gardens without you."

But Mr. Pettibone shook his head. "I've taught you just about all I know," he said. "It's time I was moving on anyway because my seeds and bulbs are just about gone and there are some fairy lanterns and fritillarias waiting for me a little farther north."

So Mr. Pettibone shook hands with Mr. Evans and Mrs. Evans and Marilyn and Peter Evans and Mr. Lewis and Mr. Olivante and all the others, and then the superintendent personally drove him out of town.

They drove for miles, without saying a word, and then the superintendent said through clenched teeth, "Funny thing—I can usually smell a troublemaker. I knew you were one first time I set eyes on you."

And Mr. Pettibone answered, "When you build those houses out there on the hill, be sure you give them plenty of outside faucets, because those flowers will need lots of water in all that sunlight."

To himself he thought again, *Who'd ever have dreamt it would go that well, all those men getting so excited about a couple of bulbs in a flower box,* and then he looked out and saw a lovely meadow covered with wildflowers and he said, "You can just drop me here if you don't mind." And before the superintendent could recover from his surprise, Mr. Pettibone was saying, with a courtly little bow, "It was terribly kind of you to give me a lift this way." The superintendent took this for sarcasm, and opened his mouth to tell Pettibone exactly what he thought of him, but the old man with the faded yellow beard catching the sunlight stopped him with: "Now you mustn't waste your breath on name-calling, because name-calling just isn't dignified, and dignity, you know, is everything."

There was no answer from the superintendent. Time was money and he had to get back to the plant. Mr. Pettibone watched him speed away, and then wandered out into the meadow to begin filling his sack with wildflower seeds.

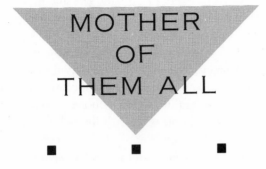

# MOTHER OF THEM ALL

It was not pain at first, only a quick flutter, and she waited, patient, almost eager for the flutter to become a stirring and then, more quickly, for the stirring to become the beginnings of pain. When she was sure, still firm and without panic, she called the doctor. She was afraid as she picked up the phone that the fear of the last few days had left her weak, for fear had been everywhere about her—in her mind the cowardly fear of the pain that would not have been so lonely with Toby there; in her womb silent fear for the safety and future of a life she had taken upon herself to push into a world that did not seem to appreciate its value; in her apartment house and in her city and radiating out toward all the borders her country was determined to preserve, group fear, the fear of millions whose minds were preoccupied with death and dying, its frantic prevention and its heroic necessity, as they vacated their homes and dug their bombproof shelters in the parks with the outward calm of people puttering in their gardens.

But now as she held the phone she felt herself beyond fear or any weakness. An hour ago, hearing snatches of people crying out their anxiety, and listening to the army trucks rumbling by with their soldiers sitting on the benches in invincible postures, she had wondered to herself, What if I do not have the strength for it? How ridiculous to conceive, suffer morning sickness, and protrude, while the embryo takes on features, real eyes and organs and feet to kick throbbing pain into my memory—to go through all that and fail now, to sink in weakness and be drowned on the shore after the channel has been swum.

She had not known where to find the strength she needed, and while she was wondering it seemed to come, an unexpected faucet turning on suddenly inside her, an independent stream having nothing to do with her mind and its doubts, filling her rapidly and efficiently with energy and physical confidence. Pushed up into the attic of the subconscious was all thought of the war that she and all the other human beings in the invaders' path had been telling each other about and trying to stop and preparing for so long now. All she knew was that the pain was on its way at last, and with that strange fundamental rightness of things this pain seemed to bring with it the sudden strength with which she was going to be able to endure it.

She had been depressed about the war that everybody kept saying would end in a matter of months or minutes and she had been depressed about the hot stirring lump within her, but now she felt almost hysterical with joy to think that she had not surrendered to weakness after all, though she had come as close as the doctor's waiting room, dingy and crowded with other women there to sacrifice their motherhood to hopelessness and fear. She remembered staring into the faces of other young women, women sculptured in sorrow because the war was already in them, forcing them to throw their babies away in mercy (as a refugee, on finding she could not be allowed to enter the haven she had struggled months to reach, tossed her infant into the sea); staring into the faces of older women on whom nature had played the practical joke of leaving them young enough for conception but too old for motherhood. She remembered the smothering sense of frustration that hung over that room, and how, at the moment her name was being called, she had run out and down the stairs and into the street.

She remembered Toby coming home that day, tall, unhandsome, good to look at, oddly unromantic in his reserve flying corps uniform, for he never looked slick in his clothes and it seemed to her his pale rugged face was too gaunt, the forehead too high, the dark inquisitive eyes lit with too much intelligence to make him look anything but incongruous in military dress. Kathy's friends considered Toby beautiful, with his black unruly hair, his nose high-bridged and well chiseled, his long face broken into interesting planes. But Kathy knew that his perfection was less in the face than in the athletic vitality of his movements, his quick and open smile, the way he set his strong mouth in thoughtful silences. Now at the telephone she remembered that scene with him, the way they had clung to each other as if trying to keep the world from coming between them, and then the way he had asked, *Honey, is it over?*

He had wanted her to do it. They had fought about it, as they had fought about getting married, with a fierceness rooted not in hate but in the depth of their love, for they realized it had been magnified, intensified and deepened by the crush of the times, by the quickening crises, by the dread of savage dislocations.

It seemed strange for a young man and woman toughened with the realism of the generation on the brink of a new war to be so thoroughly in love and yet so thoroughly divided on their problem. She had wanted the marriage and he had not and she had wanted the child and he had not, yet each could accuse the other of being unrealistic. It was never a case of one being right and the other wrong, for they were like the positive and negative sides of a battery which, when wired together, produces current.

So she had sensed that note of hope in his *Honey, is it over?* and she had fought it. "Toby, I thought I could, but I couldn't. I want to have it now. I'm going to have it."

"Now, Kathy, for God's sake." His young face seemed drained of its youth. "Do you know what we've been practicing all week?" The anger in his voice wasn't really anger. It was frenzied anguish trying to be hard-boiled. "Bringing down enemy bombers over the city. It's just a game of cops and robbers among friends so far. But now that they're mobilized along the border, we're liable any moment to begin playing for keeps."

She had answered with more than stubbornness, full of defiance and life. "If they kill us, they kill us. That's the chance we have to take. But Toby, I *want* to take that chance. I want to have it. Please, Tobe, want to have it with me."

That made his eyes tear as he kissed her in little private places, earlobes and the tip of her nose. "Look, honey, you know how much I'd get out of it with you—if it was only five years ago or. . . ." He paused, angry at himself for crying, for these were not times for tears, these were days with a war almost here. And he was never meant for war. That was not what he had learned at school all these years, what he had studied in the university, worked long hours with low pay for as an architect's apprentice until now he felt ready to interpret his dreams into action. Toby's dreams were girded with stainless steel, walled in with poured concrete, new materials for dreams, but then these dreams themselves were new: low-cost housing, clearing out the slums. But not this way, not slicing them in half or splintering them into the air with no warning for the occupants that their homes were to be blown off the earth, along with all the fathers and mothers and brothers and sisters who happened to be with them when the bombs struck. ". . . If it were only ten years ago, or ten years ahead. But now you have to be able to travel light. You have to be ready to run when the siren screams. Down into shelters or out into the country. You can't do much running with a baby at your breast. And even if you could, what sort of infancy is that? Honey, can't you see? It's the wrong time."

Now at the phone, feeling those muscles tighten, untighten, tighten, the rhythm still slow and casual, abdominal flux almost but not quite pain, she was surprised how their words rose out of a blur and came into focus. It was all so sharply remembered:

"But, Toby, just because there's liable to be a war . . . we can't stop living. And there's still hope of peace, if—"

Toby interrupted her. Bitter. "If. The lives of people aren't hanging by a thread. They're hanging by an *if.*"

That wasn't the whole fight. That had only been part of one and that one had only been part of many. They had argued over it, fought and cried over it, but she had clung to it, with moral arguments and regenerate instinct, and in the end she had won. Though victory had seemed pyrrhic when, at the six-month stage, the staccato boot steps of the invading battalions threatening new conquests echoed in their own little apartment, for the government was mobilizing its own troops in defense and Toby had been called. Historians may argue as to the day war began but for Toby and her it began the night he kissed her too quickly, said *Take care of yourself* in a voice that was not quite as casual as he meant it to sound, turned stiffly and hurried out, afraid to look back for fear of starting all over again. She watched him from the window as long as she could and then, because sitting there thinking about it was the worst thing she could do, she became very busy putting his things away, the drafting board with its half-completed plan, the clothes to be stored with mothballs, pipes, the toothbrush he forgot to pack. When she realized she was putting things away for no reason at all, she felt so lonely she climbed into the double bed, on her own side from force of habit, curled up beneath the blankets the way she used to as a child afraid of the dark, the lonely blackness bounding her consciousness the way it did that of the inner life her body could no longer conceal.

It was not the same with Toby gone and war uncurling from its own great womb. It was after that that the moods came, fits of depression when she would sit for hours in a thought-vacuum, or suddenly feel like screaming out that Toby had been right, that she was a fool not to have gone through with it that afternoon she was so close, that now they were caught together, she and it, trapped by each other, and it held some of the horror for her of a live man chained to a corpse. She even thought of going back to that doctor and finding out if it wasn't too late yet, but something always seemed to interfere, one day not feeling well enough to make the trip, or having to wait for registered mail from Toby, until at last she began to realize that nothing was stopping her but herself, that no matter how much reason hammered at the bars of her mind, deep down where we are bloody landscapes with a magnificent system of trellised canals, the undying and antidying force of renewal would prevail.

"Hello, Dr. Mank? Kathy. They've begun, Doctor."

"Good. How often?"

"Oh, every half hour or so."

"How do you feel?"

"OK. Except when it grips me and it's hard to breathe but . . ."

"Fine. Sounds normal. Nothing to be frightened of. You have plenty of time."

"Shall I hurry over? Get a friend to drive me?"

"No, I want you to walk."

"Walk?"

"Yes. Walk over slowly. You have hours yet."

"But . . ."

"Walking will do you good. Makes it easier going. Are you worried?"

"No, I don't know why, but I'm not. Not any longer."

"Good. These are tough times, for all of us. See you at the hospital."

When she entered the street it was dusk but people were not in their houses. The routine of their lives had been gradually transformed, perhaps forever, but they already were beginning to take the new life for granted. The men, dry-eyed and grim, were leaving their homes again, the children jammed into trains for the country, perhaps to preserve them for future wars, the women and the old men and the young boys had been working through the week with quiet fury to give the city its nightmare appearance with the sandbags, the barricades and the trenches cut deep into the streets.

She brushed by two middle-aged women on the corner with gas masks slung casually over the shoulder. "I absolutely refuse to wear it," one of them was chatting, as if discussing hats. "It's the most uncomfortable old thing. Why, I can hardly breathe in it."

Kathy had to laugh to herself, thinking how very silly but wonderful it was for people to be able to worry about the discomfort of breathing in a gas mask when the only alternative was the discomfort of not being able to breathe at all.

Over the city lay a nervous calm. Last night and the night before, at the signal of sirens, screeching up one street, down another, millions of people had blacked out millions of lights, plunging the city back into Stone Age night before men invented fire. Tonight, working under streetlamps that had begun as symbols of public safety but were becoming looked upon as targets of public death, the people were stripping the city of whatever could be quickly saved.

Not calm but cool, fighting off the pain within and without, she smiled as she passed the art gallery where volunteers in two lines like ants were transferring works of art from the ancient building to the waiting trucks. She smiled because she knew that even now, when the droning of planes and the whistle of bombs could make the preservation of paintings seem ridiculous, these people, without quite knowing why, would go on saving and salvaging, defending and conserving all that had been built and passed down and improved and passed down again, a fine hopeful line from the cavemen all the way down to Toby and Kathy, to Kathy's baby still curled in the dark peaceful womb. As she walked slowly through the unrecognizable city of her childhood, Kathy was gripped by a great coolness, an inexplicable pride to belong to the force of human life that was *going on*. Though she might have been afraid, she felt too strong to admit these qualms, for she was not alone, even with Toby vanished somewhere into the sky; she was not alone, for these desperate unpanicky people saving their works of art were one with her, though they might not know her as she passed them at this moment. She knew that if she had stopped to tell them of her uncertainty in these last nine months and to ask them what they would have done, their answer would have been her own, the answer she was walking slowly toward the hospital to find.

Several blocks further she had to step down from the curb and walk along the gutter, for the corner was piled waist-high with sandbags surrounding a government building. One little boy was standing on top of the sandbags looking down at another, somewhat smaller, lying on the pavement crying.

Especially drawn to any suffering now, she stopped, helped the child to his feet and tried to check the quiver of his shoulders with her hands.

"There. You're all right. Don't cry."

For there is too much to cry about, she thought. And all we need is to have someone start us, the tears of all of us flowing and flowing until the dam breaks and the very city is flooded, drowning us in our own sorrow.

The little boy blurted his rage through his sobs. "He pushed me. He knocked me down."

She brushed him off and looked up into the face of the larger boy, who was still perched on the sandbags, staring down at them with undisguised hostility. She scolded him with motherly patience.

"You didn't really mean to hurt him, did you? You look like too nice a little boy to be a bully." And we have too many of those in the world now, she thought.

The larger child whined his defense: "Well, he pinched me first. So I tried to pinch him back and he fell off."

Queer the way he wasn't able to doubt that he was in the right and the smaller boy had started it. All that morning waiting until it was time to call the doctor, she had tried to keep her mind free from war the way he had cautioned her to. She had just one job now, Dr. Mank had reminded her, and she had to give it all the strength and concentration she had. But there beside the sandbags and this tiny war oblivious of the enormous one into which it fitted, it was impossible to forget another bully's words, *We will match bomb with bomb*— what a roundabout way of saying what did not need to be said at all, because everyone's consciousness pounded with it already, *We will bomb your cities or blow you off the face of the earth or go down in flames ourselves!*

"But aren't you two boys friends?"

"No," the smaller boy raged. "He's my brother and I'm going to kill him." He started climbing up the sandbags in pursuit, but the shiny coin that she held out to him checked the attack.

"Here," she said. "One for each of you. Now, why don't you trot on home like little men."

It frightened her, saying that. Absurd, really, calling these babies in all their injured innocence *little men.* She wondered if she said that because there was no time for children anymore, because the children could be sheltered from the harshness and cruelty no more than the grownups, so that their lives must be sinister and violent from the day of birth, running to avoid shells instead of each other in a game of tag, playing a grim new game of hide-and-seek, in bombproof cellars where death was always "it" and where they could lose but once.

"We're waiting for Mother to come home," the younger one answered. "We don't know where she's gone."

She felt as if they belonged to her, with their shabby clothes and their little pinched faces, playing on the barricades like puppy dogs. I am your mother, she wanted to say, I am going to give birth to you tonight. And you must promise me to be good boys and stop fighting, you must promise me not to die, because if you die . . .

She caught herself, reminded by a sudden twinge at the pit of her stomach, more definite than any before, that she must go on more quickly. So she left the children, begging them not to hurt each other again, and when she looked back they were sitting on the edge of the sandbags together, swinging their legs and flipping the mysterious coins in their hands.

Dr. Mank had left word for her to be placed in a room with another woman, red-faced and robust, whose child had been born a few days before, and who looked comfortably settled and established in bed, surrounded by newspapers on all sides.

The rhythm of tension down her sides and through her abdomen, recurring, disappearing and recurring again, each time with greater force and for longer intervals, was not painful enough to prevent conversation.

"Any hope of peace?" she asked.

"Peace!" The woman seemed to spit the word out. "There won't be any hope of peace till those madmen are in padded cells. Some of their troops are over the border already. They've been shooting back and forth all afternoon."

Perspiration was beginning to form in tiny beads across Kathy's forehead. The dilation pains had set in now, tidelike contractions breaking over her in little waves, followed by the ebbing relaxation, giving her time to catch her breath.

"No," she protested, "they can't start it, they mustn't, they . . ."

The rhythm was quickening, knotting so long she felt something was trying to strangle her, not around the throat but through the waist.

"Here," the other woman said. "If you don't believe me, read it yourself." She passed the papers over, black with headlines and pictures of men preparing to kill one another.

Kathy reached out her hand for them, but midair the hand faltered, like an injured plane, and flopped down to clutch the edge of the bed. She was not engulfed in pain yet, she could still feel the core of it shooting out along her thighs and down her legs, the dark weight in her pressing back the walls, cutting its way down with the infinitesimal movement of a glacier.

She lay back with her teeth clamped so hard together the nerves began to ache. She was stiffened and crying and absolutely silent.

The woman began to talk to her again, calmly speculating as to when the war would come, but Kathy, straining through her tears and sweat, could no longer hear the words, only the sounds. And this time a nurse put her finger to her lips to silence the hearty convalescent.

She lay back, staring at the ceiling, at the sandbags, at the little boy crying, at Toby. Hello, darling, she said, all to herself, her mind chattering away, hello, darling, do you know where I am? Maybe you were right because you always did say you didn't want me to go through it until we could be sure of being together, and now we've lost each other, maybe even forever, and here I am at the hospital about to do it anyway. And don't be afraid, Toby darling, because I'm not, not *too* afraid, and don't think I'm silly because it isn't silly to think that this is just as important as war, is it? Nor heroic either, for

I know I'm neither of those, I'm not trying to do anything great because of war, I'm just trying to be myself, a young woman in love about to have a baby.

All day she lay there softly moaning, fighting her quiet battle, no longer seeing the other woman, sensing people walking in and out only as shadows gliding through darkness, catching only a word here and there that winged out from the flock of words flying back and forth around her. "Shhh . . . raid . . . shouldn't . . . hours more . . . husband is . . . tonight? . . . brave . . . sterilize . . ." the words forming a dim, meaningless pattern as her mind coasted on.

She wasn't unconscious, simply preoccupied with pain, for the timing was reversing itself now, the moments of wrenching seeming to last for hours, the lulls hardly long enough to brace her for the next attack. The impact reminded her of a swing, each time shoved off returning faster and farther, until pain had begun to glaze her eyes and draw the nervous moisture from her pores. But she was still composed because she did not fight the pain, feeling equal to it, giving her body to it as if she were embracing it.

Then a strong hand was at her chin, and a firm voice spoke: ". . . Ready for the delivery room."

"Toby?" she said, reaching out her hand, and the strong hand held it.

"Don't leave me, Toby."

"I'm right here. I won't leave you," said the young doctor.

It was strange, moving through the halls with that strong hand, Toby's—yet knowing it wasn't—Toby's only in that it was young and strong and loving, Toby's in that it would rather sow life than death; coasting through the white halls, remembering the first time her hand ever touched Toby's, that night when peace still seemed the normal way, Toby a tall, intense stranger with a fine unhandsome face, speaking to her and the others with none of the arrogance of a public lecturer, *Only fools and rats refuse to fight until they're cornered. The chief difference between us human beings and the other animals is that we can remember the past and envision the future. So, as fellow human beings, let us weed out the fools and rats and lock arms to check aggression while it may still be done in peace.* She would never forget his quiet simplicity, scorning orators' tricks. And yet no one else had ever made her feel that war was so hideous or peace so possible. When the meeting ended, she had rushed up to tell him this, though she had never done anything like that before, surprised to find how young and shy he was, earnest but blushing too as he answered, "Thanks a lot. This is a war where we can use"—pausing a bashful moment— "pretty young girls in the front lines." Then their hands clasped, and she liked the solid way he shook her hand, as if man to man. She would always remember his hands, long and narrow, with white tapering fingers that might have looked feminine if they had not been so strengthened with nervous energy. And now, for by this time she had forgotten, it was good to feel Toby's hand on hers again, reassuring to know that even if what she was tensing her body against was not the worst of it, his closeness would ease the pain.

"Toby," she murmured, "you won't take your hand away, will you? Hold it tighter." And her fingers tightened around the hand convulsively, pressing so hard they trembled, as the hand's voice floated down to her like a cool breeze. "I won't leave you. I'm right here." This man who was more Toby than the young architect up there in the dark, poised to kill other young men in defense of the sky.

She was not being rolled through corridors any longer. She was lying still in a white room, surrounded by white bodies, among them Dr. Mank's, when suddenly she was crushed in a vise of pain so powerful that she knew everything she had endured so far had not been pain at all, merely the prelude to pain. Everything before had only been a hurt, for hurt is specific, in definite places, she had felt it localized all day, able to put her finger on it, but now the pain was not inside her at all, but she inside it, there she lay squirming in the womb of pain, so absorbed in it she could not cry out, dumbly exultant, no longer thinking she had to be brave because suddenly bravery had become instinctive, not a virtue but a reflex.

Then, at the moment when she thought she must explode, the vise released her and she sank down limp and faintly conscious. Her hand crept blindly to the edge of the table and Toby's was there to meet it again. Toby had tried to prevent it but nothing could stop it now. After the peace rally they had talked the night away and then had watched the dawn come in together, Toby saying softly, *If contrast makes beauty, we're seeing the most beautiful sky in the history of the world, for it's a sky full of fleecy clouds instead of enemy planes, and the crimson light spreading across it pours from the sun, not from incendiary bombs.* And that was the way they spoke their love, not in romantic phrases in idyllic spots, but through whatever they were doing, peace meetings, lunch hours and bicycle trips, arguing modern architecture and modern ideas for the preservation and extension of human living, knowing the world was a serious business but helping each other to play in it too. They were able to skip the maneuvering stage between meeting and adjustment, ready at once to share each other's life, hopeful, hectic, doomed and unafraid. If these times were too highly charged for low-current happiness, at least they were alive and together, and those factors, multiplied, produced the positive result of wanting to go on.

Three months after they met they were talking marriage. But one evening, with the date already set, they were slowly strolling arm in arm when Toby broke a queer, long silence by suddenly blurting out: "Kathy, I've been thinking it over. I . . . I think we better call it off."

She had halted, her flesh pimpling with chill but her dark eyes steady. "But we love each other."

His restless eyes avoided her and then, obviously struggling to overcome weakness, he raised them to hers. His voice had the firmness of decision after long agony. "They took another country today. You know what that means. War is just a matter of time. If that's the logic of it, then love is illogical. The more attached we are to each other now, the more we'll have to suffer when it comes between us. I love you, Kathy, I always will, but . . . love in these times is a luxury we can't afford."

She had fought the first shock impulsively, the words seeming to reach her lips before her mind. "Toby, don't be a coward. You're running away."

They had not been able to keep their voices from being angry with each other, even though both knew the irritation was only a superficial sign of the grief dividing them. "Coward? I'm just trying to make myself face the truth, no matter how it hurts. Kathy, don't you see what's ahead? The closer we cling to each other now, the more unbearable it'll be when we're torn apart. I'm not being cowardly. Just goddamn realistic."

On the surface she could understand his words and they made a kind of sense. Until this moment she had not quite realized how violent life had become, twisting love itself into a denial of life. But there was no hesitation. For reasons she hardly recognized or understood, she knew that denial must be checked and routed with all the persistence of her mind and body. "Who's talking about *clinging*? I'm thinking about *living*. We've got to go on on doing that, no matter what happens. And that means breathing, eating, thinking, loving each other. If you run away from this, you'll run away from something else, and then something else, until finally you know what the logical step will be, to decide that breathing isn't worth doing in these times either—because living itself is a luxury you can't afford."

She paused, the two of them there in the darkness, victims of a war that had not yet begun. "Toby," she said, "what you're trying to do to us *is* brave. But it isn't brave enough. Living is harder now than it ever was before. But it's just as necessary. So is loving. Maybe more so. These times make us belong to each other more than ever—not to escape from life into each other, but to love each other so much that we want to keep life going on."

It had seemed a long time, reliving that. Now she was shocked to realize it could not have been more than a few seconds, for the moment of release was already ended, and pain was crashing around her again, waves of pain looming higher and higher, carrying her up, up, up, and smashing her down again into a violent sea of pain, foaming around her, breaking over her and rushing through her. But she held on, biting her lip into silence, knowing this terrible unleashed fury was life, her triumph, born in pain and blood.

Because the spasmic rhythm had taken the place of any concept of time, she couldn't tell how long it had been before she realized that the scream she was hearing was not her own but the shrill cry of the siren, that the terrible rumbling, louder and louder, was not the whirring of her own brain, that these white walls were not the boundaries of the world, for alien sound was penetrating them, the ominous sound of fears she had forgotten in her self-absorption. But as pain finally ebbed, the movement and speech sharpened for her, the doctors and nurses staring up as if believing their eyes could drill holes through the roof, the way fear was passed back and forth from face to face, the hoarse whispering: *My God!* and *Air raid!* and *It's begun!*

All of them heard the first blast, at the far end of the city, the roar muffled but the vibration strong enough to make the hospital walls shudder. One of the nurses turned to run, and Dr. Mank's voice barked *"Stay,"* and then they heard, louder and closer, the second blast and Kathy's body shook to it, not knowing where the pain of the city began and her own left off, screaming at last as she saw through eyes tightly pressed together the bombs, plowing through buildings, the floors falling away into little pieces, the sky full of bits of glass and human beings, everything falling, falling, the sirens rushing down the streets screaming through human mouths. All this she felt, her whole body suddenly filled with destruction and terror, the thought scurrying through her mind like a maniac that she was being bombed while the city was giving birth, for it had become all one, one long and ugly suffering.

She saw the little boy sitting on the sandbag, waiting playfully to catch the bomb in his hand like a shiny coin. She tried to break away from the many hands that held her, for he was her child, the child Toby had not wanted her to have for just this reason, because the bombs were falling, and she had to save him because in another second . . . *darling don't stay there run away help help they're killing him* fighting off the hands that held her *let me go do something don't let him die. . . .* They tried to tell her that she had no child out there, that her child was here, safe and not quite born, but she knew better, she was the mother of all the children in all the cities where bombs were falling, she would lie there in pain forever, giving forth child after child, feverishly trying to replace the thousands being slaughtered tonight while playing, while nursing at their mothers' breasts, while saying *Now I lay me. . . .* while sitting on their potties, while being born.

There was another thundering blast and she screamed again, thinking the hospital was hit, feeling the walls collapsing around her, the glass shattering, ceilings tumbling down through floors tumbling down through ceilings—but this time the only explosion was within herself. She trembled violently with the impact, throwing her head back, her hair soaked and matted with sweat, her eyes bulging, the cords in her neck straining as if they would break. No longer embracing pain. She was fighting it now, hating it, screaming at it. She wrenched her hand away savagely from the one that had been holding it. You aren't Toby! What made you think you were Toby? Toby is out there, trying to stop those bombs. But he isn't stopping them. I can hear them falling. He's only dying.

Everything is dying. My little son on the sandbag is dying. I'm dying. My baby is dying. This pain that's in me and that I'm in isn't birth. It's death. She screamed again, *It's dead, it's dead, it's dead!*

The voice in her ear was like the distant roar in a seashell, *Steady now, steady, we're almost done,* but she wanted to fight them off, these fools who insisted on going on dealing with life when the world was full of death. Toby, can you hear me? Toby, you were right! What am I doing here, what am I bringing into the world, another target for bombs, flame-throwers and poison gas? Toby, I must've been mad, forcing a living baby out into this dying world, where the only air his lungs will ever breathe is lethal gas. Oh, Toby, you've won! It's not too late not to have it. I'm not going to let it be born. I'm just going to lie here motionless and not give birth to it. Then we'll both be dead, Toby, and that will be right because that is the way the world is going (tonight I heard the bombs fall, darling) and I can't populate the world single-handed with all those bombs against me.

Dr. Mank bent over her tensely. "Please—you've got to help me."

"I won't," she screamed. "I won't. You're trying to fool me. You only want more soldiers. But I'm not going to give them to you. Toby was right. No time for marriage, or children, or . . . Let it die. Let us both die!"

"More gas," Dr. Mank whispered. "A little more gas."

"Gas!" she screamed.

"Want to put her under, Doctor?"

"No. Just enough to quiet her. She has to work with me. Its position is very bad. If she doesn't help me . . ." He shook his head.

She fought the gas. "Poison," she sobbed, too weak to scream now, "the planes are . . . spreading poison gas. I feel . . . all full of death."

Bending over her, the doctor pleaded, "Bear down. Bear down harder. *Harder!*"

And if I don't, she thought. Toby, you'll forgive me if I don't.

Overhead more planes droned. Explosions were coming regularly now, a new rhythm of pain.

She lay there trembling, numbed with pain, struggling against an instinct no longer controllable. Eagerly the doctor worked with the life force as the momentum of her labor began to carry her through. . . .

Consciousness trickled back slowly, white shadows piercing the blackness, the shadows slowly forming patterns, becoming objects, until the sense of her body began coasting back into her mind again. Finally she began to realize where she was, back in the double room she had left the evening before. There seemed to be something changed about the room. Gradually she discovered what it was: the other woman was gone and even her bed was missing. That was pleasing, just to lie there, saturated with listlessness, surrounded by whiteness and solitary quiet here in this peaceful and empty room. I feel like this room, she thought wearily, emptied and peaceful too. She tried to tell herself she was glad the child was gone, but it wasn't gladness, only the backwash satisfaction of resignation. It is best, she thought, and Toby is right. What is birth today but the beginning of pain our child's being spared?

At the sound of a door opening she made an effort to turn her head but she could not see Dr. Mank until he was standing over her.

"Congratulations. A husky young man. Eight and a quarter pounds."

She began to cry, ecstatic as steeple bells ringing. I always wanted him, she thought, animation suddenly covering fatigue. No matter what Toby said, it's what I wanted.

"Thank God," she said. "Thank God. Thank God."

He smiled through darkly circled eyes. "How about thanking me?"

"I had a dream," she said slowly. "I dreamed he died . . . and that an air raid . . ."

"I wish you *had* been dreaming."

"Oh?" Her voice nose-dived. Far, far away she heard the echo of the sirens and the bombing planes, barely remembered, like childhood scars.

"We're evacuating all patients tonight. Feel up to it?" He reached for her pulse.

All she seemed to remember was that stream of ants, lugging their paintings to waiting trucks when they might have been rushing out into the country to save their lives. Only suddenly those weren't canvases on their backs, they were patients, handled tenderly as masterpieces, and as she paused to watch them being saved, somehow Toby was there looking on beside her and she was explaining to him: *That's what I mean by living. We have to go on doing that no matter what happens.*

"I said we have to move tonight," he repeated. "I wish I could tell you it was going to be easy—or safe. . . ."

She wondered when words like *safe* and *easy* would be used again. "I'll be all right, Doctor. I'll have to be." *Isn't that what I'm supposed to say?* And then, as if the war had never begun, as if bombs had never fallen: "Where is he? Can I see him now?"

# LOVE,
# ACTION,
# LAUGHTER

■    ■    ■

Larry Moran was a bareback rider in a circus who broke into the movie game in the early days as a double for a Western star who couldn't ride a horse.

The hero would always learn in a very dramatic scene that the damsel was in distress and he would run for his horse and then Larry would carry it on from there—riding to the rescue from every possible angle—all afternoon.

Every girl in the company used to look up when Larry did his stuff. He was a feverish young man with an almost primitive force. He had a strong sensuous face, a well-trained body and an athletic mind. His agility and eagerness were electrifying. He was violent, he could walk faster than most men run, he was aggressive and nimble-brained; no wonder he climbed the Hollywood ladder two rungs at a time.

Larry spent two months riding to the rescue with the wind in his ears and the dust in his mouth before he caught on to the movie racket. One day he raced over a bump and swal-

■

lowed too much dust; he coughed and spat and had an inspiration.

"Why must I keep racing through this lousy dust?" Larry asked. "Why don't you shoot lots of cameras at me at once from different angles, and get the whole chase knocked off at one crack?"

That was one of the most brilliant things that had been said in Hollywood up to that time. The director shook his head in disgust.

"When I want advice from you," he bellowed, "I'll ask for it."

Larry's suggestion had never been tried before and it was obviously ridiculous. The director told him to keep moving. Those were the days when anybody who knew how to fit a crank into a camera was a cameraman and a director was the guy who could yell the loudest.

Larry was convinced that either he or the picture business would have to go. "This game is nutty," he said. "For a calm, quiet, sensible life, give me a circus any day, you nippleheaded fuck-up."

Just then a little man, who called himself a producer, one of the first to suspect that people would actually pay to see pictures moving on a screen, reached out and drew Larry back into the industry.

The producer told him he had heard his idea.

Larry told him he could take the idea and do with it as his imagination directed.

The producer told him his idea would cut a shooting schedule on a Western in half—he must be a genius or something.

Larry told him he thought he could direct pictures a whole lot better than that clown behind the megaphone.

The producer said, "Kid, you've got the job. I'll put you on at seventy-five a week."

Larry said, "That's pretty cheap for a genius, but I'll take a stab at it."

Larry's stab cut deep into Hollywood. He became the industry's first great Western director.

Hollywood was rising like a new world out of the sea, and on its highest peak stood Larry Moran, circus performer.

Larry Moran helped to give America something to do in the evening. He was God's gift to the moment. He was an artist and a pioneer and a drunkard and a tough guy and he caught the fancy of a nation.

Dames wanted Larry Moran for a thousand reasons. Society women winked at his vulgarity—he was a target for every little girl whose insides squirmed with the itch for a career. When he walked through the studio he left a wake of sighing secretaries.

But there could be no permanence for Larry Moran; life was a grab bag, he could reach into it to his elbows; every month there was a new picture and a new salary and a new fame.

Larry's mind was always leaping ahead, inventing new camera angles, improving the lighting, speeding up the tempo—and going on the most complex and rambunctious binges known to man. Larry's hair grew gray, his pictures were longer and more mature—Larry and his industry were growing up. It was 1925 and he was thirty-one—he had lived ten years in Hollywood, a lifetime long enough to span the conception and revelation of a new world that lived and trembled on a thousand silver screens.

The late twenties were a nightmare to Larry Moran. Suddenly the silent screen stood up and screamed, trying its voice like a new baby, and the sound split the earth, and futures and careers and fortunes were swallowed up—and among them, suddenly shaken from his pedestal and devoured by oblivion, was Larry Moran.

For it must be told, it cannot be explained. Hollywood swallows its children. Watch, as it bears them, suckles them and suddenly leaps upon them from the rear and gulps them down.

Time caught up with Larry Moran and gave him the razzberry as it passed him by. People told one another how sorry they were for him. His money ran out—there had always been a leak at the bottom. Then his health ran out—an unkind columnist said his mind was pickled in alcohol. One morning he woke up in a Hollywood hotel with a bad hangover and very little more and he looked at himself in the mirror. His face was lined with purple veins from too much drinking and his eyes were glazed and sunken with not enough forgetting.

"Larry," he said to himself, "I knew you when. If you don't get yourself a job today, I'll see you in hell, and that's a place inhabited strictly by agents and supervisors."

He sent his suit out to be pressed. He gave the bellboy the line about it being easier to tip him in a lump sum at the end of the month. He drew his clothes on gingerly, to save the creases, and took the redcar to Classic Pictures, Inc. Classic Pictures was the brainchild of Sammy Glick, Hollywood's boy producer, an amoral young man with a cold eye and a quick head. Maybe Larry wouldn't admit it to himself, but he picked Glick because the older producers knew him too well for what he was. His virility made him sense their pity and resist their condescension.

Larry was tense inside and trying to be as casual as possible when he gave his name to Doc, the receptionist.

"Larry Moran!" Doc said. "I thought I remembered you."

"That's great," said Larry—he wished people wouldn't remember him. "I want to see Sammy Glick."

"Any special business?" Doc asked.

"Hell, yes," said Larry. "I was toying with the idea of going back to work."

Doc called Glick's secretary, Judy Becker.

"Larry Moran's out here," Doc said. "Goes back aways." Remember him? He wants to see Mr. Glick."

Larry Moran? Larry!

Judy was almost thirty-five. She had been one of those secretaries on the old lot. She had the same feeling now she used to have when she watched Larry Moran drive into the studio in his Austrian limousine, the only one of its kind in the country. One day she had been sent down to give him a message on the set; she remembered how he strode across the set to her, making a riding whip whistle in the air—she remembered being frightened by his youth and his fierceness.

She was young enough to be shy and excited then, and her message slipped under her tongue. It was a desperate moment and he had put his arm around her in front of the whole company, saying, "Take it easy, sister." He was a fresh guy and she should have minded; she looked up into his face and told him the whole message and she was all mixed up. She wished it were longer and she was sweating and blushing and glad it was over just the same.

"Can you hear me? I said Larry Moran's out here," Doc repeated. "The old-timer."

"Oh," Judy said, making a nonstop return flight. "Send him right in."

She had thought he was dead; it was such a dreadful thing to think. She looked into her mirror; it was such a silly thing to do, he wouldn't even notice her. She daubed a bit of rouge on her cheeks to hide that studio pallor.

She could hear him coming. Should she recognize him? She didn't want to hurt him. She felt choked up. She didn't want to see him again, ever. She stared at the door, waiting for him.

Larry entered as jauntily as possible. This job was now or never and he must be casual—don't let them get inside you—that's it, smile, wink at the secretary.

"Hello, honey, is the boss in?"

"It may take a little doing, Mr. Moran. I'll remind him who you are. Won't you please have a seat?"

"Thank you," Larry said quietly.

Judy had expected him to tell a dirty story about waiting rooms. She had found the change she feared. He was like a great volcano that has become quiescent. He seemed to be a

much smaller man that she had remembered. And not as handsome. The shock of thick, brown hair that had given him a
wild, careless look was gone. His hair was thinned now, and
tamed. Everything about him was thinner and tamer.

There was a long silence. She had waited so many years to
see him that she couldn't think of anything to say.

Larry waited an hour and fifteen minutes to see Mr. Glick.
She wanted to remind him of the time he put his arm around
her absentmindedly on the old lot—she wanted to tell him
what it meant for her still. She was copying her shorthand
notes and banging the typewriter as loud as she could.

Finally she said, "You can go in now, Mr. Moran."

Larry went in and found a little fellow, a dark man with an
unattractive puss, behind an enormous desk.

Sammy Glick was friendly and smiling—he came forward
and shook Larry's hand softly.

Sammy knew the old-timer wanted a job; he couldn't insult
him, and he hoped to pass the whole thing off as a social call.

Larry could see what Sammy was trying to do. Did this
young punk think he was a complete rum-dum?

"Listen, Sammy," said Larry. "You and me know our business. I'm not the kind of a guy to beat around the bush. You've
proved that you've got the courage of your convictions—
you've got a fresh slant on this racket, and you're going up.
I was the biggest director in the game and I wouldn't take up
your time if I wasn't sure I could still deliver."

"Sure," said Sammy, "everybody knows what you've done,
but the business is changing. You were tops in the blood-and-
thunder days. I guess you could still give us cards and spades
on mellerdrammer, but times have changed. That old hokum
is dead and buried; the people want something new, something fresh and light; they want young love, action, music and
laughter."

"Listen," said Larry desperately. "Everybody in town says
I can't come back. If you give me a break you'll be the white-
haired boy."

"Why kid ourselves?" Sammy said. "I already am."

Larry beat a retreat.

"How about your second-unit stuff?" he asked. "God knows I know enough about this business to swing those—"

"But the tempo's changed," said Sammy, less politely. He didn't have time for this. "I said all the people want now is young love, action, music, and laughter. I don't think you've got the pace for that sort of thing anymore."

Larry stood up. He felt leaden inside.

Sammy put his hands in his pockets. He was uncomfortable; he didn't want an old-timer like Larry Moran going out hating his guts—it hurt his pride; it wasn't good for his reputation.

"Listen," Sammy said, "we all have our ups and downs, that's the law out here." He fished into his pocket and said, "Take this C-note. And there's no hurry about paying it back."

Larry clenched his fists. This had never happened before. He was wondering if he could squash this cockroach on the big green blotter of his big shiny desk.

And then something strange happened. Something hidden in Larry Moran, some alien thing that Larry did not recognize, reached out to grasp that bill. A broken voice inside him said, "Thanks, Sammy," and his hand slipped into his pocket, where the bill rested quietly, hiding from the shame.

Sammy Glick's phone rang. It was Tony Kreuger, the agent, one of his pals.

"Hey, Tony, howya, baby?" he said. "Naw, I'm not busy, lay it on me." Then he laughed. "That's right. Always ready for a good lay. You kill me, Tony."

Larry walked slowly out of the office, his head hanging down as if his neck were broken.

When he came out Judy tried to look at him without pity, and she was able to, because she loved him. To Judy Becker he was still a force and a danger.

For Larry the show was over and he didn't have to act any more.

"Well, girlie," he said, "it looks like the curtain on the third act for me. It's all over but the piano playing as you walk out."

"What did he say?"

"He says he wants young love, action, music and laughter," Larry said. "He says he wants four things I ain't got."

He looked her over once more. For some crazy reason he hoped Sammy Glick didn't get to first base with her. Then he gave her an informal salute.

"Take it easy, sister," he said, and started out.

Judy watched him walking out of her life. She was frantic for a moment and then was sure.

"Larry, wait."

He whirled around in surprise.

"It isn't too late," she said, "believe me, Larry."

He smiled faintly. "What's it to you?"

"Everything," she said. She knew it sounded too dramatic, but she didn't care. This was no time for caution—you don't think of subject and predicate when you've wanted a man for sixteen years.

"On the level," she said. "I used to watch you on the old lot. It's been that long."

Larry looked at her. He believed her, "This is one screwy day," he said.

"Larry, let me see you tonight, let me help you."

"Don't waste your time," Larry said. "I'm old hat. I told you what he said. I can't give you young love, action, music and laughter—that's what you want—that's what we all need."

"I never did like formulas," she said, "and anyway, I'll take my chances."

"No," he said, "it's crazy, it's too late."

"Not for me," she insisted. "It's my turn. The old wheel has finally stopped on my number."

Judy knew there must be something about this moment that would burn them both. She knew that this was the last time, that if he walked out into the street now, and she went back to her dictation, that was the end for both of them.

"This will sound nutty," she said. "I've been in love with you for sixteen years. I was in love with you when girls buzzed around you like bees. I was in love with you when you went off on yachting parties and stayed drunk for weeks, when the scandals came and the papers had to be hushed up. I was in love with you for a million years, and now—"

Larry looked at her hard and wrinkles spread in ripples from his eyes as he smiled.

"You win," he said.

"Call for me at the Villa Carlotta at eight o'clock."

"Okay," he said, "what's your name?"

"Judy," she said. "Judy Becker."

"I'll be there, Judy," he said, "in tails—we're going formal."

Larry was back at eight. He had downed four highballs. His dress suit was tight around the shoulders and slightly faded. He drove up to the Villa Carlotta in a taxi; the fare was ninety cents. He gave the driver his hundred-dollar bill. The driver laughed and said, "I haven't seen one of them things since the Depression."

"Okay," Larry said. "Then wait here. We can use you— we're going places."

Judy came down in a purple evening gown. She must have spent a lot of time on her face—it didn't look so round and white. She took his hand and squeezed it hard twice. She had been very excited all afternoon thinking of this and now she was subdued and slow moving.

He helped her into the taxi almost too elegantly and said, "To Chasen's." He turned on the radio. It played too loud at first, and then too soft, and this was very funny and they laughed at it together.

In the taxi Judy teased him, "It looks like you've got a head start on me," and Larry said, "I have a feeling this is one race we're going to end up together." The radio swung with Artie Shaw. Larry looked at her and said, "I wish you had forced this on me fifteen years ago," and Judy answered, "Don't be silly. It couldn't have happened then. You were too busy."

They kissed then, for the first time, and the driver looked around and grinned and said, "Here's Chasen's."

"Just like in the movies," Judy laughed.

"I haven't felt like this since I was a kid," Larry said as they went in. "Young-love Sammy Glick should see us now."

Nearly everybody who eats in places like Chasen's watches the door, lapping up the success with their filets, eager to see the new people who are entering the charmed circle. When Larry came in with Judy on his arm, people put their heads together and wondered who they were, and one lady thought she had seen Judy at some party the week before and then Wally Connors, Judy's boss when he was production manager for Larry on the old lot, looked up and said, "Jesus, that's Larry Moran—haven't seen the old cock in years."

Connors walked over to Larry's table and seemed very glad to see him.

"Hello, Larry," he said, "where've you been keeping yourself?"

"Hello, Wally old kid, I've been traveling," Larry said.

"Abroad?" Connors asked. "Why didn't you look me up when you got back, you dog?"

"I've just been traveling from one hotel to another, jumping the rent," Larry said.

Connors threw his big head back and roared. "Still the same old Larry Moran," he said. "But on the level, you're looking great. Things must be picking up for you."

"Can't complain," said Larry. "Korda wants me to make a picture in England, but you know how I feel about this town."

"Sure do," said Connors. He was glancing over toward his table. He couldn't quite make Larry out, and he'd rather let it go at that before he got involved.

"By the way," Larry said, "you know Miss Becker, don't you? Used to be with us on the old lot."

"Of course," said Connors, vaguely, "good to see you again."

There was an awkward silence. Connors glanced over at another table and waved. "There's Lolly Parsons," he said. "Gotta see her a minute. Give me a ring, Larry, and we'll have lunch sometime."

"He and I used to be great pals," Larry said.

"I can see that," Judy said.

"See," said Larry, "they still come over to me—we're in, kid."

He picked up the menu and read it from cover to cover. It gave him a kick to see those prices again. Then he beckoned the waiter with an authoritative wave.

"Why isn't the 1931 Liebfraumilch on the wine list?" he demanded.

"I'm sorry, sir," the waiter answered, "we have the 1933."

"But the 1931 is the best year," Larry said triumphantly.

Larry leaned back. He had won his right to belong again. He ordered the '33 and lobster Thermidor. He squeezed Judy's hand. "Baby," he said, "I haven't felt so good in years."

"You didn't have to order all that," she said, "it's too expensive. We don't need all that stuff to have a good time."

She was wondering how he could afford it. He told her not to worry, just leave everything to him.

Larry was getting drunk, and pretty soon Judy had a glow on too, and more people stopped over to say hello, and Larry leaned back very full and comfortable. He was beginning to feel his old warmth.

He asked for a phone extension and called Ciro's and said, "Reserve a table for two for Mr. Larry Moran," and he hung up and blew Judy a kiss.

Judy was drunk, not from wine but from the exquisite illusion of being out with the Larry Moran they all wanted to know. And I always thought I was a little too heavy to play Cinderella, she smiled at herself in her little makeup mirror.

"Snap out of it, Judy girl," Larry said. "You're a million miles away."

And Judy snapped, giving herself to the moment. She'd forgot about thinking, she wouldn't look before or after. "I'm right with you, Larry boy," she said. "Have you heard the one about the Polish starlet who went to bed with the writer . . . ?"

They both howled then, and started out, Larry yelling back to the headwaiter, "Next time have that 1931." And they roared with laughter, all the way out to the taxi. "Next stop, Ciro's," Larry shouted, "and step on it, we open the show!"

"Young love, action, music and laughter, yowzer!" Larry Louis-Armstronged, and then he sang the words in time to the radio, "Young-love, action-and-music, laughter, do-dee-o-do. Can you imagine that little shrimp saying I don't know anything about young-love, action-and-music, laugh-ter? Wait'll I get one good picture under my belt, I'll show that little worm—I wouldn't have him as my office boy. Judy baby, you brought me luck—I love you, we'll knock this town dead."

"We?" Judy asked.

"Damn right!" said Larry, "we're made for each other. We'll fly down to Tijuana tonight and get hitched."

"Kiss me," Judy said.

"Are ya happy, honey? Say something."

"Hold me, Larry," she said. "Just hold me."

Ciro's was filling up. There was an air to that place with its smart patterns of black and white, the rustle of evening gowns, the seminude cigarette girls, the tailored moguls and their panting stooges, ingratiating agents doing business after dark, beautiful women with wet lips and cool mascara still searching for something, and poised ladies who had arrived, leaning back to watch the procession. With a well-practiced professional grin, the bandleader was driving his musicians through an impassioned *cha-cha-cha.*

It was not quite real, this topsy-turvy world into which Larry and Judy entered, holding hands and laughing—laughing because all of a sudden life was just too funny for words.

They were led to a table in a corner, ordered more wine and joined the dancers on the floor. As they whirled, they were tighter and tighter together until they almost fell. Somebody said, "If that's what you want to do there's a motel across the street." It was Tony Kreuger, the tough little kid who used to be California lightweight champ until he met Sammy Glick and found out it was a softer racket to be a ten-percenter.

Larry and Judy just laughed at Tony, and Tony didn't like it. But he didn't know who Larry was so he couldn't come on too strong until he found out.

Now Larry was making love out loud to Judy, and the waiters smiled, and Judy shook her finger, but Larry only kissed it noisily, saying, "We got a right—this is our engagement party! Hey, waiter, another bottle of champagne for me and the bride."

When they got up to dance again, they noticed that Tony Kreuger was sitting right behind them with a blond showgirl.

"Those guys give me a royal pain," Larry said. "Just another Hollywood tough guy. Like to see him get tough with me."

When the floor show began, Larry didn't bother watching it, he was too busy watching Judy. His eyes made love to Judy.

"As soon as this is over," he said, "as soon as they wrap up the floor show we're heading for the last round-up."

Tony Kreuger looked over and glared. He had found out who Larry was. "Shut up," he growled.

Larry stiffened. "Who do you think you're talking to?"

"Don't give me that act," Tony said. "I heard all about you from Sammy Glick. Just because he's nice enough to give you a handout today you think you can come here and be a big shot."

This was a shock to Judy. She must have loved Larry from way back because she still didn't pity him; she understood—nothing was going to come between them.

"Larry, sit down," she begged.

Her voice pierced the fog that was settling around his head.
"Sorry, baby," he said. "Let's blow—let's have some fun."

Tony felt very proud of himself; his eyes shone like a cat's.

Larry staggered out, Judy trying to help him without appearing to. They tumbled into the taxi, and Larry pulled all the bills he had left out of his pocket and told Judy to count them. She did, fearfully. There were fifty dollars left; she would like to tell him to save them, to take it easy, but there was no time, no time like the present, no time but this for young love, action, music and laughter; time was ticking, time was chasing itself around the block; last call for fun. So she shut her eyes again, they would loop the last loop together, and she said, "Fifty bucks, honey," and he grinned and yelled two loud words to the driver, "Clover Club," and he grabbed her chin and kissed her possessively and said, "Now we're gonna see some action!"

And Judy said, "I'm right with you." If Larry was going to lose his last fifty bucks, he was going to lose sight of Tony Kreuger, too. This night he would lose his shame and his weariness. Judy was with him. She was going to hold on to him; he could lose everything but her.

The Clover Club was one of those quiet, swanky places where big men threw away big money with such ease you forget it was money at all. It was very exclusive, for they had to be careful whom they took their money from. Larry and Judy climbed the steps to the door, and a dark face looked out at them from a peephole.

The face said, "Sorry, boss, don't know you."

Larry said, "That's your fault, I'm Larry Moran."

The face was puzzled. It said, "Wait a minute," and disappeared.

In a moment it bobbed up again with another face. The new face started out more diplomatically. "I'm sorry, sir, I didn't get the name."

"You better get the name," Larry said, "Or you'll get a lot more than that."

Larry pranced on the step like a mad bull; he puffed fury into the air; he held his head high in the air and looked down on these guardians of the gate.

He had won. He heard the bolt sliding and the knob turning. The big door swung open to them.

Inside, Hollywood was having an expensive good time. Larry stormed in; Judy thought he would make everybody look at him. She caught a glimpse of Wally Connors, and there was Sammy Glick, but Hollywood has always suffered from convenient nearsightedness. Nobody turned, nobody seemed to look, the rhythm of the Clover Club flowed on unchanged.

Larry shouldered his way into the crowd at the roulette table and asked Judy, "When's your birthday, child?" "August fourteenth," she said, and without hesitating he put five one-dollar chips on it.

The wheel spun and the little ball did its dance.

The wheel slowed, the little ball let each number catch it for a moment, then jumped away again, like a flirtatious girl, until it hopped securely into the arms of fourteen.

Judy said, "Try twenty-eight, that's the year we first met," and the wheel spun once, and spun again. But twenty-eight didn't seem to show, and Judy was nervous—it had to for her sake; and the third time the ball leaped in, as if it knew it was overdue.

The wall of blue chips in front of Larry was growing higher. The man next to him said, "You're getting to them," and Judy noticed that several others looked over. Larry hadn't time to look up.

Then Larry put all forty blue chips on red, the whole stack, and the weasel looked up in appreciation. And Judy prayed, and red it was, four hundred dollars in chips, sliding across the table to them; that little ball was human, it understood them, and knew their needs.

Larry and Judy and the wheel were going crazy; they were
all spinning around together; they were hoping to spin forever. It seemed to Judy that they were out in a wonderful sort
of snowstorm; it was snowing blue chips that would become
a great fortress to protect them against the world.

When Judy saw the wall of blue chips grow higher and
higher, she asked, then begged, "Let me cash in half of that
for you—and play with the rest. Let's see what it looks like—in
real money."

She came back from the cashier's with a thousand dollars in
cash—two five-hundred-dollar bills that first felt cool and crisp
and then grew warmer and warmer until her hand began to
perspire from their heat.

Back at the table Larry was drawing a crowd. A waiter was
serving Scotch-and-sodas, courtesy of the house. The Bern-
heimers who owned this elegant casino—illegal but winked at
by the local DA—only did this for their best customers. Larry
drank his quickly, too quickly Judy thought, and sprinkled
chips across the board like seeds. He and Judy were the center
of a circle of amazement and envy. "Who is this lucky sonofabitch?" somebody asked. Someone thought he was a big devel-
oper from the east. Someone else had heard he had made
millions running in booze from Canada in the Prohibition
days. Then Sammy Glick came up behind him, watched him
hit again, watched him take another highball from the tray,
and said, "You don't know who that is? Larry Moran. The
director. He was in my office just today. One of my oldest
friends."

Larry was ahead three thousand and the wheel was still
spinning. Wally Connors said, "Larry—he's been making pictures in England. Helluva guy, Larry. One o' my favorite
people." And he went through the room proclaiming to everyone that his pal Larry Moran was hitting the wheel like his feet
were attached to secret pedals and he owned it.

The name was hoisted above the room like a flag. Larry
Moran had ten thousand dollars. Everybody saluted.

"It's time to cash in," Judy said.

She was right. The room was buzzing with Larry Moran. With every moment and every dollar he was becoming a better director. "He can still do a better job than half these punks drawing down big dough," one producer said. "He had a great touch," another said.

"The touch of a winner c'n make a lousy actress look good." The old producer came up to him and shook his hand. "Congratulations, Larry," he said, "glad to see you back. I've got a hunch Hollywood needs you more than England does. How would you like to meet me at the Vendome tomorrow at one o'clock?"

"Okay, pal, you got it." Larry said. This time the ball bounced out of fourteen, but what's a hundred dollars?

"Why, hello, Mr. Glick," Judy said.

It was Sammy. He put his arm around Larry and whispered into his ear.

"Listen," he said. "I happened to hear what A.D. said to you. How about dropping into my office first, about ten? I may have something hot for you."

Larry nodded. The wheel was still spinning. He was hot. He would rub one producer against another like flints. He would start a real fire again.

Judy's "cash in" seemed to be lost in the buzz of excitement building in volume around Larry. Like a star down front center stage, he took a stack of blue chips and set them on fourteen again. A blonde, a little tipsy, a bit player hungry for stardom, leaned over and kissed Larry on the check and set a few chips on top of his. "Lucky you, lucky me, baby," she said.

The little blonde took the loss of her chips like a good sport. "Lose some, win some," she said, moving in between Larry and Judy, handing Larry another drink and taking one herself. "My name is Penny. Your lucky Penny. My birthday's June sixth. Sixth month, sixth day. Let's play her together, honey."

"Larry, it's time to cash in," Judy said, trying to push between them. "Cash in, Larry."

"Spoilsport," Penny said. "Party-pooper. Go away. We're havin' fun."

This time the little ball came to rest on double-zero. The croupier raked in Larry's stack of chips. "Double zero." Judy said to the blonde. "That's your birthday. Double-zero."

When Larry blew another stack, and then another, the little blonde pouted. "Boo hoo, there goes my paycheck," and then eyeing Larry's dwindling but still substantial stack, "You give Penny five o' yours, I'll win it back. When's your birthday?"

"He already played his birthday, and won," Judy said. "You only have one birthday a year."

Larry looked over at her, almost as if he had forgotten she was there.

"I need that grand," he said.

Judy's hand tightened around the bills. "No, Larry, please."

"My dough," he said. His words were beginning to thicken. "Give it to me, Judy. Gotta get more chips."

People were beginning to notice them, in a different way. Some edged away. Nobody likes trouble. Especially in a casino. Things have got to flow nice. Nice when the money flows in. Flows in flows out. But don't make waves.

Judy wanted to put that money in a bank for Larry. Give him some breathing time. Space to move back into the stream again. But Larry didn't have a bank. He had a few chips in his hand and the wheel and his head were spinning together. When Judy held back he made a sudden move, grabbed the bills from her hand, and asked the croupier to turn them into chips to be placed on lucky numbers and rebuild the blue castle around them.

Judy wasn't a partner anymore, merely a bystander, a witness to a night of wonders turning into a horror show, like the old Academy Award winner she had seen, the splendid Dr. Jekyll becoming the grotesque Mr. Hyde.

Ten by ten and then five by five the blue chips, as if drawn to a magnet in the croupier's hand, moved back across the board from Larry's dwindling pile. Judy watched and felt hopeless as five hundred dollars' worth of new chips followed the other back to the croupier.

Larry just shrugged, had another drink and tried again, and again. He looked around for his little blonde mascot but Penny had moved on. David Selznick had just came in and he was flashing money at the crap table and beginning to draw a crowd. Judy didn't really have to look around to know what was happening. The little blonde knew her Hollywood. D.O.S., as the insiders called him, was hot and famous after *Gone With the Wind,* and now with a new hit with Hitch . . . "Hey, David," she was saying, "remember me, at the Spiegel party? Penny—I'm your lucky Penny . . ."

All the chips he had left Larry could hold in his own hand now. His eyes were a little glassy and the big smile of the early winner now seemed to be frozen on his face. Wally Connors glanced over at him and said to a friend, "Well, I guess once a lush, always a lush." Other players at the table drew away from him as if he were suddenly infected with a deadly disease. No sweet smell here. The sour odor of failure. The Hollywood disease. Worse than TB in the old days. Worse than VD terminal.

Sammy Glick came by on his way to smooch D.O.S. and got the picture on the run. "Blew it again," he said. "I knew it. Hit me for a hundred in my office and blows it. Fuckin' has-been."

Larry heard that and wheeled around. "Listen, you little sonofabitch. I heard that! I got more talent in my little finger 'n' you've got in your whole—"

Two Clover Club bouncers straight out of Warner Brothers B-movies closed in.

"All right, Mr. Moran, it's good night now." Judy followed in a kind of cold trance, as they started moving him toward the door. "Wait a minute—wanna see the boss—sign a chit—five-hundred-dollar credit . . ."

Judy saw how they were able to move him without roughing him. Almost without making a scene. Though Errol Flynn said to his date, who looked like a cheerleader from Hollywood High, "Hey, I remember him. Larry Moran. Made one of my first pictures. Been wondering where he went." To which the little jailbait beauty, who was not as dumb as she looked, said, "Well, now you know."

Outside the club Larry was ready to pound on the door and demand his rights, but somehow Judy managed to get him back to the cab.

"Nex' stop, Barney's Beanery," he said. "Open all night. Barney's a pal."

"Next stop, bed," Judy said.

"Yours or mine?" Larry laughed. How could he still laugh, Judy wondered. Or maybe that's how he went on winning, or losing and laughing.

"I'll drop you at your apartment," Judy said.

There was nothing to say now, so Larry whistled the "Hi-ho" theme from *Snow White*. In a few minutes they were at Larry's apartment, a run-down three-story stucco on Yucca north of Hollywood Boulevard.

"Sure you don' wanna come in?"

"I'm sure," Judy said, thinking of all the times she would have said "Yes! Yes!" in her fantasies.

"Well, we had a run for our money," Larry said. He was actually grinning. He wasn't part of the tragedy. Only she was. Now he was the onlooker.

"I'll call you—how's for lunch at the Derby, OK?"

She nodded, thinking, almost admiring—how will he pay for it? He never worries: When he sings, "Life is just a bowl of cherries," by God he means it . . .

He wasn't too drunk or too broke to notice the look on her face, and he wouldn't have been Larry Moran if he hadn't wanted to leave her with an upper—"Come on, baby, it's singin' in the rain, let a smile be your umbrella, 'member what your boss Sammy said, what they want now is young love, action, music 'n' laughter!''

She watched him manage to both lurch and swagger his way to the door of the faded yellow-brown stucco apartment. And she wondered when he'd find the hundred-dollar bill she always carried in her change purse.

Now if this had been one of Sammy's movies, Judy was thinking as she slowly drove home, Larry would have multiplied his thousand by ten, marched out in triumph, signed a new contract and she would have become Mrs. Larry Moran.

But this was Hollywood, the dream factory, with emphasis on *factory,* where she wasn't Loretta Young, and Larry Moran wasn't Larry Moran anymore.

BUDD SCHULBERG's career as a novelist began with the meteoric success of *What Makes Sammy Run?* Among his other novels are *Waterfront, The Harder They Fall, Sanctuary V,* and *The Disenchanted,* which Anthony Burgess included in his *New York Times* list of "The Ninety-nine Best Novels of the Twentieth Century."

Schulberg won an Oscar for his screenplay *On the Waterfront,* several awards for his film *A Face in the Crowd,* and a Tony nomination for his Broadway adaptation of *The Disenchanted.* He attributes his ability to adapt his own work to stage or screen to his upbringing in Hollywood, where his father ran a major motion-picture studio.

Currently he is writing the screenplay for *What Makes Sammy Run?,* scheduled for production early in 1990, coinciding with the publication by Random House of the anniversary edition of his celebrated novel.